A dark passion was their destiny . . . A shocking secret, their fate.

Angèle Roget – for the exquisite Creole beauty, love was a liberator . . . and a destroyer.

Philippe de l'Eglise – for the exiled French aristocrat, desire was a power to use . . . and abuse.

Minette – for the sensuous octaroon courtesan, passion was her legacy . . . and her revenge.

Jean-Philippe – for the handsome young rogue, obsession was his inheritance . . . and his doom.

Love's Sorcery

VIRGINIA NIELSEN

Headline

Copyright © 1986 by Virginia Nielsen

Published by arrangement with Dell Publishing Co, Inc,
New York, USA.

First published in Great Britain in 1987
by Headline Book Publishing PLC

All characters in this publication are fictitious and any resemblance to
real persons, living or dead, is purely coincidental.

British Library Cataloguing in Publication Data

Nielsen, Virginia
    Love's sorcery.
    Rn: Virginia Nielsen McCall   I. Title
    813′.54[F]   PS3525.A126

    ISBN 0–7472–0019–X
    ISBN 0–7472–3015–3 Pbk

Headline Book Publishing PLC
Headline House
79 Great Titchfield Street
London W1P 7FN

Printed and bound in Great Britain by
William Collins Sons & Co Ltd,
Glasgow G4 0NB

To Frances St Martin Dansereau,
who introduced us to French
Louisiana and its history,
and fabulous Creole cuisine.

Prologue.

Louisiana. 1830

*Y*ESTERDAY I rode up the choked drive to La Sorcellerie, a path I had thought never to take again. But she whose pride its elegance was, that proud and wilful lady who was my mother's cousin, is gone now. Two days ago we laid la Marquise de l'Eglise beside her father and mother in the brick mausoleum behind the cathedral, crowned—fittingly—with the angel pointing one marble hand to heaven. Is it too much to hope that we laid to rest those other unquiet spirits who still people La Sorcellerie in my dreams?

Like so many days in Louisiana, yesterday was still and slumberous. I did not tell anyone where I was going when I ordered my mount saddled and brought around from the stables at Bellemont. It was hot, and the air was heavy with unshed tears. Overhead, those fantastic clouds that build up over the gulf and drift across the Mississippi delta were massing in puffed layers, but along the bayou where I rode, no breath stirred the gray moss hanging from the ancient oaks.

We moved slowly, my mare and I, she shiny with perspiration and I feeling a heaviness that was due to more than the moisture-laden air. Where I rode, the bank was high and grassy, cleared of all but the great oaks with their long gray beards turning black beneath the surface of the bayou. On my right the cane—that sweet "golden grass" that pours such unbelievable wealth into our hands—stretched away in a dense thicket eight feet tall.

The bayou itself lay black and sluggish, its smoky surface crinkled by darting water bugs or an alligator's bony snout. Across the bayou was a remnant of the virgin cypress swamp that once surrounded New Orleans, an impenetrable jungle of vine-choked trees with their knobby roots in stagnant water.

Gradually, as I rode, I was leaving behind the cane fields on my right. I was entering the untended grounds and gardens surrounding La Sorcellerie. I passed near enough to recognize through the encroaching creepers the old grinding rock that the mules once pulled round and round in season while slaves tended fires under the sugar pots.

The ground was spongy, returning to swamp now that the slaves no longer tended the drainage ditches. My little mare shied suddenly, rolling her eyes back at me, and I held her firmly as a cottonmouth moccasin slithered away through the wet grass. And then, through the dim greenish light, I glimpsed peeling white pillars.

I forced my mare through a curtain of creepers, and there it lay before me: La Sorcellerie. I had prepared myself for decay, yet recognition came with a shock. Grass grew high between the ancient oaks bordering the long drive, trees almost unrecognizable beneath the creepers binding them in a deadly embrace.

When the house was built, in the 1790's, the bayou was the only thoroughfare. La Sorcellerie faced the bayou, so I had come upon it at an angle. Slender pillars extending through two levels of wide galéries to support the sloping roof marched all around the rectangular house, and even now I marveled at the sorcery of its perfect proportions.

The wide stair leading up to the galéries was still intact, but the ground-floor storage area was almost hidden by rank weeds growing between the square brick supports.

My heart began beating heavily. I had reined in my horse beside the *garçonnière* and had not even recognized it through the green gloom. Philippe's rooms had been in the *garçonnière*, that bachelor dwelling of the old plantation home, and I knew them well.

There, too, was the octagonal *pigeonnier,* but no doves had flown up with beating wings to circle it at my approach.

A shutter hung awry from one of the French windows on La Sorcellerie's upper galérie. Was that the room in which I had wakened, opened my door, and rushed out to see Cousin Angèle on the stair below me with her pistol in her hand? I started, hearing again that haunting cry of my name: *Melodieee!*

But it was only the long imitative trill of a mockingbird lost in the foliage surrounding me.

My throat chokingly tight, I held my mare quiet and took it all in: the moldy paint, the soft brick that crumbled so quickly in this humid heat; the small animals scurrying through the ivy, its green dulled by countless spider webs; the mass of ragged untrimmed camellias that struggled up through rank undergrowth toward the sun. . . .

Behind my blurring tears I was seeing the fragile wine goblets and heavy silver on Cousin Angèle's bleached Belgium linen, the crystal chandeliers twinkling with myriad reflected candles under which I had once danced the daring waltz with Jean-Philippe and Jeffery, whirling from partner to partner in a dizzying pas de trois.

I seemed to hear a well-loved voice saying: *Cette terre douce, cette terre, douce et condamnée.*

"This sweet, doomed land . . ." But it had not been the land that was doomed. I felt choked, suddenly, my eyes brimming with the tears that blurred the scene before me.

I know it all now . . . all, from the beginning.

And I shall not come this way again, I thought, turning my mare. I did not care to pass through those once-beautiful doors into the high-ceilinged rooms of my innocence and see grackles roosting in the marble fireplaces or hear rats scrabbling behind the moldering draperies.

I do not want to know whether the blood stains have faded from the cypress plank floor. . . .

Part I

Chapter 1

Louisiana. 1803.

A familiar sound reached the ears of Etienne Roget, spending an indolent Sunday afternoon with his family on the front galérie of his plantation house. He lifted his grizzled head and called to the naked black children who were making a game of scything the long grass around the brick supports of the pillars and the steps to the galérie.

"It's ma'am'selle! Quick!"

With cries of excitement the children dropped their scythes and tore across the circle of grass and down the long drive between the oak trees as the cloppety-clop of a galloping horse grew louder from the road along the bayou.

Etienne's guest, Philippe, the marquis de l'Eglise, pulled up his elegant long legs and straightened in his chair to stare as an astonishing equipage came into view, but Madame Roget and seventeen-year-old Clothilde smiled in recognition. It was a single-seated carriage pulled by a single spirited horse, and its driver was an equally spirited young woman. She was sitting erectly on the edge of the seat, the whip in her hand, leaning forward from her hips to urge her horse even faster. She had

3

turned into Etienne's drive and was galloping her horse pell-mell toward his closed gate!

"Mon dieu!" exclaimed the marquis, jumping to his feet. It looked like a race to see whether the carriage or the running children would reach the gate first. "What insanity!"

Etienne Roget chuckled. "Relax, my friend. Mademoiselle never wins."

"But who is this crazy female?"

"She is my Cousin Angèle," Clothilde said, her dark eyes sparkling with fond laughter.

Etienne looked at his daughter with his eyelids drooping to hide a surge of extravagant love. She was a beauty, this only surviving child of his. Sometimes, looking at Astride, grown stout with their prosperity, a faint dark mustache like a shadow on her upper lip, he could not believe the two of them had produced this beguiling creature.

He had not missed the tender looks she and his guest had been exchanging. Any day now the young marquis would approach him to ask for Clothilde's hand. He would assent, in spite of the marquis's present impecunious state, for there was no doubt that Clothilde was in love.

After all, we have all had our ancestral estates in France confiscated, Etienne reminded himself. And look at us now! There were still opportunities here in Louisiana for a young man of quality. He signaled the slave hovering in the background to bring more wine, and told the marquis, still watching the approaching carriage, "The young woman is my late brother's heiress."

"An independent young woman," Madame Roget added, in tones that managed to convey both affection and disapproval.

"Indeed she is!" Philippe agreed wryly.

"Angèle is an original," Clothilde told him, laughing. "You will like her, m'sieu."

Philippe moved to the rail and watched, his aristocratic face alight with interest and amusement as the race ended in what was close to a dead heat. The children, screaming, "Enter, m'selle! Enter, enter!" threw wide the wrought-iron gates just seconds before the horse galloped through them and continued at a breakneck speed up the drive to the galérie, where his mistress turned him smartly at the foot of the ascending stair.

Philippe drew a long breath. "Magnificent, mademoiselle!"

The young woman lifted her head and flicked a brief glance at the man bending over the rail, then threw her reins to the groom who waited, and jumped down from the carriage.

She wore a straw hat on her thick dark hair, and a prim light-colored dress that defined a pretty bosom and fitted over narrow hips above a flaring skirt. But it was her look that had given Philippe a curious shock—it was very direct, from the coolest of blue eyes ringed with sweeping black lashes.

Philippe was not an excessively conceited man, yet he had grown accustomed to a certain expression in the eyes of the women he met. Whether gentle and soft or discreetly bold, it was invariably a look of approval. He was so tall that he gave an impression of slenderness although his shoulders were broad. He had melancholy dark eyes, and his creamy skin with the rosy cheeks often seen on young French boys were in striking contrast to his velvet black brows and hair; but it was something more subtle than his looks that moved women to instinctive approval and had led a doting aunt to exclaim that he had the face of an angel.

The truth was that Philippe had a genuine liking for and a rare sympathy with women. They sensed it in the deep interest with which he listened to what a woman said. They trusted it even when he teased them. They read it in his expressive eyes and were melted by it. It amazed him sometimes how quickly they melted.

But this woman! Her look was one Philippe had never encountered before, and it intrigued him, because he was not sure whether it was meant to convey a challenge or merely a cool indifference. There seemed to be something of both in it, yet he did not think she was being deliberately provocative.

Coming up the steps to the galérie, she was calling in a low thrilling voice, "Good morning, Nonc' Etienne and Tant' Astride! Good morning, dear Clothilde!" She bent over her aunt and uncle, kissing their cheeks. Only then did she acknowledge his presence, with a question. "And m'sieu. . . ?"

Clothilde had risen to greet her cousin. "Angèle, may I present M'sieu le marquis, Philippe de l'Eglise? My cousin, Mademoiselle Roget."

"Enchanted." Again Philippe met that cool, measuring look.

It provoked him into saying, "You are a superb driver, Mademoiselle Roget, but I confess I thought to see a waste of prime horseflesh when you slammed into a closed gate."

"Spoken like an Englishman, Philippe." Etienne chuckled. "Everyone knows they hold their horseflesh more dear than their women."

Angèle ignored the remark. "My uncle's slaves will never permit me to reach a closed gate, m'sieu." She extended her hand with a faint smile.

He kissed her fingers. "I hope not, but if I were your husband, I am sure I would not allow you to risk your pretty neck in such reckless fashion."

"That, m'sieu, is exactly why I do not have a husband."

Etienne Roget's deep laugh rumbled. "Do not believe her, m'sieu. The real reason is that my niece refuses to turn La Sorcellerie, her inheritance, over to a man."

"Indeed?" With practiced ease Philippe catalogued her features. In spite of an almost masculine directness, she was both feminine and extremely attractive. "I foresee that someday some man will change your mind, mademoiselle."

"Many have tried," her uncle said, "but she has refused all offers, preferring managing her plantation to marriage. Now she is twenty-three and drying up."

"Etienne!" his wife reproached him.

Angèle's lashes drooped over her eyes and her lips quivered, but she said nothing.

It was the first hint of passion she had exhibited. Philippe was intrigued. He persisted, "Admit that a man is better suited than you, mademoiselle, to manage a plantation."

Her blue gaze flashed upward. "I admit nothing of the kind! I am quite capable of managing my plantation, m'sieu, and no one could care as much for La Sorcellerie as I do."

"Ah, but affection does not necessarily make a good stewardess."

Clothilde was looking alarmed. "Come, Angèle! Do you not wish to remove your hat and freshen yourself before dinner? You look somewhat heated."

"Thank you, Clothilde."

The two girls excused themselves and went into the house. Madame Roget left also, to see how the meal she had ordered

6

was progressing. Philippe remained standing, looking out at the naked children straggling back between the magnificent oaks. "My niece is an orphan," Etienne rumbled behind him, and Philippe turned to listen. "She lost her mother when she was ten. From that time until his death she was her father's sole companion, riding over the plantation with him daily. She has managed La Sorcellerie for the past three years, and the plantation has prospered. So she has convinced herself that she does not need a man." He shrugged.

And what of her emotional needs? Philippe wondered, but thought it would be imprudent to ask.

"Of course, she also finds the law which gives a husband absolute control over his wife's property unacceptable," Etienne said with a wry smile.

"A most unusual woman, obviously. I'm sorry that I baited her." Philippe genuinely regretted it. "I don't know why. . . ."

Etienne chuckled. "She is a challenge to our masculine pride, no? We do not like to think a woman can prosper without us."

Inside the house the two girls had reached the top of the staircase and entered Clothilde's pleasant bedroom with its high, gauze-draped bed, and its long French windows open to the shaded upper galérie to let the faint coolness from the bayou steal in. Angèle removed the pins from her hat, saying, "Who is that odious man?"

Clothilde's delicate skin flushed the color of a pale rose, and distress darkened her eyes. "Oh, Angèle, how can you call him oc ious? I did so want you to like him."

"Who is he? Why haven't I met him before?"

"He has been in England since the Terror. He has only recently arrived in New Orleans. Papa met him at the Exchange." Her eyes were suspiciously bright.

Angèle looked closely at her young cousin. "What have I said? Are those tears?" she asked in surprise.

The younger girl turned quickly away. "Of course not! But don't you find him handsome, Angèle? Admit at least that you find him attractive!"

"You know that I find very few men attractive, Clothilde," Angèle said, shrugging. She was still annoyed with the marquis. "Is he so important to you, *chère?*"

Clothilde didn't answer at once. Then she said, "Maman thinks he may offer for me."

Angèle heard her with a tiny shock of dismay. But she took the younger girl by the shoulders and turned her around, kissing her. "Then I am happy for you," she said fondly. "So you will be a marquise!" She added, ironically, "For what that is worth today."

"A marquise without a home," Clothilde confessed. "Philippe's father's estates were confiscated, but he still believes he will regain his inheritance one day and return to France."

"What émigré doesn't!" Angèle said cynically. "Except Nonc' Etienne, who is a practical man."

"Papa tries to convince Philippe that his fortune lies here in Louisiana, now that we are again a French colony." Clothilde's cheeks were scarlet. "I did so want you to like him, Angèle."

"Dear Clothilde!" Angèle was filled with remorse. "If you are fond of him, that is all that matters. You know I shall like him too." But she was surprised by the strength of her instinctive rejection. Something in her was insisting, I do not want that man in the family! Ever since her mother's death she had considered Nonc' Etienne's family her own. Papa and his brother had always been close and Tant' Astride and Clothilde were like mother and sister to her.

Probably she would resent the intrusion of any outsider, but she and this arrogant young émigré would not agree on anything! She could see herself sparring with him, spoiling every family gathering. She did not ask herself why, but she knew it would be intolerable.

They said no more about it, Clothilde turning the conversation to the new gowns made for her on her mother's dressmaker's recent visit to Bellemont. When the bell rang for Madame Roget's Sunday afternoon dinner, the two girls went down the staircase arm in arm.

Clothilde's mother set a bountiful table. For the first course there were succulent oysters from Barataria, with a peppery sauce. The marquis was seated at Madame Roget's right hand, and Angèle on her left. Clothilde sat between Philippe and her father. This placed Angèle directly across from the marquis. She felt his speculative gaze on her, but avoided it as much as

8

possible. When their eyes accidentally met, she felt such a thrill of dislike that it confused her, and her confusion irritated her.

Clothilde watched Angèle and the marquis uneasily. She could feel the antagonism between them, and was distressed by it.

The second course consisted of braised partridges in a delectable sauce, and with it Etienne called for an imported wine.

"Smuggled in by the Baratarians," he confided to the marquis. "Now that Bonaparte has made peace with England and the English have lifted their blockade, it should be easier to obtain. But the Spanish have turned pirates, and we must contend with our former rulers! I fear I will still be going to Barataria."

Philippe laughed.

Etienne lifted his glass. "To Napoleon, who freed us from Spanish domination!"

"And who has not yet got around to sending us a French governor," Angèle said dryly.

"Tsk!" Etienne said in annoyance. "Bonaparte knows what he is doing, my dear."

"To the ladies," Philippe returned, looking at Clothilde, who colored becomingly.

Madame Roget beamed on them both, but Angèle barely touched her glass to her lips.

It was hot. The French doors to the galérie were shuttered, with open louvers to allow the air to circulate, but this afternoon the air was heavy and still. Madame Roget gave an order, and several black children came in with palm fans to circulate the air in the high-ceilinged room with its pale blue wainscoting and its plaster cherubim circling the point from which the crystal chandelier was suspended. Etienne was in good spirits. "So your family fled from Paris to England during the revolution?" he asked genially. "That was their choice, ah?"

"I remember little of that flight," the marquis confessed, "except that the excessive swaying of the coach at the speed we were traveling made me ill. We took the quickest road from our country place to the coast, which led us to Dieppe. At Dieppe we took the first ship. It was bound for the Netherlands, and from there we crossed to England."

"But what did your father find to do in England, m'sieu?"

"He spent his time until his death plotting to retrieve his estates."

"Ah, just so! My brother and I chose to come to the colonies, where it would be possible to build up another estate. Unfortunately we were scarcely settled in Saint Domingue when that black fellow who called himself Toussaint L'Ouverture led our slaves in a bloody revolt. Believe me, m'sieu, that was a narrow escape! If one of my brother's house servants had not warned us—"

"Oh, Papa, not again!" cried Clothilde, who had heard the story a hundred times and assumed it would be as tiring to the marquis as she found it.

Her father silenced her with a *tsk!* "We left at night, taking our jewels and valuables, our terrified women and children, and a house servant each of us trusted, and set out in a small boat for Florida. My sister-in-law Lisette was frail. She did not long survive that terrible voyage. . . ." He tossed off the last of his wine and the house servant behind him refilled his goblet.

"It was such a dreadful time," Madame Roget said. "Do we have to talk about it, Etienne?"

He paid no attention to his wife's interruption. "And now my brother Angel is gone too," he told the marquis. "Dead in his bed, of a natural affliction. But Angel and I, we escaped both the guillotine and the machete!" he finished, throwing up his grizzled head in pride. "And look at us now! Are we not comfortable in this tropical Nouvelle Orléans? The Good Lord has been generous."

Although Clothilde had begged her father not to tell their story again, she saw an opportunity to break down the hostility she sensed between two people she loved. "Cousin Angèle was a skinny ten-year-old when we fled from Saint Domingue," she told the marquis, "and I was not yet five. Angèle held me in her arms all through that dreadful voyage, while her mother was dying. She is very dear to me," she finished, her eyes, soft with love, going from his face to Angèle's. "I hope you will be good friends."

"I hope Mademoiselle will allow me to be her friend," Philippe replied. "But I fear she does not have a high opinion of my sex."

"Or you of mine, m'sieu!" Angèle retorted.

10

"On the contrary, ma'am'selle." The deep twinkle in his eyes annoyed her. "Tell me, what is your principle crop at La Sorcellerie?"

"One day it will be cane." She flung it at him like a challenge, but said no more.

"My brother became very interested in sugarcane during our two years in the West Indies," Etienne said. "He began experimenting with it as soon as we purchased our land here. Angèle and I both watched his experiments with great interest."

"Indeed?" said the marquis. "I find West Indies sugar far superior to that which is locally grown. Louisiana sugar is often only half crystallized."

"True," Etienne said, "but in a few years—"

Angèle cut in pointedly. "Clothilde, you must bring M'sieu le marquis to La Sorcellerie while he is your guest and let me show him our experimental cane fields."

"We will ride over tomorrow morning," Clothilde said, smiling with relief at this evidence of her cousin's goodwill. "Would you like that, m'sieu?"

"It would give me the greatest pleasure," Philippe said, smiling.

But Angèle read into his smiling reply a tolerance she found disparaging, and closed her lips on the tart response she would have liked to give him. She did not understand why she was spoiling for a fight, but she longed to fly into a passion and rage at him. It would have relieved the tension that had been building inside her ever since she met him.

The roast of venison was just being served. It would be impossible to leave for over an hour. Angèle set herself to concealing her thoughts from her aunt and uncle, and as soon as she could courteously do so after dinner, ordered her carriage brought around.

She took great pleasure in urging her horse to a furious gallop on the heels of the children who raced ahead of her to open Nonc' Etienne's gate. Their screams of delight at winning the race rang in her ears as she dashed recklessly after them as they pushed the gate open. With the thrill of danger she felt one carriage wheel lift a bit as she turned sharply onto the bayou road.

Behind her, she imagined she heard Philippe de l'Eglise

laughing, although she was much too far away to have heard him.

By the time she reached La Sorcellerie, scarcely three miles away, Angèle was calmer. As always, at her first glimpse of the house her father had built, she was suffused with the pleasure of homecoming. The house faced the boat landing, but she approached it from one side by the new road which cut off a bend in the bayou. The afternoon sun threw diagonal bands of brilliant light across its creamy walls and dark blue shutters.

La Sorcellerie was not so different in style from other French plantation houses along the bayous fanning out from the Mississippi. It rose two-and-a-half stories to bring the living quarters above the flood level when the river overflowed its levees. Almost square, La Sorcellerie had the typical steep four-sided roof that extended over upper and lower galéries, both of which entirely circled the house.

Its special charm lay in the delicacy of the slender pillars rising from their square brick bases through both galéries to the roof. It was a style influenced by the tropical planters' houses they had become acquainted with in the West Indies, and it was perfectly suited to the Louisiana climate.

Camellias and azaleas Angèle had planted before her father's death surrounded the house with masses of pink and rose every spring, and they were dazzling in the lowering sun. Admiring them, Angèle realized she was seeing her beloved home as she imagined it would look to Philippe de l'Eglise, and she thrust the thought of him away with irritation.

There was no gate at La Sorcellerie. At the broad steps to the lower galérie her groom waited to take the reins and drive her carriage to the stables behind the house where two stable boys would rub her horse down and feed and water him. A dignified white-haired man who had been her father's valet and was now her majordomo opened the fanlighted door for her.

"Thank you, Duval." She went past him into the comparative coolness of the house. "Where is Mimi?"

"I am here, m'selle." A slender quadroon who looked to be about Angèle's age but was actually ten years older, appeared at the top of the graceful staircase rising from the foyer. Angèle climbed toward her, her hand unconsciously caressing the

South American mahogany of the balustrade, beautiful in its simplicity.

"Prepare a bath for me, Mimi. A cool one, please."

"Ah, yes, poor dear." Her voice was dark and rich, and her French was perfect. "You are wilted, no?" She was looking with compassion at the curling damp tendrils of hair around Angèle's face.

"Yes, it's hot, hot!" Angèle went impatiently past her into her bedroom.

Mimi had a unique position in her household. She had been Angèle's nursemaid in Saint Domingue and her personal maid since she had grown up. Now that Angèle spent so much time in the management of her plantation, she depended on Duval to keep her other four house servants, consisting of a cook, two young maids, and a footman, disciplined and industrious. But Mimi had become her assistant as well as her confidante, often the liaison between her and Duval. Angèle's nerves were jangling, and she knew it was the thought of Clothilde's marriage that bothered her. What Clothilde had told the marquis about their closeness was true. Angèle's love for Clothilde had something maternal in it, and it probably did have its beginning in that time of terror and the dangers of their voyage when she had tenderly comforted and cared for her young cousin while the adults, both black and white, were concerned with reaching a safe harbor, and with the alarming frailty of her mother.

It was not that Clothilde was too young to marry; at seventeen she was already past the age when most Creole girls were given in marriage. No, it was the man she had chosen, and Angèle was at a loss to explain why her instinct to fight the proposed match was so strong.

Mimi brought one of the young black maids carrying a steaming kettle of water, and directed the girl to set it down while she pulled the tin bathtub from a closet. It was Mimi, daughter of a West Indian planter and his mulatto mistress, who had warned them about the slave revolt and helped them flee Saint Domingue.

Long afterward Angèle had a glimmer of understanding why Mimi had done it, but it was an insight she had pushed from her immature consciousness, remembering only how tenderly the dusky-skinned girl had cared for her mother until her death, and for herself, a bereaved child.

"Minette! Ouma!" Mimi called sharply, as they heard childish voices on the stairs.

The two children straggled down the hall and into the room, carrying buckets of cool water to mix with the hot. Neither of her children resembled Mimi, whose full curving lips and slightly flattened nose were more eloquent than the café-au-lait skin of her African heritage. Both of Mimi's children were lighter than their mother, their delicate features showing their French blood.

Minette had always been a beautiful child, with sparkling dark eyes, and shining hair which clustered around her piquant face in soft biddable curls. It was Angèle's father who began calling her Minette, "kitten," and the nickname stuck. Mimi had taught her child to set a proper table when she was still too small to reach it without standing on a wooden box. But looking at Minette's budding breasts and the tiny jutting buttocks that Angèle realized were typically African, she knew that the girl would never be content to be a house servant.

There were other paths open to a beautiful octaroon, and Minette showed promise of great beauty. Angèle resolved that she would speak to Nonc' Etienne about the child. Until then she would put this faint anxiety about her out of her mind.

There would be a place for Minette's brother Ouma at La Sorcellerie. A sturdy boy of fourteen, he said little, but his black eyes saw everything. If her father were still living, he would have Ouma educated. She would have to consider that.

The children poured water into the tub, and at their mother's bidding, ran from the room. While Mimi added hot water to her bath, Angèle pinned her heavy cloud of hair high on her head, then stood to let Mimi unbutton her dress and slip it down over Angèle's arms and her narrow hips so she could step out of it. Next Mimi untied the light corselette that squeezed her waist and pushed up her small round breasts.

The tub was too short for Angèle to stretch her long legs, but it had a sloping back, and she leaned against it, relaxing sensuously as the tepid water cooled her blood. Looking down at her flat abdomen and the slender thighs rising to her bent knees,

Angèle had a sudden startling vision of Philippe de l'Eglise as he might look in his bath.

It was not difficult to imagine his elegant long-limbed figure unclothed. Daily she saw her slaves with their bodies bared to the waist, their muscles rippling under the glistening ebony skin as they worked. Philippe's paler skin would glisten like gold in the sun, but the muscles of his broad shoulders would ripple in the same way. That his long legs were as straight and shapely as her own, had been clearly evident because of the tight fit of his fine cloth breeches.

But what shocked Angèle was the vision that immediately followed. Too quickly for her to prevent it, the slender white curves of Clothilde's young body leaped to her mind, and she saw it pressed close to Philippe's, their arms entwined—lovers in a naked embrace.

Hot blood suffused her, undoing the effect of the cooling water. Angèle put her hands to her flaming cheeks, and Mimi looked at her curiously. "Are you feverish, m'selle?"

"No, no, Mimi. I don't think so. Just overheated."

"Shall I bring more cool water?"

"No, never mind." Angèle was appalled at her thoughts. She did not want a man in that way, and particularly not a man Clothilde was interested in! But her body was playing cruel tricks on her. She straightened in her bath and stood up, letting Mimi envelop her in a towel.

"M'selle Clothilde has a houseguest," she told Mimi.

"Oui, m'selle?"

"A young man. A marquis. I think he likes her very much."

"That is good, no?"

"Yes, Mimi, it is good. I think I shall entertain for them at La Sorcellerie before m'sieu returns to New Orleans."

Yes, that was what she would do. She would give a ball! There was little time to prepare a really special entertainment, but Tant' Astride would help. They had often pooled their household help when Bellemont or La Sorcellerie entertained, and their slaves enjoyed those rare opportunities to work and feast while visiting.

Her aunt and uncle would be pleased, and she would become used to seeing Clothilde and her marquis together.

Chapter 2

WHEN Angèle heard the rat-a-tat of cantering horses on the drive at ten o'clock the next morning, her nerves tightened as if to meet a challenge. She was sitting before the mirror in her bedchamber while Mimi put the finishing touches to her coiffure. Ouma's young voice floated up over the galérie as he shouted, "I go, m'selle! I go!"

Mimi shook her head in smiling exasperation. "Now he tries to be your groom! That boy worships you, m'selle."

"They're here! I must hurry, Mimi." Ridiculously, there was that same hollowness in Angèle's stomach she had felt when she was summoned to the Mother Superior during her school days in the convent of the Ursuline nuns.

My word! Was she not a grown woman now, and a plantation owner? The days when she and her friends at the convent had been vulnerable to emotional storms of the heart were long past. She schooled herself to impassivity.

Nevertheless when she went out on the upper galérie to greet Clothilde and her guest, her cool expression concealed a curious fluttering of her nerves. Philippe de l'Eglise was impressive astride Nonc' Etienne's large black stallion. Mounted, he lost the illusion of slenderness that his height gave him, appearing broad and muscular and more formidably masculine. Mon dieu! Happy or not, if she married him Clothilde would have a husband to be proud of!

Clothilde sat at ease on her own dainty mare, looking fresh and charming in a riding skirt, a small straw hat perched on her pinned-up hair. She would be a prize for any man, Angèle thought fondly.

She leaned over the rail. "Come up for coffee before we give m'sieu the grand tour," she called.

Clothilde looked up and waved gaily. "Thank you, Angèle."

Angèle ran down the stairs and emerged on the lower galérie just as Philippe jumped down, tossing his reins to Ouma, who had come running around the house with Jules, who held Clothilde's horse. Philippe walked around to help Clothilde dismount.

The young black boy was studying the finely dressed marquis with wide eyes but a touching dignity. Angèle called down, "Let Ouma give the horses water, Jules. You saddle Jolie for me."

"Oui, m'selle."

Philippe watched Ouma as the slaves led the horses away. "What a handsome boy!" he said, following Clothilde up the steps. "Was he bred on La Sorcellerie?"

Angèle's lips tightened. She glanced at Clothilde, but the younger girl did not meet her eyes. "He is the son of my maid, a West Indian quadroon," Angèle said curtly. "One day he will be my majordomo."

Philippe nodded approval. "Excellent stock for house servants," he commented, "but not husky enough for labor." He saw the anger she could not conceal then, and raised velvety black eyebrows. "Forgive me if you think me indelicate, mademoiselle, but surely you cannot be offended by such discussions of plantation management?"

Was there mockery in those dark eyes? She managed a shrug, but her smile was glacial. His first casual question had sunk deep, touching that moist festering wound all Louisiana women kept hidden under a bandage of pride. Philippe was a newcomer to New Orleans; still, he should have known better.

He did know, of course. What he was saying was that her management of the plantation absolved him of the necessity for treating her with the delicacy due a woman in civilized society. Being hospitable to Clothilde's guest was going to tax all her social resources.

With a wave of her hand she invited them to enter through the wide fan-topped doorway. Philippe looked around the high-ceilinged entry, noting its bronze and crystal chandelier and glancing up the handsome staircase to the landing where light streamed in from the upper galéries.

"A splendid house, mademoiselle."

"My father planned it," she said coolly. She turned to her majordomo, who stood by the stair. "Duval, please show m'sieu where he may wash while I order the coffee. You may take him to Papa's old room. Clothilde, Mimi will assist you in mine. Coffee will be served on the galérie."

Clothilde smiled at Philippe. "We live on our galéries, m'sieu."

"A charming custom in this climate."

When Clothilde preceded Philippe upstairs, Angèle entered the salon to jerk the bell pull that would signal the kitchen they were ready for the coffee and tray of sweet cakes she had ordered.

Conflicting impulses were warring within her: to make the marquis acknowledge that a woman could manage her own inheritance, and to show him that she could still be a woman. This morning would not be easy for her.

But why should she care what he thought? she wondered. It was, of course, for dear Clothilde's sake.

When they were seated around the silver coffee service on the galérie, Angèle asked pleasantly, "How long will you be at Bellemont, m'sieu?"

In his eyes she clearly discerned his knowledge of the secret fury that still burned in her breast, but he was smiling at her and she fancied he was amused. "Another fortnight, mademoiselle."

"Excellent," she said brightly. "Clothilde, I would like to give a ball honoring your guest. Don't you think that will be pleasant?"

"Dear Angèle!" Clothilde exclaimed, delighted. "It's charming of you! Maman will be so pleased."

"I'll send out invitations immediately," Angèle declared. "Shall we say Saturday after next?"

"You are very kind, mademoiselle." The glint in Philippe's eyes had grown more pronounced, making her uncomfortable. She and Clothilde discussed the guest list for some time, then Angèle suggested that they commence their ride before the sun climbed too high.

Their horses were brought around and they set down their small coffee cups and went leisurely down the steps to mount, the marquis helping first Clothilde and then Angèle. Resting her hand on Philippe's shoulder to steady herself as she placed her foot in his palm, she felt the movement of his muscles as he lifted her. It seemed disturbingly intimate. Quickly she touched her mare's flanks and trotted in the lead.

They rode around the house beneath magnolia trees where black gardeners were raking the earth, and passed the detached kitchen. Smoke hung in the heavy warm air, and the aroma of baking bread followed them.

The lane was strewn with sand bordered with whitewashed stones, but on each side of it the earth was black and moist. The way led between two rows of cypress cabins, also whitewashed. Black babies played in the doorways, while behind them dark figures stood in the shadowy interiors, gazing impassively at the passing riders. Angèle thought that Philippe looked closely at the sturdy infants. He said nothing, but she was made aware that none was as light-skinned as Ouma, and her lips tightened again in dislike.

Beyond the slave quarters they turned right and rode past the thatch-roofed grinding shed with its huge flat stone and the long sweep which lay idle. "When we are grinding cane," Angèle told Philippe, "the sweep is fastened to a yoked mule and he walks round and round, turning the stone."

"I have seen similar mills in the West Indies," Philippe murmured.

"The stone was shipped from Saint Domingue," she admitted.

"Crude, but effective," he said, dismissing it.

She tightened her lips.

Beyond the crushing shed she pointed out the boiling pots in which the cane juice was cooked until it became liquid sugar. "I grow little cane beyond what we can use on the plantation," Angèle explained. "But I have several small experimental fields where I am trying to develop a strain which will crystallize in this climate."

"M'sieu de Boré is also trying to crystallize Louisiana cane sugar without much success," remarked the marquis.

Angèle flushed. "M'sieu de Boré and I compare results of our experiments," she said stiffly.

But she could see that in spite of his skepticism, Philippe was genuinely interested. His eyes were alert, and the expression on his face was beginning to show more than a casual interest. Gradually Angèle regained her composure. She sat her mount confidently, mistress of all they could see. Here she was in her element. This was the life she had chosen: to follow in her father's footsteps, turning her back on the usual role of a Louisiana woman as mistress of her husband's home and mother of his bouquet of children, although not without some doubts about the sacrifices it required.

But as she described the operation of the plantation and the extent of her experiments, she grew completely absorbed, her enthusiasm vibrant in her unusually low voice. Her cheeks warmed with color.

Indigo grew beyond the cane. "An old field," Angèle said, pointing it out. "Not very productive. We have a problem with a parasite which attacks the plant."

Beyond the indigo an irregular dark line marked the beginning of the cypress swamp that lay behind New Orleans and all the plantations along the river. There the trees and intertwining vines grew so thick that the sun could not penetrate its oppressive gloom, but as they rode nearer, they saw an occasional flicker of reflected light on black stagnant water. Large birds flew up as the sound of their horses' hooves reached the swamp, flapping their wings and disappearing into deeper gloom. Turtles and alligators slid off logs, disappearing beneath the opaque water.

The heavy characteristic smell of the swamp was in the air, an aroma composed of rotting leaves, damp air, and a dank animal odor. Along its border fifteen or twenty slaves, naked to the waist and standing in black mud that coated their legs, were sluggishly digging a trench. Sweat dripped from their bodies, and in the sun their skin shone like oiled ebony.

"Mon dieu, what hot work!" Philippe muttered. "What are they doing?"

"They are making a canal which will drain the swamp."

To the rhythm of a slow chant they were throwing mud up on the sides of the trench, which filled with water as they dug. The mud was slowly drying in the sun, forming a path of fairly solid earth along the bank of the new canal. Along this levee the overseer, a big half-Spanish mulatto with a short-clipped beard, came walking toward them.

"In a year or two," Angèle explained, "when the cypress dries out, we will begin cutting it for lumber. Eventually the roots will be burned out and I will be able to plant more cane."

"You assume your experiments will succeed, then," Philippe commented, it seemed to her with an amused condescension.

"It is only a matter of time, m'sieu, before we will have a commercial crop of sugar as good as that imported from Saint Domingue."

"Angèle is so clever!" exclaimed Clothilde, who had been listening admiringly.

"You are looking a long way into the future, mademoiselle. A lifetime, perhaps."

"La Sorcellerie is my life," Angèle said simply.

Philippe looked at her out of expressive eyes and murmured, "All of it?" Something in the way he said it, and the way he looked at her, caused a twang along her nerves, harsh as the accidental pluck of a guitar. There was no doubt whatever as to what he wondered!

She turned abruptly to her overseer and spoke crisply with him for a few minutes about the drainage trench, then they turned back. The sun was high, and their sweating horses moved slowly. It was a great discomfort to be so aware of the man on Nonc's black stallion, and the subtle but very physical way he constantly challenged her. Was Clothilde seeing this byplay? Her gentle cousin must not marry this man! she thought. He would break the heart of any woman so foolish as to give him her love.

At La Sorcellerie Clothilde went up to Angèle's room again

to sponge the heat of the ride from her face. This time Angèle accompanied her. Mimi awaited them in Angèle's room, whose colors—mostly cool blues and greens—gave it an illusion of comfort. The shutters were closed on the French windows looking out on the upper galérie, and the white bed was shadowy behind its mosquito netting. Mimi poured water for Clothilde from the tall porcelain pitcher into the fluted white porcelain basin.

Clothilde thanked her with a sunny smile, then turned to Angèle. "Philippe was fascinated," she told her. "He is impressed by your remarkable knowledge and ability."

"Indeed?" Angèle said dryly.

Her cousin dipped her hands into the cool water. "Men just won't believe a woman can do such things." She raised dripping hands to her flushed face. "But really, Angèle," she said seriously, looking up through drenched lashes, "he is very understanding. He is a man who knows without being told just what a woman is thinking and feeling. Sometimes it's uncanny!"

"Indeed!" Angèle repeated. Her mouth was actually dry.

"I can hardly wait until the ball," Clothilde chattered on, catching up the towel Mimi handed her. "You always give such wonderful soirées at La Sorcellerie! Just like Nonc' Angel used to give."

"My dear, I planned his soirées from the time I was thirteen! I shall address the invitations this very evening," Angèle promised.

"I can't wait!" Clothilde said again. "Perhaps he will have spoken to Papa before then!"

Angèle stared. "But surely you would not want to announce your betrothal at my ball?"

"Oh, no! Maman will want to give her own reception for that. Can't I do something for the ball? Please let me help."

"Thank you, Clothilde. You can help with delivering the invitations. I should like to have them delivered as quickly as possible. Perhaps Nonc' Etienne's driver can help Jules tomorrow, for he cannot do it in one day. I'll send Jules to New Orleans. If your Bris could ride toward the lake—"

"Of course! Shall I send him over for the notices in the morning? No, I have a better idea. Why not come to Bellemont for coffee in the morning and bring those invitations with you—"

"And you shall help me plan the entertainment."

Now why had she agreed to that? Angèle asked herself. She had no wish to drive to Bellemont again while the marquis was a guest there.

Clothilde kissed her. "It will be such fun! Until tomorrow morning, dear Angèle."

They returned downstairs, where the marquis awaited them, his expressive eyes admiring them both. Philippe was thinking that the young girl, all softness and color, was like a luscious fruit ripe for picking, but the woman's beauty was mysteriously different, spiced with a tangy wit and a subtle challenge in her flashing eyes. He took her hand, brought it to his lips, and was stirred when he felt its delicate quiver.

"Until tomorrow," he murmured, with a speaking look, and was amused at the brisk way she responded as he and Clothilde took their leave.

Angèle was still irritated with herself in the morning as she set out for Bellemont with the invitations, and her annoyance made her drive her horse faster than her usual breakneck speed. She had spent several hours during last evening addressing the notes, and then stayed awake chastising herself for even thinking of giving a ball. She was still wondering why she was doing it.

Why on earth should she? she asked herself. She did not wish to encourage this betrothal. If it should come about, she would be obliged to give more parties. Where had she mislaid her judgment?

Her mood was reckless when the low stone fence with its closed iron gates came into view. She raised her whip and urged her horse even faster. The screaming black children were still pushing open the gates when she dashed through them and thundered up the drive to the galérie. No one was on it but Philippe de l'Eglise, who was standing at the rail, gripping it.

Even from below she could see how white his knuckles were as he stood there, glaring down at her. In a low, angry voice, he said, "You're tempting fate, you little fool!"

Shocked at his tone, but with a curious thrill of satisfaction, she tossed her reins to the black groom who stood waiting, and ran up the stairs with the same verve she exhibited driving her coach.

"Were you speaking to me, m'sieu?" she asked coolly.

"You know damn well I was!"

He moved toward her with his hands lifted as if to grab her by her shoulders and rattle her teeth, but he stopped dead when Etienne came out of the house behind him, rumbling, "Angèle, dear!"

Startled and shaken, Angèle murmured, "Uncle!" as he kissed her cheeks.

She stole a glance at the marquis. A polite mask had slid over his aristocratic face, but his eyes were still furious. Her heart pounded with a wild exultation. So he was not as self-possessed as he appeared!

I'll show you, you arrogant Bourbon! she thought.

Clothilde came out of the house, her hands outstretched, her face alight with innocent love. "Cousin Angèle! Did you stay up all night addressing those invitations for your ball? Give them to me and I will send Bris off immediately. Maman is delighted."

For a moment Angèle stood still. The wild thudding charge of excitement drained out of her until she felt almost ill, and for the space of several heartbeats she was disoriented—a stranger in a strange landscape. *How extraordinary!* In shock she asked herself what was happening. Whether Clothilde's suitor approved of her actions or not was nothing to her, she told herself.

Then she regained her composure and embraced Clothilde. She disliked the marquis even more now than before, she was thinking, even while greeting her young cousin and pulling the bundle of invitations from her reticule.

"Sit here and talk to Papa and M'sieu while I attend to these," Clothilde said. "Or do you wish to go upstairs?"

Angèle met Philippe de l'Eglise's eyes. They were so knowing! He knew exactly what she was feeling. He expected her to flee the galérie, and would no doubt congratulate himself on disturbing her calm.

"No, thank you, dear." Angèle seated herself with a show of composure she did not feel, and turned brightly to her uncle, resolved to take care not to find herself alone with the marquis again.

She was grateful for Nonc's presence, and that his nattering kept the marquis occupied until Tant' Astride appeared, a maid following with the coffee tray. Astride greeted Angèle warmly, thanking her for helping to entertain their guest. A moment later Clothilde brought the news that her share of the invitations had been dispatched. From that time on they discussed nothing but Angèle's plans for the ball, with many offers of help.

Driving back to La Sorcellerie with her head full of things to do, Angèle thought briefly about that astonishing moment when Philippe de l'Eglise had been so angry with her and she had exulted in his fury. The look in his eyes, disturbing in its intensity, kept coming back to her, and she decided she'd been right to instinctively mistrust him.

He was too attractive. Even she, who had long ago resolved that no man would possess her, had been stirred to unladylike passion when he accosted her with anger. Soberly she said to herself, "I am concerned for Clothilde. I am afraid he will hurt her."

For the next ten days Angèle was kept too busy to make her usual calls at Bellemont, and when Clothilde and Tant' Astride came, they were delivered by Nonc' Etienne's coachman. Etienne, they said, was keeping their guest amused, with hunts and cards. Angèle knew she would not see Philippe de l'Eglise again until the night of the ball.

For days the kitchen servants had been preparing pastries and fancy little cakes, and now they were starting on the daube glacées. Others had been giving the house a special polish. La Sorcellerie had never looked lovelier. The wide plank floors and the furniture gleamed in the light of hundreds of candles. They blazed in all the rooms in chandeliers and wall sconces, and in paper lanterns Angèle had directed her servants to string on both upper and lower galéries.

The drawing room and dining room, two large salons to the left of the entry, were open to form one room extending from the front to the rear of the house. Each room had two sets of wide French doors opening to the galérie. In one corner of the ballroom thus formed, a dais had been brought in for the musicians. The chairs and lounges were ranged around the walls, but the dining table had been moved across the hall to what had been her father's study. On it was a large silver bowl and silver cups for the gentlemen interested in the potent punch for which her father's soirées had been famous.

Carriages began arriving at dusk. The women of the Creoles —as the colonists of French and Spanish descent called themselves—favored white dresses, and they alighted and swarmed up the steps to the galérie like a bevy of white butterflies, calling to each other in high sweet voices in a shower of laughter and greetings.

Angèle was busy with her guests when Nonc' Etienne and Tant' Astride arrived with Clothilde and their guest. Her first sight of Philippe de l'Eglise was one she would never forget, and once she saw him she could not take her eyes from him. He, too, was dressed in white, with a pale blue waistcoat, and the contrast his velvet-black hair and brows made with his embroidered coat and knee-length breeches was very effective.

She told herself that it was because he was half a head taller than the other men present that she was always aware of his position as she moved among her guests. It was not difficult to avoid him. He was finding favor with her other guests, and they were keeping him occupied.

She greeted an old friend and former admirer, Henri Devaux. He had been one of the most persistent of the young gallants who pressed their suits after her father died. With Henri was a stranger.

"I crave your indulgence, dear Angèle. I have brought a friend with me. May I present M'sieu Bellamy? He is an American business associate of mine who is establishing himself in New Orleans."

"Any friend of yours is welcome, Henri."

"I am charmed, mademoiselle," said the American.

Angèle looked at him with interest. He was a robust young man with steady hazel eyes and a thatch of hair the color of chestnuts. His hearty voice suggested a man of the frontier, but he spoke surprisingly good French.

"Where is your home, m'sieu?" Angèle asked him.

"In New Orleans, mademoiselle," he replied with a twinkle, "but I come from Philadelphia."

"An American?" Clothilde had appeared at Angèle's elbow.

She was sparkling with pleasure, and Angèle thought she looked especially lovely. "Clothilde, may I present Henri's friend, M'sieu Bellamy?"

Clothilde laughed her bell-like laugh. "But you cannot be American, m'sieu! Surely you are French, with a name like Belle Aimée."

Angèle saw the glaze that came over M'sieu Bellamy's eyes as they took in Clothilde's fresh young beauty. "I would like to think my name was originally French, mademoiselle. However, I fear it has long been anglicized."

"And are you 'beloved,' as your name suggests, m'sieu?" Clothilde asked mischievously.

"Alas, no, mademoiselle," he said, with a look that left an impression on Angèle.

"You have made a conquest of M'sieu Bellamy, Clothilde," she whispered to her cousin after the men had excused themselves and moved on.

But her cousin whispered back, "Isn't Philippe marvelous? Have you noted what a sensation he is with your guests?"

"Certainly with the women," Angèle said tartly.

Poor Clothilde! Quite apart from his striking height and appearance, Philippe de l'Eglise was a man who would always be attractive to women. As for herself, she thought, the less she saw of him the better.

When the musicians began playing, the marquis made his way toward them, smiling. "Oh, there you are, m'sieu!" Angèle said. "Will you and Clothilde lead the dance?"

"Isn't it customary for the guest of honor to lead his hostess?" Philippe said, giving Angèle a look of invitation so soft and glistening that she could not meet it.

"No, no," she exclaimed. "Clothilde is your hostess as much as I. I insist, Clothilde."

It was only later, when she saw the significant glances and heard the whispers of her guests, that Angèle realized what she had done. It was tantamount to announcing publicly that the marquis was seeking Clothilde's hand! She saw envious looks on several young faces, both male and female, as they watched the handsome couple perform the intricate steps of the dance. She must quickly apologize to Tant' Astride, she thought.

Angèle soon realized that she had only succeeded in delaying what she dreaded, for Philippe returned to her to claim the next set. Reluctantly she gave him her hand.

Angèle was taller than most of her Creole friends, a match for Philippe's height. She was not as curvaceous as Clothilde, being slender and strong from her daily hours on horseback, but she had a natural grace. Immediately she sensed a physical rapport with the marquis. She was aware of the touch of his hand in a curious way throughout her body. It was light and courteous, yet she felt as if their hands had fused and that she would never be able to withdraw her fingers from his.

The air was fragrant with the scent of jasmine carried on the balmy night air wafting in from the bayou. The shrill chorus of the tree frogs and the deeper croaking of bullfrogs came through the open doors to mingle with the strains of the violins and guitars of the musicians. Philippe's dark eyes smiled down at her with admiration and a secret awareness of the response she was feeling as she turned and bowed before him.

She felt her cheeks grow hot, and wondered if the dance would ever end. Tearing her gaze away from the hypnotizing eyes of her partner, she looked for Clothilde. Her cousin was dancing with M'sieu Bellamy, who was obviously entranced.

Clothilde's happiness was overflowing, Angèle thought; she was spreading it recklessly around her. Again Angèle felt a chill of premonition.

"Clothilde looks so happy tonight," she told Philippe, and added, hoping to provoke him, "M'sieu Bellamy seems quite taken with her."

"She is   delicious girl, a confection!" the marquis said, with obvious appreciation.

"What a curious thing to say!" Angèle exclaimed coldly. "It is like smacking your lips, m'sieu."

He laughed.

She wanted to ask him bluntly whether that meant he was in love with Clothilde. Did a man in love speak of his future wife as a confection? But the music had ended. Angèle sighed with relief and moved quickly away from Philippe, determined not to dance with him again.

He had no lack of partners, but all during the evening she was aware of his eyes, looking over the heads of her guests and finding her. Her own eyes constantly sought him, but it was to enable her to avoid him. When he moved in her direction, she immediately found it necessary to see to the comfort of Tant' Astride or to seek out one of her waiters with an unnecessary reminder to replenish the punch bowl for the gentlemen.

At midnight the silver bowl was moved to a sideboard and the servants laid out a supper of glacées of meat and crusty bread, fruit and pastries on the dining room table. The musicians were still playing, but softly, languidly, and no one was dancing. Guests were filling their plates and moving with them out on the galéries, where small tables had been set up under the paper lanterns.

Angèle came out of the pantry where she had been speaking with her cook about replacing some of the dishes in the dining room, and turned out of the hall onto the rear galérie for a moment of privacy and fresh air. No tables had been set here, and she thought the galérie was deserted until she smelled tobacco smoke. Looking along the row of slender white pillars, she saw the glow of a small cigar and recognized Philippe's white form between two of the pillars.

He threw his cigar over the rail into a flower bed and came toward her. "You have been avoiding me, mademoiselle."

"I have other guests also, m'sieu." She turned to go back into the house, but he moved quickly, and taking her arm, turned her to face him.

"But I am your guest of honor," he said, smiling, and in the light from the open French window she saw the teasing gleam in his eyes. "Surely you can spare me a moment to tell me why you are so determined to dislike me, Mademoiselle Angèle."

"Do not feel flattered, m'sieu. I dislike most men."

"That I find hard to believe." The caress in his voice alarmed her. She tried to pull her arm away, but he held it tightly. The warmth from his hand traveled up and spread to her head, flaming in her cheeks, and when he refused to release his fingers, it flowed down through her body in sensuous waves.

A panic was beginning to swell in her, warring with the delightful sensations rippling out from the bare arm he had captured.

"Why are you frightened? Is it my touch that alarms you?"

"What an egoist!" she scoffed tensely. "Why should I be frightened?"

"Why, indeed?" He was pulling her toward him. "You are not a bud anymore, my dear. You are a woman, a lovely long-stemmed rose of a woman. You have so much to offer a man."

"Me, I have nothing to give." She shrugged. "And I want nothing from any man."

"You are a woman with a woman's needs," he insisted. "I will show you, Angèle."

"I don't need you," she said, feeling desperate. "And you are Clothilde's!"

His fingers tightened on her arm. "No woman has a claim on me, Angèle. Not Clothilde, nor anyone else."

She was shocked and angered, remembering Clothilde's transparent happiness. "And no man shall ever have a claim on me!" she retorted.

A look came into his face, so intense that she mistook it for anger. But before she could draw back, he had slipped his free hand into the décolletage of her gown and taken one soft breast into his fingers like an apple.

She recoiled in shock from the intimate touch, but it ignited a passion that blazed with such suddenness and power that she was for a moment helpless in its grip. He slipped his arm around her, still holding her breast in his sinuous fingers. When his lips met hers, it was as if another creature possessed her, a self she had not known existed. She swayed toward him while her world rocked around her and her breasts flamed.

The kiss lasted for a long moment, and then she wrenched herself out of his hands and was running, appalled, into the pantry. Her precipitateness had twisted her breast, but stronger than the pain was the thrill of passion that still throbbed in it.

She wanted to hide from her guests and from what had happened, and from herself—this self that had betrayed her, this new self she could not accept.

She did not want Philippe de l'Eglise, she told herself, denying the clamor of her blood. She could not possibly want a man she so disliked.

And he was Clothilde's. He was Clothilde's!

Chapter 3

*I*N the deserted pantry Angèle stood in the shadows beyond the circle of light thrown by an iron candelabra. Her hands were pressed to her burning cheeks, and she was taking deep breaths to slow her racing heart. She had only minutes. At any moment a servant would return to pick up one of the trays of food arrayed on the work table in the center of the room. All her senses were keenly alive, alert for signs that she had been seen or that Philippe had followed her.

From beyond the pantry wall came a medley of voices and the tinkle of silverware against china as her guests continued around the buffet table set up in her father's study. Across the hall the musicians were still playing softly in the near empty ballroom, the piercing sweetness of the violins almost drowned by the singing of the tree frogs in the trees between the rear galérie and the kitchen.

At the sound of a soft step behind her, Angèle whirled around. When she saw the familiar dusky face, she sighed, "Oh, Mimi," and laid her head on the quadroon's shoulder.

"You overheated, m'selle!" Mimi exclaimed, feeling Angèle's

body heat through the soft cotton of her dress. "You must go sit with your aunt for a quarter hour and enjoy a cool drink."

"I can't. My guests—"

"You won't be missed. Everyone's having a good time. Your ball's a grand success, m'selle." Mimi, as tall as Angèle and only slightly heavier, moved to a low table which held a basin and a pitcher of water. She poured water into the basin, dipped a kitchen towel in it, and wrung it out.

"Here, cool your cheeks with this."

Angèle buried her face in the cool damp cloth while her heartbeat slowed and she gained control of herself. At last she put down the towel and straightened her shoulders.

Mimi looked her over critically, tucking a stray lock into her coiffure. "Your aunt is taking her supper on the front galérie. I'll send your lemonade."

With Mimi nodding approval of her appearance, Angèle, feeling sixteen again, walked out of the pantry and down the corridor past the ballroom. In a swift glance through the door to her left, she saw Clothilde at the buffet table between Philippe and M'sieu Bellamy, advising the American which of the Creole dishes to try. As if he were listening for her step, Philippe raised his head. His luminous eyes met Angèle's for a jolting second as she passed.

Taking another deep breath, she pushed through the front door and joined Tant' Astride and two of her aunt's friends, who were eating their supper at a small table.

"Where is your plate, Angèle?" Madame Roget chided her.

"I'm too hot to eat now, Tant' Astride. Perhaps later."

Ouma arrived, carrying her lemonade on a silver tray. He was wearing white trousers and a white shirt, which contrasted handsomely with his café-au-lait skin. He looked both proud of his new clothes and self-conscious about them.

"Thank you, Ouma." Looking into his serious young face, Angèle heard an echo of Philippe's lazy voice saying, "A handsome boy," and a tremor passed through her limbs.

"Did you shiver, Angèle?" her aunt said in a startled voice. "You're not taking a fever, are you?"

"No, Tant' Astride. It's nerves." She called Ouma back. "Tell Mimi to send the children with fans now, before the mosquitoes devour us."

"Oui, m'selle."

"You can slow down and take your pleasure, my dear. Your party is a great success."

"Thanks to your charming guest," Angèle returned automatically.

Her aunt nodded toward the azaleas below the galérie, making Angèle aware of the small dark forms hidden there. She saw flashes of the whites of enrapt eyes. The young slave children were enjoying the ball vicariously as they watched their older brothers and sisters station themselves near the tables with their waving palm fronds. Angèle and her aunt exchanged amused glances.

But Angèle's amusement evaporated when a radiant Clothilde came out on the galérie, followed by M'sieu Bellamy and Philippe. "You must sit with us, Angèle," she ordered gaily. "Poor M'sieu Well-Loved lacks a dinner partner."

"It's your duty as my hostess," the American reminded her with a twinkle.

"Then of course she must," Tant' Astride said, smiling her dismissal.

"But first I must fill a plate," Angèle said, avoiding Philippe's eyes. She stood up to flee, but M'sieu Bellamy was ahead of her.

"Please take my plate, mademoiselle, and I will fill another."

There was nothing to do but follow Clothilde to another table.

A panic seized Angèle as Philippe fell in behind her. She thought, What am I going to do? Her imagination leaped ahead, through countless parties she would have to attend if Clothilde was betrothed to this odious man. If Clothilde married him, she would naturally expect Angèle to be her attendant.

But Clothilde must not marry him! Angèle thought, resolving to do everything in her power to prevent such a marriage. Had not Philippe de l'Eglise revealed his true colors in that shocking familiarity that had made her completely lose her head? A word to Nonc' Etienne about that incident was all it would take . . . if she could bring herself to confess that she had neither screamed nor fainted.

Clothilde was sparkling tonight, her gentle nature made confident by the admiration of two handsome young men. It was an effort to join in her lighthearted banter with the American while ignoring Philippe. The marquis was saying little, but she was very conscious of him leaning back in his chair across the table from her, eyes half closed, the expression on his handsome face both disturbing and infuriating. In spite of his remote look, he seemed to listen for her voice and to be particularly intent when she spoke.

When he said something, his voice stroked her senses, exciting her, and she struggled against its affect. At last she looked at him, and was surprised by the worldly knowledge in his eyes. It was as if he saw her inner turmoil and viewed it with comprehension. Angèle rejected that look with all her power, finding it intolerable.

Tomorrow morning, she told herself, she would mount her favorite mare and inspect the experimental cane field with her overseer, and they would discuss her plans for the next planting. This temporary madness would fade into the insignificant thing it was, and tonight would be as if it had never happened. She would excise this self she did not recognize, this stranger-self who had taken possession of her body and had allowed Philippe's kiss.

She reminded herself that she had everything she wanted at La Sorcellerie except a family. In a way her slaves, her everyday familiars, filled that lack. And at Bellemont she had thrifty Nonc' Etienne, who teased her and gave her shrewd advice, and Tant' Astride, whose comfortable affection had buoyed her since her mother's death, but who never tried to impose her wishes on her strong-willed niece. And dear Clothilde, who was like a younger sister, and whose love was precious to her.

Do you really want to deny yourself the love of a man and the children he could give you? she thought, and stifled the unbidden question. Philippe de l'Eglise was not that man in any case, she told herself.

It was a relief to Angèle when the first carriage was brought around. For the next hour she stood at the entry bidding her guests good-bye as their equipages rolled up to the front steps in a steady stream. The Rogets and their guest were the last to leave. After their affectionate farewells Angèle went up to her room feeling emotionally exhausted, but when she was in her canopied bed with the gauze mosquito netting closed around it, she did not immediately fall asleep.

In fact she had never felt more wakeful. There was a singing along her veins, oddly like the anticipation she had felt before attending her first ball. How old had she been? Sixteen? It seemed a lifetime ago.

She set herself to doing mental arithmetic, adding up the acres of cane it would be possible to plant when the drainage ditches she envisioned were all in place. But the breast Philippe had held in his hand so tenderly, felt swollen and heavy, and she wondered if she had bruised it when she tore out of his grasp.

She was acutely aware of her body in a way that was both new and disturbing; there was a secret warm glow deep in its most intimate core. In the pale folds of the mosquito netting at the foot of her bed, an image of Philippe appeared as he had looked tonight, his dark curling hair in sharp contrast to the elegant white coat and white breeches that both revealed and enhanced his long limbs. He looked down at her with his faintly melancholy, intimate gaze and his knowing half smile, and a warm flush swept in waves over her. She was feeling again the pressure of his firm-muscled body against her own, and she experienced in memory the delightful weakness of melting against him.

Then she realized what her physical reactions signified, and she recoiled from confronting the implications of her own sensuality. She was beginning to envy Clothilde, who looked forward with such innocent confidence to the love and companionship she expected to find in marriage. For a few heart-stopping seconds Philippe's kiss had beguiled Angèle into thinking she glimpsed paradise!

Soberly she looked down a long tunnel of years, when she would live out her days as mistress and sole heiress of her beloved La Sorcellerie while longing for Clothilde's husband, and she made two vows: she would prevent this proposed marriage any way she could; and she would strangle the intolerable attraction she felt for Philippe de l'Eglise.

Finally, toward morning, she fell into an exhausted slumber.

The sun was high when Mimi's daughter came into her room balancing a large tray containing café au lait and rolls and set it down on a table beside the bed. Minette pulled back the mosquito netting. "Sun up, m'selle," she caroled, and went to open the shutters to the galérie.

"Hasn't Mimi taught you the proper way to waken your mistress?" Angèle demanded crossly.

"Oui, m'selle, but my mistress doesn't like to sleep late," the girl said pertly. "She prefers to ride out in the cool of early morning."

The child was growing tall. Her breasts were definitely budding, and those little jutting buttocks were somehow impudent. How old was she now? Thirteen going on fourteen?

Angèle was made aware of the passage of time and her advancing age. She could remember when Minette was born, shortly after they arrived in Louisiana after their ordeal in fleeing Saint Domingue, with Ouma still a babe in Mimi's arms. It occurred to her now that Mimi must have been carrying Minette when they made that perilous voyage from the West Indies.

But as usual she refused to think of Minette, whose arrival had been Angèle's first experience of a birthing. Ten years old and momentarily forsaken as her mother lay dying, she had gone down to the slave quarters looking for Mimi, stumbled on a Gothic scene in the candlelit room, and fled in horror. She remembered only that back in her own bedchamber she had been violently ill. All that remained in her consciousness was the faint revulsion she had always felt toward Mimi's daughter.

Her father, entertained by Minette's kittenish ways, had spoiled the little slave, Angèle thought with a flash of bitterness. Minette was not as biddable as her brother Ouma. There was a streak of independent mischief in her that not many slave owners would tolerate. It would be insupportable when she matured.

"Maman say I should help you dress." Minette's voice was shy, with a hint of childish pride.

Angèle told her shortly, "I won't need you, Minette," and looked away from the girl's disappointment.

She dressed in her coolest riding habit and went downstairs, where she found Mimi and a small army of black women cleaning up after the party. Angèle ordered her mare saddled, and with a straw hat protecting her head from the sun, rode out to inspect the work on the canal.

The morning was lazily humid, but she found the workers cheerful. Last night's ball had meant music and dancing in the slave quarters as well, and the leftovers of good food that would spoil quickly in this climate were always distributed among them. The chanting that accompanied the digging was vigorous, and there were smiles and good-natured taunts for Jean-Baptiste, her stern Spanish overseer.

After discussing the work with him, Angèle turned her mare Jolie back toward the house. It was nearing ten o'clock, at which time she usually took coffee on the galérie.

As she rode, Angèle surveyed her tall waving cane, green in the morning sunlight, lightly dusted with the lavender of tasseling just beginning. Warm pleasure curled around her heart. Soon the great stone wheel would be turning for the grinding, but now it lay idle in its bare-earth circle, warmed by the sun. From the slave quarters, shaded by the trees her father had planted, came the muted squawking of hens carrying across the field, and the shrieks and laughter of the children chasing them. Beyond the cabins rose the white columns of the second galérie of La Sorcellerie, serene and lovely, a cool refuge which beckoned her with its promise of morning coffee, perhaps with a ten o'clock caller.

As she came nearer the grinding stone, she saw a lone horseman riding out of the lane between the cabins toward her. She recognized her uncle's stallion but it was not Nonc' Etienne astride him. Hot blood rose to her head. M'sieu le marquis's audacity in coming alone to call on her—and so soon!—took her breath away.

But immediately she welcomed the opportunity to do what she had to do. She spurred her horse toward the marquis, which made him smile and lift his hand in welcome.

"Good morning, mademoiselle."

Angèle looked at him coolly, not answering his greeting. "I had not thought to see you out so early after your late night, m'sieu. But I am glad we have met this morning, for I have something important to say to you."

"And I to you, mademoiselle." He sat the stallion with an easy grace. His skin was clear and rosy; his eyes had lost the melancholy cast that tugged at a woman's heart, and were brilliant in the morning light. The stallion was restive, and Jolie wheeled nervously in the narrow cane road. Smiling intimately, Philippe urged the big stallion closer, until their horses' flanks touched. Jolie flinched and tossed her head, and Angèle flushed with annoyance.

"It is this," she said coldly. "You will not make an offer for my cousin Clothilde. I must warn you that if you persist in paying court to her, I will be forced to tell my uncle exactly what happened between us last night."

His eyes danced. "Everything?" he asked.

She felt a twinge of delicious pain in her bruised breast, and her cheeks warmed.

The glint in his eyes became one of suppressed laughter. "That will not be necessary, my dear Mademoiselle Angèle, unless, of course, you wish to confide in him. I have no intention of offering for your cousin."

She stammered, disbelieving, "You—you have no *intention. . . ?*"

"None."

After only a slight hesitation, she said, "That is wise of you." She was surprised by the ease of her victory, but contrarily, she was furious at how carelessly he could throw off Clothilde's infatuation, even though Angèle really thought it was for the best.

The marquis was looking at her with unsettling intensity. "In fæt I came this morning to warn you that I intend to ask your uncle for your hand, Mademoiselle Angèle."

She stared at him in shock. "For *me?* M'sieu le marquis, your arrogance is undoubtedly bred by your title, and so perhaps can be excused," she said icily. "But you should be aware that French royalty has little status today, even with the colonials."

"Indeed?" he said wryly. "I have not found it so." But he had reddened, and she felt a thrill of triumph.

She gave a shrug that said there was no accounting for tastes. "Do not waste your time, m'sieu. I am not my uncle's ward. No man can give me in marriage."

His eyes had narrowed; now they gleamed. "Then, mademoiselle, I shall ask you. May I have your permission to pay suit?"

Outraged, she cried, "How can you do this to Clothilde? You

must know that she is expecting you to offer for her. You have given her every reason to expect it. And she loves you!"

"And don't I have anything to say about it, you exasperating woman? I haven't been able to think of anyone else since I saw you in that little two-wheeled contraption, galloping your horse straight at a closed gate. I decided then that I must marry you to keep you from breaking your beautiful neck."

"You are making sport of me, m'sieu! I will not listen to such—"

"On the contrary, I am totally serious. God help me! You are a foolhardy driver, Angèle, and in England, if not in France, you would be ostracized for sitting your mare like a man, but you are a distractingly handsome woman, and I'm madly in love with you."

In spite of her fury, her heart gave a startled leap. She made her voice even icier. "That is unfortunate because I do not love you."

"Then I have a rival?" he asked, so lightly that his tone disposed of any possible contender as negligible.

She made an impatient gesture. "My uncle told you when we met that I am resolved never to marry."

"But I refuse to believe it, mademoiselle. You're skittish, like your mare, but you revealed yourself last night as a passionate woman, a woman made for love. You must know that."

The sun was warm on her shoulders. It reflected from his gleaming boots and made his brows drop deep shadows over his eyes. She could not believe they were sitting their restive mounts in this bright morning light and talking of passion.

Angrily she said, "I am a gentlewoman, m'sieu. Don't think because I ride like a man and manage my own plantation that you can make improper remarks to me!" Did he actually think, because she was unmarried at twenty-three, that she was a fallen woman, no longer a virgin?

"Don't deny your feelings, Angèle," he said gently. He reached for her hand on the reins, but Angèle touched Jolie's flanks with her heels, and her mare moved sideways, kicking up her heels.

Angèle could not have borne his touch. Her rage was mixed with a stifling panic. She said thickly, "I must ask you to leave my plantation, m'sieu."

His face stiffened, and it occurred to her that a marquis might never have considered the possibility of receiving such an insulting ultimatum. He regarded her steadily for a moment. As the silence lengthened, the look in his eyes began to disarm her. It was changing from one of icy offense to one at once tender and amused. A strange regret crept into the tangle of her emotions and she fiercely repressed it.

"Certainly, mademoiselle. But I warn you that I will come again." He touched his hat, then dropped his voice to a low murmur. "And again and again, until you return my love—"

"You will not be welcome at La Sorcellerie!"

Again his proud lips tightened. But he asked, softly, "Can you really be so cruel, Angèle?"

She distrusted his tone of rueful reproach, but it still affected her. When she felt the sudden welling of tears, she turned her head so he would not see her weakness, but she sat stiff and unrelenting astride her mare. After a moment she heard the restless pawing of the stallion settle into a rhythm as he cantered away.

When man and horse disappeared around the house, she walked Jolie to the stables with tears running down her cheeks.

Each morning after that when Angèle stepped out on her galérie to walk down the steps to where Jules waited to help her mount Jolie for her morning inspection, a distant figure appeared on the bayou road at the end of her oak-bordered drive. As soon as Angèle lifted her head, Philippe reined in the black stallion, doffed his hat, and bowed, then cantered on in the direction of New Orleans.

She made no acknowledgment, but on the fourth morning she did not order Jolie saddled, and spent the day unhappily inside, upsetting Mimi. Usually Mimi ran the household with no interference from her young mistress, who preferred the concerns of the planting and the crushing.

On the fifth morning Angèle rose earlier, and although she had not sent word to Jules, dressed for a ride. A glance at the bayou road revealed it to be empty, and she was chagrined at her fleeting sense of loss. She walked around the corner of the house to the stables and saw Philippe. He had dismounted and was standing beside the black stallion, talking with Jules, her groom. Angèle hesitated. She and Philippe regarded each other.

Neither of them spoke, but the tension was so thick that Jules backed into the stables, out of her sight.

"M'sieu, I have told you that I do not welcome your attentions," she began, thickly. "Must I—"

He interrupted in a choking voice, "I could not stay away. . . ."

Then she was in his arms, her heart pounding in her breast and her senses reeling as he kissed her, the sweetness of his lips invading her blood with their tender hunger.

The sharp rat-a-tat of a trotting horse recalled her from the exquisite fantasy to which she was surrendering, and she wrenched violently away from him.

On that morning Clothilde stood behind the French windows of her bedroom and watched Philippe ride away from Bellemont. For the fifth straight day he had failed to ask her to accompany him on his morning ride, leaving earlier than she usually rose. She found this so pointed after their pleasant custom of riding together, that this morning she was fully dressed, having left orders the evening before to be awakened.

A low whistle brought her groom around with her mare. She closed the shutters and went through her room to the hall. Passing her mother's closed door, she paused when she met her mother's *femme de chambre* coming up the stair with a tray of coffee and rolls, and said, "Tell Maman I've gone riding."

"Oui, m'selle," the black woman said.

Once mounted, Clothilde waved back her groom, who would have followed her, and trotted her horse down the drive. She waited while the children who were just straggling up from the gate turned and ran back to open it again. She had no clear idea of where she was going, but desperation had driven her to following Philippe this morning. With his stay at Bellemont drawing to a close, he had apparently lost all interest in offering for her.

He was calling on someone else, she was certain. And at so early an hour, she concluded, he could only be riding with someone. There could be no other reason for avoiding the morning ride they had fallen into a habit of sharing. She felt shamed by what she was doing, but was frantic to know who had so intrigued him at Angèle's ball, for it must have happened then.

What was inexplicable—and unforgivable—was that while he was with her at Bellemont, Philippe was as tenderly attentive as ever. She loved him more than ever, but not as happily—her love poisoned now with distrust. And Maman was beginning to notice.

The black stallion was already out of sight when she turned out of the drive.

"Michie ride that way," the children cried, pointing.

The slaves always knew what was happening, Clothilde thought in despair as she turned her mare in the direction they pointed. Philippe could be stopping at any of the plantations along the bayou. He could even be riding into New Orleans. She seized on the slight hope that thought offered, telling herself that he could be on his way to arrange for living quarters when he left her father's hospitality, for he was not yet settled in the colony. But why should he not confide his plans to her . . . if he loved her?

And what was she doing here on the bayou road, hoping to spy on him? Clothilde felt black despair.

Her gentle mare had gradually slowed her pace, reacting to Clothilde's unhappy indecision. She jogged along while the sun rose slightly ahead to the left, catching diamondlike points of reflection in a thousand drops of dew in the rank grasses along the bayou. Clothilde no longer hoped to see Philippe ahead of her. He had gone swiftly wherever he'd gone. Did that mean he was indeed on his way to New Orleans on some business which was no threat to her hopes?

Oh, may le bon dieu make it so! she wished.

Riding in the direction of La Sorcellerie, it occurred to her that it would be a comfort to talk to Cousin Angèle, although she would never confess her humiliation, not even to her beloved cousin. Not that it would be necessary, she realized, tears starting to her eyes. Angèle always knew what she was feeling. She watched for the glimpse of La Sorcellerie's slender white pillars through the trees, and with a sense of comfort guided her mare into the drive leading to her cousin's serenely beautiful home. As she cantered up to the front steps, Ouma came running around the house, crying, "Welcome, m'selle!"

"Where is your mistress, Ouma?" Clothilde asked. "Is she riding this morning?"

He shook his head and made a vague gesture toward the stables.

Clothilde dismounted, gave him her reins, and walked around the corner of the house, where she stopped in dismay. Her father's black stallion stood in front of the stables, his reins dragging. A few feet from the horse Philippe and her cousin faced her.

Clothilde knew immediately.

They were standing apart, but as if they had just been wrenched away from each other. The space between them crackled with tension, and Angèle's mouth looked swollen, as if it had just been passionately kissed. The revealing tableau lasted only seconds. Then Angèle started toward her, hands outstretched.

"Dear Clothilde!" she exclaimed, making no effort to hide her distress. "Do not trust your love with this man. I must warn you, he is not trustworthy."

Clothilde did not even look at Philippe. Her stricken eyes were on Angèle.

"Do you imagine that he is loyal to you?" Angèle said. "I—I must tell you—" She gave a distraught little laugh. "Why, he even talks of marriage to me!"

Marriage to *Angèle?* Clothilde swayed, suddenly feeling the morning heat like a crushing burden. "And you have said yes?" she asked faintly.

"No, Clothilde!" Angèle cried. "That is not what I meant to say! I have told him I will never marry!"

Clothilde stood very straight, willing herself not to faint. When she thought she could manage her voice, she said, "But you will say yes, dear Angèle. How could you resist?" And she turned so brilliant a smile on Philippe that a barely perceptible flush crept into his face.

"Your cousin finds it easy to resist, Mademoiselle Clothilde," he said wryly.

"But not you, m'sieu." Her voice had an excessively polite tone that sounded false even in her own ears. "I must be going," she said. "I just came by to tell you I have not stopped hearing how entertaining your ball was, Angèle." She turned and began walking rapidly back to where Ouma stood holding her mount.

"Clothilde!" Angèle begged. "Pay no attention to what I said, please. I was understandably upset. Please stay. M'sieu le marquis is leaving." She turned a fierce look on him, but Clothilde was not looking back to see it.

"Thank you, but I am on my way to call on Adele Dupré," she lied, desperately. "I had thought to ask you to go with me." She was almost running.

"I will go with you," Angèle called. "Please wait, Clothilde!"

To Ouma, wide-eyed, Clothilde muttered, "Help me mount. Be quick!"

Ouma cupped his small hands to support her foot, as he had seen Angèle's groom Jules do. He staggered a little when she put her weight on him.

"Adieu!" Clothilde cried, and dug her heel into her mare's flank so sharply that she galloped off while Angèle was still running toward her.

Angèle turned back to Philippe, tears running down her cheeks.

He held out his arms, his face mirroring her distress. "Angèle, my dearest one—"

"Go!" she cried. "Please go! Don't you see what you have done?"

"My darling—"

"You are not welcome here. You must never come back." Catching her breath in a great sob, she turned and ran for the steps.

Inside the fan-topped entrance Mimi opened her arms and Angèle fled into her embrace. "Oh, Mimi, I'm such a fool!"

"No, not a fool," Mimi murmured. "Just a woman in love."

Angèle moved her face from side to side against the comfort of Mimi's shoulder. "No, no, no . . ."

Silently Mimi held her while the clop of the stallion's hooves died away on the drive.

Clothilde made no pretense of going in the direction of the Dupré plantation, but headed toward Bellemont, galloping the whole three miles.

When she saw the gates of her father's plantation and the

children, still halfway from the house, coming to open them, she thought of how they raced to meet their beloved M'selle Angèle's carriage, and a wild recklessness seized her. She urged her mare faster and faster toward the closed gates, and felt the gentle beast's terrified hesitation as she confronted them.

I will be killed, Clothilde thought, and closed her eyes.

But the brave mare gathered her feet under her and soared over the barrier, scattering the small slaves, then galloped up the drive to the house with Clothilde clinging to her. Clothilde threw her reins at her groom, thankful to have escaped her father's notice. Her mother came out on the galérie as she reached it, but Clothilde rushed by her and up the stairs to her room.

She got out of her riding clothes and allowed her maid to sponge her body with cool water. Then she lay on her bed, motioned for the mosquito netting to be closed, and said no, she did not want to eat anything this morning. She did not want to be disturbed.

At ten-thirty her mother came into her room to ask if she was ill. Clothilde had scarcely moved. She was not feverish, her mother decided. In spite of the warmth of her room, her face was pale.

"M'sieu le marquis has returned and is asking for you. I have ordered coffee on the galérie, as usual."

"Please ask him to excuse me, Maman," Clothilde said in a faraway voice. "I will take coffee in my room this morning."

Madame Roget had suspected for several days that there had been a lovers' quarrel. She said equably, "Very well, my child."

A few moments later she was back. "Angèle has ridden over. She asks if she may have her coffee up here with you."

"Tell her I would be very poor company this morning and I would prefer to sleep."

Madame Roget's eyebrows rose, but she said, again, "Very well," and went downstairs to entertain her two young guests, who seemed very formal with each other this morning.

After she heard the sound of Angèle's mare leaving, Clothilde lay in a self-induced state between waking and sleeping, wishing to die. Most of the time her eyes were open, staring at the ceiling, because the instant she closed them she saw again the terrible, revealing tableau that had made everything known to her—and then her imagination would begin supplying her with all too vivid pictures of the kiss she knew her arrival had interrupted. Beyond that point she could not let her mind go.

In summer the entire household rested during the hottest hours of the afternoon. It was after Madame Roget had risen from her nap, been refreshed by a cool bath, and conferred with her cook about dinner, that she again climbed the stairs and knocked lightly at Clothilde's door before opening it. Her daughter was still in her bed behind the mosquito netting, her hair clinging in damp tendrils around her unhappy perspiring face.

"You have a caller, my dear."

Clothilde turned her face away.

"I told him you were not feeling well, but he has come such a long way that I have invited him to stay for dinner."

Clothilde turned back, looking faintly interested. *"He,* Maman?"

"Henri's friend, the American."

Clothilde's eyes opened wider. "M'sieu Belle Aimée is here?"

"He is here. He has ridden through the afternoon heat from New Orleans, which no Creole gentleman would do, and I have no doubt it is you he has come to see. Since he will be staying, you have plenty of time to make yourself beautiful again."

Clothilde did not smile. Her face took on a surprisingly firm look, one that gave the startled Madame Roget a fleeting glimpse of the woman her seventeen-year-old daughter would one day become.

"Thanks, Maman. I do believe I will feel better if I get dressed. My headache is almost gone."

Chapter 4

*A*ngèle had not seen the black stallion for two weeks, so when the splendid animal appeared on the bayou road, she felt a tremor of anticipation. But this morning it was Nonc' Etienne who trotted his favorite mount up her drive.

"Good morning, Angèle," he called cheerfully up to the galérie, giving his reins to Ouma, who had outrun the groom rounding the corner of the house. "Have you a cup of coffee for a wandering rider?"

"Always for you, Uncle." She nodded at the young footman who had appeared, grinning, at the corner of the galérie to see what Michie Etienne wanted.

Etienne climbed the stairs at a deliberate pace. "I have come to bring you the news, since you do not come to see us," he said pointedly.

Angèle had not visited Bellemont since Clothilde had refused to have coffee with her the day Angèle wanted to explain about Philippe's compromising presence at La Sorcellerie. Perhaps time would help heal Clothilde's hurt, she had thought, but even now she could not explain to herself why she had lost her head for the second time, nor could she appease her nagging guilt. Clothilde's distress had been very upsetting.

"I've been busy. I'm trying to calculate the best time for cutting my cane," she defended herself. "It requires my daily attention just now."

"Excuses," he grumbled. "A woman can always find one. But once she has made up her mind what she wants, she must have it the day before yesterday."

"Indeed? What is this news that displeases you?" Angèle asked apprehensively.

"Did I say I was displeased? I am merely puzzled by woman's inconstancy." He settled himself comfortably in a chair at one of the small tables on Angèle's galérie. "It is Clothilde's wedding, of course."

A surprisingly painful anxiety gripped Angèle as she waited for him to go on.

"We—Astride and I—thought the marquis was on the verge of offering for her, and Clothilde seemed very much attracted to him. But now she seems wholly smitten by this M'sieu Bellamy. Astride says there must have been a lovers' quarrel."

He stopped and looked inquiringly at her, his eyes shrewd under the grizzled eyebrows.

She looked away, to hide her shocking relief. "Clothilde has said nothing to me of . . . of a quarrel with M'sieu le marquis, Uncle."

"No? Perhaps you knew that he has left Bellemont?"

She shook her head.

"He has returned to the house of his kinsman, M'sieu le comte, the mayor of New Orleans. . . ." He paused, sent a keen glance at her, and when she said nothing, went on. "A few days ago something curious happened. Philippe came out from New Orleans, not to call on Clothilde but to discuss the situation with me. He did so, he explained, because he intends to press his suit for your hand."

Angèle drew a quick breath and muttered, "Incredible!"

Should she tell Nonc' Etienne why she thought Clothilde was fortunate not to be marrying Philippe de l'Eglise? Heat rose to her face as she tried to imagine what words she could possibly use to convey to her uncle that unthinkable incident on her galérie the night of her ball. And now she feared she would have to explain that she had allowed herself to be kissed a second time, an indiscretion in which she had been discovered by Clothilde!

"I will enjoy my coffee," Nonc' Etienne said, patiently reminding her of her duties as his hostess, "while you explain to me whether you have come to your senses and decided to marry like other people."

Angèle leaned forward and poured a demitasse of the black liquid while she debated how much to reveal to her uncle.

He took the cup and beckoned the footman, who had retreated just far enough away not to be accused of eavesdropping. "Bring me some brandy," he ordered. "I must flavor this brew."

"You don't like my coffee, Nonc'?"

"Don't change the subject, my dear. Are you going to marry the marquis or not?" He added, wistfully, "It would be pleasant to have him in the family."

"You know me better than that!"

"I'm not sure that I do," her uncle said. "I'd have wagered my black stud there that our Clothilde was in love with Philippe de l'Eglise. But no! She must have this Yankee merchant." He gave a sigh. "It's a pity. I enjoyed conversing with the marquis."

Angèle hesitated, turning this information over in her mind. Could Clothilde have fallen in love with M'sieu Bellamy so quickly? Was it possible that she had only been blinded by the glamor of Philippe's title and his Old World manners? No, she thought. She could not be so mistaken.

"M'sieu Bellamy is very genteel, and I think that he is very fond of our Clothilde," she said carefully. "You must have noticed how much they were enjoying each other's company at my ball."

"That is reason enough to marry?" her uncle asked tartly.

"He speaks excellent French."

"That's in his favor," Nonc' Etienne conceded. He took the crystal brandy decanter from the tray the footman had brought and poured a generous dollop into his cup.

Angèle was silent. She feared that Clothilde's decision to marry M'sieu Bellamy meant that her cousin was rushing into a loveless marriage because she had lost Philippe. But Angèle would not reveal her private misgivings about the proposed wedding.

"I am investigating M'sieu Bellamy's credentials," her uncle said at last. "He brought the necessary baptismal records from the Baltimore diocese." He sighed again. "I promised Astride that Clothilde would not be forced into a marriage not of her choice, but never did I dream that I would have *an American* for a son-in-law."

Angèle winced at his tone of contempt. "M'sieu Bellamy is from a very different class than the frontiersmen who bring the flatboats down the river," she reminded her uncle.

Ignoring that feeble recommendation, he drained his cup and stood up. "Well, I thought I should tell you these things before Clothilde rides over. She will be certain to ask you to be her attendant."

Remembering their last encounter, Angèle was not so sure. But she said, "I'll be very happy to." Less sincerely, she added, "Perhaps she will enlighten me about the change in her sentiments."

"Let's hope so," her uncle said, and signaling her groom to lead up his stallion, he walked heavily down the steps.

But Angèle saw Philippe before she saw Clothilde again.

It was a few days after Nonc' Etienne's visit. An overcast of moisture-laden clouds had trapped the humid heat, pressing it down upon bayou and swamp and the bands of arable land between them. No air stirred the hanging beards of moss on the trees, and no birds sang. It seemed an effort to breathe, and everyone in the house moved as if wading through molasses.

The effect of the weather on Angèle was to make her feel heavy and swollen, as if there were forces bottled up within her that could burst just as the clouds, when they grew too heavy, released their burden of moisture.

She was alerted by one of her servants to the approach of a visitor: a gentleman arriving in a coach. She left her father's study, where she had been drowsing over some entries in her plantation books, and stepped onto the front galérie to see who was calling on this day made for sleeping. It was a hired coach. Its driver was an elderly black man whose bare head was covered with a short fuzz of gray hair.

A deafening rat-a-tat of rain struck the overhanging roof of the galérie just as the coachman turned his pair and came to a stop in front of the steps. The dark clouds that had been rolling in from the Gulf of Mexico all day had opened and relieved themselves with the characteristic suddenness of the tropics. While Angèle watched incredulously from under the shelter of her roof, Philippe de l'Eglise jumped out of the coach and ran up through the drenching rain to join her.

He doffed his soaked hat. Water was rolling down his smooth cheeks, but between his drenched eyelashes, his eyes were glowing with an admiration that pierced her torpor, making her feel beautiful and desired even while this imposition on her hospitality ired her. The anger she felt at his intrusion sent a freshet of energy flowing through her veins.

She greeted him coldly. "Apparently you have forgotten, m'sieu, that La Sorcellerie's doors are closed to you."

"Even in a downpour, mademoiselle?" he asked, smiling.

"A convenient one for your purpose, was it not?"

Philippe viewed her heightened color and her spirited response with obvious pleasure. "Ah, so you know the purpose of my visit."

"I know that you have spoken to M'sieu Roget about me, which I consider a gross impropriety, since I don't encourage your suit."

"I didn't make the gross error of asking him for your hand," he assured her, a glint of humor in his eyes. "I merely wished to inform your uncle of my intentions." He saw the gathering storm in her eyes and added swiftly, "I felt obliged to do that since you had told me that his daughter entertained hopes about me."

"Oh, you are without shame!" she exclaimed. "Clothilde is well rid of you!"

"You have a low opinion of me, mademoiselle. In my defense I will confess that although I have tried, I could stay away from La Sorcellerie no longer. And you are too hospitable to put me out in a storm."

It was a challenge that called her attention again to the heavy clatter of rain still pounding on the roof of the galérie. Water was running from the eaves in a transparent sheet through which she had a blurred vision of the coach. Her groom clung precariously on its step as it was being driven swiftly around the house to the shelter of the stables.

Seething with a mixture of impotent anger and a dangerously unstable excitement, Angèle affected a shrug and led the way into the drawing room.

"Coffee or brandy, m'sieu?" There would be exquisite release in letting her temper explode, but she dared not reveal how easily just seeing Philippe de l'Eglise could disturb her composure.

He gave his dripping hat to a servant who offered him a towel. He took it and strolled past her into the drawing room. With it he dried his face, while over it his appreciative eyes traveled the length of her slender body, not missing the color in her cheeks nor the telltale quiver of her hand as she raised it to the bellpull.

He read the signs expertly, catching his breath at the beautiful curve made by her perfect breasts as she raised her arm, and admiring her proud pretense at self-control even as he plotted how to destroy it.

She was vulnerable beneath that pride, the more so because she did not realize how very vulnerable she was. He had seen her outrage at his assumption that she was no virgin, flung at her mostly as a challenge, and he sensed that in spite of her maturity and her trained planter's mind, she was unaware of her own sensuality. At the thought of awakening her, a wave of passionate love suffused him.

I must have her, he thought.

He handed the towel to the servant, who knelt and wiped away the perfectly round drops rolling down his well-oiled boots. The footman returned with a coffee tray. Angèle sat on a damask double chair and poured, but Philippe remained standing, taking his cup to the hearth.

Her heart was beating too fast, Angèle thought. He was very attractive standing there, so tall he looked deceptively slender, the melancholy cast of his eyes in his long oval face promising a romantic illusion of love that her cousin had found completely false. She groped for strength to steel her heart against his seductive charm.

"What will the rain do to your cane fields?"

She was surprised that he should ask. "Nothing, unless it

stays too long." In spite of her annoyance with him, her face relaxed in an expression of pleasure as she added, "I can almost see it growing taller in weather like this."

"You have a genuine feeling for your land, no?"

"Does that surprise you, m'sieu?"

He did not answer her immediately, thinking of the land that was his birthright. "My father's country estate, which would have been mine but for the revolution, is very different from your land, Mademoiselle Angèle, but I love it as you love La Sorcellerie."

Something in her heart turned over in response to his obvious sincerity. Her parents, forced by the revolution to flee their ancestral estates to a faraway, very different land in the New World, had suffered a trauma she was too young to appreciate at the time. The marquis, too, had been taken to a strange country, and he must have been old enough to feel his loss.

"It is sad to lose a home whose soil is in your blood, m'sieu."

His eyes warmed on her. "It is a pain that wasted my father. For the rest of his life he dreamed of regaining his estates. Now I dream of doing it in his memory."

Angèle shook her head in a scornful pity. "Thousands of émigrés cherish that dream, m'sieu, but hasn't the revolutionary government been selling off all the confiscated royalist lands?"

"Some, not all. Many houses and estates, including mine, are still boarded up and posted: 'government property'."

"How can you be sure yours is one of them?"

"Émigrés in London were able to get information from Paris even while England and France were at war. It is more difficult now that I am in Louisiana." His gaze softened. "Sans Souci lies to the southeast of Paris in a region of orchards and vineyards. If it were nearer Paris, it would have been sold long ago. My father reasoned that as long as there is no new owner, there is hope for the old." His expression softened still further, his eyes filled with childhood memories. "I think you would find my château charming."

Angèle felt drawn to him in spite of her prickly distrust. "I should die if I lost La Sorcellerie," she said simply.

With understanding in his dark eyes, he said, "And that is why you resolved never to marry."

Angèle stiffened. How neatly he had brought the conversation around to marriage! "I will tell you exactly why, m'sieu, so you need never ask again. If I marry, I will put myself in the position of being powerless under the law to prevent my husband from selling La Sorcellerie, or even losing it at cards—as one of my father's friends did. That I could not tolerate."

"A man who loves his home could not do that. Nor could a man who loves you do that to you. But I understand your concern."

"Do you? Can any man truly understand?"

"Our laws under the *ancien régime* were not fair to women," he acknowledged. "But the revolution that destroyed the Bourbon monarchy brought equality to the women of France. A Frenchman can no longer dispose of the possessions of his wife or a child without penalty. Nor does he have unlimited power over their lives."

"Your revolution had little effect here, m'sieu. You forget that we were governed by Spain then, a country which is no kinder to its women. I don't know what our fate will be under Napoleon Bonaparte. I do not trust Bonaparte. Unfortunately, since we are once again a French colony, any law Napoleon is able to put into effect will apply to Nouvelle Orléans as well."

His thick dark eyebrows rose questioningly. "You seem well informed, mademoiselle. Are you and your uncle revolutionists, then?"

She retorted, "You, m'sieu, would be happy to return the Bourbons to the throne, wouldn't you? After all, are you not of the blood?"

His face closed. "You are jumping to conclusions, my angel."

Her heart jerked with startled anger at the endearment he had created from her name, but he appeared not to notice her reaction.

"I favor Napoleon, actually," he said, sipping his coffee. "France needed him to eliminate the excesses of the infamous revolutionary Directorate and to stabilize the government. And he is intelligent enough to see that in order to do that he needs the return of the émigrés. Of course, I consider him an interim remedy for France. After he restores order, perhaps a constitutional monarchy, like England's—"

"My uncle says Bonaparte is an ambitious man," Angèle warned him.

54

Philippe laughed. "I would help him achieve his ambitions in order to achieve mine."

"That is the remark of an opportunist."

He laughed.

She studied him. Nonc' Etienne had reacted with fury to the choice of Napoleon as First Consul and to the expansionist wars of France under him.

Philippe walked forward and placed his empty cup on the tray before her. "Come! Let us talk of our future instead of Bonaparte's."

She stiffened. "We have no future, m'sieu."

"No?" He sat down on the small settee beside her, took her cup from her suddenly limp fingers and set it on the tray beside his own. "Let me tell you what it will be like."

Her fingers trembled in his. This near to him, she felt his personal charm like an overpowering force.

"We will be married—"

She tried to pull away, but he held her hand tightly in his grasp. His dark eyes were alight with tenderness.

"And I will love you with every caress you have dreamed about," he said softly. "I will love you in sunlight and in moonlight and under the moonless stars. I will worship your lovely breasts with my hands and my lips—"

"Mon dieu, m'sieu! You would seduce me with words?" She jerked her hand away and stood so precipitously that she nearly upset the tray. Her heart was pumping with terrified speed. "You presume too much! I must ask you to leave, storm or no storm!"

He had risen too. "Be honest, Angèle. I have felt your passion, and I can sense your response to me. This masquerade of taking your father's place is only a game you are playing."

"It is no game!" she said furiously. "You think because I manage my own plantation that I am playing at being a man? You are insufferably self-esteemed to think so!"

He reached out and pulled her into an embrace that brought her close against his chest. With the clean smell of his tunic in her nostrils and the sound of his pounding heart giving away his own excitement, she felt the hostility drain out of her. She melted into his embrace, making no effort to evade his lips. Drowning in the sweet rapture of his kiss, she marveled at how familiar, how warm and protected, it felt to be in his arms, and how cold and lonely it would be outside them.

Had Clothilde imagined this rich fabric of love and concern surrounding her when she thought he was going to offer for her? Angèle wondered. But how fragile had been Clothilde's dream!

When he sensed her submission, he raised his lips to murmur, "We'll be married lovers, Angèle, and you will always be in my arms, like this." He kissed her again, and said, "I will treasure you and cosset you. . . ."

"You are dreaming, m'sieu," Angèle said crisply, "if you think I will ever put my life and my fortune in your hands."

Philippe thrust her away from him, and she was abruptly aware of the force of his sudden anger, just as she had been that morning on Nonc' Etienne's galérie when he had castigated her for the way she drove.

"Mademoiselle, I am not a fool!" His face above hers was furious. "Do you imagine that I wish to marry you in order to gain possession of your plantation? What would I want with your swamps and your sickly indigo and cane? I want only my inheritance, my vineyards and orchards outside Paris! That is my goal, and that is what I intend to have."

"Then we have nothing to give each other—"

"Only love, sweet Angèle, but I am beginning to believe you are incapable of loving."

"You can say that?" she cried. "You who have made love to my cousin and are breaking her heart?" Wrenching herself from his grasp, she said, "The rain has slacked, m'sieu. I shall order your coach."

With the quiet arrogance of his royal blood, he replied, "But I'm not ready to leave, mademoiselle."

"I shall call my servant to put you out!"

His head jerked up. In a deadly quiet tone he said, "If your majordomo lays a hand on me, I will kill him."

"If you lay a hand on me, M'sieu le marquis," Angèle retorted, "you will have to kill him, or be killed!"

For a long moment they stood glaring at each other. Then Philippe took her roughly in his arms again, and before she could cry out, gave her a kiss such as she had never experienced, thrusting his tongue into her mouth with a shocking intimacy and arousing in her a feverish excitement that she resented, but could not conceal.

With the sweet taste of triumph, he let her go as abruptly as he had seized her, and said softly, "To kill me isn't at all what you want, my dear angel. Dream about me tonight."

She could not even move to the bellpull. She stood where he left her, beside the table with its coffee tray, while Philippe strode out on the galérie and called imperiously for his coach. The young footman appeared at the door, his look questioning.

"Take M'sieu le marquis his hat, then come back for this tray."

"Yes, m'selle." The young black hesitated. "The bayou has risen and is flooding the road, m'selle."

"M'sieu wishes to leave," she repeated inflexibly, and went across the hall to her father's study. But she looked down at her books, unseeing, while her nerves vibrated to the sound of the hooves and the wheels pausing at the steps and then creaking down the drive, carrying Philippe away.

An hour and a half later she heard cries of surprise and distress and left her desk to see what was happening. A muddy, bedraggled man was walking up the oak-lined drive leading a horse. He walked stiffly, as if he had been thrown. After a few moments, when he had come closer, Angèle recognized the driver of Philippe's coach.

Two servants were running to meet him. As soon as he was near enough, Angèle leaned over the rail and called to him, "Where is your master?"

"He's not my master, m'selle. I am one of the free people of color. This morning m'sieu hired my coach, which is now stuck fast in the mud of the road in two feet of water."

"Where is m'sieu?" she demanded.

"Me, I advise' him to remain in the coach while I ride back to ask you for the help of strong men—"

She gasped. "You left him, with the coach filling?"

"If the water rise high, he can sit on the roof, no? My horses don't take kindly to carrying mens on they backs. After all, *they* carriage horses," he said with dignity. "As you see before you, m'selle, I was thrown but I pick' myself up and come through the mud on my foots while m'sieu wait for me."

Angèle called Duval and gave him instructions to send Jules

to the stalled carriage with an extra horse to bring M'sieu le marquis to La Sorcellerie.

"It will probably be necessary for m'sieu to spend the night," she said, "but I will not receive him. Have a bath prepared and a change of clothes—you can find something in my father's armoire, surely. Put him in my father's bedroom, and arrange a place for his driver in the quarters. Choose some slaves to go for the coach when the rain stops."

"Oui, m'selle."

She then rang for Mimi, ordered dinner served to m'sieu in the dining room, and instructed that her dinner be sent up to her on a tray. Having settled all that, she retired to her room, claiming that the exceptionally humid day and the heat had given her a violent headache.

As she ascended the stairs, Angèle had a panicky feeling, somewhat as if she were a leaf afloat on the river when it was in flood, being swept along until it was engulfed in a whirlpool.

The Fates were against her. Philippe was returning to La Sorcellerie, and this time she could not turn him away.

Chapter 5

TOWARD evening the storm passed over, moving to the north. The air cooled somewhat, although it was still heavy with moisture. Angèle had remained in her room, but her headache, which was not in the least an imaginary one, hadn't improved. She'd heard Philippe's arrival and the murmur of his and Duval's voices from the room across the broad hall from hers, listened to the sounds of Philippe's bath and the selection of his clothing from her father's armoire. Her reactions ranged from anger to shame at her wanton imagination, which was portraying vivid pictures of him in his privacy.

She heard him going downstairs to dinner, and his step when he returned. He met Mimi in the hall and asked how her mistress was feeling. The tone of his voice was warm and solicitous. Angèle's surprise was accompanied by a flicker of pleasure which she immediately repressed. Surely he could not fail to understand that by not appearing in the dining room, she was refusing to receive him!

As the sounds from below died away and the voices of the servants leaving the house for the slave quarters floated up to her room, Angèle began to feel feverishly nervous. She was not alone in the house—Duval had a small room off the pantry; she could ring him, or the cook and her helper in their rooms in the kitchen compound—but she knew she would not be able to sleep tonight with Philippe in her father's bed.

Lying perfectly still, she listened to Philippe's preparations for bed in the room across the hall, feeling a guilty pleasure in imagining each step he took. Later, when the house was quiet, she was still too restless to pretend any longer to be sleeping. Telling herself she would not be discovered if she did not light the candle, she slipped into a light robe, carefully made her way to the long windows, opened them, then threw back the shutters to let the ragged moon shine into the room.

The air felt marvelously balmy after the heavy humidity of the day, and she stepped out on the side galérie to draw great draughts of it into her lungs. To her left, beyond the kitchen buildings, the double row of slave cabins was cloaked in darkness. A low-hanging mist had been left by the storm, and under the piecemeal moon, the familiar shapes of moss-hung trees to her right and the gleam of bayou water through their branches were part of a vague and mysterious landscape.

The perpetual cacophony of sound from the swamp, so steady it became part of the silence, was a familiar lullaby. But when its rhythm was broken by the bark of an alligator and a splash from near the boat landing, Angèle's imagination peopled the night with unseen life.

She saw the amphibians lying with their long ugly snouts barely raised above the surface of the black water, only a bubble marking their location. She heard no bird song, but she could picture owls perched in the darkness, swiveling their heads with their great unblinking eyes from side to side. She saw deadly water snakes, the moccasins and cottonmouths, curled up in the shelter of cypress roots knee deep in swamp water or in the wet grass on the banks of the bayou. And in the room across the hall, Philippe slept in her father's bed.

Angèle shivered.

A faint sound caught her attention—not every creature was sleeping. Turning her head in the direction of the slave quarters, she was startled into a gasp as a pale figure appeared at the far end of the galérie.

"P'pa!" she whispered, for a moment swept into unreality.

Almost at once she realized she was seeing not an incarnation of her dead parent, but Philippe clad in a summer robe of her father's. It had been her father's favorite in hot weather, and its soft, porous cotton had been laundered many times. Quite obviously Philippe wore nothing under it. It was almost as revealing of his shapely muscular body in the filtered moonlight as the sheer robe she wore must be of her own.

The realization should have sent her flying into her room to slam and bar the shutters, but she did not move, frozen by her recognition of the inevitability of this moment. He came silently toward her on bare feet. Trembling, she awaited him.

"Did I startle you?" His low voice was tender.

"It's the robe," she whispered. "For a moment I thought—" Her eyes were blind with tears.

He immediately grasped what she was saying. "It was your father's, wasn't it? I'm sorry."

She drew a ragged breath. He stopped so close to her that she could sense his presence through her pores like an animal senses danger. She was still shaken by that imagined glimpse of her father and her emotional reaction to it.

"Mon dieu," Philippe murmured, "how beautiful you are in this moonlight!" He raised his hands and gently traced the curve of her breasts beneath the thin robe.

"Ah, how shameless you are," she murmured despairingly, but swayed into his touching hands.

"You are without shame, too, my reckless beauty," he said, his low laugh suddenly confident. "You want me as much as I want you."

It was true, but she couldn't admit it. Yet when he drew her against the firm muscles of his chest, she could not protest, because the touch of him everywhere was melting her flesh.

Slowly he moved his hands up her body until they clasped her neck in an erotic caress while his lips moved from her temple down her cheek, murmuring between kisses, "You want this . . . and this . . . and this . . ."

He paused to nibble at her ear, then strewed kisses down the curve of her slim neck to the base of her throat. She was motionless in his arms, unresisting, but with no reaction except trembling until he touched her lips. When his mouth covered hers, his tongue seeking, and he pulled her closer, she felt his powerful arousal and the gathering storm within her broke, flooding her with a desire that swept every other thought from her mind.

He wanted her as desperately as she wanted him, and nothing else mattered. She threw her arms around his neck and pressed her breasts against him with an abandon that made him catch his breath.

Mimi stood in her open doorway, the first in the row of cabins facing the rear and side of the "big house," as transfixed as her mistress by the sight of the tall man in the familiar summer robe.

In the darkness behind her, Jean-Baptiste slept in the bed they shared, and beyond it in the curtained alcove, Ouma and Minette slept on their cots as if drugged. The unbearable humidity that preceded the storm and still weighted the air, had exhausted them all, and the cramped room still imprisoned the torpid heat of the afternoon.

Mimi, who spent her days until M'selle Angèle retired in her mistress's relatively cooler house, had been unable to sleep. She stared at the white-robed figure and gasped, *"Michie!"*

Her heart began pounding and her hands shook. *Oh, michie, michie, what brings you back? What terrible danger calls you from your rest?*

Had someone's obeah brought him back against his will? For a few hard heartbeats her soul was a-tremble with the old superstitions.

Then she saw in the misty moonlight the other figure in sheer white who waited beside the railing, and she knew who the tall man was. As in a trance she watched him approach her mistress, and while she waited in spirit with the waiting woman on the galérie, a rush of memories held her motionless . . . the broad graceful fronds of the banana and the coconut palm . . . the red and yellow fruit of the coco plant as big as a man's head . . . her homeland, Saint Domingue, where she had first learned what a man was, what he could do to her, and what the consequences were. The askance looks and the turned backs of the other slaves, and the way they had stopped talking when she entered a cabin. In her ignorance she'd thought it was because of what she was carrying beneath her heart. . . .

Now she knew it was simply that they could not trust her.

And they had been right. She had warned her master of the planned uprising, and fled with her white family. She had done it to save the children—her own Ouma, and Minette, yet unborn—and the little girl she adored, who had grown into the woman now being carried into her bedroom in the arms of their visitor, the woman Mimi sometimes thought of not as her mistress but as her eldest daughter.

The shutter was left open, but no candle was lit. From this distance Mimi could hear no sound, but she knew only too well what was happening in that moonlit room—La Sorcellerie would have a new master.

Standing motionless in the shadowy doorway, she thought about what that would mean to her and her family. There was a deep affection between her and M'selle Angèle. The color of their skins had never mattered to the small pale girl, but it was in those hours on the open seas in a small boat, when everything had become immaterial measured against the peril they faced together, that their love had been cemented. It had approached a mother-daughter relationship in the years since Madame Roget's death. But looking up at Angele's dark window, Mimi felt a certain chill in her heart. It had to be an unequal love when one person held the power to destroy the other's happiness, even her life itself. Didn't it?

Not that she doubted M'selle Angèle's genuine affection, nor that her need was real. Over the years her childish voice still called, *I need you, Mimi!* La Sorcellerie is my home, she thought, the Rogets my family. But a new master had no love for an old master's slaves. A new master could sell Jean-Baptiste as if he were a horse—or Ouma, or Minette—and M'selle Angèle could not prevent it. That thought crawled like a snake in Mimi's belly.

For a long time she stood in her door, looking up at the big dark house. At last she turned inside and slipped into the bed beside the big hot body of Jean-Baptiste. He stirred and muttered, "Mimi?"

She rolled close to him, almost drowning in his body heat, but welcoming it. "I'm so afraid," she murmured.

"What you 'fraid of?" her husband asked sleepily.

"Ah, Jean-Baptiste," she sighed, "I have fear for us all."

He folded his great arms around her slender body and held her in a loving embrace.

In the handsome house that the émigré Angel Roget had named Sorcery, Angèle lay naked in the arms of her first lover, her breasts heaving rapidly as Philippe with exquisite skill initiated her into the sorcery of love.

Later, lying unfulfilled and wondering in his relaxed embrace, she murmured, "You could enslave a woman, Philippe."

He knew what she was admitting, and he felt a powerful wave of emotion. "A virgin," he marveled. "A twenty-three-year-old virgin! Angèle, it is you who have enslaved me."

She ran tentative fingers through the dark silky curls forming a wedge on his chest. She was both frightened and inexpressibly happy. She marveled that a woman as self-sufficient as she thought she was could find such delight in being picked up like a child and carried to her bed. And then, afterward. . . ! The unimaginable wonder of skin touching skin with no barriers, the new sensations aroused by his skilled caresses, the heart-stopping excitement overriding the pain, the foretaste of an incredible pleasure that ended too soon—mon dieu, how little she had known!

He took her hand in his, spread her fingers and began kissing each one, murmuring, "Your skin is like satin, and your face when you are enjoying me is like a saint's with her eyes rolled up in ecstasy."

"Hush!" she protested in a shocked whisper. "That is a sacrilege!"

"Is it? What is nearer to godliness than love?" He began kissing her breasts and stroking the smooth slender lines of her thighs. In a few short minutes they were both aroused and made love again, this time with more pleasure for Angèle, after which they slept.

There were faint lines of light between the wooden shutters when Angèle opened her eyes. She was not alone in her bed, she realized with a thrill that was half pleasure and half panic.

She imagined she heard soft steps outside on the lower galérie, and whispered urgently, "Philippe, wake up! You must go across the hall to your room before the servants arrive with our morning coffee."

He opened his eyes and leaned over to kiss her. Before the kiss could deepen she slid out of his arms and the bed, leaving the mosquito net parted. She found her robe and wrapped it around her. His robe lay on the floor where he had dropped it. She picked it up to throw at him, but he let it fall across his body, ignoring it. Taking her pillow and stacking it on his own, he propped himself up on them and watched her through the mosquito net as she went to close the long shutters they had left open for air.

Coming back, she paused to feast her eyes on him, the reality so much more than she had imagined in her fantasies the night before last. Her gaze moved from his thick hair, so black against the pillows, down across the powerful shoulders, then above his slender rib cage to the beautiful hands lying on the white linen that covered him to his waist. She was quivering inside with that new emotion that was part apprehension and part joy.

"Get up!" she ordered again. "Someone will be coming up directly."

"Is that any way to speak to your lord and master?" he chided her.

"You are ever my lord," she answered him sweetly, "but you will never be master here."

"No? When we are married I shall certainly be master, here or wherever we are."

"Then I shall not marry you."

In a tone of amusement, he said, "It's too late for that, my love. I've accepted your exquisite surrender."

"I surrendered nothing, Philippe."

"No?" It was a lazy challenge.

"Only my virtue, and that was a gift from me to you."

"Indeed?" There was a look of startled query in his dark eyes.

"It is something rare and precious—after all, it can be given only once." She saw the flags of anger rising in his cheeks, and warned lightly, "Do not ask me for more gifts."

"By God, but you're a stubborn, hard-headed woman!" he swore. "It's you I want, not your damn gifts!"

"Be quiet!" she hissed. "Do you want to tell the servants you spent the night in my room?"

"Damn the servants!"

There was a tiny knock at the door before it was pushed slowly open. Minette stood there, her face alight with glee above the oversized silver platter she carried.

"Good morning, m'sieu and m'selle. Your coffee!"

Philippe stared at her as if struck dumb.

Angèle demanded, angrily, "Why did you bring m'sieu's coffee to my room?"

"Because he is here," Minette answered, looking in wondering innocence from her to Philippe's bare chest, for he had not yet picked up M'sieu Roget's robe, which lay across his legs.

Was it innocence or insolence? Angèle reminded herself that Minette was still a child. "How did you know that?"

"M'ma say—"

"Mimi told you to bring m'sieu's coffee here?"

"Yes, m'selle." With a smile that showed beautifully white even teeth, she set the tray down on Philippe's knees. He groaned, and she laughed happily. Her clear young skin was a golden ivory, her nose as straight and narrow as Angèle's, but her great mysterious brown eyes were Mimi's.

And how had Mimi known Philippe would be spending the night with her? Angèle asked herself. It was just as she and Clothilde had often observed: their slaves knew more about what they were doing than they knew themselves.

"Say nothing of what you see here. Do you understand, Minette? Not to anyone."

"Yes, m'selle."

"You may go now, Minette."

"Yes, m'selle." With a saucy smile, Minette skipped out of the room.

Philippe was laughing. "Who is she?"

"The child of my maid," Angèle said without expression.

"Ouma's sister?"

Angèle looked at him curiously. "You remember his name?"

"Of course. He is extraordinarily handsome for a slave, and so is his sister."

"She knows it and is insolent," Angèle said, shrugging, and wondered again what she should do about the child. She resolved to speak to Mimi as well as to her uncle about Minette's future. "Please leave now, Philippe. You are embarrassing me."

"There is no need for embarrassment, dear Angèle, since we are betrothed."

"We are not betrothed! How many times must I tell you before you will understand that I do not intend to marry?"

"If you keep saying that, I will leave you to rot in your black swamps full of repulsive reptiles," he threatened.

"To speak ill of my plantation is no way to induce me to love you, m'sieu!"

"Ah, sweet, if you could see my land with its vineyards and orchards and its placid hills, you would never want to return. Look! If you will go to Paris with me to reclaim my estates, I will sign away my espousal rights to your property here."

"Of course you will," she said, heatedly. "Such an agreement would not hold water in any French court!"

"The devil! Can't you trust my word?"

"I trust no man where La Sorcellerie is concerned."

"You she-demon!" he exclaimed, and leaped out of bed, naked as a newborn. She screamed and picked her father's robe off the bed to throw at him, but before she could complete the throw he had grabbed her, pressing her slender body hard against his own. "Is that your final word?" he demanded, his face glowing with life.

"Yes," she gasped, and he kissed her so thoroughly that she pulled away from his lips to catch her breath.

"Yes?" he challenged.

"Yes!"

They were laughing, but their gasps of laughter turned into those of passion, and no further thought of the slaves moving around the house in their usual tasks prevented them from going back to bed.

After breakfast they sat on the galérie, enclosed in privacy by the frequent heavy rains. Philippe talked about his years in school in England and his dappled childhood memories of France, while the trees around them dripped moisture, and in the stables Angèle's slaves cleaned and repaired the freedman's coach and curried his horses.

When the hour for siesta arrived and they went upstairs, it

was to Angèle's room. There they closed the door and the shutters and stripped off their clothes. She went into his arms eagerly.

"Where is your concern about appearances now?" Philippe asked her, tipping up her face with a finger under her chin. "What about the servants?"

"Do you imagine that little minx Minette has not told what she saw this morning? By now they know everything."

Philippe laughed.

But Mimi had already known, if Minette had told the truth. Angèle would never admit it, but what Mimi thought mattered to her. But when Philippe kissed her, Mimi vanished from Angèle's mind. She was drugged with love, all her senses filled with the sight and touch and sound of her lover. His laughter was music in her ears; the fragrance of his skin was sweet in her nostrils; the brush of his silky hair against her breasts made her almost swoon with pleasure. Quivering with anticipation, she let him lead her to her bed. She pulled the gauze around her bed to enclose them in a shadowy private world, and surrendered to his seeking lips.

By evening the stars were out and fireflies appeared under the oak trees. They separated at last to dress for dinner, which they were served in the candlelit dining room on a table set with the china and crystal her father had ordered from France to replace that which had been left behind.

"A male guest brings out the best in my cook," Angèle observed wryly, seeing the array of game dishes and sauces set before them.

"But of course," Philippe told her. "She knows by instinct that all true gourmands are men."

"Poppycock!"

"And that the gourmet chefs are all men."

"You are insulting my cook, Philippe!"

He gave her an infuriating smile. "Furthermore, the world's best chefs are all Frenchmen, working mostly in Paris. England's food is terrible, except for the kitchen of that rare duke who has been able to persuade a Parisian chef to enter his service."

"And in Louisiana?" she asked with dangerous sweetness.

"Louisiana's food is passable, passable," he conceded maddeningly. "After all, her cooks have been trained by French palates."

"So!" she pounced. "You admit that French women also know good food! Because it is they who train our cooks."

He shrugged. "Their men are demanding. And the kitchen is their domain."

She was becoming angry. "But the cane field is not? How illogical you are!"

His eyes gleamed with amusement. "Now that you mention it . . ."

When she saw that he was goading her, expecting her to explode, she began to laugh. He looked chagrined, like a little boy whose scheme has misfired. For some reason that look made her heart turn over. A message flashed between them, speaking eloquently of the night that lay ahead of them, with its promise of joys to come.

I am shameless, indeed, Angèle thought guiltily. But that did not lessen her pleasure.

In the morning the sun came out, the flood receded, and the road soon dried enough to make travel possible. Philippe left La Sorcellerie reluctantly for New Orleans.

It was unsettling to Angèle that the house should suddenly seem emptied and lonely. She sent word to her groom that she would ride out to the cane fields, and was about to go upstairs to change clothes when she saw Clothilde on her mare trotting up the oak-bordered drive, her groom following her on his pony.

Angèle walked out on the galérie and awaited her cousin with an anxiety suffused with guilt. What could she say to Clothilde? What would her cousin say to her? Her body still throbbed with physical reminders of Philippe's love. Would it show? Or had Clothilde already heard what everyone at La Sorcellerie knew by now—that the mistress had taken a lover.

Nervously, Angèle ordered coffee and the little mushroom sandwiches that Clothilde loved, then stood at the top of the galérie steps to greet her.

She came with her customary greeting on her lips, reaching out her hands. Although she had been riding sedately, she sounded slightly out of breath as she announced, "I've come to ask you to be maid of honor at my wedding, dear Angèle!"

Immediately Angèle sensed a new air of maturity in Clothilde; it was as if in anticipation of her marriage, her cousin was already in the process of changing herself from a young girl to a young matron.

"Next month I shall become Madame Hector Bellamy."

"Dear Clothilde!" Angèle grasped her hands in congratulation and kissed her on both cheeks. Even as she did so, she was thinking that a few weeks ago they would have embraced. Now she felt unhappily as if they were playing a part on a stage. "Nonc' Etienne gave me a hint. He was wondering what it would be like to have an American son-in-law."

"He'll get used to it." Clothilde's smile was ravishing.

"But M'sieu Bellamy! After all, you have known him only since my ball, haven't you?"

Clothilde withdrew her hands. "If you are asking me if I know my own mind," she said lightly, "the answer is yes, I know what I am doing."

Angèle could feel Philippe's love wrapping her like an aura, and she had the curious notion that Clothilde could see it. It was impossible for Clothilde not to know they were lovers. She and her young cousin had been too close. The knowledge hung in the air between them.

"Please," she said miserably. "I didn't mean to offend by my question."

Clothilde shrugged, the gesture showing her surprising new maturity. "Do you want to be my attendant?"

"I should be very hurt if you had not asked me. When is the wedding?"

"As soon as the banns are published. The first one will be announced next Sunday."

So soon! Angèle wanted to protest, but a look at Clothilde's closed face silenced her. Her cousin was not going to confide in her again. Just as she could never speak to Clothilde about Philippe's love. She sighed for their lost innocence and the intimacy that Philippe had shattered, knowing it would never return.

"Will you be married at Bellemont?"

"Yes. Maman is in a fit, begging us to give her at least two months. But Hector has business in the United States capital and wants to take me with him to meet his family. The ship leaves for Baltimore in a few weeks."

Voices were so revealing, Angèle thought. In spite of its bright air, Clothilde's light voice was not the voice of a happy bride.

"Can Madame Breaux make your wedding gown so quickly?"

"I will be married in Maman's wedding gown. I've always planned to. Do you remember when we tried on our mothers' gowns, and I showed it to you? All lace and white silk embroidery?"

"Indeed I do. You will be an exquisite bride in it."

"It will fit admirably, with only a little taking in. And do you remember that lovely blue gown you showed me, the one Tant' Lisette brought from France?" Her smile had a surface luster, but it was very different from the gentle childlike gaiety that had been so much a part of Clothilde's charm.

Angèle nodded, her throat tight.

"I should like you to attend me in Tant' Lisette's gown."

"Of course, my dear."

Clothilde still loved her, Angèle thought, blinking back tears, even though she had forfeited her young cousin's trust.

They discussed her wedding plans for half an hour over coffee and sandwiches, Angèle offering her own and her servants' help in preparing for the ball at which the Rogets would introduce M'sieu Bellamy to their friends. After that, Angèle knew, there would be soirées and suppers nightly until the wedding rites.

"Where will you live?" Angèle asked.

"Hector has bought a house in New Orleans. It will be our town house, but Bellemont will always be our home."

It was only as Clothilde was leaving that she tossed over her shoulder, "I'm sending an invitation to Philippe, of course."

Angèle could only say lamely, "Of course."

There was one thing more. Clothilde paused at the first step, and with an obvious effort said, "Hector is asking both Philippe and Henri to be part of the wedding party."

Angèle caught her breath as Clothilde ran down the steps to where her groom waited patiently with her mount. She would be constantly thrown together with Philippe during the pre-wedding festivities, and the thought filled her with a terrified joy. She would not be able to resist him, and everyone would know.

Everyone would be saying that the eccentric Roget heiress, the talk of the parish because she had vowed never to marry, had met her match.

Chapter 6

*A*NGÈLE took Mimi and her cook with her to Bellemont to help her aunt prepare for Clothilde's wedding. Mimi did not want to go. She pursed her pale pink lips and observed that M'selle Clothilde's haste was indecent.

"Besides, how can I leave that Minette of mine at La Sorcellerie with Jean-Baptiste in the fields all day? She's Petite Mischief herself!"

Angèle was annoyed. "Are you afraid Jean-Baptiste will find another woman while you're gone? Petra can keep an eye on Minette." Petra was the big black woman who would rule the kitchen in the cook's absence. "I can't get along without you, Mimi," she insisted.

She sent the two servants and her small trunk with Jules in a cart, and drove herself over in her cabriolet.

It was a time of frenetic activity, cleaning and preparing Bellemont's rooms for overnight guests and arranging quarters for their valets and maids, planning and gathering supplies for the cooking of gargantuan amounts of food, and finding time for fittings of the gowns for all the bridal party. To avoid the bustling women and their seamstresses and servants, as much as to furnish some game for the cooks, Nonc' Etienne went hunting.

Through it all Clothilde moved like a wind-up doll, remote from all of them, a situation that made it hard for Angèle to sleep at night. Lying awake in the gauze-draped bed in Tant' Astride's guest room, worrying about Clothilde and haunted by memories of those two ecstatic nights she had spent in Philippe's arms, Angèle was suffering excruciating pangs of guilt.

She worried about the future. Everything was changing, and she accepted her responsibility for the change, but regretted the consequences of her impulsive decision to oppose Clothilde's betrothal to Philippe de l'Eglise. Things had moved swiftly out of her hands in an appalling direction. And what would happen to them all now?

She had heard nothing from Philippe since he had literally left her bed. His silence magnified her guilt and was gradually undermining her self-respect. What had she done?

On the Wednesday after Angèle left La Sorcellerie, Philippe presented himself at the plantation and was told by Duval that she would remain at Bellemont until her cousin's wedding.

"Did she leave a message for me?" Philippe asked.

"No, m'sieu."

Philippe was puzzled. Angèle had mentioned no wedding. What cousin? Did she have another besides Clothilde Roget? Philippe was not only disappointed, but annoyed. He debated remounting to ride the three miles farther to Bellemont, but on reflection requested instead that he be served some refreshments before he returned to New Orleans.

While he sat on the front galérie and waited for his tea, he became aware of how much Angèle's absence changed the atmosphere at La Sorcellerie. The house was unchanged, yet he sensed a hollowness at the heart of its beauty, diminished vitality in the slower pace of the household.

He did not know that both the cook and Mimi, Angèle's most powerful assistant in the running of the household, were also absent. For him the strong personality of its mistress had given La Sorcellerie that fillip of excitement that made it seem so attractive. Without her it seemed dull as whist.

Damned nuisance, riding all this way for nothing, he thought, bored.

When his tray arrived it was carried by Angèle's maid's child, Minette, and Philippe surveyed the girl's slender figure with interest. Her skin was lighter than her brother's, a pale golden color that gave her a healthy glow but was as creamy as old ivory. She was filling out remarkably. He could swear her little breasts were larger than they had been last week.

"Your tea, michie," she said, shyly lowering long black lashes, then flashing him a beautiful smile as she raised them to reveal her lively brown eyes.

Philippe was charmed. "You carried my breakfast tray one morning, didn't you?"

"Yes, michie." The lashes fluttered again, but her eyes were innocent of any reference to finding him in her mistress's bed.

"Do you carry all the breakfast trays, then?"

"No, michie, but many of our peoples went with m'selle to Bellemont, and Maman told me to help Petra. Petra is cook's helper," she explained.

Her French was not as crisp as her mother's; her speech had a distinctive rhythm. African?

"I see." He nodded his thanks as she poured tea into his cup.

"Sugah 'n' milk, michie?"

"Neither."

She gave him a sunny smile, revealing gleaming white teeth.

A beautiful child, and a natural coquette. In a few years she would be breathtaking. He wondered about her background. New to the colonies, he knew little about the Africans, but he had already picked up some fascinating gossip in town about La Sorcellerie and had learned that Angèle and her father were both considered somewhat eccentric.

"Angel Roget, that one that died, he was too easy on his slaves," one Creole told him. Then, with a significant look, "You've heard about the uprising a few years ago, when that planter upriver and all his family were murdered in their beds? That one, *he* was too lenient with his slaves. You've got to keep the whip hand, no? Now the other Roget, Angel's brother, he's a wiser master."

Looking at Minette's delicate features and clear ivory skin, Philippe speculated on that conversation.

Sitting on the galérie, drinking his tea and looking out to the shimmering bayou, Philippe saw a scarlet bird flash across the lawn and admitted that this tropical land had its attractions. But at once that inner vision of Sans Souci that had been at the core of his nostalgic moods since childhood, returned with its haunting recollections, and he wondered what Angèle would think of his estates.

In England he had learned that a title was not as important as being an Englishman or having money. The English had the same scorn for foreign titles that they had for foreigners, especially if they were held by impecunious émigrés.

But here the people he met spoke his language, and many were also émigrés. His introduction as a marquis had opened many doors, that and his kinship to the mayor. Angèle, alone, had been singularly unimpressed. He chuckled, remembering. She had won him with her first cool appraising look.

It was her independent strength and her sense of her own individual worth that appealed to him—the very qualities that made the colonists regard her as eccentric. But he would be at a loss to explain why such a woman, undeniably beautiful, had immediately established such power over him. Her great show of remaining independent mattered little to him, because beneath it he had discerned her passionate femininity. She was a woman who could be ruled only by love. He recalled her awakening passion with delight. How had she remained a virgin so long?

My gift to you, she had said.

Remembering, he was swept by love for her. He was convinced that if he married Angèle and took her to France, she would see how infinitely superior the ancestral estates of his family were to these colonial plantations. France was Angèle's homeland, too, he reminded himself. With Angèle at his side, how he was going to enjoy exploring those civilized delights of Paris his father had so often described.

Thoughts of Paris immediately brought the subject of his finances to mind. His stay in England had been one all too familiar to émigrés, a time of penury and pinch penny. It was after he had set sail for the New World to seek his fortune in the colonies, that he had learned Bonaparte was encouraging the return of the émigrés. But he didn't even have money enough to return, let alone to finance a campaign to regain his lands.

His kin, the mayor, had advised him that the quickest way to a fortune in Louisiana was to marry the daughter of one of the prospering planters. Clothilde Roget, an only child, had seemed the obvious choice, and he had found her very desirable. He might have married her quite happily if he had not met her cousin.

Angèle was pretending to resist marriage, but he was determined to have her, and he never doubted his eventual success. But his instincts, usually reliable where women were concerned, told him it would be a mistake to follow her to Bellemont.

He could be patient. Draining his cup, he shouted for his horse.

When he reached his rooms in the mayor's house, he found an invitation to Clothilde Roget's wedding to the American, Hector Bellamy, waiting for him, and cards for several soirées and balls in their honor.

A wedding made in heaven, Philippe thought with satisfaction. When Clothilde was happily married, Angèle would surely entertain thoughts of marrying him. It was probably her affection for her cousin that was the chief barrier to his suit. The prospect of success brought a dozen sensuous memories tumbling into his head, and his frustration at not finding her home was greater than it had been at La Sorcellerie.

Thumbing through the other notes, he found one from the American bridegroom. It was a request that the marquis honor the wedding party by acting as one of the bridesmaids' escorts, and Philippe's frustration vanished. Now he knew his strategy was correct. Angèle would be one of the wedding party. There would be ample opportunity to be at her side during the coming season of parties for the betrothed couple.

With the help of his valet, Philippe removed his coat and boots and cravat and sat in his open-throated shirt, contemplating his future. The long windows to his small balcony overlooked the courtyard, and smells of the mayor's stables and of the unseen river stole into his room. The creaking of carriage wheels and the ring of horseshoes on cobblestones mingled not unpleasantly with the cries of the oyster hawkers on a distant street.

Over the roofs of the houses between the mayor's house and the river, he could see the masts and furled sails of a large ship protruding above the levee, and he thought, *Next year at this time we will be on our way to France,* and sincerely believed it.

Clothilde was standing for a final adjustment of her mother's gown, her mother and Angèle watching critically while Madame Breaux, their dressmaker and herself a guest at the wedding, kneeled in her gray silk dress and bonnet to straighten a tiny dip in the hem, pins in her mouth.

Downstairs the other guests were gathered, and the musicians were tuning their instruments. They were waiting for Father Antoine, who was coming out from New Orleans to marry them.

The bride and groom planned to spend their wedding night aboard the ship, now riding at anchor in the river at New Orleans, which would leave on the early morning tide for Baltimore. In twenty-four hours, Angèle thought, Clothilde would be on her wedding trip, and it would be too late to mend the estrangement Angèle still felt between her and her cousin.

"If only I can escape mal de mer!" Clothilde exclaimed for the dozenth time.

"If you don't, it will be your own fault," her mother retorted. Madame Roget's plump face was red with exertion and nervousness. "You should have given us and yourself more time. Parties every night, and our preparations continuing night and day. You are already exhausted, and the day's only beginning."

"I'm perfectly well, and I've been having a wonderful time," Clothilde protested. But Angèle looked at the shadows under her young cousin's eyes and wondered if she had been sleeping well.

"Whatever is keeping Pére Antoine?" Madame Roget worried.

"He's probably riding out on his little donkey!"

"Don't be sarcastic, dear. Your father sent the carriage for him, of course."

Just then a servant appeared in the door to report that the priest was at the gates.

"I must meet him and offer him some wine and a place to prepare himself for the ceremony." Tant' Astride kissed her daughter and told her, "You are divine now, my darling. Perfection itself!"

Madame Breaux took the pins from her mouth and bit a thread, then rose to her feet. "A vision!" she pronounced.

But Clothilde still turned this way and that before the mirror, studying the reflection of her lovely old wedding gown with dissatisfaction.

"Leave us now, madame, if you please," Angèle told the dressmaker after Tant' Astride's departure.

Alone with Angèle, Clothilde avoided her eyes, fussing with her veil.

"You are so beautiful," Angèle said softly. "Oh, Clothilde, are you truly happy?"

Giving her veil a tiny impatient tug, Clothilde exclaimed, "Will you stop asking me that, Angèle?" although it was the first opportunity Angèle had had to ask her. "Why should I not be happy on my wedding day? Or do you also think that Hector is not good enough for me?" Her usually gentle voice had a bite.

"No, no, dear. I like Hector very much." Angèle hesitated. For three weeks she had tried to get Clothilde alone, and had not been successful until now. She plunged swiftly. "But why do I have this feeling that you have not got over Philippe?"

Her cousin turned on her. "Oh, marry him and have done with it!"

Angèle gasped, "Clothilde!"

"Do you think I haven't seen how you look at each other, or how he attaches himself to you at every soirée? He touches you constantly!"

A slow hot tide traveled up Angèle's body as the memory of Philippe's hands on her became so vivid that she could actually feel them and see the lambent look under those shapely dark brows which her fingers longed to trace.

Clothilde was watching her with sad, knowing eyes. She said more gently, "You are not the kind of woman who can enjoy living in sin." While Angèle's cheeks bloomed scarlet, Clothilde picked up her rosary from the dressing table. "Now I would like to be alone, dear Angèle."

Angèle stumbled out of the room. It was humbling and a little frightening to hear that Clothilde had noticed how single-mindedly Philippe was pursuing her, and how flimsy had become her resistance to his charms. Was it obvious to everyone? she wondered.

Going downstairs, her gaze immediately roved across the heads of other guests, and fastened on Philippe. His face and form were perfect in her eyes. Inwardly she traced the brows, so perfectly curved above the long slender Gallic nose; in her imagination she ran her finger along his firm upper lip, which contrasted so movingly with the sensuous fullness of the lower one.

He lifted his head and smiled at her, and her heart jumped with a ridiculous joy. Infatuated, like a schoolgirl, at twenty-three!

Tant' Astride met her at the foot of the stairs. "Come, it's time! Are the bridesmaids dressed? Père Antoine is ready to begin the ceremony."

"They are dressed and waiting, Tant' Astride."

"And the bride?"

"All ready."

"Good. I will collect Hector's young men." She signaled the musicians to begin, and the conversation of the guests dwindled as the priest, the bridegroom and his friends took their positions in the drawing room.

A few minutes later Clothilde began descending the wide stair with her attendants following her. Nonc' Etienne waited below, his expression as he looked up at his daughter conveying both love and regret. Low *ah's* of approval rose from the guests when they glimpsed Clothilde in her flowing ivory gown. Lowering her gaze, mysterious behind the veil of fragile old Belgian lace, she placed her small hand on her father's arm and advanced slowly to the altar, behind which Père Antoine awaited.

Hector Bellamy, unusually pale and serious, and looking unfamiliar with his wedding collar and cravat so high that his chin pointed somewhere over the short priest's head, stepped forward as Nonc' Etienne released her, and the two young people stood together before the priest to exchange their vows.

Angèle, behind and to the right of Clothilde, had not expected to respond emotionally to the ceremony, but her cousin's haunting beauty and the vulnerability of her youth were very moving, and she could not dismiss her feeling that it was in some mysterious way tragic. She wondered what Philippe's feelings were at this moment, but did not dare let her eyes wander to him, standing with Henri Dévaux at Hector's left. Her feelings had already brought tears to her eyes.

Other weddings had not affected her in this way. She knew that a tremendous upheaval was taking place in her life, as well as in Clothilde's. Nothing would ever again be the same, and it wasn't only because Clothilde was leaving Louisiana for an indefinite stay. She herself had changed.

The bride's expression was not perceptible through her still lowered veil. When at last she raised it, a married woman, for Hector's kiss, the audience burst into applause. While the guests came forward to congratulate the couple, servants removed the chairs. When all had presented themselves to the newlyweds and the bride's parents and been thanked for coming, the musicians struck up a waltz which had been Hector's somewhat daring request, and the floor was cleared for the young couple to dance.

Tant' Astride watched them with damp sentimentality, and after they had made the first round, she and Nonc' Etienne joined them. Philippe claimed Angèle as the other attendants moved out on the floor.

As Angèle moved into his light embrace, the significance of what had gone before paled before the pleasure of being in his arms. A kind of joyousness spurred her, and she entered into the waltz with vivacity. White-coated waiters moved among the guests with trays of wineglasses, and after the first wedding party danced, Nonc' Etienne proposed a toast. When all had drunk to the happy couple, he signaled the musicians and claimed his daughter as his partner. The guests joined enthusiastically in the dancing.

Wine flowed until midnight, when a wedding feast was served, after which most of the company piled into waiting carriages drawn up behind that of the bride and groom. Clothilde took Angèle upstairs with her when she went to get out of the elaborate wedding gown and into a traveling dress.

"We must hurry," Clothilde said, signaling her waiting maid to unbutton her dress. Her face was flushed now with wine and compliments, and her smile was dazzling. "I'll miss you, dear Angèle! You need have no worries about me. I shall be very happy!"

Angèle, too moved to speak, embraced her, and they clung to each other for a moment before Angèle stepped back to allow the moist-eyed maid to help Clothilde. When the bride had changed, they went downstairs together.

Angèle had eyes only for Philippe, waiting at the bottom with Hector. He took her hand and they ran out to the waiting carriages, after Hector and Clothilde. Nonc' Etienne and Tant' Astride were already seated with Father Antoine in the carriage directly behind the bride and groom's.

Philippe helped Angèle into a small glass-enclosed carriage with a coachman on the box and a single luxurious seat. He immediately imprisoned her hand. "This wedding has given me many chances to see you, but never alone!" he complained.

The bayou water had a black gleam, and the half-eaten moon threw ghostly light on the strings of moss hanging from the branches of the oaks along the bayou road. Against the perpetual background of night songs, bullfrogs croaked a wedding march in deep bass. The air was balmy, damp and sweet-smelling with the fragrance of Tant' Astride's flower gardens, strong enough in spring to overwhelm the swamp odors. Angèle's hand trembled in Philippe's.

Drivers flicked their whips and shouted orders, and the long train of carriages lurched off on the bayou road to New Orleans, their occupants singing all the way. But in the third carriage the glass was cloudy, giving the hungry lovers a modicum of privacy. They melted into each other's arms for the stolen kisses that had been denied them since those memorable two days of the storm.

When at last Philippe raised his head, the moonlight illumined Angèle's cheek and he saw her tears. He said, with tender reproach, "I wouldn't have thought a woman like you would cry at weddings."

"What kind of woman do you think I am? Why is she marrying him when she loves you?"

"Darling Angèle," he said, "she is only seventeen. Shall I tell you how many seventeen-year-olds have imagined themselves in love with me?"

"Oh, doubtless!" she said, and blew her nose into her handkerchief. "You probably collect them like trophies."

"The love of a seventeen-year-old isn't much of a trophy. At that age they are in love with love."

And wasn't she in love with love? Angèle wondered. It was so new to her. She could not stop thinking of her lover. He came between her and every other thing that had been important in her life; he was her first thought in the morning when she awoke, her last thought at night. She resented that, but could not prevent it.

She sniffled. "How worldly of you!"

"That sounds like jealousy. Are you jealous, my darling?"

"Insanely. But Clothilde is the sister I never had, the daughter I will never—"

"I know," he said, caressing her. "My darling, I know. But don't say *never.*"

No other man in her world would have said "I know" in just that way, she thought. He did know. I shall have to marry him, Angèle told herself.

He kissed her again, long and lingeringly. Angèle lifted her fingers and lightly traced the lines of his mouth, then touched the tip of his nose and followed its straight line to the curve of a brow, murmuring, "I've been wanting to do that all evening." She lifted her fingers to his hair, tracing his hairline as though she were trying to see him through her touch.

He caught her hand and kissed the fingers separately. "If I promise never to interfere with your management of La Sorcellerie, will you marry me?"

In a muffled voice she said, "I'd want that in writing, Philippe."

His hand stilled on hers. "As you have already pointed out, such a document would have no meaning in a French court," he warned her. When she was silent, he said with laughter in his voice, "You see, you have no choice but to trust me."

She sighed, leaned against him, and raised her lips for more kisses. There was no more conversation on the road to New Orleans.

When the carriages lined up on the levee above the anchored vessel and Nonc' Etienne's guests spilled out of them, Angèle came out of Philippe's arms bemused and disoriented. The bridal couple, whose luggage had been put aboard by their servants earlier, lingered on the levee as if reluctant now to end the festivities and face this final parting.

It was a glorious night in the city, with the moon soaring above the rooftops. The same lopsided moon was throwing a pathway to the tall-masted ship anchored alongside the pier below the levee. The buzz of insects and other night sounds were not as loud here as the slap of water against the boats along the wharf, or the creak of hawsers as the larger vessels swung in the current.

There was a fragrance of flowers on the balmy air but it was overlaid by stronger waterfront odors, some of them unpleasant, but exciting because they suggested exotic places and strange novelties. It was past curfew, the time when slaves and sailors must be off the streets, but there were still many citizens abroad, and it was obvious that not all sailors who had returned to their craft in the river were in their berths.

On a flatboat tied up at a pier a little distance upriver, some Yankee rivermen rose abruptly to their feet and threw their caps in the air with a great cheer, almost as if they were cheering the wedding party. Some began singing lustily in incomprehensible English.

Clothilde's and Hector's friends crowded around them for a final good-bye, saying that never had there been such a wedding party. Some of them trailed after the couple as they started down the grassy levee to the pier where the vessel's boat waited to take the newlyweds aboard. Philippe and Angèle started down with them.

Up on the levee there was a small commotion attracting more and more spectators. One of the men was shouting something at them, but no one paid him any attention.

Then Nonc' Etienne, who with Tant' Astride was descending the levee with slow care, told them to wait, and motioned the man forward. He came sliding down the slope toward them, a bearded man whose face reflected some great emotional excitement.

"What did you say, m'sieu?" Etienne asked him.

"Bonaparte has sold us to the Americans!"

"What? You're drunk, man!"

"It's true! He has sold all of Louisiana to the Americans for three million U.S. dollars."

"Impossible!" Nonc' Etienne said loudly, with conviction. "We have only just been informed that he completed negotiations with Spain for the return of Louisiana to France! Why would he turn around and sell such an excellent port to Britain's revolutionists?"

"For money to carry on his wars, of course. I tell you it's true, man! Word came on yonder vessel. God save us, we are all Americans now!"

"The traitor! The stinking traitor!" Nonc' Etienne shouted in a rage, as excited now as his informant.

All around him Creole men took up his cry. Were they to be made Americans against their will? Just when they were rejoicing over having become French citizens once more? Whether of Spanish origin or French, American citizenship was the last choice many of them would have made. It was insupportable! But what was one to do? Except curse that upstart Corsican general, Bonaparte! May all his hair fall out! May his teeth rot in his head and all his mistresses be unfaithful!

"Why are you so upset?" Madame Roget asked her husband. "Isn't your son-in-law an American?"

"He will make a better Frenchman than I will make a Yankee," said Etienne, whose surly judgment of the new nation was based almost entirely on his impression of the rough rivermen who brought the flatboats loaded with cotton, hides, and tallow down the Mississippi, then roamed the streets, drunk and looking for women.

A little farther down the grassy slope Philippe, his blood on fire with Angèle's kisses, put his arms around her quite openly. "We shall return to France, my love," he whispered exultantly in her ear. "I am a Frenchman, after all."

We? Angèle thought dizzily. But she did not contradict him, even though she heard a woman behind her whisper, "There will be another wedding soon, no?"

Chapter 7

C*LOTHILDE* did not return for Angèle's wedding. She wrote that she was enceinte and Hector's family insisted on keeping them in Philadelphia for her accouchement. The American city was grand, she said, but neither as gay nor as punctilious about proper behavior as Nouvelle Orléans. She found English difficult to learn. She missed them all. Nevertheless she was supremely happy, and as tenderly cared for as if she were at Bellemont.

Tant' Astride was beside herself with worry because Clothilde was having her first child so far from home, and in order to occupy her mind she threw herself into the preparations for Angèle's marriage rites.

The wedding promised to be the high point of the social season, and not only because of Philippe's title and his relationship to the mayor. All of New Orleans was intrigued because the strong-willed Roget heiress was actually putting her neck into the marriage yoke. The men were gossiping over their coffees at the Exchange, and the women behind their fans at the soirées, about the story Angèle's lawyer could not resist telling his best friend, M'sieu DuBonnet, who told *his* best friend. It was a story no one could be expected to keep, and soon all the town was highly diverted by it.

"Before Angèle Roget would consent to the banns being posted, she insisted that Philippe de l'Eglise sign away his rights to her property."

"No!"

"Her lawyer told Mademoiselle Roget that the paper would be worthless if challenged in a court of law, but she said that the honor of the marquis was at stake."

"And the marquis? What did he think of that? He is an émigré, after all, and not a rich man."

"He is said to be furious, but he signed."

"He must be besotted with love for the woman!"

"He is not the only man who has knocked at that door—only the first to be admitted."

"But at what a price!"

Eventually the gossip reached the ears of Philippe's kinsman, the mayor. By that time the pasquinades had begun to appear. Since the West Indian émigré's newssheet carried only news from France and Spain brought by vessels arriving in port, these amusing lampoons were posted at street corners, on the walls of tradesmen's buildings, or on the picket fences surrounding houses and gardens. When the mayor called them to Philippe's attention, Philippe flew into a rage.

"That bastard of a lawyer! I'm going to call him out!"

"Swords?" the mayor asked mildly, picking up his snuff box.

"Or pistols! His choice! Will you be my second?"

Taking a pinch in his deliberate way, the mayor said, "Certainly. But I am sorry for him because he is no match for you, and he is not entirely at fault."

"Then who is?"

The mayor could not repress a smile. "Do you think anyone could resist talking about such a woman as Angèle Roget?" He kissed his fingers and rolled his eyes in a pantomime of ecstasy.

Philippe flushed dark red, and for a second his kinsman was in danger of receiving a blow. Then Philippe turned away and rang for his servant. Ordering a horse, he rode out to inspect the pasquinades. He needed to see only one. It was a crude satiric drawing of Angèle wearing breeches and astride a horse! Within minutes he was riding hard toward La Sorcellerie.

The longer he thought about the lampoons, the angrier Philippe became. By the time he reached the plantation he was fuming. He leaped off his mount—one of the mayor's geldings —and flung the reins to Jules, ignoring the groom's polite "Good morning."

Running up the stair to the galérie, Philippe almost collided with Minette as the slave girl came tearing around the corner of the building and slid to a halt. Breathlessly she cried, "Good morning!" Her eyes widened at sight of his face and she blurted, "You're angry, michie?"

Philippe fought for self-control. "Not with you, child." He drew a deep breath into his lungs, oblivious to the heavy sweet odor of crushed cane it carried. "Where is your mistress?"

Just then the front door was opened by Duval, who scowled when he saw Minette and jerked his head to send her back to the kitchen annex. Angèle appeared behind her majordomo, wearing her riding costume. She handed her riding crop to the servant and dismissed him with a soft, "Thank you, Duval," then held out her hands to Philippe, her lively face alight with pleasure.

"What a lovely surprise! Have you come to watch the crushing—" she began.

"I've had a very *un*pleasant surprise!" he snapped, and she saw with alarm that his face was pale with anger.

"What's happened?"

"The whole town is laughing at me. Is that what you wanted?"

"What are you talking about, Philippe?"

"The mayor has heard from several sources of your request that I sign away my rights to your property. Every one, he says, found it extremely amusing."

"My lawyer would not reveal my intimate business!" she gasped.

"No? If you think that, you're a fool!"

She stiffened.

"Either he has told his wife, who is a gossip," Philippe said violently, "or his clerk has babbled in the Merchants Exchange.

88

Who knows? At any rate, you've made me the sport of all the town wits with your stubborn independence."

With flags of high color in her cheeks, she said, "I thought you loved me for my independence."

"Do you understand what I am saying? There are vulgar lampoons about us on every street corner. My kinsman tells me they are all over town. And everyone is *laughing.*" His eyes were as stormy as on the first day they'd met, when he had come close to grabbing and shaking her because of what he called her reckless driving.

Angèle looked him in the eye and said scornfully, "You, a 'prince of the blood,' are intimidated by the laughter of the people?"

"I am not intimidated, I am *furious!*" he shouted, coming so near that she felt the vibrations of his anger in tiny shock waves against her nerves. "But what can I do? Must I call out the entire male population? You have placed me in this humiliating position with your open lack of trust in me. *You,* who say you love me!"

Her heart was beating so fast, its rhythm was like a desperate dance, but her eyes did not waver from his. "Do you want to end our betrothal, Philippe?" She had paled, and her body was braced as if against a blow.

He heard her through the red haze of his fury, and a shock went through him as he realized what she was offering. Her head was high as she proffered him his freedom, in spite of the irretrievable disgrace it would mean for her if he accepted. His fury collapsed under a wave of admiration and love.

"Mon dieu, Angèle, don't quarrel with me when I'm angry," he implored her. "Anything could happen!"

She laughed shakily as he pulled her into his arms with a heartfelt groan. She felt as if she had been battered by the force of his emotional storm and come at last into quiet waters, there in his arms, in the hall of her own La Sorcellerie.

"I love you," he said against her hair. "That's all that matters. And I ask only one thing of you, darling Angèle."

She loved hearing him speak her name in that caressing tone. Her own voice deepened with love. "What is that, my Philippe?"

"That we leave for France as quickly as possible after the wedding."

She drew back in alarm. "To France?" *Leave La Sorcellerie?* And what of all the lives that depended on her here? "So soon? I cannot possibly leave before all the cane is cut and crushed and processed! I have invested so much time, so much hope in this experimental crop!"

"There is no time to lose if I am to succeed in recovering my title and estates."

"And that is everything to you?" She raised clear, questioning eyes.

"No!" he said violently. "If you must know, it is you who are everything to me." He pulled her head down against his shoulder and murmured above it, "Sometimes I resent that."

"Yes," she said, and heard herself echoing him when she said it, "I know. Yes," she repeated more softly. "It is our fate to love, Philippe, but perhaps not our fate to love happily, no?"

He raised her chin, lowered his mouth to hers, and drank deeply of her sweetness, feeling her passion swell to complement his own arousal and glorying in it. "Are you happy now?" he challenged her.

"Supremely," she gasped with her first breath.

"Well, then?" With his arms still around her, he moved toward the stair.

His long intimate kiss had started needles of flame throughout her body. She ached with an intolerable desire for his love after the near calamity of their quarrel. "Please, Philippe, you must not kiss me like this until we are wed."

"I make no promise," he said hoarsely, "because you have already extracted my vow. You could not enrage me so if I did not love you with my whole being. I may kill you one day, but I will never wed another."

"Nor I," vowed Angèle.

Mimi was quieter than usual brushing Angèle's hair that evening, not exactly morose but not her usual cheerful self.

"What's the matter, Mimi?" Angèle asked her. "You look as if you've lost your last friend."

"Maybe I have," Mimi said heavily.

"Have you and Jean-Baptiste been quarreling?" Angèle asked

idly, her thoughts still roaming in the pleasure fields of Philippe's lovemaking.

"Jean-Baptiste never quarrels with me, m'selle. When I feel like quarreling, he goes back to the fields."

Angèle laughed. "What is it, then?"

Mimi brushed in silence, drawing the long dark tresses out in a way that she knew made her mistress feel languorous and well cared for. Presently she said, "We're going to have a new master, no?"

Angèle was annoyed because she was guiltily aware that Mimi had known from the beginning all about her stolen hours with Philippe. "You know that I am betrothed to the marquis, Mimi. What is it that you want to say?"

The black woman asked softly, "Is this man the right one for you?"

Angèle closed her eyes, her head bobbing slightly with the pull of the brush. "He is." Her tone was relaxed and ripe with sensual pleasure.

Mimi murmured, "Will he be a good master?"

Angèle's eyes flew open in irritation. "Nothing will change. I will still be mistress of La Sorcellerie." She caught herself, and added, "Except that when the cane is all harvested, the master will be taking me back to France with him."

Mimi's hand jerked the brush and was momentarily stilled.

"You will go with me, of course."

"I?" In the mirror Angèle saw Mimi's eyes widen in fear. "Go to *France?* Oh, no, m'selle!"

"No?" Angèle said, startled. "Why not?"

"I can't leave my children! And Jean-Baptiste, he's my proper husband! I don't want to lose him."

"They belong to me, not to you," Angèle said coldly.

Mimi caught her breath. "Oui, m'selle." She brought her lips together in a straight line and began brushing again, in a silence that lasted.

"Of course you will go with me, Mimi!" Angèle said, breaking the silence. "You know I couldn't get along without you."

Mimi said nothing.

"We'll come back here, you know."

Mimi heaved a deep sigh.

"Anyway," Angèle said at last, "it's a long time in the future."

She dismissed Mimi and got into her bed. It still smelled faintly of Philippe's body, but Angèle's enjoyment of remembered ecstasy was spoiled by what Mimi had said. Her words had brought unwelcome pictures of Mimi in the embrace of the huge black Spanish-mulatto foreman Mimi had called her "proper husband," an image Angèle found strangely uncomfortable.

Her wedding day dawned fair after a week of torrential rains that had everyone worried. The ritual was to be celebrated in the St. Louis Cathedral in New Orleans. Philippe's wedding gift was delivered to Angèle at La Sorcellerie by his kinsman, the mayor, who rode out to La Sorcellerie early.

"Philippe would like you to wear this today," he told Angèle, handing her a silken case.

She unrolled it and gave an exclamation of pleasure. Taking out the exquisite necklace of sapphires and diamonds, she held it up to show Tant' Astride and Nonc' Etienne, who had come to drive her to the New Orleans cathedral.

"It is an heirloom in his family," M'sieu le mayor said. "He told me his father had pawned it three times in England to feed and clothe his family, but he refused to sell it. It is the last piece of jewelry left to Philippe."

"Magnificent!" Tant' Astride breathed.

"Priceless," Nonc' Etienne said gruffly, and Angèle wondered uncomfortably if he were imagining it on Clothilde's white throat.

"My gift for Philippe is much more practical," Angèle said ruefully. "I mean to present it after the ceremony."

"I am sure it will be as much appreciated," the mayor said, with a sly smile that hinted he had guessed what it was.

When Angèle had dressed, with the help of Mimi and Tant' Astride and Minette watching in excitement, ready to run any errands, Tant' Astride fastened the precious necklace around her throat, filling the rounded décolletage of her wedding gown, then kissed her with tears in her eyes. "If only your dear mother could see you!"

They rode into town in Nonc' Etienne's carriage, the horses

slogging through mud. The unpaved streets of New Orleans were muddy, too, although the pedestrians had banquettes made of cypress planks. Tant' Astride and Nonc' Etienne were more nervous than they had been at Clothilde's wedding.

"If I were mayor, I would see that these streets were cobblestoned," Tant' Astride grumbled.

"And where should M'sieu le mayor get the stones," Nonc' Etienne demanded, "in this land of trembling prairies that was designed only for muskrats?"

"From the ships which carry rocks for ballast," Tant' Astride said triumphantly.

"You've thought it all out, ah?" her husband said dryly.

"At least there is no dust," Angèle, who was as nervous as they were, pointed out as their carriage approached the side door of the cathedral.

Mimi, riding beside the coachman, carried a reticule containing Angèle's comb and brush and other necessary toilet articles. Jean-Baptiste accompanied them on horseback, given the honor of carrying Angèle through the mud from the carriage to the robing room where Mimi and Tant' Astride would help her remove the traces of her journey and adjust her veil.

The cathedral was filled to overflowing. The mayor was both well-known and well-liked, and his kinsman, the marquis, had cut a dashing figure in the town. His interest in the eccentric Roget woman had intrigued many townspeople and disappointed some; and there had been those amusing lampoons. All wanted to witness the wedding, and since the mayor was a public figure, the wedding assumed the proportions of a public ritual.

There were gasps of admiration when Angèle appeared on the arm of her uncle. It is the necklace, Angèle thought. But Madame Breaux had outdone herself in producing the wedding gown of soft white silk. It followed the simple classic style introduced by the revolution, was eminently suitable to Louisiana's climate and sublimely becoming to Angèle's tall, slender figure.

The design cleverly separated her gently rounded breasts and lifted them with crisscrossing strips heavily encrusted with seed pearls. From these bands the narrow skirt fell in soft folds, ending in a very short train. On her flowing dark hair she wore a tiara of pearls from which her veil cascaded in a semicircle, leaving her expressive face uncovered.

Hers was not a classical beauty, Philippe's kinsman noted, nor could it inspire the dreamy illusion of great beauty that had drawn men like flies to her young cousin. This bride's face was a unique combination of direct blue eyes, a nose that was proudly straight, and a mouth that was not only generous but could change in a moment from a forbidding firmness to a smile that quirked with humor. It was an unusual face, so lively that it would be remembered longer than one that was conventionally beautiful.

When his young kinsman stood beside her, tall and handsome in a style everyone recognized as that of the aristocracy of the *ancien régime,* they made a striking couple. They would always command respect, the mayor told himself with satisfaction. No sound was heard in the cathedral except the rustling of petticoats as the congregation knelt and rose again, as the rites bade them. In the rapt silence a sonorous chanting rose to the arches as the couple knelt before the altar for the blessing of their union.

After their triumphal march down the aisle, they emerged into the square, where Angèle's wedding gift to Philippe awaited them—a handsome barouche in glittering black, decorated in gold with Philippe's own crest and drawn by two shining black horses with white feet. A look of pure pleasure came into his face, then he looked into her eyes with such love that she felt weak with emotion.

He handed her into the carriage. Its flexible top was folded back and Angèle looked across the Place d'Armes, where the sun shone on the muskets and on the polished boots of the city guard in their sky-blue uniforms, drawn up in parade at the request of the mayor to honor their nuptials. As she turned toward them, they raised their muskets, shifted them to the opposite shoulder, raised them again and returned them to the original position in salute. She waved her gloved hand, and they cheered. Beyond the parade ground and the barracks, she could see over the levee the tall masts of ships in port from the States, Europe, and the West Indies.

Inevitably the sight brought Angèle memories of Clothilde's wedding night—the night they learned they had become American citizens in Louisiana Territory. Americans had been streaming into New Orleans ever since, offending everybody with their proprietary airs and their ungracious way of doing business. But there was no escape from them. Some had even appeared inside the cathedral just now!

Dear Clothilde, she thought. If only she could have been here today! Instead she was far away among those ill-mannered and ungracious people, and pregnant. . . .

Angèle turned, looked into her husband's eyes, and felt herself drowning in the love she saw there. He picked up her hand, the one wearing the heavy gold band that had been his mother's and his grandmother's before that, and brought it to his lips.

The congregation streamed into the square and followed the carriage as it conveyed the newlyweds the short distance to the ballroom for the public reception. There, they stood in their wedding finery and received the congratulations of the people of the town including, Angèle whispered to Philippe, those who had laughed at the pasquinades. When the musicians began playing, Philippe led her in a waltz while their guests applauded. Then the mayor and his lady and Tant' Astride and Nonc' Etienne joined them in another waltz, and soon the floor was filled with the elite of the town whirling in three-quarter time.

When everyone was dancing, Angèle and Philippe murmured their good-byes to Tant' Astride and Nonc' Etienne and slipped down to the street, where Jules and Mimi and Jean-Baptiste waited with the new carriage. They were driven back to La Sorcellerie, where a feast was being prepared for all the slaves on the plantation, to celebrate the marriage of their mistress and to introduce their new master.

Still wearing her wedding dress and her sapphires, her veil secured by the tiara of pearls, Angèle stood beside Philippe, who was magnificent in his own wedding costume of dove-gray breeches, cream waistcoat, and a coat of pale gold embroidered in deeper gold. They received the good wishes of her servants, field workers as well as house servants and grooms, and afterward drank a toast and retired to the master bedroom suite, which had been her parents. Later they reappeared on the rear galérie to watch the Africans dance in the light of the huge bonfire that had been lit in the open space between the great house and the slave quarters.

The drums of Africa set up their throbbing rhythm, and in the light of the fire, the silhouettes of the dancers became angular and exotic. The children were dancing, too. Watching them Angèle thought, *There will be an heir to La Sorcellerie, and perhaps a daughter like Clothilde,* and wondered how she could ever have considered remaining single.

When the slaves were completely absorbed in their dancing, Philippe drew her through the wide-open French windows and into the room that had been her mother's, where Mimi waited to help her undress, as Philippe left to go to his own valet.

"Handle my gown gently," Angèle told Mimi. "One day my daughter will wear it."

Mimi, stroking its silken folds, looked up with a fleeting, ineffably wistful expression. "Oui, madame," she said, with a faint emphasis on Angèle's new title, and they smiled at each other.

When Angèle was ready, she dismissed Mimi, and in her negligée walked through the connecting door into Philippe's room. He had just sent his man away and was standing in the center of the room in his silken robe. She took two steps and paused.

He looked at her with intense love. "Drop your robe," he said hoarsely.

She loosened the ribbons at her breast, and shrugging out of the sheer robe, let it fall around her feet. Philippe threw off his robe and stood before her for a moment, his masculine beauty and his passion fully revealed, his glowing, dreamy eyes reflecting back on her such a loving image of herself that she felt more beautiful than she had ever imagined she could be. He came toward her, dropped to his knees, and putting his arms around her waist, began kissing the soft skin of her abdomen and her thighs, worshiping her body with kisses.

Angèle dug her fingers into the soft dark curls of his hair. When she began moaning, "Philippe, oh, Philippe!" he rose, lifting her in his arms, and carried her to their bed. There in the light of a single candle they made love, while the distant African rhythms throbbed in the night.

Chapter 8

A man made such a difference in a house. It had been three years since a man's laughter had echoed from La Sorcellerie's high ceilings, or a man had shouted cheerfully from the galérie for an ale instead of using the bellpull to summon a servant. There was the delightful novelty of waking mornings with the sweet weight of a man's arm lying across her breasts, and turning blissfully to inhale the warm odor of his skin before even opening her eyes.

They had fallen easily into a routine. For a few weeks after their wedding Philippe rode out with Angèle on her morning inspection of her fields, but since he did not share her absorbing interest in the cultivation of sugarcane, he soon found reasons to be driven in the new carriage and pair into New Orleans, where he met his friends for coffee at the Exchange and picked up secondhand news from London or Paris brought in by the vessels tied up at the wharf below the levee.

He still rode with Angèle at least twice a week, and spent the rest of the morning writing letters to friends and relatives abroad who might help him persuade Napoleon to return his ancestral estates.

On the days when he went to New Orleans, he brought back news of what was being talked about among the other planters who were turning to sugar and the merchants who were buying it. In the evenings, when they sat on the galérie with the older black children waving their fans to keep the insects away and the young ones chasing fireflies down under the oak trees, he told her what he had heard and asked many questions about her plans for marketing the sugar, which interested him more than its cultivation.

The magic of their pleasure in each other did not dim. When they went upstairs to their rooms, they made love. Afterward Philippe tenderly sluiced her heated body in the cool bath they had ordered prepared before dismissing their servants, and she performed the same loving service for him. Then they slept together in her father's big bed, through the cooler hours until daylight. It was an idyllic time, and Angèle was supremely happy.

Two months after the wedding another field of experimental cane was ripe for harvesting and the cutting and crushing were resumed. It was sweltering weather, the air heavy with the sweetened smoke as fires burned under the pots of boiling syrup. In spite of the heat Angèle rose early and kept a close watch on every phase of the operation, from the cutting of the ripe cane to hauling it in oxen-drawn carts to the crude stone mill where it was washed and crushed and the juice run off into the black pots for the lengthy boiling.

All day and night the steam rose in sweet clouds above the perspiring slaves who piled wood on the fires and stirred the bubbling syrup. The heavy, sickening odor spread upriver on the breezes blowing in from the gulf.

Philippe persuaded some merchants to come out from New Orleans to inspect the crushing and speculate on whether the sugar would crystallize properly this time. He talked optimistically of going back to France when the sugar crop was harvested and sold, but to Angèle it was talk that did not touch her, busy as she was.

She was feeling the heat and the humidity more than ordinarily this season. The second crushing was running into November, and it was still hot, hot. The crushed cane quickly fermented, and its overpowering odor sometimes made her feel squeamish.

She came in one morning white and nauseated, and Mimi put her to bed with cool damp towels covering her body, muttering, "What is the master thinking of, letting you stay out so long in this heat?"

"He doesn't tell me what to do!" Angèle said sharply. "I have always kept an eye on the harvest."

"But you are a married woman now, madame," Mimi murmured, replacing the wet cloth on her forehead. "Perhaps you are enceinte?"

Angèle's eyes widened and she silently began reckoning the days that had passed so happily and swiftly since her wedding.

Mimi laughed at her. "It is possible, no?"

"Yes, Mimi," Angèle said in a bemused voice as a warm wonder filtered through her thoughts. "It is quite possible." She thought of Clothilde, who was carrying a child so far from home, and wished they were nearer to each other so they could share this awesome experience. Though expected, it was an emotional shock now that it was here.

She waited until she was very sure before telling Philippe. He had been in New Orleans all day, and was driven up in the carriage just after Angèle had risen from her nap and bathed and dressed in a light cotton dress. When she heard him calling "Angèle!" as he ran up the stairs, she dismissed Mimi and waited for him in her room.

He looked elegant in his well-fitted clothes, not at all wilted from the heat. She loved the way his face brightened when he saw her. The thought that she made him happy gave her intense pleasure. She moved toward him with her hands extended. "I have some news, Philippe."

A faint shadow crossed his face. "Good news, I hope?"

"I hope it will please you. I . . . we . . ." To her astonishment, she found her tongue suddenly awkward, and she blurted, "We're having a baby."

The joy that flooded his face spilled over into her heart. It was one of those moments when their union was the mingling of two currents of life in the same way that two streams mingled and flowed together in flood time, moments Angèle was hoarding in her memory.

He took her in his arms and rocked her tenderly. "A son! You're giving me a son!"

A laugh bubbled up in her throat. "I hope you won't be disappointed if—"

He did not even hear her. "An heir!" he exulted. "And he will be born on French soil!"

She drew back and looked up at him in surprise. "Philippe?"

Smiling down at her, he said, "I have news, too, darling. Today I arranged for our passage on a Yankee schooner sailing for France next month."

"France!" Angèle pulled out of his embrace. "You will cancel it, of course."

With a quick frown, he asked, "Why? The cane will be harvested. There is no reason to stay here."

"Only the most important reason—that I am enceinte!" she exclaimed. "My son must be born on La Sorcellerie. It is his heritage."

Anger colored Philippe's face. "Your son, madame, will inherit *my* title, and one day, I hope, be master of Sans Souci. Of course he will be born on French soil! He must be a French citizen."

She knew it had been a terrible slip of the tongue to say *my* son, but she was helpless to mend it when she had no control over the anger that had leaped up in volatile response to his own. It happened frequently that way; she reacted helplessly to his every change of mood. Besides, she thought what he was suggesting was so utterly mad that even he must see it. So she made a second mistake.

"Your title counts for nothing under the Directorate, Philippe. Whether we like it or not, our son's destiny is here. French citizenship would only handicap him. Here he will be master of La Sorcellerie, and sugar will make him rich!"

Philippe looked at Angèle's vivid face with mixed anger and rue. He had brought this on himself. He thought fleetingly of Clothilde Roget, who would never have questioned his judgment in such a matter.

"The Bourbons are not finished, madame, however little you

may value my title. As an American you could not be expected to realize its importance to our son."

Angèle paled at Philippe's insult. She had always considered herself French and had been as shocked and angered as every other Creole by the stroke of Bonaparte's pen that had deprived her of French citzenship. Now she was being told she did not value her husband's distinguished heritage! She still considered herself more French than American, but she was also the daughter of a Roget, and her father had been—like Nonc' Etienne—a practical man who saw the necessity for adapting to one's environment.

But it was not so much Philippe's words that hurt her so badly. It was his anger. Frightened, she threw her arms around his neck, trying too late to undo the damage her tongue had done. "Listen to the two of us," she exclaimed with a shaky laugh, "quarreling about nothing! We could have a daughter, you know."

He did not respond to her teasing. "It makes no difference," he said coldly, "since we will be going to Paris in any case."

"Philippe, please be sensible! I do not refuse to go to France with you. But I cannot undertake a long and difficult journey in my condition. Let us go next year."

He threw off her arms with a furious gesture. "You still pretend to misunderstand. It is your condition that makes the journey urgent. Our passage is engaged. We sail in four weeks."

Angèle cried, "I cannot bear your anger! A moment ago we were so close I thought we were as near to being one soul as two people could come. I thought that—" Her voice broke. "Oh, Philippe, I thought you were happy. . . ."

He understood too well what she was feeling, and with his special gift saw even more than she could reveal. He reminded himself that Clothilde's sweetness had ended by boring him, while Angèle's personality had affected him like an astringent aperitif on a hot day. His anger crumpled into remorse. He took her in his arms again, holding her tenderly.

"Darling Angèle, forgive me. You've made me truly happy, and I'm a beast to be shouting at you." He picked up her hands and kissed each one tenderly. "I will love our child. You know that, don't you? It is because of my great love that I do what I do." He kissed her deeply, and responsive as always to his change of mood, she felt every bone in her body melting with surrender.

Soon he was caressing her with urgent lips and seeking hands, and she was just as urgently sliding her fingers beneath his coat to hold him closer, opening herself to him unreservedly. Their quarrel had raised their emotions to such a pitch that when lovemaking followed, it was like a cataclysm.

Afterward, lying exhausted but happy in his arms, secure again in his love, Angèle said tenderly, "Next year we will go to France, I promise you."

Philippe was silent a long moment. When she shifted her head to look at his face, he said, "I'm sorry, Angèle. Napoleon is at peace with England, but it's an uneasy truce. We must go now, before another blockade prevents us from making a French port."

So nothing was changed.

Her heart sank like a stone, but she had no fight left. Philippe obviously expected war with France and England to break out again. If it did, they would be trapped in France. How long would it be before she could return to her beloved La Sorcellerie? She wondered.

Yet she knew she would go. For if she refused, what would be the end of it? Would Philippe go without her, and be unable to return?

She did not dare risk it.

But to leave La Sorcellerie! *What had she done?*

Mimi still did not want to go to France, and Angèle was insisting she needed her. But Angèle was urging her with a cruelly divided mind. How could she face a difficult journey without the woman—nurse, confidante, and conscience—who in her childhood had been, next to her father, the most important person in her life? On the other hand how could she leave La Sorcellerie, for who knew how long, without leaving Mimi and Jean-Baptiste in charge—under the supervision, of course, of Nonc' Etienne?

When she confessed her dilemma to Philippe, his solution was swift and decisive. Without even looking up from the papers on his desk, he said, "Leave her. It will be necessary to engage a Parisian woman as soon as we arrive anyway. You will need someone knowledgeable in high fashion and protocol. They say the First Consul maintains what is essentially a court at the Tuileries."

"And what will I do for a maid on board ship?" Angèle demanded.

"Do without. I'll be with you."

"Can you dress my hair?" she scoffed.

"You can let it hang down, which I find most charming."

Secretly pleased, Angèle gave a delicate snort. "Will you think I am charming if I am suffering from mal de mer?"

Philippe looked up. "You will not, I hope, my love?"

"I *am* enceinte," she warned him.

He grimaced. "Take the girl. Minette."

"She is useless. Besides . . ." I do not really like her, Angèle thought, but did not say it.

"She can bring your food to the cabin, and clean you if you are ill. Mimi can train her to do your hair, can't she? She's old enough. When you hire a Parisian woman," he said carelessly, "the girl can help in the kitchen."

They boarded the schooner in December after tearful farewells with Nonc' Etienne and Tant' Astride, who still had not heard when Clothilde was returning and had tried without success to persuade Philippe to wait until spring. At least the season of hurricanes was over, those wicked storms that blew in from the gulf in the fall months. The winds now came from the north, bringing chill temperatures but less destruction.

Their ship was a three-masted schooner with a complex rigging of sails, and it had a look of swiftness and elegance about it. Nonc' Etienne and Tant' Astride and a few friends accompanied them to say their farewells on the levee, but Mimi had been forbidden to come. She was desolate about sending Minette in her place, and had to be reassured over and over again that Philippe and Angèle would protect her child from "those Yankee sailors." She was going to miss Mimi sorely.

Knowing from his previous experience in crossing the Atlantic Ocean how cramped the space would be, Philippe had had the forethought to engage adjoining cabins for their use. Minette, whose spirits swung amusingly between fourteen-year-old self-importance, feverish excitement, and simple terror of the ocean, would have a pallet in Angèle's cubicle.

The pilot came aboard, the mate shouted orders in his gruff Yankee tongue, and the sailors fell to unfurling sails and raising them aloft. The ship, its wooden joints creaking, moved out into the current. Gradually the waving friends they were leaving behind on the levee grew indistinguishable, and then the Place d'Armes and its surrounding square of buildings, and finally the town itself, grew more distant and were soon out of sight around the bend in the river. It would be hours before they emerged from the tortuous channel through the many-mouthed Mississippi into the Gulf of Mexico and returned the pilot to his boat. Angèle prepared a short note to send back to Nonc' Etienne with him, containing messages for Mimi and Jean-Baptiste, the last she would be able to send for some time.

The gulf was comparatively calm, and Angèle enjoyed the snap of the wind in the taut sails and the buoyancy of the swift, silent schooner skimming the blue water, so much bluer than she had imagined. She also enjoyed relief from the heat of the summer and the sickeningly sweet odor of fermenting cane. The sea breeze was fresh and cool, and it was exhilarating to walk the deck with Philippe in the morning before breakfast in the salon.

What enchanting adventures marriage to Philippe was bringing her! If she had not fallen in love, her life would have continued at La Sorcellerie in the pattern it had taken since her father's death, when she had assumed his responsibilities. She marveled now at how she had fought Philippe over this trip to France she was finding so pleasant. To live in a floating abode with one's beloved on turquoise and emerald seas frequently within sight of tropical islands—at one of which the schooner stopped to unload cargo and take on fresh fruit and produce—was like playing house; and to make love in a small bunk which rocked like a cradle with the rise and fall of the inconceivably vast waters beneath them, was a new experience.

It was after the first weeks, when the schooner emerged from the comparatively placid waters of the Caribbean Sea into the south Atlantic, that Angèle's ordeal began.

The weather turned gray and the waves rose threateningly, seeming at times to tower so high above the schooner that Angèle marveled that their vessel was not buried when they crested and toppled over. Instead the *Julia S.* rose with the next swell from the trough in which it lay, giving the boat a peculiar motion which combined a forward-and-back pitch with a dizzying roll from side to side. It was more than her stomach, already queasy in the mornings, could take, and she became violently ill.

She spent the rest of the voyage in her cabin in her bunk, refusing most of the food that Minette brought her from the galley, mostly tough fowl, salt beef, and biscuits. Philippe checked her condition each morning, sometimes accompanied by the captain, who assured them that she was suffering from nothing more than mal de mer and offered her a lemon from his private stock, replenished when they reached the islands off Portugal.

Angèle was scarcely aware of Philippe's visits, or of Minette, beyond accepting her inexperienced ministrations. Nothing existed except her misery and her will to survive and to keep the life within her safe.

When they finally reached the coast of France, Angèle was thin and weak, having been unable to keep any food down. The captain had planned to sail up the Loire River to Nantes, from which a good carriage road existed to Paris, but a strong rain-bearing wind carried them past the river mouth and he put in at Quiberon bay.

The wind continued in strength, preventing them from returning to the Loire, and Philippe, eager to get Angèle on solid ground, arranged for their trunks to be carried from Nantes to Paris when the vessel reached that port, and asked the captain to put them ashore.

"An excellent plan," said the captain, who wanted his passenger off the ship before she might die. "Madame will recover once she steps on solid earth."

Philippe agreed. Once she quit the ship, Angèle would no longer suffer from mal de mer. Alarmed by her pallor and lethargy, he had her carried ashore at Quiberon. The coastal inn to which they were taken was one used by the crews of the fishing boats that filled the small harbor; its public rooms were small and dark, with low ceilings blackened by the smoky hearth fire, and so redolent of sour wine and the stinking clothes of its fishermen patrons that Philippe put a handkerchief to his aristocratic nose.

That was why Angèle was surprised when one of the fishermen rose from his place by the hearth and accosted Philippe familiarly. He spoke in English, and Philippe replied impatiently in the same language. Angèle grasped without understanding them that Philippe was telling the man his wife was ill and he had no time for him. She was still feeling too weak and ill to question Philippe about the incident, and soon forgot it. He engaged a bedroom for Angèle and Minette and instructed the black girl to bar the door while he went to engage a carriage to take them immediately to Nantes.

"Mon dieu, I can't travel today, Philippe!" Angèle protested wanly from the bed.

His nostrils curled. "You can't remain overnight in such a place."

She had a curious impression that fear was mixed with his distaste. But even the rough character of the inn was preferable to traveling. "Philippe, I must. I can't take a coach today. It's too much!"

"Angèle, you would suffocate in this air that reeks of fish entrails! It's worse than your stinking cane."

She reacted immediately, her direct gaze suddenly blue flame. "That stinking cane paid for your stinking voyage, M'sieu le marquis!"

Blood stained his cheeks, already burned by wind and sun from pacing the deck of the *Julia S.* But Philippe said nothing, studying her. Already some color had returned to her face, brought on by her outrage.

"You can rest here while I hire a coach. Give her water, a little at a time," he instructed Minette, "and encourage her to take a little food, if you can."

"Oui, michie," the girl said, her great dark eyes eloquent with compassion and concern.

Those eloquent eyes stayed in Philippe's thoughts as he descended the narrow stair, and avoiding the common room, went to the kitchen to see for himself what kind of refreshment the innkeeper's wife could offer. He was thinking about the lively child whose impudence had amused him when he first saw her. He had suggested bringing her with them largely to avoid further arguments with Angèle, and she was now behaving with unexpected maturity.

106

Philippe was determined to leave this obscure port at once. Seeing the royalist Véry here, disguised as a common fisherman, was an indication something was afoot that Véry wanted to involve him in, something that could ruin his hopes.

The kitchen was cleaner than he had hoped to find it, and the fish soup the innkeeper's buxom wife had bubbling in a great blackened pot suspended over the hearthfire smelled delicious. He asked to sample it, and found it coarse but hearty fare, full of fish and seafood and the vegetables they had missed on the ocean voyage.

When he returned to the room, followed by a serving girl carrying a tray with two bowls of the bouillabaisse and a loaf of bread, Angèle turned her face to the wall. He put his hand on Minette's shoulder. "I don't know what we would have done without you, Minette."

Pleasure suffused her face, lighting it with a dazzling glow, and he saw, stunned, that she was also beginning to reveal the potential of an extraordinary mature beauty. He remembered that he had caught a hint of it once before—when she had entered Angèle's room the first time he had shared it, with a breakfast tray that almost hid her. He turned brusquely away, saying, "Take good care of your mistress. I'll get us out of here as quickly as I can." He tossed a coin on the serving girl's tray and went out of the room.

Left in surroundings such as she could not have imagined, alone with the one person who had always given her a feeling of uneasy dislike, Angèle stared from her dingy bed at a smoke-blackened ceiling and thought about her ordered daily routine at home. She wondered if Jules was exercising Joli, her spirited mare, and whether Jean-Baptiste had replanted the cane. She thought about Mimi, missing her quick sympathy. But most of all she wondered what Angèle Roget of La Sorcellerie was doing in this place.

"Do you know what has brought me to this, Minette?"

"Madame?" the girl asked anxiously.

"Love." Angèle laughed, making a wide gesture that took in the small blackened hearth, the fire Philippe had ordered built, the small deep-recessed window with its battered wooden shutters banging against the stone walls from the wind off the coast, the unclean bed on which she lay. "It was love brought me from La Sorcellerie to this."

Her red-rimmed eyes rested on the servant whose skin was nearly as fair as her own and whose eyes reminded her uncomfortably of Clothilde's. "And you with me, Papa's 'little kitten'."

After a startled moment Minette began to smile, and then giggle. Angèle laughed until the tears ran, then said, "Wash my face and hands, Minette, and serve me that soup. I must feed the child within me."

When Philippe returned after two hours, wet and fatigued but with a hired coach, he found Angèle much improved and declaring herself ready to leave the ill-smelling inn. They set out an hour later in a cold drizzle of rain, wearing almost all of the clothes they had with them in several layers. When Angèle saw the coach waiting in the inn courtyard, her steps faltered. It was a decrepit carriage pulled by horses that looked as if they might not make it to the next post. The driver placed heated bricks at their feet, and told Philippe in an accent Angèle could barely understand that they could reheat them when they changed horses en route to Nantes.

Philippe was not only wet and fatigued, but humiliated by his inability to find a decent equipage. He knew Angèle was appalled, and he acutely shared her distrust. The travelers sat on two seats covered with crimson satin worn thin by many bodies, and trimmed with tassels of silk yarn which were matted and sparse, Minette beside her mistress and Philippe facing them. Moisture dribbled on their heads and shoulders from tiny leaks in the carriage top, and the chill wind whistled in at the carriage door and windows.

All of this Angèle could have borne, but once they left the village, the road was so pitted with great mud-filled holes into which the wheels sank and bumped out, that they were all thrown around like rag dolls. Furious, Philippe leaned out into the rain and called up to the coachman, "Slow down, man, for the love of God! My wife is ill."

The ruffian shouted that if he did as the gentleman requested, a wheel could drop into a pocket and stay there and they would never reach Nantes.

"You insolent pup!" Philippe shouted back. "You'll be glad to reach Nantes in one piece, if you don't take care!"

"We'll none o'us reach Nantes if we loiter here, m'sieu," the coachman's warning came floating back over the wind. " 'Twas just here a diligence was set upon by bandits that live in this dark wood. Sixteen were robbed and half a dozen murdered."

"Ah, mon dieu!" Angèle cried, and Minette cowered in her corner with her large eyes growing bigger.

Philippe, glowering, held Angèle tightly in his arms to try to spare her the worst of the bouncing as they were carried at a full gallop through the wood. Nevertheless when dark fell and they pulled into the courtyard of a roadside inn some leagues from Nantes, she was bruised and in pain. It was still raining, and she was stiff with cold. The small inn was clean, and so comfortable after the miserable coach ride that it seemed a haven. But sometime in the night Angèle wakened and discovered she was bleeding.

Distraught, Philippe wakened the innkeeper and his wife, who told him the nearest doctor was in Nantes. But in spite of Philippe's gold, the innkeeper protested he couldn't send man nor beast through that storm before morning. Long before then, while the wind howled around the inn, whipping the trees along the road outside the courtyard until they almost bent double, Angèle and Philippe lost the heir they had been prepared to welcome with love and delight.

Madame Pitou, the innkeeper's wife, although not a midwife, was a compassionate woman experienced in matters pertaining to her sex. When she had made Angèle as comfortable as possible, she opened the bedroom door to Philippe and left them alone.

Philippe advanced to the bed with a haggard face. In a voice choked with grief, he said, "My son . . . my son . . ."

Angèle closed her eyes in exhaustion.

"We should have stayed in that sinkhole of a swamp—I should have listened to you." He knelt by the bed and laid his head on her breast. "Forgive me, my darling."

Without opening her eyes, Angèle said tonelessly, "I don't know if I can, Philippe."

Chapter 9

Paris, 1804.

*T*HE house on the rue de Nevers was narrow and high, as were its immediately adjoining neighbors. The garden at the rear of the house, enclosed by a high wall, was no larger than her camellia beds at La Sorcellerie. In this cold month of March it was brown and bare. A more pronounced contrast to the year-round sunny tangle of green and blossoming shrubs among the vine-wrapped trees at La Sorcellerie, bearded with moss and wearing garlands of mistletoe, could scarcely be imagined.

Awakening here in her bedroom two flights up, Philippe sleeping warmly beside her, Angèle did not hear the warbling of mocking birds and the soft whinnies from the stable where Jules was feeding the horses, but the incessant and monotonous twitter of sparrows signaling the approach of the hawkers from Les Halles or from boats tied up on the nearby Seine. Their musical calls, muffled by the morning mists that gathered along the river, grew steadily louder until they were below her windows: "Oy-y-ysters! . . . Fresh ma-a-ackerel! . . . Li-i-ive herring!"

Then, moments later, in a quick staccato bass: "Fresh-baked rolls! Baked apples! . . . Fresh-baked rolls!"

She lay with her eyes closed, listening for the soft pattering on the stairs as the servants ran down to intercept the strolling tradesmen and gossip with other servants while they made purchases of the food they would serve "m'sieu and madame."

Even the city odors were different, she thought, remembering how the wood smoke from the kitchen fires at La Sorcellerie blended with the musky aroma of rotting leaves from the swamp. Early morning in Paris smelled of fish, fresh-baked bread, and steaming biscuits of fresh horse dung.

On that March morning she heard a new voice, a baritone singing on the street below, "Portugal! Portugal!"

"What is he selling?" she asked Philippe, whose eyes were still closed. But she knew he was awake. She played with the soft black curls on his chest, twining them around a finger.

"Oranges," he murmured. "They are shipped from Portugal." He captured her hand and brought her fingers to his lips.

Then he threw back the covers and got out of bed, causing her to cry out at the draft of cold air to which he had exposed her. The house at number 10 rue de Nevers was always cold and dark, which continued to distress her. It was so different from the tropical warmth at nearly all seasons, she thought, and the shuttered light in all the airy rooms at La Sorcellerie.

Philippe laughed at her cry, but turned back to bend over her and tuck the covers tenderly around her shoulders, kissing her before he went through the connecting door to his own chamber, where his coffee and his valet awaited him. He would be out most of the day, Angèle knew, seeing the influential men who could help him win favor with Napoleon. Leaving her at home, she reminded herself, to twiddle her thumbs and worry about the new crop of cane ripening at La Sorcellerie in her absence.

Since her convalescence from the effects of that dreadful journey from the coast to Paris, they had not breakfasted together. They had come close again in a deep and tender passion, but although Angèle knew that Philippe grieved over the loss of the heir he had expected, she had not been able to share her complex sorrow with him. Neither of them had ever referred to the bitterness she'd revealed the night of her miscarriage.

Moments after Philippe left there was a light knock at her door. "Enter!" Angèle said.

Minette came in with coffee and rolls and silently put her tray down on a round, draped table beside the canopied bed. Angèle slid up against her pillows. "Good morning, Minette."

"It is not good, madame, but rainy and cold."

Mimi's daughter had grown taller in the months since they had sailed from New Orleans, and the little mounds of her breasts had grown as round as the Portugal oranges. But her eyes were no longer laughing and mischievous, and the beauty of her face was marred by a surly expression. As always, Angèle felt a disquieting unease in the girl's presence.

She knew it was not the Parisian winter alone that caused that look, although she knew Minette hated the cold as much as she did. The "little kitten" was not happy about being assigned to the kitchen down on the ground floor, where the burly chef Philippe had engaged—a Monsieur Breva, who had been out of work since his former employer was carried off in a tumbril—ruled like an autocrat.

In the street below, carriages were beginning to pass, their wheels and the shod hooves of the horses sliding off the wet cobbles and making a sound Angèle had learned was characteristic of wet weather in this place. She sighed. "I'm told spring comes to Paris most felicitously. Until then we must be patient."

Minette's sulky eyes met hers so directly that Angèle experienced a tiny shock as she realized just how unhappy Minette was. "You're getting good experience here, Minette," she said sternly. "When we return to La Sorcellerie, you will have skills in housekeeping that even your mother lacks."

For a brief second Minette's expressive eyes flashed, and Angèle's nerves tightened in anticipation of her protest. Then she lowered her sweeping lashes. "Oui, madame," she said with resignation.

Mademoiselle Heureux entered Angèle's chamber, frowning in disapproval as Minette left. Fortyish, with sharp features and gleaming black eyes, she was the "Parisian woman" Philippe had insisted Angèle engage to help her prepare for consular court society. She had been found for them by Madame de Rémusat, the wife of Philippe's kinsman, August de Rémusat, who was Napoleon's protocol officer. It was a sign of the changing times, Philippe said, that the First Consul had made an aristocrat responsible for maintaining the rituals of court etiquette, placing Madame de Rémusat in charge of the four ladies who attended Josephine, his wife.

Claire de Rémusat was also supervising Angèle's preparations for entering court society, but doing it through Mademoiselle Heureux, who had coiffed and dressed and attended to the wardrobe of a fashionable aristocrat who had lost her head during the revolution. Philippe had called on his kinsman immediately upon their arrival in Paris, but Angèle would meet the de Rémusats for the first time at a dinner party on the following Tuesday evening.

Mademoiselle Heureux went to the huge carved armoire and took out one of the new dresses Angèle had had made in Paris. "I suggest you wear this for your visit to your dressmaker this morning, madame." She planned to accompany Angèle to order a gown for the dinner with Philippe's formidable kinsman and his lady.

Angèle shook her head. "Something warmer."

"This, then, madame." The dress she held up was a deep rich burgundy trimmed in black braid, a most becoming color with Angèle's glossy dark hair. It had a graceful bodice, with sleeves that ballooned at the shoulders and a straight skirt that began just below her breasts, in the simple style affected since the revolution.

Angèle nodded. While she sipped her café au lait, Mademoiselle Heureux suggested, "Perhaps we should also discuss with your dressmaker a gown for your first appearance at court."

Angèle hesitated, not certain she would not be giving offense. "Madame de Rémusat may wish to attend me—"

"She is entirely too busy supervising Madame Bonaparte's wardrobe ladies," mademoiselle said firmly. "Besides, Madame de Rémusat trusts my taste implicitly." She lowered her voice. "The Bonapartes are commoners, you understand. Josephine de Beauharnais, whose first husband was also a general, likes the trappings of aristocratic life and the First Consul, who is very much in love, indulges her. They say that he himself is happiest living quite simply, like the soldier he is, but he does not deny madame a fine carriage and sumptuous gowns for the opera and the balls she enjoys giving."

When she saw she had Angèle's attention, mademoiselle's

eyes glistened. "Velvets and satins have lately become much in vogue. And jewels! Such a pleasure to see those drab clothes of the 'citoyennes' fall out of favor!" She finished, "Shall I ring for your bath, madame?"

At ten o'clock mademoiselle sent a servant to procure a carriage-for-hire and they set out.

Paris must be the largest and the most beautiful city in the world, Angèle admitted grudgingly as their carriage emerged from the narrow streets of the old quarter onto the quai opposite the old palace of the Louvre. Her first impressions had been formed while she was confined to her cold chamber on the second floor, listening to the rain and the chill winds whistling in the crevices between the houses. But March was ending, and April would bring its intimations of spring. Now that she was able to go out in the carriage, she was seeing a different Paris. With its handsome stone bridges across the Seine, its spacious squares and parks surrounded by imposing five-story buildings, and the brisk traffic on its newly paved boulevards giving it an air of prosperity, it was a city to make New Orleans look like a village. Angèle had her first glimmer of understanding of Philippe's obsession with their native land.

She had to admit, also, that the gaunt sophisticated dressmaker to whom Mademoiselle Heureux had taken her made an amateur of Madame Breaux with her needle. Angèle spent two hours amiably ordering gowns in which she could conquer this remarkable city.

It was when they returned to the house with a servant carrying the boxes of hats and gloves and other accessories for the ordered gowns, that Angèle found waiting for her the first letter to arrive from Bellemont. It was addressed in Nonc' Etienne's meticulous hand, and it contained a careful accounting of the business he had transacted for her and a draft on a New Orleans bank.

"You would not recognize Nouvelle Orléans," she read. "It is overrun with Yankees. They come to our balls and insist the musicians play a 'jig,' which is a ludicrously undignified dance. M. de Boré, who is now mayor, has had to order alternate French and American dances to prevent fisticuffs on the floor!"

Tant' Astride had added several pages in her round, childish writing. It was from them that Astride learned that Clothilde had been delivered of a beautiful little girl and was even now returning to Bellemont with her husband and child. Tant' Astride was ecstatic with joy.

Angèle felt a sharp pain in her midriff. Clothilde's safe delivery inevitably turned her thoughts to her own loss. She let the pages fall into her lap. Mademoiselle had finished opening the boxes and putting away the new bonnets.

"Please ring downstairs for coffee for me before you go," Angèle said. "Tell them to send Minette."

Mademoiselle made a moue of disapproval at the last request. "If madame will pardon me, she should not allow the kitchen girl above stairs. It would be more seemly if I brought—"

Angèle gave the woman a cold stare. "I do not need assistance in managing my household, mademoiselle."

Mademoiselle Heureux flushed and tilted her chin, but she murmured, "Forgive me, madame," and left the chamber.

A few minutes later Minette slipped in through the door with her tray, silently placed it on the table beside Angèle's chair, and turned to go.

"Stay, Minette," Angèle said. "I have a letter from Bellemont."

Minette halted and turned smoldering eyes toward her. But there was something in their dark depths that twisted Angèle's heart. She read aloud Nonc' Etienne's few sentences saying that La Sorcellerie was prospering under the guardianship of Jean-Baptiste in the fields and Mimi in the house, then read Tant' Astride's description of Clothilde's first child, who had been christened Melodie.

Minette listened, her hands clasped. "A name that sings," she said softly, her large eyes now luminous. And then, crossing her arms over her ripening breasts and rocking back and forth, she breathed, "Ah, madame, how I long for home!"

"I too," Angèle whispered, her own eyes glazed with tears.

When she left the master suite, Minette started up the stairs to her little room under the eaves. The tears that had lain frozen in her breast, piled up like the snow she had seen for the first time in this strange, overwhelming city, had been thawed by hearing news from La Sorcellerie. It was proof that her home still existed; that the other children still played in the haylofts in

115

the stables, from where they could hear the soft babble of African voices from the garden, where the women tended the vegetables; that when dark fell they still chased fireflies under the great oak trees, and later lay on their pallets and listened to the sad African songs their parents sang, sitting on their stoops in the warm nights. These past months she had sometimes wondered if she had dreamed the plantation and the wonderful freedom she had had there, or if it had ceased to exist once she was taken from it.

She had truly believed she would never see Mimi and Ouma and Jean-Baptiste again. The distance she had come to this place was too great. Knowing they were still in that familiar place that was no longer her home, made Minette feel both warm and weak. She needed to hide her head under the worn cover on her bed and let the tears flow until her heart ran dry.

But at that moment Madame Arquet, the housekeeper, left her comfortable room at the head of the stairs and began descending. "Where are you going, young lady? You should be in the kitchen, helping M'sieu Breva prepare the vegetables."

"Oui, Madame Arquet," Minette said obediently, keeping her eyes lowered to conceal their moisture. "I will be down immediately."

"See that you are," said the housekeeper.

When Minette entered the kitchen a few minutes later, M'sieu Breva scowled fiercely at her and twirled one end of his mustache in nervous vanity at the same time, making her want to giggle. But he was nothing to laugh about, that one. He frightened her with his shouted demands and curses. But she was even more frightened of his clumsy attempts to caress her whenever Madame Arquet's back was turned.

He growled now, "About time. Where've you been, Mademoiselle Lazy? Sleeping?"

"I took madame's coffee tray upstairs."

"Scullery maids don't carry trays," he snarled.

Jeanne, the maid, agreed spitefully. "That's my job, scullie."

"She asked for me," Minette protested, determined not to mention the letter that had arrived, with messages that completely dissolved her.

"Who says?" chef Breva roared. "You're as deceitful as you are pretty, aren't you?"

Hearing that, Jeanne flounced across the kitchen.

"Mademoiselle Heureux said madame wanted me to bring it."

"Is this true?" inquired Madame Arquet sternly.

"Oui," Jeanne admitted.

Madame Arquet's lips tightened. She knew that Mademoiselle Heureux knew better. "I will speak to madame," she informed them. "She is still uncertain of our French ways."

Minette was shattered by the possibility that these people could cut her off from her one link with home. "But I have always carried ma'am'selle's trays!"

"She is no longer 'ma'am'selle,'" Madame Arquet said firmly. "She is Madame la marquise de l'Eglise. You are now in *Paris!* You must get that through your shallow head."

Minette sat on her stool and bent over the vegetables the chef poured in her lap. She managed to control herself until he sent her outside with her peelings. After she had dumped them, she escaped blindly to a shadowed corner of the garden, where she let the long-stifled tears flow. She started as michie's familiar voice teased, "Is that the playful little kitten—*weeping?* What is it, Minettte?"

"They don't like me," she said in a choking voice. "They make fun of the way I talk, and they all hate me because madame asks me to carry her trays. Michie, will you tell them I have always carried her trays?"

Philippe had walked out into the garden to check on a rose bush Claire de Rémusat had sent from Josephine's conservatory, and had seen the huddled figure in the shapeless dark shift at the far end of the garden. He remembered that Angèle had complained about her father spoiling the little slave, and that Minette's mother, Mimi, was both a privileged house servant and one of those maternal women who seem to exude love from every pore. He reflected that it was probably the first time little Minette had experienced dislike.

Stooping before her, he said tenderly, "Don't you know why they are cruel to you, petite?"

She shook her head.

"It is because you are so beautiful. They know you are too beautiful to remain a scullery maid, and they are jealous."

She stared at him. "Do you think I am beautiful, michie?"

117

He made himself say evenly, "I know you are, Minette, and so do they. Very beautiful."

"Perhaps . . ." she said thoughtfully, her tears drying on her cheeks. She paused.

"What is it?"

"Perhaps that is why even though Michie Breva is always scolding me, he . . . touches me?"

Philippe stiffened. "Where does he touch you?"

"Here," she said simply, lifting a breast in one hand. The erect little nipple showed plainly through the thin stuff of her shift.

Philippe caught his breath. "We must do something about that." He started to put his hand over hers, then thought better of it. "Don't weep, Minette. I will speak to madame."

She lifted her gaze, her magnificent eyes drenched with adoration.

When Angèle descended the stairs to the salon where Philippe awaited her on the evening of his kinsman's dinner party, she knew she was beautiful. Her mirror had told her so even before she saw the light of passionate admiration leap to Philippe's eyes. But it was her excitement at the prospect of a social evening of the kind she had enjoyed in Louisiana, which had been so long denied her, that put the color in her cheeks and the sparkle in her eyes. Her satin gown of deep blue emphasized the creaminess of her skin, visible in the deep décolletage and a striking contrast with her dark hair, which mademoiselle had wound artfully with a string of pearls atop her head, accompanying the swift skill of her hands, as always, with imparting bits of her extensive knowledge of fashion.

"High coiffures, but no birdcages," she decreed. "Aristocracy may be back, but no one wants to return to the *ancien régime!* Madame Bonaparte sets the style, of course, and she has a taste for simple elegance." She followed Angèle downstairs, carrying her velvet wrap.

Philippe met them at the bottom, and raised Angèle's hand to his lips, murmuring, "Exquisite! Mademoiselle Heureux, my congratulations!"

As always Angèle responded to his approval like a flower to sunlight, but she felt a flicker of irritation because he was giving her Parisian femme all the credit for her glamorous appearance. But he looked wonderful, and as always, impeccably assured. Angèle's momentary displeasure evaporated under the light shining from his liquid gaze.

He accepted her cloak from mademoiselle and placed it around Angèle's shoulders with a loving tenderness that was almost a caress. The carriage was waiting when they emerged from the ground floor. It was a clear dry night, and the stars in the strip of sky above the narrow street shone with a cold brilliance. Breath from the patiently waiting horses misted in the chill air. Philippe helped Angèle into the coach, and the driver slapped the reins over the backs of his pair with a clucking sound that started them smartly trotting.

When they turned out of the narrow street into the broader quai, they joined considerable carriage traffic. It increased as they made their way toward the boulevard which carried them to the fashionable Place de Vosges. The Place was an attractive square park around which impressive residences had been built in pleasing architectural harmony, exquisitely revealed through the bare branches of the trees in the square.

The de Rémusats, who moved with other intimates of Napoleon and Josephine between the Tuileries and Josephine's Malmaison, were entertaining tonight in the home of their friends, Colonel and Madame Soutard. The carriage left them at the door of number 24, and soon Angèle was meeting the woman she had been hearing so much about from Mademoiselle Heureux.

Claire de Rémusat was a strikingly handsome woman with a high forehead, a long aristocratic nose, and beautiful gray-green eyes that sparkled with intelligence. There was approval in them as she swiftly appraised Angèle. "I have been looking forward to this moment."

"We both have," Monsieu de Rémusat added warmly.

"I am delighted to be here," Angèle said simply. "Philippe has spoken of you both with so much affection."

They were escorted into an inner salon furnished in the elegant Louis XV style, the pastel upholstery of the chairs and divans keyed to the soft colors of a magnificent Aubusson carpet. In corners of the room several large Chinese vases were set on the floor, holding arrangements of flowers five feet high—

gladioli, obviously out-of-season, in the soft colors of the carpet, spiced with huge white and gold chrysanthemums—but on the tables and consoles there was little bric-a-brac.

Philippe and Angèle were introduced to the other guests: pale young Viscomte Roulade; blond, sharp-eyed Mademoiselle Berthaud; smiling Madame Soutard and her very military husband; and Monsieur Fouché and Madame Diderot, who was one of Josephine's ladies-in-waiting. The conversation their arrival had interrupted continued after the introductions. August de Rémusat's guests had been discussing rumors circulating in the First Consul's court which, scarcely a decade after the revolution, was apparently awash with talk about France again becoming a monarchy.

"You have come home at an auspicious time," Monsieur de Rémusat told Philippe. "Many of our leaders believe that now that the revolution has accomplished its aims, only one strong man can bring back the order we need."

"Napoleon?" Angèle exclaimed, remembering Nonc' Etienne's assessment of the First Consul as "an ambitious man."

Madame de Rémusat looked doubtful. "A commoner on a throne?"

But her husband said, "Of course, Napoleon. Who else could accomplish what he has already done?"

"Exactly," said Colonel Soutard.

"It seems clear what Napoleon is thinking," Madame de Rémusat admitted. "After all, he has surrounded himself with émigré aristocrats. When I remarked on the sumptuousness of Josephine's last court ball, Napoleon explained, as if he were excusing it, that the French love monarchy in all its trappings."

Angèle risked an exchange of glances with Philippe, then complimented Madame Soutard by admiring the flowers, saying, "It's wonderful to see them in such a cold winter!"

Madame Soutard smiled and said, "They are from the conservatory, of course. I have Claire to thank for them."

"You are accustomed to a warmer climate, no?" Madame de Rémusat remarked. "Do you have flowers in winter?"

"But yes, madame! Just now, the azaleas and rhododendrons. Many flowering shrubs and trees." This led to a lively discussion of Louisiana and its differences from the south of France, which Angèle had not yet seen, while they sipped aperitifs. Meanwhile, Angèle noticed, Philippe and his cousin were carrying on a semi-private conversation.

After half an hour Madame de Rémusat led them into the dining room on Philippe's arm, her husband offering his to Angèle. The others followed, Colonel and Madame Soutard coming in last, having surrendered the duties of host and hostess to the de Rémusats.

The table was set with an elegance that could make one doubt there had ever been a revolution. Wine was poured into fragile crystal goblets, and candlelight from a crystal chandelier of great beauty sparkled on the array of china and silver. Angèle was seated at the right of her host, facing the young viscomte. The daunting Monsieur Fouché, who seemed to have something to do with the police, was to her right. Philippe was at the other end of the table, between their hostess and Madame Diderot, facing the lively Madame Soutard.

At the table the conversation returned to politics when Monsieur Fouché responded to a question from August de Rémusat.

"It is these worrisome assassination plots—we have uncovered several, you know—that have made us think a crown is necessary to keep Bonaparte safe," he explained to Philippe. "After all, an assassin thinks twice about attacking a royal ruler whose office is consecrated by God."

"And is he not making overtures to the Pope?" asked Madame Diderot.

"I find his pretensions quite entertaining," remarked the viscomte in a languid voice, "after the appalling crime he committed in executing a prince of the blood."

"That ill-timed unfortunate affair makes me wonder if he is as hospitable to returning émigrés as I was told," Philippe said ruefully.

"Le duc de l'Enghien was not executed by Bonaparte's direct order," Monsieur de Rémusat corrected them sharply. "On the contrary, the unfortunate duke faced a firing squad just two hours before Bonaparte's messenger arrived with orders for the general to spare the duke's life."

A liveried servant began serving them a buttery, garlicky appetizer of escargots.

"But didn't he give the commission he appointed to investigate the conspiracy authority to punish the would-be assassins?" The young viscomte's voice, Angèle thought, was salted with mischief.

Their host reacted angrily. "That was scarcely permission to execute a Bourbon! The general himself had qualms, and sent a note to Bonaparte asking for his permission, which Bonaparte refused."

"Which refusal Bonaparte delayed sending until it was too late," the viscomte pointed out.

"Napoleon was furious, let me tell you!" de Rémusat exclaimed. "He locked himself in his study and refused entrance to everyone, including Josephine. Believe me, he knows he needs the Bourbons to back up his authority."

"But he is not willing to let a Bourbon become the monarch he thinks France should have."

"Because he knows the citizens are not yet disposed to accept another Bourbon," Fouché insisted.

"It is done, gentlemen," Madame Rémusat reproved them gently, "and whether or not he planned to seize the government, no amount of talk will bring the unhappy duke back. Isn't it more profitable to discuss the future than the might-have-beens?" She signaled her servants to remove the plates to make way for the next course.

"How wise you are, madame." Angèle detected the faint mockery in the viscomte's tone. She had listened to the argument without full understanding, but with fascination. She decided she disliked the young viscomte, but when he turned his attention to her, asking her about "conditions in the late colonies," she answered his questions and before long found herself discoursing, over the excellent sole and braised partridge, on Nouvelle Orléans, the territory of Louisiana, and even of La Sorcellerie and her experiments with sugar cane. Meanwhile Philippe talked long and semi-privately with his kinsman's wife.

"And Bonaparte sold that promising colony!" the viscomte commented, and Angèle felt a rapport with him.

By the time dessert and a sweet wine had been served, the company was quite compatible.

Philippe was euphoric during their carriage ride home that evening. He was assured of de Rémusat's help in getting an interview with Bonaparte. "And who is in a better position than my cousin to arrange it!" he exulted.

His enthusiasm infected Angèle. "Or his wife!"

She liked Claire de Rémusat, impressed by her quick mind and the ease with which she spoke it. She had also enjoyed the lively and sometimes irreverent Madame Soutard. Several times she thought her stiffly military husband had secretly groaned at some of his wife's impulsive remarks. Angèle put what she had heard this evening together with Mademoiselle Heureux's gossip and decided that the women of Paris were extremely independent and assertive. These women of the revolution were more her kind than the submissive Creole ladies of Louisiana Territory who had thought her eccentric. Perhaps Philippe had been right in bringing her to Paris.

She added, "Madame de Rémusat is very close to Josephine, after all."

"As much as Napoleon dotes on his Creole wife, I doubt if he takes her advice in matters of state," Philippe said wryly.

Stung by his tone, she said, "Your inheritance is hardly a matter of state, is it?"

To her surprise Philippe responded to her thoughtless retort with rare sarcasm. "I'm quite aware that it is a small matter to you, my angel!"

Still edgy from the nervous strain of this first important step into Parisian society, sponsored by Philippe's kin, she over-reacted. "And I'm aware that you're obsessed by it just as your father was!"

"You call me obsessed, madame?" he said cuttingly. "You, who were willing to humiliate me publicly in order to keep me merely your guest at La Sorcellerie?"

She looked at him in astonishment. "You are still smarting over that?"

He had not mentioned the affair of the lampoons since their marriage. It devastated her when he called her *madame* in such an icy tone. It had happened on several occasions since her miscarriage, which seemed to have made her more sensitive to his moods. She thought of them as being joined by bell ropes—when Philippe pulled on his, hers rose, lifting her emotionally off her feet. Thus her response to his every emotion was direct and involuntary, as his seemed to be to her.

The carriage rocked through the lamplit streets, lively even at eleven o'clock at night, filled with passing coaches and pedestrians who were leaving restaurants and theaters. But Angèle was aware only of the tension tightening between her and the man beside her. Now and then Philippe's shadowed face and beautiful eyes were briefly illumined as they passed a lamppost, and she was torn between anger and her love for him.

When the carriage stopped before their door, Philippe jumped out as if he were going to stalk into the house, leaving her to the assistance of the coachman. But he had never been rude, and she felt ashamed of her thought when he turned and extended his hand. When they touched, a shiver passed through her. She raised stricken eyes to his face and saw his deep misery. Surprised and moved, she had made a heartbroken sound and his arms went around her, hard and forgiving.

"Philippe—"

"Don't talk," he warned against her hair. "Our nerves are strung too high tonight."

The coachman on his perch coughed. "M'sieu . . ."

Philippe found some coins to hand up to him. The driver touched his hat in a salute and drove off. Philippe got out his key, but before he could insert it, the door opened. In the dimlit foyer they saw Minette, standing back to let them enter.

"Are you still up, Minette?" Philippe asked in a tone of surprise.

She gazed at them, her great eyes going from Philippe to Angèle with a strange expression that both baffled and annoyed Angèle, even though it seemed to consist mostly of stunned admiration.

"I heard the carriage. . . ." she murmured in a vague voice.

Angèle realized the girl had never seen them dressed for an important evening, but her heightened emotions abruptly focused on Minette. "It was quite unnecessary for you to stay up," she said, her tone sharper than she had intended. "I suppose mademoiselle is in my chamber?"

"I can help madame—"

"No!" It had burst out of her, simply the way she felt, and it was too late to soften her refusal.

"Please do not waken any of the servants, Minette," Philippe cut in. "We will not need anyone tonight." His voice had a tone of repressed passion.

Minette looked from one to the other, her face going blank. She turned away to lock the front door, then followed them up the stairs, going on to her room on the third floor. Angèle forgot her immediately, her thoughts returning to Philippe and the frayed nerves that had almost resulted in a quarrel. She was aroused, and the tone of his voice just now had suggested he was too. She climbed the second flight with a fantasy of unbuttoning Philippe's shirt and sliding her hands around his bare waist while she leaned into the curve of his shoulder.

But hardly had Philippe closed Angèle's bedroom door behind them than he turned to her, his face so unexpectedly furious that she recoiled.

"What is it, Philippe?" she asked, her voice cool but her heart hammering like the hooves of a runaway horse. So it was anger he was trying to control, not his passion for her! She knew she had made a good impression on his kinspeople. What had she done to anger him so?

"I must ask Mademoiselle Heureux to teach you how to treat your servants," he said icily. "I should have thought you'd realize Minette is something more than a possession."

Angèle stared at him in astonished anger. "She is my slave! I am not a hard master."

"You treated your little riding mare at La Sorcellerie better!"

With quick, cold fury, Angèle retorted, "Jolie is the more valuable."

Her pulse pounded in the veins at her temples. He was interfering in her domain, and she fiercely resented his criticism. Today, of all days, she felt it was undeserved. Had she not shared her news of Mimi and Jean-Baptiste with Minette, shared her own homesickness for her beloved La Sorcellerie? But her pride and a certain guilt over her instinctive dislike of Minette had inspired her cynical response.

"You would do well to remember where you are. France no longer tolerates slavery."

When she saw contempt in Philippe's eyes, ordinarily so affectionate, she felt herself breaking up inside. With sublime irrelevance she cried, "I hate it here! Do you know what it is not to have my stables when I have been riding every morning of my life since our flight from Saint Domingue? Or to have nothing to do except wait for you to come home, when I have been responsible for sheltering and feeding fifty slaves, and managing the cultivation and marketing of the crops of hundreds of acres—"

"Covered mostly by cypress swamp."

That was partly true. "Oh!" she cried, in sheer rage. An appalling sob rose in her throat, and although she tried to suppress it, it escaped through her stiff, cold lips.

Philippe had never been able to remain unmoved while a woman cried. He pulled her into his arms in an embrace that was compounded of both anger and passion, barely resisting the urge to shake her. She suffered his embrace with her arms at her sides.

"I shouldn't have said what I did about Minette, but you might consider whether or not the girl is homesick."

"Of course she is! So am I!" Angèle cried.

He ignored that. "She is unhappy in the kitchen—"

"It was you who insisted I must have Mademoiselle Heureux!"

"I was right. You obviously did need her! But why throw Minette to the wolves? She is young, the servants are jealous, the chef is probably bent on her seduction—"

"That is something Madame Arquet should be able to handle. Philippe, I have managed *La Sorcellerie!* Do you think I can't manage a small household such as this?"

"Pardon, Angèle, but you're in a different world now."

She brought up her hands and pushed violently against his chest. "And I want to go home. . . ." she said, her voice breaking on a sob.

The sight of his proud wife in tears, begging to go home, twisted his heart and brought a wave of pitying love that instantly aroused him.

She was close enough so that she felt the movement against her thigh, and a weakening emotion flooded her.

He kissed her passionately. "Darling Angèle, your home is with me." Her lips were salty with tears, but she was still angry, as much at her own weakness, he knew, as at him. The knowledge moved him even more.

In moments they were caressing and tasting each other as if

they could never be satiated. He pushed the satin gown off her shoulders and gently bit the creamy flesh he exposed. The satin fell into a shimmering blue pool at her feet. He flung his elegant suit piece by piece at a chair.

They came together, naked, and she moaned her need. In her bed he took her in a fever of desire almost unbearably heightened by their quarrel.

Chapter 10

A few weeks later Philippe made a trip to his former estate, Sans Souci, leaving Angèle in Paris. "I have no idea what condition I will find at the château," he told her. "I prefer to make sure it is habitable—or not already inhabited!—before I take you to see it." He would be gone possibly for several weeks, depending on what he found there. Angèle reluctantly let herself be persuaded to remain in Paris, although she felt she would die of loneliness in this cold city without Philippe.

One afternoon shortly after he left she was informed that she had two gentlemen callers. Viscomte Roulade was at her door, accompanied by a friend. She instructed her servant to show them up to the salon on the first floor and to bring a tray with sherry and coffee when she rang.

When she entered the salon, both young men rose to their feet. The viscomte murmured, "Charming!" in bold admiration, and raised Angèle's extended hand to his lips. He introduced his friend, a Monsieur Delroix. Both men were younger than Philippe and somewhat shorter. The viscomte was slender with narrow shoulders, eyes she remembered as perpetually amused and somewhat malicious, and an air of frail health. His companion was more robust and youthfully attractive.

"I hope we are not intruding, Madame la marquise," Viscomte Roulade said. "We come as suppliants, not for ourselves but for a good friend."

"You intrigue me." It was significant, she thought, that he had used her title. With composure Angèle gestured for them to be seated and arranged her skirts about her on a chair facing them. "Who is this good friend?"

The viscomte stepped into the doorway and looked into the hall before he answered her. "You have no doubt heard of Madame de Stael?"

"No, m'sieu."

The two young men looked at each other, eyebrows slightly raised in amused disbelief.

"That will be distressing news to the lady," the viscomte said in his faintly mocking way. "Madame de Stael is the wife of the Swedish ambassador. Her father is a well-known French banker, highly respected because of the government's dependence on the large loans he is able to arrange."

Monsieur Delroix laughed.

"Her salon has attracted some of the most powerful men in Paris," the viscomte continued, "and formerly was noted far beyond the borders of France. Distinguished visitors frequently asked to meet her."

"And?" Angèle asked warily.

"She has expressed a desire to meet you."

"Why should this woman wish to meet an undistinguished visitor like myself?"

"Undistinguished, madame? I have to confess that I was impressed enough when we met at Madame de Rémusat's dinner to tell Madame de Stael about the beautiful American marquise. Madame has a great interest in America, which she hopes to visit one day, and she was interested to hear of a woman who managed her own plantation with slaves. She has sent Delroix and myself to bring her your promise to attend her tomorrow evening."

"It is very kind of Madame de Stael, but my husband is presently away at his country estate—"

"It is not M'sieu le marquis who interests madame," Delroix remarked with a disarming smile.

"On the other hand, you may be able to further his interests by going with us," said the viscomte. "Madame de Stael also has a great interest in Napoleon, and she was intrigued by your husband's kinship with de Rémusat."

"You believe that you know what my husband's 'interests' are?" Angèle asked, coolly masking her growing excitement. Perhaps she *could* help Philippe regain the estates that meant so much to him.

"I keep my ears open. M'sieu Talleyrand is a friend of Madame de Stael, and he could have a great deal to say about the return of your husband's title to his property."

Since Angèle was finding the life of an unknown colonial lady in Paris not only lonely with Philippe away, but quite boring, the invitation seemed heaven-sent.

"Please tell Madame de Stael I am honored."

Arrangements were made for both young men to escort her to the lady's salon on the following night, and the gentlemen took their leave, again with flattering compliments. Angèle mounted the stairs to her private sitting room with the purposeful walk that had been hers at La Sorcellerie. At last she had something constructive to do.

She dressed carefully for the evening in a gown with a deep décolleté and small puff sleeves. It was made of rich silk of a soft rose color, and had its own matching velvet cloak. With some trepidation she allowed the viscomte and Delroix to hand her into the coach they had engaged. To her surprise, the house of Madame de Stael, set back from the road in a long garden, was a considerable distance in the country.

The woman to whom Angèle was presented when they arrived at the house was large and formidable, astonishingly ugly except for her magnificent eyes, which were almost magnetic in their force. On this evening her other guests were all men, except for one young woman of striking beauty.

Angèle's heart skipped a beat when she was introduced to the renowned Talleyrand, but that gentleman said little, although his keen hooded eyes appraised her in unsettling detail. It was soon obvious that the chief entertainment of the evening was to be in far-ranging witty conversation, at which it was also obvious Madame de Stael excelled. The other female guest posed languidly, as though her purpose in being present was mostly as an ornament.

Monsieur Talleyrand discussed the pleasures of a good table with amusing gusto, but much of the talk concerned Napoleon's plans, and the politics of France and her European neighbors, making Angèle realize she was quite uninformed in such matters. But she also found an astonishing interest on the part of Madame de Stael's distinguished guests in what she could tell them about Louisiana and her cultivation of sugarcane there in competition with the West Indies product.

"I do not believe I would be considered an eccentric here," Angèle ventured. "It seems to me that Parisian women such as yourself wield great influence."

"Indeed," Talleyrand said. "When Bonaparte first came to Paris as a young officer a decade ago, he said that a woman, in order to know what is due her and what power she has, must live in Paris for six months."

"And this year," Madame de Stael said sardonically, "with his Code Napoleon, he has thrown us back into a patriarchal society!"

She was disappointed to learn that Angèle had no knowledge of New York State, saying she was probably going to lose money on investments she had made there.

At the end of the visit Angèle felt she had acquitted herself well and learned a great deal that might be of interest to Philippe.

"We must meet again, dear Angèle," Madame de Stael said with surprising affection when she took her leave.

"Monsieur Talleyrand seems to have a great fondness for her," Angèle remarked in the carriage as the viscomte and his friend took her home, and was chagrined when her remark provoked great amusement in her escorts.

"He's one of madame's former lovers," Delroix explained.

"*One* of them?" Angèle could not repress the exclamation, creating more merriment in her new friends.

"You reveal your provincialism, dear marquise. You are in Paris now."

"I wish I were not," she said, provoked by their laughter.

She had the satisfaction of observing that she'd shocked

them. There was no place on earth worth living but in Paris, they assured her. Admittedly, it was a sophisticated society. Had she not heard of Josephine Bonaparte's remark that the new moral codes were not intended for the upper classes?

They argued amiably and quite charmingly about that during the rest of the long ride back to Paris, and Angèle enjoyed their outrageous wit.

But the pleasures of the evening were wiped from Angèle's mind by finding the household at number 10 awake and in a turmoil when they left her at her door. She was met by her servants with the news that the scullery maid, Minette, had disappeared.

"What do you mean, 'disappeared'? Was she sent on an errand?"

"No, madame. No one saw her leave."

Holding up her silken skirts, Angèle climbed the narrow flight of stairs from her chamber on the second floor to inspect Minette's room in the servants' quarters. It was the first time she had seen this floor, and the dark low-ceilinged room touched some long-forgotten memory which she could not quite dredge up but which filled her with revulsion. The maid, Jeanne, checked Minette's few possessions and reported nothing missing.

Was Minette so unhappy that she would walk out in the simple shift she was wearing? Angèle wondered. "Has she left the house alone before?" she asked the servants.

"She sometimes walked in the garden in the evening."

A cold dread encircled Angèle's heart as she remembered how glibly she and Philippe had assured Mimi that they would keep her young daughter safe from harm. Had Minette left of her own choosing, or had she been carried off? "What has been done?" she demanded.

"Nothing, madame," the servants told her, "since we lacked orders. What do you wish done?"

She sent one of them out on the street to find a gendarme. He came, an unsmiling rosy-cheeked young officer who asked precise questions in a deferential but dogged manner.

"You say a servant is missing? Has anything been taken from the house?"

"No, m'sieu, nothing. She did not even take a change of clothing."

"What, then, is her crime?"

Angèle stared at him. "She is a runaway slave!"

His eyebrows rose. "Do you mean that she was indentured?"

"No, she is my African slave. I brought her with me from Louisiana."

The officer's face broke into what was almost a smile. "Ah, you are an American, then? I once had conversation with your so charming M'sieu Franklin, madame."

Angèle said blankly, "Who?"

"The old gentleman who always wore a fur cap and spectacles. He came as an agent of your government—now I have it, his name was Benjamin, as in the scriptures. You did not know him?"

"America is large," Angèle said dryly, "and I have been American only since your Napoleon sold us to the United States last year. I have always considered myself French, m'sieu."

"But French women do not have slaves."

"They did in Louisiana."

"Your pardon, madame, but slavery was abolished under the Directory in 'ninety-four, both in France and the colonies."

"While Louisiana was a Spanish territory. Please, officer, I am concerned for my slave's safety, that is all. She is young and attractive, and unused to a large city."

"Attractive? And she was a kitchen girl, you say? How would you describe her? Dark hair, dark eyes, dark skin—"

"No, her skin is quite fair."

"What language does she speak?"

"French, of course."

Again his eyebrows went up, his eyes bright with curiosity. "And you say she is attractive." He put away his notebook. "You will probably not see her again, madame."

Angèle's heart sank. "You will not look for her, then?"

"Oh, yes, we will ask questions, and we have informants. But there is little chance of finding such a young girl as you describe in this city," he said with a bluntness that was still oddly deferential.

The words stabbed her with guilt. Had Minette been so unhappy that she would prefer any kind of life to the life she was born into?

The officer bowed. "I regret, madame."

Angèle thanked him for coming, and had him shown out.

She waited anxiously for Philippe's return, fearing he would accuse her of having been cruel to Minette; dreading the letter she must write to Bellemont with the sad news for Mimi; and feeling crushed by guilt, because among her worries, she thought she detected a certain relief to be free of Minette at last. It was that knowledge that persuaded her to enlist the help of her new friends.

In spite of Mademoiselle Heureux's warning that no revolutionary Parisian would be eager to help someone find a runaway slave, and that certainly she should not approach the de Rémusats about such a matter, Angèle sent a note to Madame de Stael, begging that forceful woman to tell her what a veritable stranger in France could do in such a dilemma. Her note was returned with a message saying Madame de Stael could be reached at her father's castle near Geneva, where she was preparing for a trip to Italy.

Days passed and Angèle heard nothing more from the police. She put off the letter she must write to her uncle, both longing for and dreading Philippe's return from the country. At last he arrived, one afternoon, coming straight to her sitting room. She rose from her chair so precipitately that she dropped the needlework she had taken up out of utter boredom. Philippe took her in his arms, kissing her hungrily.

"Ah, Philippe, how I have missed you!" she said, when she could get her breath.

"Next time you will go with me," he promised her. He looked wonderful. The sun had laid a golden cast over his skin, and the smell of the country clung to his clothes.

"The château was not burned, fortunately. All its furnishings have been carried off, but I expected that. I wonder what I would find in the cottages of the tenants who persuaded me they would be happy to have me as seigneur in residence in the château?" he mused wryly. "I rode over all the land and am convinced that tenant life goes on much as it did before the revolution, except that half of my former tenants now own the lands they till."

"No!" Angèle exclaimed.

"But yes, my dear. Talleyrand and his men have allowed those tenants who were able to raise a small amount of money to purchase the land they work. I suspect de l'Eglise silver and paintings bought some farms. Half the land in France is now owned by peasants! All that is left to me is the château and its park and a small vineyard. And the château is at present uninhabitable."

"Oh, Philippe! I am so sorry!" She was afraid her expression was revealing the tiny hope that sprang to life. Now would Philippe be willing to return to La Sorcellerie with her?

He did not seem as unhappy as she would have expected at such news. He seemed more exhilarated, as though by a challenge. Cradling her in his embrace, teasing her with kisses, he asked, "What have you been doing to forget me?"

"How could I forget you when I was so lonely? But we did have an . . . occurrence." It was not quite the word she had meant to use—it minimized her anxiety about Minette—but her unease about how he would take the news had made her awkward. Drawing a deep breath, she said, "Minette has run away."

Philippe pushed her away and regarded her sharply. "What? Run away? When?"

She was relieved that he did not ask "Why?"

"It was one night a few days after you left. I was invited to meet Madame de Stael that evening, and when I came home, the servants were all upset because they had no one to wash the pots and pans. I sent for a gendarme—"

He interrupted her, frowning. "Madame de Stael! How do you know her?"

"Do you remember Viscomte Roulade, whom we met at your kinsman's? It was he who brought me her invitation. He and a friend escorted me," she added hastily as storm clouds further darkened Philippe's expression.

Philippe said furiously, "Do you imagine I am jealous of that whelp? Anyway, it's said he does not prefer women. But *Madame de Stael!* What was that woman doing in Paris?"

"Actually, she was not in Paris. We drove out in the country—"

He had released her from his embrace to pace her sitting

room. "For good reason! She has been exiled from Paris! Napoleon has forbidden her to come within forty leagues of Paris!" He looked at her accusingly, but she kept still, although she knew she had not traveled forty leagues from the city.

"If Bonaparte thinks we have a connection there, I am ruined. And he will learn you have seen her—he has spies everywhere!" He turned on her and demanded, "Is it this way you hope to make certain we do not remain in France?"

She had been so worried about his reaction to the news about Minette that she was momentarily disoriented by his attack. Anger came to her aid. "You are being hasty, Philippe. I was trying to help you. If you were not so afraid of my challenging your authority, you could see that. I met several gentlemen there who are ministers to Napoleon."

"Naturally. They want to know what mischief de Stael is planning for him."

"Monsieur Talleyrand was one!" she flung at him.

"Mon dieu!" Philippe sank down on a chair and put his head in his hands. "How many times have you called on this woman?"

"Once, but . . . I asked her help in finding Minette," she confessed. "I received a message saying she was in Geneva."

"Where she has been ordered to remain! Who knows you saw her?"

"Only the viscomte and Monsieur Delroix. And the gentlemen who were her guests. And another woman, a Madame Savarat."

He groaned.

She stood above him, her lower lip caught between her teeth, churning with anger mixed with the anxious fear that she had, indeed, made a dreadful blunder. Yet it gave her an involuntary pleasure to realize that Napoleon feared her new friend's influence.

"You called the gendarmes?" Philippe reminded her in a weary voice. "Of what did you accuse Minette?"

Her head snapped back. "Nothing!" she said, furious. She moved to the window and looked down on the cobbled street. A chimney sweep was passing by, followed by a grimy boy dragging a voluminous sack over one shoulder. "I asked the officer to find her," she said after a moment.

"What did he say?"

"That I should not expect to see her again," she admitted reluctantly.

Philippe was silent, and Angèle held her peace with difficulty. Finally he rose. "Do not mention Madame de Stael to anyone," he said in a cold voice. "Don't ever speak her name." He left her room.

Angèle remained at the window, chewing her lip to keep from bursting into tears. At last she sat at her desk to write the difficult letter to Bellemont asking her uncle to give Mimi and Jean-Baptiste the distressing news.

Philippe's disapproval had left her feeling bereft, but that night he sought her bed and she welcomed him with tears of joy.

In May Napoleon Bonaparte was proclaimed Emperor of the French Republic by the Senate and the Tribunate, a hereditary title, and two days later a plebiscite of the people gave him over three million votes. All Paris began preparing for his gala coronation, which was to take place in December.

Roses bloomed in the parks, and the trees that had worn a delicate green aura were now decked out in dense emerald. Angèle was presented to the new emperor and his beautiful extravagant wife, and invitations began arriving at the house in rue de Nevers. She found Napoleon extraordinarily handsome but rather daunting, although he was no taller than she. When she was introduced, he looked at her with keen eyes and spoke bluntly: "I'm told women find your husband irresistible. Why do you think that is so?"

"Because he listens to what a woman has to say," she replied.

The emperor's gaze dropped to her décolletage, which revealed the rising curve of her breasts. "It is not what a woman says that interests me, madame," he said significantly, but so impersonally that she was not certain whether she should feel insulted or complimented.

She thought the Empress Josephine charming.

The next months were too busy for Angèle to be homesick. There were new gowns to be ordered, since she and Philippe were invited everywhere, thanks to his relationship to the de Rémusats. But everyone in Napoleon's court was so involved in preparations for the coronation and the arrival of the Pope, who had agreed to consecrate the new emperor, that Philippe still had not been able to get a decision on the return of what was left of his estate. As for the title that had been his father's, he simply continued to use it, as he had since his father's death.

What Napoleon had observed was true. Philippe was enormously popular with the ladies, and Angèle knew exactly why. She had seen him bend the same attentive gaze on a pale and retiring young woman who was only too obviously aware of her plainness as he did on a great beauty, and then seem unaware of the chit's grateful adoration. Angèle tried to control her twinge of jealousy. It was because Philippe was caring and sympathetic and could uncannily sense a woman's secret fears and longings that she had been unable to resist falling in love with him.

She felt more secure when he was carried off as soon as they arrived at a ball, not by one woman but by three or four. She had her own group of admirers, including Viscomte Roulade and Monsieur Delroix, and gradually they made her aware that in Paris it was quite common for each partner in a marriage to have a lover, and that several men were offering themselves for her choice, just as women were parading their charms before Philippe.

Angèle had developed considerable skill in friendly flirtation during the years she had avoided marrying the New Orleans suitors who had besieged her and had enjoyed the game. But Paris games were more serious. It was a different world, as Philippe had told her—and yet she did not think the emperor would be any more willing to share Josephine than she was to share Philippe.

About Josephine, she was not sure. Greeting them at a ball at the Tuileries, the empress looked at Philippe—elegantly tall and slender in the soft blue coat and breeches and cream waistcoat that was both subdued enough to satisfy the revolutionists and rich enough for a reincarnated aristocrat—and murmured, "You will have all the ladies swooning tonight, M'sieu le marquis."

Philippe bowed and returned, "You, madame, have us all at your feet."

Josephine acknowledged the compliment with a gracious movement of her fan. "Here comes the first of your admirers, m'sieu." She nodded toward Madame Chouinard, the wife of a minor minister, who was moving determinedly toward them, and teased Angèle, "That one is very clever. You must keep an eye on her."

"You're not jealous of Madame Chouinard, surely?" Philippe asked Angèle with a smile of disbelief. "She is only an unhappy woman whose husband treats her abominably and who cries on my shoulder—"

"And would gladly let her head remain there!" Angèle could not keep a twinge of annoyance from her tone.

Philippe let his eyes rove over her in appreciation, and said fondly to the empress, "My wife is looking very lovely tonight, isn't she, madame?" His gaze moved from Angèle's lustrous dark hair, which Mademoiselle Heureux had piled high and bound with a ribbon over which a few soft curls fell, to her bodice—fitted closely in the current fashion, just under her breasts—and on down her elegant narrow skirt. It was a style perfectly suited to her tall, slender figure.

Josephine met Angèle's exasperated look with amusement.

Philippe sighed as Madame Chouinard moved on her course toward them. "There is so little love in the world, and so many women hungering for it."

"And you believe it is your destiny to satisfy their hunger?" Angèle challenged him dryly.

Philippe laughed aloud. "No, my darling, but I wish I were less aware of it." He kissed her hand, and before he turned to Madame Chouinard, murmured, "It is my destiny to love you." Angèle's heart leaped in pleasure.

Josephine had watched the little interchange with amused interest. "I see now why my ladies tell me your husband is irresistible. He is a man who truly likes women, and they sense it."

"He understands me better than I understand him," Angèle admitted. "Sometimes I wish he found me more of a mystery."

Josephine laughed. "Don't try to fight it," she advised before moving on to another of her guests. "He is charming, your husband."

Angèle moved toward Viscomte Roulade, who was approaching her, smiling.

Philippe watched her go, his own words echoing in his head

while he listened to what Madame Chouinard was pouring into his ear. He had spoken the truth when he said he wished he were less aware of the miserable situations in which so many women found themselves. He knew more now about Mademoiselle Chouinard's marriage than he cared to know. He knew that she was starved, not for physical love but for recognition, and sincerely wished it did not arouse his emotions to see a lovely woman so little appreciated.

Angèle thought of Philippe's remark often in the months ahead, as the city careened giddily toward the establishment of an empire and Napoleon dickered with the Pope, who at last agreed to come and give his blessing to Napoleon's coronation as emperor. Early in December Angèle stood with other ladies of the court in the congregation at the cathedral of Notre Dame, watching Napoleon being anointed by the Pope. He then crowned himself and stooped to place a circlet of diamonds on the beautiful head of his Josephine, kneeling before him.

"Like a chattel," Angèle murmured to Claire de Rémusat beside her. Like Madame de Stael, she was outraged by the new Code of Laws, which over the objections of some of Napoleon's advisers, destroyed most of the freedoms the revolution had given to women.

"Hush!" Claire warned.

The pageant before them would have done credit to the greatest and most powerful of monarchs; which the new emperor now was, Angèle reminded herself with resentment. The hero had assumed the powers of a despot. If it was not yet clear to the populace, no woman could fail to understand it. The new form of government made Philippe's title secure, but she wondered if he would ever regain his estate.

Much later, when her social life had quieted somewhat, she described everything that happened that day in December in a letter to Clothilde:

Philippe's cousins were involved in the careful planning of the coronation—they studied old court rituals, Claire told me. Even the procession from the Tuileries to the cathedral of Notre Dame was planned to the least detail, with Napoleon's generals in full dress in regal carriages, followed by marching army units in colorful uniforms.

The dressmakers and milliners of Paris have been working frantically for months to supply Josephine and her court ladies with new costumes. Josephine wore the crown jewelry and rode with Bonaparte in the coach marked with a royal *N* and drawn by *eight* horses. Napoleon wore *purple* velvet embroidered with gold and adorned with sparkling gems! I did not see all this pomp and show because we were already gathered in the cathedral, where we waited, shivering, for an hour.

Napoleon and Josephine both wore elaborately furred and decorated coronation robes. He came first before the Pope, who anointed and blessed them both. *Napoleon placed the crown on his own head!* Then, very tenderly, he placed a diadem on Josephine's hair as she knelt before him, making her his empress. Her long slender neck looked so vulnerable, one could not help thinking of the last poor queen. It was most affecting.

But that has not ended the round of parties and balls, because the Pope is finding Paris such a beautiful and pleasant city that he is staying on! It has been an exciting winter, and believe me, dear Clothilde, winters here need excitement to be endured. I am wearied and long for the lovely warm days at La Sorcellerie when I rode through my fields, and the peaceful nights listening to the singing from the slave quarters. And I long to see your Melodie, and your dear self; and Tant' Astride and Nonc' Etienne. And Mimi. How I miss you all!

Angèle laid down her pen and sprinkled sand over what she had written. Letters from Louisiana came very infrequently now that France was again at war—this time with nearly all of Europe, since most of the monarchs, fearful of Napoleon's ambitions, were allied with England. The last letter from Clothilde had been so full of little Melodie's charm and beauty and sweetness of character that Angèle had been much depressed after receiving it.

She had not told Clothilde that for months she had been disturbed by imagining she saw Minette when she went abroad.

Whenever she was driven through mean streets, she scrutinized the women they passed: a dark tangled head above a ragged shawl would hold her undivided attention until she could see the woman's face, too old and hardened to be Minette's. Or she would watch shudderingly a pretty painted wanton for minutes, until the carriage came close enough to show her the girl's nose was too broad or her lips too wide, or her neck too scrawny to be Minette.

Angèle picked up her pen again and wrote a postscript: "Minette was never found."

Chapter 11

*E*VEN if Philippe had been willing to return to Louisiana, it was not possible while Napoleon was confiscating every French vessel for his planned assault across the Channel. Just as Philippe had feared, Napoleon's truce with England had lasted only a little over a year. Once he had been recognized as emperor by all the governments of Europe except England, Sweden, and Russia, Napoleon offered to make peace with George III and was spurned. Angered, the new emperor devised a complex plan to lure the British fleet over to the West Indies, leaving England vulnerable to an invasion by his Grande Armée.

Nor was it advisable to take ship from a Spanish port, since British raiders were attacking the vessels of that French ally. Under the circumstances it was not strange that few letters with bank drafts made their way across the Atlantic from Nonc' Etienne. Fortunately, due to Philippe's close connections with the imperial court, his credit was almost inexhaustible.

While war raged, the matter of Philippe's estate was of no importance to anyone but him. Besides, not only was Napoleon away from Paris, but Claire and August de Rémusat were following him and his Grande Armée, with Josephine in their care. There was nothing to do but wait out the war.

Meanwhile, as Philippe pointed out to Angèle, war or no war, they could not sit at home twiddling their thumbs. They missed the de Rémusats, their pipeline to the Tuileries, and the absence of Josephine from the city dimmed the brilliance of the social scene. But Parisian life was still far from dull. Invitations poured in for the young marquis and marquise. The haute monde still took their entertainment at the opera, the Théâtre Française, or in the new restaurants of the Palais Royal, opened after the revolution by famous chefs to the aristocracy who lost their positions when their former employers lost their heads.

There was Véry's, one of the four finest restaurants in the city, and the most fashionable—everyone of any importance could be found there at one time or another. But there was also the popular Café des Mille Colonnes, with its sumptuous Salle de Trône, its green marble columns and bronze ornaments multiplied dizzyingly in glass panels, its revelry presided over by the stately blond wife of the café's owner. She was known as *"la belle reine limonadière"* because she sat on a genuine antique throne behind an array of goblets of silver and crystal, wearing a diadem of precious stones.

"Who would know France was at war?" Philippe asked, unabashedly enjoying the Salle's luxury.

"And stunningly successful at it!" Viscomte Roulade exclaimed.

In June Napoleon had brought several Italian states into his empire, alarming Austria so much that she joined the Third Coalition of allies against Napoleon. He promptly abandoned his plan to invade England, and leaving Admiral Villeneuve in charge of searching out and destroying the British fleet, marched his Grande Armée across France. He had taken Josephine with him to Strasbourg, where he left her in the care of the de Rémusats while he went to meet the Austrians.

"But why does he have to always be at war?" Angèle cried in exasperation. They had moved on with a small party of friends to dine at the Frères Provenceau, another popular restaurant famed for its *brandade de morue,* a delectable cod.

Viscomte Roulade, who had suggested the restaurant, was sitting at Angèle's left. He answered, in his sardonic way, "To

144

justify his title. It is not enough to be Emperor of France. He must be Emperor of Europe."

"My uncle characterized him as an ambitious man when he first came into prominence after the revolution," Angèle told him.

"Your uncle is an astute man to have perceived that at such a distance."

"Perhaps it is his distance from Bonaparte that allows him to be that astute," Madame Soutard suggested, smiling. "Our emperor has considerable personal charm."

Philippe shrugged. "Do you know that in England, where he is hated, he is called 'Boney'?"

"You were raised in England, no?" the viscomte said idly, but Angèle recognized the glint of mischief in his slitted eyes.

"And France. I was ten years old when my father and I fled to England."

"And what is your opinion of 'Boney'?"

"He is the man of the hour, the strong man France needs to restore order after a decade of terror and destruction. I have expressed myself on that score often enough."

"He is also the man who could restore your estates. But he has not done so, has he?"

Philippe's eyes gleamed with sudden anger. "Are you asking if I am an English sympathizer?"

The viscomte paled. "No, no, m'sieu, I meant no offense!" he cried comically. "If I have offended, beat me with a broom, but do not, I beg you, call me out! I have an unconquerable aversion to pistols!"

As Angèle was sure young Roulade intended, his little speech provoked laughter all around the table. After a tense moment Philippe laughed, too, but he growled, "Then you had better bind your tongue."

In the carriage on the way home, he said, "Do not accept any invitations which are likely to include the viscomte. I have had quite enough of that popinjay!"

In his irritation, he sounded so dictatorial that Angèle was provoked. "He amuses me."

"During my absences, no doubt."

"And why not? You go often to your Sans Souci, but you have yet to take me there."

"Because it is uninhabitable," he snapped. "But that is beside the point. I am telling you I do not wish to see Roulade again."

"And I am saying I will see whom I please!"

When Angèle shouted in a temper, she flung her arms about. Their incipient quarrel ended abruptly when she inadvertently touched Philippe's hand. She flinched, and a delicious heat flowed through her body, warming her skin and making the remnant of her perfume more volatile, so that it suddenly filled the small closed-in space of the coach.

Philippe had seen her start and felt an immediate response. Still angry, he pulled her into his arms for a long punishing kiss that soon turned into increasingly frantic caresses. So absorbed were they that the coachman had to cough several times before they realized the carriage had stopped before their door, and Angèle had to make hasty adjustments to her bodice.

But when they made love later in Angèle's bed, it was with as much anger as passion, and in spite of her physical satisfaction, Angèle was left with a hunger and a longing for the sweet, somnolent honeymoon days at La Sorcellerie. They had not shared a bed all night since their arrival in Paris, and it seemed to her a pity. But although she knew she had been contrary— she did not like young Roulade any better than Philippe did— she did not apologize.

One evening shortly after that, Angèle decided to wear the elegant sapphire-and-diamond necklace that had been Philippe's wedding gift, and found it missing from its satin case. In great agitation she called Philippe.

When he came into her bedroom, his eyes went immediately to the empty case in her hands, and his look told her that he already knew the necklace was missing. "You sold it!" she gasped, paling. "How dared you sell my necklace without even consulting me?"

"*Your* necklace, madame?" he said, in the icy tone that always hurt her.

She exclaimed, "Oh, I knew I was putting myself in this position when I married! But how do you think it makes me feel to know that you can sell my jewelry, even my clothes if you choose, and I have no recourse!" She went quickly to her jewel case and opened it.

His eyes sparked with anger. "Calm yourself, madame. Your

jewels are intact. As for the de l'Eglise necklace, you will wear it again. This is not the first time it has served to spare me embarrassment."

Her gaze flew up uncertainly. "You pawned it?"

"For the eleventh time, I think. I have lost count." He sighed. "It is mine during my lifetime, after which it goes to my heir."

The word, so long unspoken between them, stabbed her with pain. She looked down at the few garnets and diamonds and aquamarines winking in the candlelight on her dressing table, all that was left of the fortune that had enabled her father to build La Sorcellerie. Nothing was missing. Understanding came to her, and with it an acute embarrassment.

"I thought to gain us something at the gaming tables," he said dispiritedly, "but I was unlucky."

"Philippe, I . . . I'm sorry. If you had only told me—"

He took her in his arms and kissed her. "The money from the necklace will tide us over until your bank draft arrives, no?"

She hid her face against his shoulder to conceal her thoughts. Mingled with her deep regret for her outburst was her buried anger at the law that had impelled her as a young woman to swear never to marry, and when she did, to force Philippe to sign a humiliating document making him dependent on her. Was that not as bad as the woman's lot she had vowed to escape?

Philippe had not thought he'd be forced to live on her money after they reached France. He had expected to regain his rentals long before this. How humiliating it must be for him! she thought, promising herself never to doubt him again. She pressed herself more tightly against him. He groaned and began fumbling with her bodice.

"Pardon!" gasped Mademoiselle Heureux, who had appeared in the doorway from Angèle's dressing room with her wrap.

"Go down and hold the carriage for us, if you please," Philippe ordered curtly.

With two spots of scarlet in her cheeks, mademoiselle obeyed. He stopped Angèle's soft laugh with his mouth. In a few moments they had shed their fine clothes. Philippe threw back the coverlet on her bed.

Angèle lay looking up at the long, beautifully tapered body

he was lowering over her, quivering with her readiness to receive him, thoughts and memories whirling through her head. A woman in love needed no laws to bind her. Love itself, with its merciless desire, destroyed her freedom. Given the choice between love and freedom, what woman would not choose as she had? Was it not the same for a man—as long as he truly loved a woman? She drew a deep breath of satisfaction as she slid her hands down Philippe's body to his buttocks to pull him more strongly into her.

When they arrived very late at Madame Soutard's soirée that evening, all talk concerned the war. Word had been received that Napoleon had won a great victory over the Austrians at Ulm and had entered Vienna in triumph.

"He is sending twenty thousand prisoners back. The rest fled toward the Russian border."

"Where Czar Alexander has his legions marching to meet Napoleon," one of the younger men pointed out.

Angèle was standing with Madame Soutard just outside the group of men. Her husband, Colonel Soutard, was with Napoleon, and she was listening as closely as Angèle to the men's conversation.

"The news is not all good, gentlemen," a tall, stooped man stamped with the look of a bureaucrat said quietly. "It will soon be common news, so you may as well hear it from me. A dispatch came in from Spain just before I left the Tuileries. Our navy engaged Lord Nelson's fleet off Cape Trafalgar."

A circle of silence fell around them and expanded until everyone in the room stopped talking to listen.

"Napoleon is following the Austrians toward the advancing Russians. It was my sad duty to send dispatches after him advising him of Admiral Villeneuve's defeat. We have lost twenty ships."

There were groans, and cries of "Ah, non!"

"Lord Nelson is wounded, and Villeneuve has taken his own life."

This time there was a stunned silence.

"It is the end of the French fleet," the white-haired man said heavily at last. "We can no longer challenge England's supremacy of the seas."

The news put a pall on the conversation, and the evening

ended early. The next day the long-awaited letter with enclosed bank draft was delivered to the house on rue de Nevers, brought by a vessel that had slipped through the blockade. A few weeks later, toward the end of December, news of Napoleon's victory over the Russians and Austrians at Austerlitz overcame the dour mood in the city and put Parisians in a fever of celebration.

"Bonaparte is remaking the map of Europe," Philippe remarked bitterly to Angèle, "but England still controls our sea lanes."

Angèle had not thought of Minette in some time, but the girl came into her mind that winter in a most unexpected way. She had been driven to the Palais Royal one gray afternoon to meet Madame Soutard at the Café Lembler, an establishment famed for its excellent tea, coffee, and chocolate. Madame Soutard heard frequently from her husband, and since the de Rémusats had little time to write, she was Angèle and Philippe's prime source for news from the front.

She was widely acquainted in Paris and was also the source of much entertaining gossip. It was from her that Angèle learned more about her eccentric acquaintance, Madame de Stael. She was, Madame Soutard said, the author of several books. She had earned Napoleon's bitter enmity by her political activities and her criticism of his growing despotism. He had exiled her from Paris, forcing her to live on her late father's estate near Geneva, which he still regarded as a hotbed of political conspiracy against him.

"No wonder Philippe was appalled when I mentioned meeting her!"

"You actually met her?" Madame Soutard squeaked. "In *Paris*? When was that?"

Angèle was alerted by her friend's eagerness. "Perhaps I shouldn't tell you. She was not actually in Paris, but several leagues from the city, and she said that she came to conduct some business having to do with her investments in America. Please forget I mentioned it."

Madame Soutard studied her for a moment with narrowed eyes. "Very well. Do you see that woman with the very long eyelashes, she in the blue velvet bonnet?" she was pointing out a handsome woman, very well dressed, who was enjoying coffee with two gentlemen not far from where they sat. "She is a famous courtesan. The gentleman on her left is her current lover."

"They meet so openly?" Angèle exclaimed.

"Oh, she is received everywhere, even at court. She has an apartment in the Palais Royal."

"Here?" Angèle said, in some alarm.

Her friend laughed. "Didn't you know? Many prostitutes have rooms in the apartments above these cafés and restaurants."

"But isn't the Palais Royal the most fashionable quarter?"

Madame Soutard shrugged. "Where else would their trade be more profitable or better received?"

Angèle laughed with her friend, but there was a tiny pang in her heart, a small kernel of doubt that she realized had been there for some time and that she'd been ignoring.

Perhaps because Madame Soutard had turned her thoughts toward the subject, as Angèle was being driven home she thought about New Orleans's notorious octaroon balls—never mentioned in polite society—where it was said dusky mothers brought their beautiful daughters when they were old enough to form an "arrangement" with a wealthy Creole.

Or perhaps it was meeting the handsome chaise with a single passenger while Angèle was being driven back to the rue de Nevers that brought the subject of Minette to her mind. She had long ceased imagining she saw her runaway slave in women she glimpsed on the streets of Paris, and there was certainly no reason to be reminded of Minette by this proud young woman. But ordinarily so young a woman—she looked not more than sixteen or seventeen—especially one of such startling beauty, would not be out in her carriage unescorted. The thought immediately entered Angèle's head: *A courtesan?*

Immediately on the heels of that suspicion Angèle wondered, with the unease of guilt, what had happened to Minette, and recalled how she had once planned to talk to Nonc' Etienne about Minette because she had known the girl would not be happy as a house servant. She had even pictured Minette being taken to one of the infamous balls. Angèle shook her head as if to shake the troubling memories out of it. Where was Minette

150

now? she wondered. Could she be in one of those rooms above the fashionable cafés of the Palais Royal?

In December Napoleon and Josephine returnèd to Paris to triumphant celebrations of his victories. The de Rémusats returned, also, and Angèle and Philippe held a joyful reunion with them and spent a splendid evening hearing their stories of the emperor's campaigns.

"He is certainly the hero of the hour," Philippe observed wryly. "Paris seems to have lost its sophisticated heart to Napoleon."

"I wonder if it is possible for any human to avoid having his head turned by such excess praise?" Madame de Rémusat mused.

"He has enough worries to offset the public acclamations," her husband said soberly. "He received a friendly warning from his English enemy, William Pitt, that another assassination plot against him has been uncovered."

"Mon dieu!" Philippe exclaimed in a shaken voice.

"Yes," de Rémusat nodded. "A Christian act from an enemy, no? The would-be assassin has been arrested, but Pitt warned there may be other plots. It is the price a man like Bonaparte pays."

The talk turned to Napoleon's plan to have a triumphal column erected in the Place Vendôme, formerly noted as the location of the guillotine that took the lives of the unhappy king and queen and so many of their royalist supporters. It was to be coated, August de Rémusat said, with metal taken from captured enemy cannon.

Now that Napoleon was again in residence at the Tuileries, or as often in his office in Josephine's Malmaison, Philippe renewed his efforts to get a decision on the return of his land and château. But Angèle could see that he was becoming increasingly disenchanted with his chances at regaining his father's fortune.

Although France was still at war with England, the emperor remained in Paris, busying himself with matters of administration, with placing his brothers on various conquered thrones in the Italian peninsula, with planning France's first industrial exhibition—to open at the Louvre in the fall—with the new road across the Alps, with new canals and bridges, and with the building of the Arc de Triomphe de l'Etoile on the Champs-Élysées in Paris.

In August of that year France was enlarged by the voluntary separation from the Holy Roman Empire of a number of Teutonic states that formed the Confederation of the Rhine. They proposed coming under the protection of Napoleon, making his empire approximately the size of that established by Charles I, also called Charlemagne—Charles the Great—a thousand years before. Most important to Angèle, both the leaders of England and Russia had opened negotiations for peace.

It was in September, scarcely twenty days later, that Angèle's private world was turned into a nightmare. First came the letter from Louisiana which she opened joyfully, unprepared for the tragedy it revealed. It was written by Nonc' Etienne in the handwriting of a broken old man, telling simply of Clothilde's death from yellow fever and commending her soul to God. Tant' Astride was prostrated, too shocked even to add a line, and so was Hector, who had loved Clothilde devotedly.

"It is God's will," her uncle wrote, ending the heartbroken account, "and the necessity for caring for our granddaughter, Melodie, a child as pure and beautiful as her sweet mother, will help to assuage your aunt's grief."

Angèle added her own tear streaks to those already spotting the letter. She had wondered how she could bear seeing Clothilde's happiness in her child; and now that child was motherless, and she would never see dear Clothilde again.

Philippe came home very late that night. Ordinarily he would not have wakened her, but he came into her room, sensing that she was not asleep. When he heard the news, he sat on her bed and held her tenderly in his arms while she wept again, then undressed and got into her bed with her. They did not make love, but he held her close until she slept. It was not until the next morning when she opened her eyes to find him gone, that she recalled that he had said very little.

It was Mademoiselle Heureux who brought her coffee that morning. She set the tray down beside the bed, then pulled the draperies wide and said, "You have an early morning caller, madame. She is quite insistent."

They heard her on the stairs before Madame Soutard burst

into the room. Her eyes were wild, and she had not taken time to have her pale hair dressed, but had quite uncharacteristically covered it with a babushka-like scarf. "We must stop them, Angèle!" she cried. "One of them will be killed!"

"What are you saying? Who will be killed?" Angèle exclaimed, sitting up in her bed.

"They are dueling this morning. With pistols! Gustav left a note. He will kill Philippe! Or Philippe will kill him. Oh, come with me!" She turned to the stupefied Mademoiselle Heureux, who had not moved from the center of the room. "Mon dieu, mademoiselle, get a dress for your mistress! I have a coach waiting."

"Where are we going?" Angèle said through suddenly cold lips.

"To St.Cloud."

She was still numb with shock and fear when Mademoiselle Heureux put her cloak around her and Madame Soutard propelled her through the door, calling back to mademoiselle, "Bring her coffee."

Then she was climbing into the coach and Madame Soutard was getting in beside her, taking the cup from Mademoiselle Heureux and thrusting it into her hands, saying, "Drink this."

"I don't think I want to," Angèle said faintly. Philippe was going to be *killed?*

"To the dueling grounds at St.Cloud," Madame Soutard instructed the coachman, and breathed, "Pray to le bon dieu that we will be in time."

It was a dark gray morning. There was a light dusting of snow on the streets and a cold fog rising from the Seine. The street lamps, still lit, had halos of light mist around them. The coach rocked on its wheels as the coachman whipped his horses faster over the cobblestones, urged on by Madame. Angèle's hands were shaking so badly she spilled the coffee, spotting her dress.

All she could think about was Philippe's silence last night as he held her in his arms. She had thought he was grieving with her for poor Clothilde. But he had known then. He must have been thinking of his appointment with death, and he had said nothing. He had just held her. And left her without a word.

She said aloud, "I can't bear it."

"Pray we will be in time," Marie Louise said again.

But they were not in time. Their coachman was still galloping his horses toward the clump of woods when they heard the shots, two of them, the second too close behind the first to be an echo.

Chapter 12

AHEAD of them two carriages were pulled up on the verge. Their drivers, who had apparently been enjoying a smoke together, were staring in the direction from which the shots had sounded. As Madame Soutard's coachman slowed his horses, the two men looked at each other, then started into the wood.

Madame Soutard lowered her window. "Follow them!" she ordered their driver. He hesitated, and she raised her voice. "Drive into the clearing!"

When the coach bumped its way between the trees and into the meadow, they could see that Colonel Soutard was lying on the grass with Roularde and de Rémusat and a third man bending over him. Madame Soutard screamed and leaned out of the window to wrench the door open herself. She jumped to the ground, fell to her knees, picked herself up and ran toward her fallen husband.

Angèle looked at Philippe, standing alone ten paces away from the others, his pistol dangling from his hand, his face like parchment. Her relief was so strong she thought she would faint. But the look on his face was more than she could bear.

She slid down from the coach and stumbled across the uneven ground toward him.

He turned his head slowly, as a man in a trance, but when he saw her, he shouted, "What the devil are you doing here?"

Somewhere behind her, Madame Soutard was screaming, "He's killed him! He's killed my husband!" She could see that Philippe was trembling violently. Carefully she took the pistol from his limp hand and laid it on the ground. Then she put her arms around him and held his shaking body.

In a gesture that moved her immeasurably, he leaned toward her. Over his shoulder she saw the viscomte beckon the two drivers, saw them carefully lift Colonel Soutard and carry him toward the hired coach she had just left. A stranger carrying a black apothecary's bag followed them. August de Rémusat helped Madame Soutard into the coach to receive her wounded husband. The doctor sat beside her to assist, the viscomte climbed up beside the coachman, and they drove off without a backward glance.

Monsieur de Rémusat, left behind, went back to the trampled spot in the grass where the colonel had fallen, picked up the pistol he'd dropped, and put it in the empty pistol case. He spoke to the two drivers, who walked back through the trees to their carriages, then approached Angèle and Philippe.

Philippe lifted his head and asked, "Will he live, August?"

Before de Rémusat answered, he stooped to pick up the silver-plated dueling pistol Angèle had laid on the grass and put it in the case beside its mate.

"He will die before they reach Paris. You've killed him, Philippe."

"Why?" Angèle cried, having a vision of Marie Louise Soutard holding her dying husband in her arms as the coach rocked toward the hospital. *It could have been her holding Philippe!*

"He challenged me."

"Why, Philippe?" When he did not answer, she said, "I must know."

Philippe's voice was a tired monotone. "He accused me of making improper advances to his wife."

"It should not have come to this," his kinsman de Rémusat said angrily. "*Allons!* If your honesty at cards had been challenged—but a woman? Mon dieu, every man at court could find a similar cause for dueling! And a nick would have been sufficient to make your point."

"*Marie Louise?*" Angèle said in a stunned voice. "Did you? *Did* you, Philippe?"

"Angèle, your husband has just killed one of Napoleon's officers," de Rémusat said sharply. "This is men's business."

"The devil it is!" she shouted, startling them both. "Philippe, did you make 'improper advances' to my friend?"

Philippe was smiling slightly, as if she had amused him. "Her husband thought they were improper. She was so lonely," he said ruefully. "Why is it I can't resist trying to make an unhappy woman happier?"

"Oh, how I hate you!" she cried.

"You're an idiot, Philippe," his cousin said, exasperated. "You have made some dangerous enemies this day."

Angèle slipped her icy hands into the muff attached to the waistline of her winter dress. She was remembering how Philippe had said, "There is so little love—everyone is so hungry for love," and her heart was a bitter stone in her breast.

They walked together to the carriages waiting on the verge. Monsieur de Rémusat gave Colonel Soutard's driver a coin and instructed him to go home, where he was probably needed, then helped Angèle and Philippe into his own luxurious carriage and gave his coachman the address in rue de Nevers.

They said little on the ride back to Paris, but when he left them at their door, Philippe's cousin advised him to leave the city for a few weeks.

Inside the house, Philippe instructed Jeanne to send his valet to him, and Angèle ordered breakfast in her sitting room for both of them. She followed Philippe into his chamber. "Will you leave Paris, then?"

"You heard August. It seems it's advisable."

Her rage had subsided enough so that she already dreaded his leaving. "We could return to Louisiana," she suggested.

"And admit defeat? Never!"

"Where will you go?"

"I don't know."

Her anger rose again. "You're going to Sans Souci, aren't you?"

"No. I've told you before, it's bare as a stable."

"Then where?" she demanded.

He shrugged. There was a knock at his door, and his valet entered. "Pack my clothes," he instructed him.

"How long will m'sieu be away?"

"A month or longer. Pack everything you can get in two trunks."

Part of her frustration and bitterness was that she needed to talk with him, to discover if Colonel Soutard's suspicions had any truth in them, and if Philippe had really betrayed her, why?

She heard the rattle of dishes in her sitting room. "Will you take breakfast before you go?"

He followed her into the other room. He still looked strained, and she remembered how shaken he had been. She sat down at the table on which Jeanne had placed the tray, poured his coffee, then leaned forward as she offered his cup. "Philippe, take me with you," she begged.

"How can I when I don't even know where I will be?"

She knew he was lying. He must have some plan. "How can I send you money, then?"

"I'll send word where you can get a message to me. I have a little money, and I can always win enough at cards to eat and sleep."

His gaze shifted away from her. She felt the distance between them widening, and shivered with cold. Always before, even when he was angry with her, there had been a veil of love over his expression. Today the veil was rent and she saw deeply into him, and what she saw was a stranger.

"It is better if you stay here. You can tell me when August thinks this has been forgotten and I can return."

"Philippe, we have to talk. You simply cannot go off and leave me like this. I could never forgive that!"

His wry half smile came back, and its effect on her was bruising. "You are very good at that, Angèle. You've never forgiven me for the loss of our child, have you?"

Rejected, and goaded beyond bearing, she said, "No!"

"I thought not," he said.

Two hours later he left. He took what money was in the house, but would not let her send out to get more for him. They had not made love, but he clasped her tightly and kissed her good-bye. They clung to each other, both deeply affected.

"Never doubt that I have loved you, Angèle," he said, his voice husky with emotion. "Whatever happens, never doubt that."

"How can I help doubting?" she asked in a choked voice. "Oh, Philippe . . ." She could not begin to express the confusion of feelings warring within her.

He pressed her cheek against his heart and smoothed her hair with a caress. "It's all right, my angel. I know that you love me."

"You've always known—" Her voice choked down. Better than I know myself, she thought.

He kissed her again, quickly. And that was their good-bye.

She stood at her window on the first floor, watching as he emerged from the ground-floor entry and disappeared into the carriage. She stood there while the servants mounted his trunks on top of the vehicle, wondering when she would see him again. The carriage moved smartly down the street toward the river.

Feeling both angry and bereft, she stood looking after it, and her attention was caught by a second carriage starting up just down the street. It followed Philippe's to the intersection of the rue de Nevers with the quai. Just as it passed number 10, the man inside it looked up directly into her eyes, as if he knew who she was and had known she would be standing at the window. She had never seen him before, yet when the carriage turned into the quai in the same direction Philippe had taken, a dread premonition fell like a shadow over her spirits.

Surely it could only be a coincidence, she thought. Philippe's cousin had upset her with his gloomy talk.

The de Rémusats came to take her to the mass said for Colonel Soutard at the church of St. Sulpice. The crush of the colonel's friends was so great that she was spared a meeting with Marie Louise.

"It would not be advisable anyway," Claire de Rémusat told her. "She will be told you attended." She added, in a low voice, "She feels bitterly toward Philippe just now, which is understandable."

No more tête-à-têtes over chocolate with Marie Louise, who of course was in mourning. Angèle's note expressing her sympathy and regret was unanswered. Few invitations were arriving at the house in the rue de Nevers now. Nor did Viscomte de Roulade call. After all, he had acted as Soutard's second. Was he now a "dangerous enemy"?

There was no word from Philippe.

Napoleon had gone to Poland, where he prepared to meet the Russians. But this time Josephine had been left behind, and there were rumors at court, according to Claire de Rémusat, about a dalliance between Napoleon and his beautiful hostess, the Countess Waleski. Angèle wondered if Josephine were as lonely as she was, as torn as she was—caught in a vise between hating Philippe and longing for him.

One afternoon Mademoiselle Heureux came to her sitting room to tell her that the de Rémusats were below. This was so unusual—she had never met them without advance arrangements—that she started up from her chair. Philippe's kinsman should have been occupied with concerns of the court at this hour, and Claire was seldom free from her duties as mistress of Josephine's wardrobe. She had scarcely taken two steps toward the door when Claire and August entered her sitting room, and a look at their faces told her something dreadful had happened.

"Philippe?" she gasped, certainty gripping her.

Claire came in and put her arms around her. "You must be brave, dear."

Angèle felt as if her blood were draining out of her, leaving her light and dizzy and terribly cold. "What has happened?"

August came and stood beside his wife. "Did you know that Philippe was in touch with some of his royalist friends in England?"

Numbly she shook her head.

"Fouché's spies have discovered another assassination plot against the emperor, and several of the conspirators were arrested recently in Tours."

"*Philippe?* A conspirator?" Angèle's lips had gone so stiff she could scarcely form the syllables. It was incredible. "He's been . . . arrested?"

"He was among them. They were meeting in an upstairs room in an inn popular with royalist sympathizers. When the police came, Philippe tried to escape by jumping through a window."

160

"He was hurt? I must go to him!"

"He was shot by one of the police who had surrounded the building," his cousin said bleakly. "He was taken to prison with the others, where a doctor was called for him. But he did not survive."

Angèle had scarcely heard his last sentences. She sagged against Claire, and August caught her around the waist and helped her to her chaise longue. Claire called sharply for smelling salts, and Mademoiselle Heureux, who had been hovering near the door, brought it.

"You knew nothing about his plotting?" Monsieur de Rémusat asked her again.

Angèle shook her head. Her mind was denying over and over what he had said. Philippe could not be dead. In a furious physical denial that flushed her whole body, she recalled vividly his last embraces, could almost feel his strong bare arms, the touch of his slender fingers, the thrust of his body when he entered her.

"I can't believe it! No, it isn't possible."

When his cousin persisted in questioning her, she said, "No, no! He admired Napoleon so much—why would he plot against him? He wanted so badly to serve him and have his inheritance restored to him."

"I rather think you have the order reversed," his cousin said dryly. "Napoleon was shrewd enough to see that Philippe's desire to serve was not nearly so strong as his desire for his inheritance. He longed for the privileges it had assured his father before the revolution. But he became very depressed when his requests for an interview with the emperor were constantly deferred. I believe he became convinced Napoleon was toying with his hopes."

Angèle stiffened with offense. "You encouraged his hopes, m'sieu."

"I thought there was a chance he could recover his fortunes. But it is a different world since the revolution. I don't think Philippe ever realized how different."

A desolation so appalling it was like a dark blanket of fog descended over her. What kind of world was it going to be without Philippe? "Why?" she cried out. "Why did it happen? There must be more you can tell me!"

"Only that he was shot in the chest and never regained consciousness." He exchanged a look with his wife, and added, "He could even be innocent of conspiring with his friends, but left as he did when he realized he was in the wrong place at the wrong time. They were unable to question him." His eyes were compassionate. "I ordered him brought back here for burial."

"Philippe must be buried at Sans Souci!"

"I can arrange that."

"She is still numb with the shock of it," Claire said to her husband as she accompanied him to the door. "I am sure the empress will allow me to stay with her tonight."

"I will speak to her." He left to make the arrangements for Philippe's last rites, and Claire returned to Angèle's boudoir.

When she first saw the château where Philippe had been born and lived until his tenth year, Angèle felt a numbed surprise that he could have had such intense feelings for the turreted pile of nearly windowless gray stone set in its tangle of weedy gardens. It had a cold and forbidding look, quite suitable to the season and her desolate mood. She could not avoid comparing it with the warm invitation that emanated from the graceful galéries of La Sorcellerie.

How different were her and Philippe's backgrounds! Sans Souci—"without care"—must have looked more hospitable when his family had occupied it before the revolution. But its cold, forbidding appearance now in its forlorn gardens made Philippe's passion to regain it difficult for her to understand. She reflected on how little she still understood him. Such a marriage of opposites must have been doomed from the beginning.

But how they had loved each other! Knowing he would never return had not dulled her longing for him; she still had erotic dreams of his lovemaking, still hated him as fiercely for his infidelities, real or imaginary.

The mass for Philippe was said in the chapel of his château, miraculously untouched by the vandals who had stripped the mansion of its hangings and portraits and furnishings—which said something about their identity, she thought. And so she could not appreciate the feelings of the peasants who came from

162

the surrounding small farms, so neat and scrupulously cared for, to mourn him.

"They all knew and loved him as a lad. He was a charming boy," the graying priest told her, after the brief ceremony, when Philippe was placed in the mausoleum under the imposing statue of a knightly ancestor.

"But they took his land," she said bitterly. "He cared deeply for his land."

"Not as they cared for it, madame, with the toil of their hands."

The priest's words were offensive to Angèle. Was he saying that La Sorcellerie belonged to her slaves because they toiled on it? Nonsense!

As her shock lessened, an outraged sense of abandonment grew. It was a notion that was to stay with her through the terrible weeks that followed. She refused to face Philippe's death or her grief, as she had refused to face other things in life that she could not understand. Instead she nursed her fury against Bonaparte, who had refused to help him, against the peasants who had stolen his inheritance, against Fouché's police, who had killed him. She was filled with rage because Philippe had brought her to this alien place and then abandoned her.

Sometimes her mind, almost disordered by grief, spawned wild thoughts. First Clothilde, for whom she still grieved, and now Philippe. Were they together at last in paradise? Was this her punishment for taking Clothilde's love? She knew without any doubt that Clothilde had loved him, and she feared that her gentle cousin had deliberately cleared the way for Angèle by taking herself out of Philippe's life.

At other times she felt such a longing for Philippe that she had fits of wild weeping and her hatred burned for those who had destroyed him. Even while she maintained his innocence, she speculated about an informant. There had been one, she was sure, although Monsieur de Rémusat would not confirm her suspicion. She spent fruitless hours speculating on whether Marie Louise had known about his plotting. She suspected the viscomte, remembering remarks he had made about Philippe's "English friends." She knew instinctively that the informant, he or she, had been close to Colonel Soutard.

As soon as she could think clearly again, she began making plans to return to La Sorcellerie, and asked de Rémusat if he could help her get passage on a ship to Nouvelle Orléans.

He demurred. "It's risky to travel by sea as long as we are at war with England."

"What are risks to me now?" she asked him stonily, and he promised to do what he could.

He arranged passage for her, and her anguish was diverted by the necessity for getting ready for the voyage. Gradually her thoughts were turning away from Paris and her life with Philippe, to La Sorcellerie and her life as it had been before she met Philippe. Her recollections were triggered as she supervised the packing of what she would take home with her—new fabrics, pieces of furniture, and a magnificent pair of crystal chandeliers for La Sorcellerie—and planned the gifts she would take for Tant' Astride and Nonc' Etienne. How good it would be to lay her head on Mimi's shoulder and pour out her grief and angry hurt! She must buy something for Jean-Baptiste, too, she thought, and the other house servants. And Mimi's Ouma, who would be a young man now. How wonderful it was going to be to see them all again! How she had missed plantation life!

She had just picked up the sapphire-and-diamond necklace, redeemed from the pawnbroker, and was painfully remembering when Philippe had told her it would belong to his heir, when she was interrupted by Jeanne. "Visitors, madame," she said. "A young woman who refused to give her name, saying she wished to surprise you."

Angèle was puzzled. "She has not been here before?"

"No, madame, surely not, but she has a familiar look, and she has her child with her, so perhaps she is family? She is very grand, so I put her in the drawing room. I hope that was correct, madame."

It could not be a friend from Louisiana? In wartime? Yet a wild hope filled Angèle's breast. How she longed to see a familiar face!

She glanced at her coiffure in her mirror, pulled the lace at her breast into a more becoming fichu, and hurried down the stairs. When she opened the door of the drawing room, she stopped, stunned.

"You?" she whispered.

It was undoubtedly Minette, although Angèle could scarcely believe the evidence of her eyes. She reached behind her and firmly closed the door.

"Jeanne didn't recognize me, then. I thought not."

It was no wonder Jeanne had not recognized the girl she had called "scullie." Jeanne would never wear a dress as cleverly cut and as expensively trimmed as Minette's morning gown. Nor had she seen many children as beautifully dressed in a dove gray coat, with tiny brass buttons above miniature white breeches, as was the little boy who stood, not clutching Minette's skirt, but with a separate dignity Angèle found endearing.

Still very young, Minette had gained a delicious maturity of figure. Her skin was pale gold and her features had the classic beauty Angèle had seen a promise of in her childhood. She was sure now that she had seen Minette in a carriage on the quai one afternoon, then wondered why she had been reminded of her runaway slave. The resentment that had always been part of her response to Mimi's exquisite daughter was rising to the surface.

"I always knew you would be a beauty, Minette," she said. "I see you have made the most of what you have."

Minette said softly, "Thank you, dear sister."

Angèle stiffened. The blood was leaving her head, making her dizzy. "How dare you address me so fam—fam—" But she could not get the words out. She had been abruptly transported back to that low-ceilinged cabin when she had blundered in on Minette's birthing. Her head whirled and her eyes were blind to everything but the Gothic scene unfolding in her memory. For the first time since it happened, she saw clearly that bloody scene in the ill-lit slave cabin, so shocking to a totally unprepared eleven-year-old.

She saw the child she had been—the child whose mother lay dying—go flying down the dark dirt path in search of comfort in Mimi's arms. She heard again the wild screaming that propelled her into the low, mean room to see in the dim candlelight the grotesque way Mimi lay on her bed with her legs up, the two braced women holding her bent knees while she grabbed the bedstead and pushed, her screaming face shiny with sweat. Staring, the terrified child saw the head that popped out between Mimi's legs, saw one woman reaching to pull it farther out and hold it up by a pair of tiny legs, the pale bloody thing that was to become Minette.

Just then her father moved into the candlelight with a knife in his hand. Angèle fled, too shocked to make a sound. She had vomited when she reached her room that night so long ago, she remembered, and it was as if she had rid herself of the entire experience until this moment. A question flashed through her mind but was gone before she could examine it—it had to do with what influence that early shock had had on her youthful decision not to marry, and on her unforgiving reaction to the loss of Philippe's child. She felt queasy in her stomach now, and she swallowed bile.

"Yes," Minette said. She was reading Angèle's emotions in her stricken face, but could only guess at the reason for them. Her own face closed in defensive pride. "Yes," she repeated, "I am your father's other daughter, your half-sister. But you've always known, haven't you?"

Still in the spell of that nightmarish experience she had walled off from memory until this moment, Angèle could not speak. But of course she had known. It was a knowledge that had stolen gradually into her consciousness without her being aware of it. But it was something one did not think about, much less speak of. It meant that her father and Mimi . . . Had her dying mother known? she wondered. Had she been aware that her only child ran to Mimi with her hurts as to a loved step-mother?

She could not bear to think of her mother's pain; nor could she bear to ask herself whether Mimi loved them, both her and her father, or had given what they asked of her because she was a slave, a possession of her father's.

Like the other Creole women, Angèle had ignored the whispers about the quadroon balls in New Orleans, where the lovely brown girls were paraded before the young Creoles of breeding so that alliances could be made, alliances that sometimes lasted longer than the marriage vows they preceded, or sometimes betrayed. It was something Creole women preferred not to face.

"Philippe guessed," Minette said distinctly. "He pitied me at first. And then . . . he loved me." She looked down at the dark-haired boy beside her, and said, "This is his son, Jean-Philippe."

Angèle looked at the boy's face and whispered, "Mon dieu!" The pain in her breast was like a bleeding wound. She saw that he was the image of Philippe—and he was the child of that bastard whom her father had acknowledged not only by witnessing her birth, but by himself cutting her umbilical cord!

Minette was speaking, in her soft voice. "He is very much like Philippe, isn't he? . . . He is like you, too, Angèle. After all, he has both Roget and de l'Eglise blood in his veins." She said—cruelly, Angèle thought—"He could be your own son." But then she forced a laugh, and Angèle heard the desperate pain in it.

"You loved Philippe too," she said hopelessly.

"Yes."

"And Philippe loved you." Angèle sank into a chair, feeling weak. "My father loved you. It was he who named you 'kitten.' He played with you. . . . I was jealous. . . ."

"He loved us both," Minette said softly, sudden tears in her expressive eyes. "Just as Philippe loved us both. Philippe said once that we were his night and day."

Angèle was so torn between rage and a strange compassion for all of them: Minette and her beautiful little bastard, and herself—even for Philippe, wicked, loving, dead so tragically young—that she felt paralyzed. She was enraged that he had talked about her with Minette but had never spoken of Minette to her. He had made such a fool of her. "It was Philippe who took you away from here. He lied to me. All along he knew where you were."

"I was pregnant," Minette said simply.

And I had lost his heir. Rage and pain: Angèle did not know which was greater; they seemed irrevocably joined. She looked at Philippe's and Minette's child and pain twisted her insides. He must be two years old, a little more . . .

"He's kept you"—her eyes whipped up and down the fine gown Minette wore—"in fine style."

"He bought this gown with his winnings at the gaming tables. He took me with him when he gambled," Minette said in her soft voice. "He said I brought him luck."

The revelation slashed even more deeply through Angèle's pride. So Philippe's friends all knew that he kept a beautiful mistress—and probably envied him.

No. No one envied him now. Philippe was dead.

"What will you do now?" she asked, her voice harsh.

"Find another protector."

Minette's soft, hurt eyes blazed with a determination that Angèle recognized. *Ah, but she is a Roget, no?*

"What else can I do?"

"You will have no trouble finding another man. But I have not freed you. I could take you back to Louisiana with me," Angèle said cruelly.

Minette shook her head. "You won't, because I've brought you Jean-Philippe." She gave the boy a little nudge and he took a hesitant step toward Angèle, looking at her with Philippe's luminous dark eyes.

"He is Philippe's heir. Take him back to La Sorcellerie with you," Minette said.

Angèle caught her breath. Her eyes met Minette's in instant comprehension of what she was offering, and she was immediately tempted. Minette had known how she would be tempted. It would be so easy in Louisiana to pass this boy as her son— hers and Philippe's. She studied his pale features. He bore an uncanny resemblance to his father, especially around the eyes, but his determined chin was pure Roget.

Tant' Astride and Nonc' Etienne would be surprised. They would wonder why they had not heard about this son before. But her silence about him could be explained by the long English blockade of the continent. Many letters were lost through piracy. . . .

Angèle looked searchingly at Minette. "You're his mother. How can you let him go?"

Minette glanced at the boy, who was staring with fascination at an exquisite porcelain shepherdess with a wide hat, a beribboned shepherd's crook, and flounced pink skirts she held up with a tiny perfect hand.

"Do you have to ask?" she murmured. "What have I to give him except illegitimacy and a rearing he can never live down?" Her voice had a telltale catch in it.

No, Angèle thought, she needn't have asked. They both knew what *she* could do for Jean-Philippe. Angèle's emotions veered between an unexpected humility before Minette's capacity for unselfish love, and a greedy longing for this child of Philippe's own flesh.

Minette bent down and put her arms around the boy. "I've brought you to your maman, Jean-Philippe. I told you about your maman, remember?"

He nodded silently.

"You may hug her now."

Unsmiling, the boy stepped forward on sturdy legs and lifted his hands. Angèle hesitated only a moment. She stooped and her hungry arms went around Philippe's child, the child she had been denied. When she smelled his baby scent, she buried her face in his neck and inhaled deeply. He laughed the laugh of a baby being tickled, and she knew she could never give him up. Fate had taken Philippe from her and now offered something of his to console her in her loss.

She raised her eyes to Minette and saw in them the shininess of suppressed tears. For the first time she felt a kinship with this half-sister her father had given her. "I will give you your papers, Minette. You will be free."

Minette nodded. She stooped to Jean-Philippe. "You are very happy to find your maman, aren't you?"

He nodded gravely.

"I am happy for you, Jean-Philippe," Minette said. She paused. "You won't forget your Minette?"

He shook his head.

"And I will never forget you," she whispered against his soft hair. She stood up, her eyes going fiercely to Angèle. "Take good care of him."

"He is my son," Angèle said.

Minette turned abruptly and left the room.

Angèle sank into a chair, fighting tears. She also had an irrational impulse to laugh. What crazy tricks Fate played!

Jean-Philippe, still intrigued by the porcelain shepherdess on the low table beside her chair, seemed scarcely to notice Minette's departure.

"Minette was your nursemaid," Angèle told him.

He looked at her, still watching her, and put a tentative hand on the shepherdess.

"Do you like the pretty lady?"

He nodded.

She stretched her hand toward the soft black curls that covered his head, but stayed it before she could touch them. "She is yours."

His chubby hand tightened on the porcelain figure.

"Come here, Jean-Philippe."

He came obediently, still clutching the shepherdess, and stood before her.

"I am your maman."

"Oui." It was the first word he had spoken. When she heard his childish voice, she had to resist again the impulse to hug him.

"You will call me *Maman*."

"Oui."

"Say it now."

"Oui, Maman."

She put her hands on his shoulders and looked into his eyes. "And you will never lie to me," she said fiercely.

His eyes widened, but she could not read the expression in their opaque depths.

"Non, Maman," he said.

Part II

Chapter 13

La Sorcellerie. 1816.

*T*HE first time Angèle saw Charles Archer, he was astride a satiny bay trotting up her drive, sitting between a boy who was a slender replica of himself riding a small roan mare, and Nonc' Etienne on his new gray stallion.

"Bonjour, Angèle!" Nonc' Etienne called.

Angèle rose from her chair on the galérie—she had moved her work outside to keep Jean-Philippe and Melodie at their studies at a nearby table—and went to the railing. Her visitors reined their horses just below her.

"I've brought your new neighbor, M'sieu Archer," Etienne said jovially. "M'sieu, my niece, la marquise de l'Eglise."

"Welcome to La Sorcellerie, M'sieu Archer." Angèle smiled at them, thinking, Neighbor? Where? She knew all the adjoining plantation owners.

"Your servant, madame," Archer said in passable French. He doffed his hat, exposing sandy hair, and inclined his head toward the youth beside him. "This is my son Jeffery."

Melodie and Jean-Philippe looked at each other, then in a

173

rush left their table of books and came to lean over the rail beside Angèle.

"Bonjour, mes enfants," Etienne said. "Permit me to present madame's son, Jean-Philippe, and my granddaughter, Melodie Bellamy."

"Enfants!" Melodie muttered under her breath while she dipped a small curtsey. Twelve-year-old Jean-Philippe, who was a year younger than she and already tall and manly, grinned at her from under his bow.

M'sieu Archer's cool blue gaze appraised Angèle with a glint that made her reach one hand nervously toward her coiffure. The instinctive gesture surprised her, and she checked it. She had not really cared what a man thought of her appearance since Philippe's death.

He spoke French with a decided English accent; in fact he reminded Angèle of the enemy officers taken prisoner during the British invasion, some of whom had been entertained on nearby plantations during their house arrest. He was an example of the Americans who were flocking to New Orleans since the battle, far different from the flatboat rivermen from the frontier who had seemed so uncouth to the Creole residents but had won respect in the defense of the city.

Angèle smiled at his son. "You are welcome, Jeffery. It is good to see you, dear Nonc'. Will you and your guests join me for a cool drink?"

Melodie caught the blue gaze of the ruddy-haired boy on the roan as he inspected her with interest, and she stared back, her dark eyes sparkling and defiant.

Jules and one of the stable boys had come running around the house to take the horses. When the visitors dismounted and started up the steps, Angèle saw that the American was tall, well-formed, and carried himself with a confidence that seemed to her typical of his brash countrymen.

"Ah, there you are, Ti' Mouche," her uncle called to the footman approaching along the galérie. "Bring us the good brandy."

They settled themselves around a table, and Jeffery moved toward the two at the railing. Waiting beside Jean-Philippe, Melodie looked at Jeffery Archer's reddish-blond hair and into his deep blue eyes and instantly wanted to impress him. "Where do you live?" she demanded.

Jeffery thought that he had never seen dark hair that curled so softly against a skin that reminded him of the petal of a creamy rose, nor dark eyes that sparkled like winking stars and seemed to be laughing at him. *Melodie,* he thought. What a delightful name! Overcome with shyness, he looked away and spoke directly to Jean-Philippe, who, though obviously younger, was as tall as he was, with eyes as dark as the girl's. "In a hotel in New Orleans just now. But we're moving to Bellemont."

"Bellemont!" Melodie and Jean-Philippe both shrieked, startling him.

"That's my house!" Melodie exclaimed, and Jeffery looked at her with dazed eyes. He was going to live in this exotic creature's home!

They had startled Angèle too. "Are you taking in boarders, Nonc' Etienne?" she asked, only half joking.

Mr. Archer laughed, a deep sound of genuine amusement which obscurely pleased her.

Nonc' Etienne said, "I'm leasing the house to Mr. Archer, Angèle. I've taken a little house in the quartier."

"I see." Angèle tried to keep her voice neutral, because she did see. Nonc' was trying to put his griefs behind him, just as Melodie was. Hector Bellamy, Melodie's father, had fallen at Chalmette during the battle that decided the fate of New Orleans a year and a half ago. That had been a blow to Melodie, but it had been followed by another just as traumatic when her grandmother, Tant' Astride, who had raised her since she was two, succumbed to the yellow fever epidemic that followed the war.

Melodie was left alone with her grieving grandfather, and the responsibility for a young girl approaching womanhood terrified Nonc' Etienne. He had been grateful when Angèle had immediately invited Melodie to live at La Sorcellerie, which was already her second home. Angèle had a great affection for the girl, who reminded her so much of Clothilde. She had her mother's gentle charm and beauty, spiced with mischief. And a soupçon of my independence, Angèle thought fondly.

"We shall miss you, Melodie and Jean-Philippe and I," she told her uncle.

"It's been damn lonely over there with Astride and Melodie both gone," Nonc' Etienne said. "I'm putting the plantation in trust for Melodie, with you as trustee, Angèle. If you can run La Sorcellerie like your father did, I imagine I can trust you with Bellemont."

"Of course." She was aware of M'sieu Archer's shock, and it amused her. But there was a surprising understanding in his blue eyes too; he obviously realized that she had had no prior warning of her uncle's decision, and his perception made her return his look searchingly. The pulse at her throat seemed to beat a little faster than usual.

Jean-Philippe leaned over the galérie rail and called to the stable boy, who was leading Jeffery's roan away, to hold up while he admired the dainty but spirited animal. "I have a young mare too," he told Jeffery, and offered, "We could go riding sometime, if you like."

"Glad to," said Jeffery, with a pronounced English accent.

Melodie offered, "I have my own mount too."

Jeffery's ears got red, but he did not look at her. Nor did he pick up on her broad hint. Instead he began asking Jean-Philippe if he went to school, and seemed very interested in the fact that he was being tutored at home for the time being.

"I'm going to the convent school next year," Melodie announced.

They moved to the table, ignoring Melodie, and Jeffery began examining Jean-Philippe's schoolbooks.

Melodie heard her grandpére say, "It will be good for Jean-Philippe to have a friend so near," and she scowled. Didn't he know that she and Jean-Philippe did everything together?

When M'sieu Archer answered, "Jeffery has felt the need of a friend too," she began to feel as if she were suddenly invisible. She and Jean-Philippe had been inseparable, and now, voila! He was abandoning her for this new friend. She decided that she had never disliked anyone as much as Jeffery Archer.

"Would you like to see the horses?" Jean-Philippe asked him.

"Very much," Jeffery said politely.

"Come along to the stables, then." They asked Angèle to excuse them, went around the corner, and once out of sight, raced to the rear along the side galérie. Melodie did not wait for an invitation, but hurried after them.

Ti' Mouche returned with a tray holding a small pot of very strong coffee and Nonc' Etienne's brandy, and while they drank, Angèle learned that Charles Archer was a widower from Washington who had recently come to Nouvelle Orléans to open a wholesale business. He intended to buy and transship sugar as well as the furs, hides, and lumber floated down the Mississippi river on flatboats.

"I saw many opportunities in New Orleans," he told them. "It is already an important gateway to the frontier territories, and it will become more important as more settlers move west."

He had rented a warehouse near the levee and an office on Bourbon Street. His furniture was coming by sailing ship, accompanied by a few valued house servants.

"What about Tant' Astride's furniture?" Angèle asked. "Melodie will want that some day."

"But certainly," Nonc' Etienne said. "It is all in trust for her."

"Bellemont will easily accommodate it and what I am shipping too," M'sieu Archer said. His blue gaze met Angèle's with unabashed warmth. "Please come and get anything your cousin would like to remove before we take possession. I have not yet acquired a carriage and team, but—"

"*Alors,* you may want to look at my stables," Nonc' Etienne said. "I expect to be selling some horses."

"I'd be interested, m'sieu." It was agreed that he and Jeffery would return to Bellemont with Etienne.

Charles looked warmly at Angèle. "I shall be doing some minor redecorating," he said. "I would welcome your advice when it comes to selecting fabrics for recovering some of the furniture."

It was impossible not to return his smile.

"Good idea," Nonc' Etienne agreed. "Whatever Angèle approves, I'll approve."

While the two men talked horseflesh, Angèle studied Charles. He was apparently one of a growing number of prosperous Americans settling in the city. While Creole society was still exclusive, since the war with Britain it was much less prejudiced against the citizens of their new country.

Charles Archer's parents had probably exchanged British citizenship for American, Angèle speculated. He had a fair skin, which was marked by a few faint freckles, and his hair was the color of warm sand and looked very fine. And then there were his eyes, certain to attract attention in a land where blue eyes were the exception and brown eyes the norm.

She saw without embarrassment that he was aware of her scrutiny. "Do you ride, madame?"

"Every day."

"I too. Jeffery would not consider leaving his little roan mare, so we brought our mounts with us in pens we had built for them on deck. They can't get enough exercise!"

There was a tacit understanding between them, she realized with surprise and pleasure, that they would one day ride together.

Jeffery and Jean-Philippe, mounted on their mares, came trotting around the corner of the galérie and waved at them as they headed for the drive.

"We haven't time for a ride, Jeffery," Charles reminded his son.

"We'll stay on the drive, Papa," Jeffery called back. They broke into a gallop and went racing toward the bayou road at the end of the drive. Jeffery was properly dressed—overdressed for the weather—and wearing boots. Jean-Philippe had on his summer uniform, a loose-fitting shirt, and informal trousers with bare feet tucked into the stirrups of his light saddle.

As they raced, Melodie came around the house on her little black mare. Angèle felt a pang of sympathy for her. She had been Jean-Philippe's mentor and close friend from the time Angèle had brought Jean-Philippe from Paris when he was three and Melodie four, and since she had come to live at La Sorcellerie, they had been daily companions. Now she was being abandoned for his first real friend.

Excited by the presence of strange animals, her mare was restive. Melodie walked her over to the drive, holding her in as the boys thundered back in a close heat.

"Who won, Melodie?" Jean-Philippe shouted.

"Jeffery."

"Race you again, Jeffery!"

They were off, once more leaving Melodie out of it. She loosened her hold on the reins and allowed her mount to enter the drive to be ready for the next race, but when they came back and she again pronounced Jeffery the winner, he said, "We'd better walk the horses for a while."

In spite of his shyness, he was taking charge. She asked abruptly, "How old are you, Jeffery?"

He flushed bright red at being addressed directly. "Fourteen."

Two years older than Jean-Philippe! A year older than she.

"I'm as tall as you are," Jean-Philippe boasted. "Look! Look at me, Jeffery." He pulled out of the stirrups, doubled up his long legs, and leaned his weight on his pommel as he placed his bare feet on the back of his saddle. Slowly, slowly, while his tired mare circled the front lawn in a walk, he raised himself to a standing position.

Watching them from the galérie, Angèle thought, How like Jean-Philippe! Given to impulse and sudden change of mood, he was charming enough to get away with demanding attention. Once upright he rode easily, with superb balance and grace, enjoying the sensation he was creating.

When Melodie saw the look of awe and envy on Jeffery Archer's face, she took a deep breath, and uncurling her knee from the pommel and drawing her left foot out of its stirrup, kicked off her shoes. Under cover of her full skirt, she pulled up her knees, and with her hands on the pommel, hoisted herself up, feeling with her bare feet for a foothold back of the canticle. You can keep your balance in a pirogue, she reminded herself, and with her arms outstretched, she rose waveringly to an erect position.

Her startled mare was not winded, as Jean-Philippe's had been, and still excited by the races, she broke into a run.

"Melodie!" Jean-Philippe yelled. "Mon dieu, you'll kill yourself!"

The adults on the galérie rose from their seats. Angèle gasped.

Melodie leaned slightly forward, anticipating the rise and fall of Nola's gallop, wavering as her balance shifted slightly from one leg to the other. Exhilarated, she realized she was not going to fall, and a beautiful smile spread across her face.

"Mon dieu!" Nonc' Etienne exclaimed.

Angèle moved to the rail, her heart in her throat.

"Don't shout at her," Charles Archer advised in a quiet voice behind her. "You'll only frighten the animal more."

Melodie stood with her legs apart, her head thrown back like the figurehead on a bowsprit, her black hair tossing and her white skirts flying backward, outlining her slender body. But in spite of all she could do, her feet were slipping sidewise down the mare's flanks. She curled her toes, trying to grip with them, but there was nothing to grip, nothing to stop their slide. She held the reins taut, gradually pulling them in until Nola slowed to a bouncing trot. It was impossible to stand then, and Melodie let her legs slide down into a straddle. But she was behind the saddle, hanging on for dear life to keep from sliding ignominiously off Nola's rump.

"Bravo!" cried the adults from the galérie.

Jean-Philippe and Jeffery trotted forward until they were riding one on each side of her. Jeffery's face was transfixed with an incredulous adoration, and Melodie drank it in thirstily. Jean-Philippe's expression had changed from one of anxiety to pride. "That's my little cousin!" he bragged.

On the galérie Angèle sagged with relief, but she was smiling. She did not think Melodie would be left out of their games again.

A little later the three visitors called for their horses. Riding back to Bellemont, Charles Archer began teasing his son, saying, "What did you think of Madame la marquise's young equestrienne, Jeffery? Have you ever known a girl like her?"

"No, Papa," he said, his fair skin flushing. "She was . . ." He searched for a French word. "Formidable! It was quite frightening, wasn't it? I thought she would be thrown."

"She is my daughter's child," Etienne said, "but today she reminded me of my niece. Madame used to drive her own little one-horse chaise like the devil was after her, straight at my closed gates, expecting them to be opened for her."

Intrigued and amused, Charles asked, "And were they?"

"Always. The black children knew the gait of her horse. Every time they heard her coming, they raced her to have the wrought-iron bars open before she reached them, and every time they won. It was a game we all enjoyed."

"Madame is a remarkable woman," Archer said in a musing

voice, and Etienne Roget gave him a shrewd glance. The marquis had said much the same thing the day he met Angèle, he remembered. Well, he thought, philosophically, his niece had been too long without a man.

It was ten days later when the note arrived from Charles, inviting Angèle for coffee. "Jeffery requests the pleasure of M'selle Melodie and M'sieu Jean-Philippe's company while I seek your advice on the selection of certain fabrics," the note finished. It was signed, "Yours, Charles Archer."

Melodie and Jean-Philippe were delighted.

Angèle ordered her carriage after her morning inspection of her fields, changing from her riding skirt and blouse into a cool muslin dress sprinkled with small rose flowers that had an engagingly low décolletage. There was a certain pleasure in dressing to please a man again after so long a time.

If the youngsters had not been so excited themselves, they might have noticed the nervous excitement causing her heart to flutter now and then, in a way she had not experienced since she was widowed.

At Bellemont Charles and Jeffery stood side by side on the galérie to greet them, both formally dressed in white breeches and dark blue coats. Bellemont was just the same as it had always been on the exterior, but once inside, the evidence of Nonc' Etienne's removal was immediately apparent. The large painting of Clothilde that had hung over the mantel was gone.

Angèle remembered when it had been commissioned. Nonc' had wanted her aunt to sit, also, for her portrait had been left behind when they fled France, but Tant' Astride had refused, claiming she had long since lost her beauty.

Charles complimented Melodie on her resemblance to her mother and said he regretted losing the pleasure of the portrait. Jeffery blushed.

"Jeffery, kindly take m'selle and her cousin through the rooms so she can select any furniture she wishes to have removed to La Sorcellerie, while madame and I discuss the samples."

"Yes, Papa."

When the three young people had left, Charles turned to Angèle, smiling. "You are very lovely in that gown, madame."

"You are very kind, m'sieu," Angèle returned. She looked around the room at the marble-topped carved tables and chests that had been added.

"Well, what do you think? I'm afraid my pieces are all English or English-inspired. Do they look out of place?"

"Those small tables blend rather well, but some pieces are too heavy. That credenza!" she exclaimed. "I would banish it to the attic immediately!"

He laughed. "I knew you would speak your mind."

"Isn't that what you wanted? Of course, you could have a French room and an English room and segregate the furniture."

"No," he said promptly. "I prefer to blend French with English."

Their eyes met and she read his bold meaning. Her heart gave a surprisingly loud thump. Then she said, "I think that would be my choice also."

The light in his blue eyes surrounded her with magic, transporting her into a new world. "Please sit here." He indicated a small sofa, and when she was seated, handed her some squares of damask and satin in various colors. "I have hired some painters who will come out from the city in the next few days. I will ask them to try to match the color of these walls exactly. I wish your advice on which of these fabrics to use in reupholstering the sofa you are sitting on, and a pair of chairs, all quite worn."

"I am more skilled in knowing when the cane is ripe to cut," she protested, but she took the silky squares in her hands, pairing them, discarding some and holding others up at arm's length to see them against the background of the painted wall.

He watched her closely, smiling to himself as she examined the swatches with narrowed eyes. Finally she stood up and walked to the mantel. She held two squares of fabric up against the painted wood. "It is between these two, m'sieu," she said finally. "Which of the two should be your decision."

"I'll make it with more confidence now. How could I go wrong when I have the guidance of the woman responsible for La Sorcellerie's reputed elegance?"

" 'Reputed'? You shall judge for yourself, I promise. Is there an Irishman, by chance, in your ancestry? If not, I'll swear you are French after all!" She was still examining the fabric she held to the wall. When she turned to him, smiling, he was standing very close to her. The seconds stretched into a moment while they looked into each other's eyes, and Angèle imagined she could hear his heartbeat as well as her own. Her gaze dropped to his lips, firm and shapely, and hers parted as she wondered how they would feel against her own.

Seconds later she was wondering if he had read her thought; his lips were on her own with surprisingly sweet pressure. She closed her eyes and put her arms around his neck, giving herself up to a pleasure she had known for some time only in her dreams.

His long slender hands encircled her neck and his thumbs softly rubbed her ears as his mouth drew sweetness from hers. He bent his head to kiss her throat, and she stroked the fine straight hair on his nape. It was remarkable how comfortable she felt with him; it was as if she had always known him. His hands were at her bodice, and she was only slightly surprised when he opened it, released a firm breast, and bent his lips to suck at it while waves of pleasure undulated down her body.

From somewhere in the house she heard Melodie's voice greeting one of her grandfather's old servants, and she murmured, "Charles, the children!"

"Yes," he said reluctantly, and raised his head.

Quickly she fastened her bodice and smoothed her hair.

"When can I see you again?" he asked urgently.

"I ride to my cane fields every morning at dawn," she said, a laughing challenge in her eyes. "If you are early enough you may ride with me."

The children came into the room, followed closely by one of Nonc' Etienne's servants rolling a cart which carried an English tea service and a plate of small cakes.

Angèle's eyebrows lifted. "Tea?"

"Coffee. Your uncle's servants corrected me."

She laughed and poured, adding hot milk generously to the children's cups. They listened to the chatter of Melodie and the two boys and talked with their eyes as they drank the dark rich beverage.

The next morning Charles was waiting on his big bay at her stables when she came out of the house.

Angèle greeted him briskly, mounted her mare, and led the

way down the path between the two rows of brick cabins she proudly pointed out as the new quarters for her slaves.

"My father planned them before he died. They are built with bricks made from clay we found on the plantation."

From the shadowy interiors behind the open doors, and from the kitchen garden where they worked, dark women watched them pass and speculated about the man. Already they knew he was the new master at Bellemont. Every article of his clothing, from the slant of his hat to the shine of his boots, was carefully noted.

Beyond the slave quarters Angèle pointed her whip at the primitive sugarhouse: a shelter housing the millstone, the great iron pots in which the juice was boiled adjacent to it. "That's where we crush in cutting season."

"And when is that?"

"Usually from September into December."

"And you crystallize it here on the plantation?"

"Some of it. Most of it is still shipped to Europe for refining."

"Perhaps we can do business," he suggested.

"Perhaps," she said with a smile.

As they walked their horses, she talked about her cane. "The first field you will see is ratoon cane; that is, we have allowed the shoots to come up naturally after last year's cutting."

They rode on. The climbing sun sent a pure slanting light through the young stalks of pale green. "This field was planted with shoots," Angèle told him. "A slow, laborious method, but the one most often used. It would be impossible without abundant labor."

She pointed her whip toward a sparse growth of cane in a fenced field. "Occasionally cane produces seeds. When it does, we gather them and use them for our cross-fertilization experiments." She pulled her mount—a pretty, tawny mare with a white star on her forehead—up beside the fence. All around them, surrounding them, was a sea of green cane growing tall and slender, subtly changing color as it stirred and swayed in the gulf breezes.

"Sweet grass, we call it." She pointed her riding crop. "That dark line of trees marks the swamp."

"If your design was to impress me, you have succeeded."

"That was my intention," she confessed.

He laughed. "I brought a bottle of wine and some bread and cheese. Where can we share it?"

"Follow me."

She headed toward the swamp. The house was far behind them now, hidden by the towering oaks and magnolias that surrounded it. Between them and the house were acres of shoulder-high cane. She was heading for a lone cypress at the edge of the field, where she knew a levee had been thrown up beside a bayou built by slaves years ago to drain the field. It would provide a spot of shade on the grass-covered levee. When she was opposite the cypress, she left the wagon road between the fields and headed for a narrower path between two rows of cane.

Her mare disliked going between the stalks of cane, and when she reared suddenly, refusing to go forward, Angèle urged her impatiently. Then she saw what had frightened the mare, a huge cane rattler coiled to strike. Quicker than she could think, her hand found the little silver pistol she always carried in the pocket of her riding skirt and she shot at the lifted swaying head.

Her terrified mare leaped backward, crowding Charles's mount, who was panicked by the shot. For a few seconds it was all either she or Charles could do to control their mounts, who were rearing and trying to escape their restraints, threshing around and flattening the cane.

"Good God!" Charles said when he had finally quieted his horse enough to see what had prompted Angèle to shoot. "I've never seen a snake that size!" It was as big around as her arm, and he guessed its length when uncoiled would be over five feet. The accuracy of her quick shot astounded him. "You blew his head off!"

"I could hardly miss at that range. It's a variety common to cane, and it grows uncommonly large."

The big Spanish half-breed came galloping down the cane road, and shouted across to them, "Are you all right, madame? M'sieu?"

"Yes. I've killed a snake, Jean-Baptiste. Do you want it?"

"Oui, madame." He rode through the cane to join them.

She turned to Charles, who thought she looked a little pale.

"This is my foreman. Mr. Archer is our new neighbor, Jean-Baptiste."

The foreman touched his black felt hat, then looked down at the snake, grinning. "It will make fine chops. I'll come back with a sack so it won't spook my horse."

"Good. Charles, let's find some shade."

Jean-Baptiste took a longer look at Charles, then turned his horse.

They rode the rest of the distance to the cypress tree in silence. Charles quickly dismounted and held up a hand to help her. She was trembling. "Are you all right?"

"Now that it's all over, I'm shaking," she admitted.

"I've never felt so helpless," he said angrily, "with my stallion trying his best to throw me, and me afraid your mare would send you flying any minute. I couldn't even see what you'd shot at until we'd calmed the horses." He pulled her closer and kissed her, long and deeply. Feeling her still tremble, he let her go and unrolled the quilt tied behind his saddle, revealing a bottle of wine, two silver mugs, and some packets of food.

He poured her some wine, and kept his arm around her while she drank. Then he walked the horses to a smaller tree a short distance away and tied them. When he came back he took off his coat and cravat and undid the top button of his shirt, exposing the fine drops of perspiration on his throat.

The sun, glinting through the leaves of the cypress, caught threads of gold in the hairs on his chest and made his fine cotton shirt translucent. He was solid and muscular and beautiful in her eyes, with straight broad shoulders, his torso tapering to his waist. Her lips were still wet with wine when he kissed her again. "I haven't slept since yesterday afternoon when I held you like this," he said raggedly.

"Nor have I," she confessed.

He spread the quilt on the grass and sat beside her on it, taking her in his arms again. While he was kissing her, she unfastened the buttons at her throat and exposed her breasts. He caught his breath, then bent his head to gently kiss each one. The excitement the encounter with the snake had caused added fuel to the desire that had been building since his kiss the afternoon before. A white-faced ibis flew out of the cypress over their heads with slow and powerful wingbeats and a low humming cry that seemed to express her own need.

She had thought she could never feel like this again.

Jean-Baptiste stretched the huge snake out and stepped off its length before he gathered it up and put it in the bag he had brought. Mon dieu, but it was nearly six feet long! He tied the opening of the bag and slung it over the pommel of his saddle. Mounting, he glanced over at the cypress she'd indicated.

Pére Baptiste, as the other slaves had named him out of respect for his age and his caring, was a big man, and his horse stood hands higher than other horses in the stables. Because the levee was higher than the cane field, it was clearly visible from atop his horse. It was a moment before he realized what he was seeing. Then he turned back to the cane road and galloped down to the workers he had set to weeding cane.

"Come with me," he shouted. "Madame has shot a six-foot rattler." He patted the sack hanging from his pommel. "I am going to divide with all of you!"

His offer was greeted with a cheer—the round white rattler chops were a delicacy—and the men ran behind his horse back to their quarters, where the snake was exclaimed over before it was skinned and butchered.

Late that night, when Mimi lay beside him in their bed, he said heavily, "Madame has taken a lover."

Mimi did not have to ask who. After a long time she said, "It was bound to happen, yes?" But as she had once before, she lay awake long after Jean-Baptiste slept, staring up at the whitewashed ceiling and wondering what it would mean to all of them. If your master was a man, she thought, he was either a good man or a bad master—you knew what to expect. But if you were owned by a woman, anything could happen.

She hoped it meant happiness for Angèle.

Chapter 14

La Sorcellerie. 1820.

J*UNE* heat lay heavy and moist on the land. A blue drag-
onfly hovered above the skittering waterbugs crisscrossing the
black surface of the water, where an arm of the bayou wandering behind the stables had widened into a pocket lake. There
was a small pool there deep enough for a man to swim, used by
the field workers after a steamy day in the cane and during the
day by their children.

Jean-Philippe stood naked on the bank near where the stand
of cypress began, their knobby roots protruding like knees from
the shallow water in which they grew. His gaze scanned the still
surface around the roots for a bubble that would reveal the
presence of an alligator. Most of the 'gators in this bayou were
small, and Jean-Philippe prized the tail, which the cook cut into
steaks and fried for him. If he spotted one, Jeffery could seize it
and throw it on the bank to him.

Jeffery emerged from the pool, shaking the moisture out of
his brown hair. His skin was so fair that even when he spent
most of his summer days out-of-doors, his shoulders had only a
light spattering of golden-tan freckles.

"See anything?" he asked Jean-Philippe.

"Non."

Jeffery nodded toward the younger dark children who had scampered out of the water when he and Jean-Philippe approached, but were watching from the shrubbery that screened the pool. "Shall we get them a fish?" His teasing blue eyes reflected the grin that revealed even white teeth.

"But yes, if you can catch one." Jean-Philippe was a smooth tan all over, his dark hair curling in the damp air and his moist eyes so dark as to appear a luminous black.

"Watch me!" Jeffery submerged again and moved slowly toward the bank and the nearest cypress roots, feeling among them with his right hand, his left extended for balance. He moved carefully because other creatures besides the white-meated catfish hid among the cypress roots, and the big whiskered fish themselves had sharp barbs that could tear the flesh of his hands.

He saw a gleam as a ray of filtered sun struck among the roots, and reached for it. His hand touched something cold and muscular, too slender to be a fish. With a sudden contraction of fear he gripped it with all his strength. The snake could not bite as long as he held it, but neither could he let it go. With his hand upraised, he kicked to the surface of the water.

Taking a quick breath, he shouted, "Jean! Snake!" as he threw it on the bank. The children shrieked and ran. Jean-Philippe moved quickly. Before it could coil to strike, he had grabbed the deadly water moccasin by the tail and whipped its head viciously through the air, breaking its neck.

Jeffery pulled himself up on the bank and lay spread-eagled on the coarse grass. "You were quick, Jean," he panted. The moccasins were a deadly menace in the water. Many a time Jeffery had seen boys deal with them, yet he had dreaded such an encounter, fearing he would be too paralyzed to act.

"You were quick, too, Jeffery," Jean-Philippe said, and Jeffery glowed.

They heard Melodie humming on the path through the oaks and shrubbery that hid them from the stable, and hastily pulled on their trousers.

"Oh, you rascals!" she cried when she saw the mottled brown snake stretched out limp and fat on the grass beside Jean-Philippe. "You've been prowling under the cypress roots! One of these days you're both going to be fanged, and I'll have to cut your skin and suck out the poison. I'll probably die with you."

Jeffery grinned at her. "In our grateful arms, no doubt? Melodie, the nuns have made a romantic of you."

"Grateful? You?" she scoffed.

Jeffery picked up the dead snake and tossed it back into the bayou, pretending an indifference he did not feel.

The fact that Bellemont, his home, had once been Melodie's, had always had great significance to him. He'd thought her beautiful when he first saw her with a mop of dark hair pulled up on top of her head and cascading down in back, already a daring rider and expert at handling the flat canoe the Creoles called a pirogue. She had become a companion, a thrilling member of the close threesome they formed. Jean-Philippe's mother, who was her guardian, had decreed that she be sent to the Ursuline nuns to learn how to become a young lady, but she still returned to her tomboyish ways when at La Sorcellerie for vacations and some weekends, and she still preferred his and Jean-Philippe's company to that of her school friends.

Magically, this summer she had become the most enchanting creature he could imagine, with magnolia-blossom skin so soft it gave him shivers if he happened to touch it, mischievous eyes ringed by dark, dark lashes, a tender bosom that just thinking about could send him into visions of delight, and the softest voice that ever suggested secret laughter.

Probably half the Creole bloods in New Orleans had their eyes on her, he thought, but he had already determined that she and no other would be his bride. As yet he had confided his decision to no one, not even Jean-Philippe.

She looked pointedly at their bare torsos. "You'll have to put on your shirts. Cousin Angèle sent me to ask if the two of you would join us for coffee on the galérie."

"Will we deign to join them?" Jeffery playfully asked Jean-Philippe, who exchanged a look with Melodie and said, "One does not say no to Maman."

Jeffery laughed, and they started up the trail together, buttoning their shirts and tucking them in as they walked. But when they came in sight of the serene columns of the plantation house and he saw the woman sitting behind the coffee tray on the lower galérie, he looked at her not as Jean-Philippe's mother but as the woman who controlled his destiny. She was formidable, this Angèle Roget de l'Eglise who would have to give her consent before he could marry Melodie.

She was in her forties, he guessed, but she had the lean, hard figure of a woman who in spite of her title rode out to supervise the work in her fields every day. Her dark hair had silvery glints in direct sunlight, revealing the passage of years, but her blue eyes were as direct and challenging as a young woman's, although considerably colder. He suspected Jean-Philippe himself feared her.

As she sat on her galérie awaiting the young people, Angèle's thoughts were on the stand of cane she had just inspected. It was proving to be a good strain. The crop would be good again this year, barring drought or hurricanes, and it would again be immensely profitable, even though it was necessary to send the brown near-liquid sugar in barrels to Europe to be refined. The plantings she had secured from Etienne de Boré, which her workers had nurtured and improved over the years, produced sugarcane highly resistant to the insects and diseases attacking it in Louisiana.

She was conscious of a pride in her accomplishment this morning. Over the years she had increased her sugarcane acreage considerably with drainage canals. Her plantation was one of the most prosperous in the area. Not only that, La Sorcellerie itself was famed for the elegance of its furnishings, imported from France, and for its abundance of perfectly trained servants. She was known to the merchants of New Orleans as an astute trader and something of an eccentric novelty, since few women concerned themselves with sugarcane culture, but her invitations were eagerly sought and her soirées and balls attended by all the best families.

As she watched the three young people emerge from the woods, she told herself that she had done it all for Jean-Philippe and Melodie, whom she loved equally. But even as the thought formed, she knew it was not true; her pride would have spurred her to succeed without those lovable but exasperating two. What she had done solely for them was to keep her place in New Orleans society so they would have an entrée when they were ready to join adult life.

They sauntered toward the house, talking and laughing together, and Angèle's thoughts filled with images—always the three of them together, from the time Nonc' Etienne brought Jeffery to La Sorcellerie with Charles Archer. Both young men were broad-shouldered, with the tapered loins and flat stomachs of youth, but Jean-Philippe at fifteen was more compact than his seventeen-year-old American friend, with a smooth coordination of muscles that Jeff Archer envied. In spite of the difference in their ages, they had been inseparable since boyhood, complementing each other in several ways. Jeffery was thoughtful and slow to react, a good foil for Jean-Philippe's mercurial moods and lack of patience.

As for Melodie, she was promising to be a real beauty, and so charming that she was in danger of becoming spoiled, especially since she was accustomed to taking for granted the sole attention of both her cousin and Jeffery Archer.

Angèle greeted the two young men formally, like guests. At the end of the summer both of them would go away to school, and the "Triad," as their friends called them, would be broken up. When Jean-Philippe returned from Paris he would take up residence in the octagonal *garçonnière* she planned to build for him while he was away. It was the French way of acknowledging the coming of age of their sons, and their need for privacy for those little adventures that were tacitly recognized as part of becoming a mature man. Its octagonal shape would match the much smaller *pigeonnier*, whose inhabitants' musical cooing gave the children entertainment and herself much pleasure.

They climbed the steps to the galérie, and Melodie and Jeffery sat at the table with her. But Jean-Philippe took the cup of coffee she poured for him to the railing, leaning against a pillar with negligent grace and looking down at them, a stance that suddenly reminded her of his father. He was beginning to resemble Philippe so closely that sometimes Angèle found it painful to look at him—dark hair that curled softly, melancholy dark eyes, and a slender grace of movement.

"Invitations were delivered this morning for the de Martine's ball," she told him and Melodie. "You will probably find one waiting for you at home, Jeffery."

She had often wondered how the friendship between the two young men had lasted so long, but it seemed as strong as ever.

The only trait they shared was their arrogance, and even that was different in character. Part of it was the arrogant self-confidence of youth, but Jean-Philippe's was also that of name, based on his father's hereditary title and royalist background; Jeffery's was the naive self-confidence of the American nation, an ingenuous brashness that both irritated and amused the longtime Creole residents of the new American state of Louisiana, already a century old in French and Spanish history.

Melodie's eyes were sparkling. "Now I can wear the gown you ordered for me. May I, Cousin Angèle?"

"Why not?" Angèle said, smiling. "I predict you will be the belle of the ball." She caught the anxious look that crossed Jeffery Archer's face and thought, *That young man is already putting in his bid.*

An American? Well, Melodie was herself half American. No one would be disturbed except Nonc' Etienne, who still complained about the brusque business manners of the Americans. "Never offer a man a glass of wine," he growled. "Never pass the time of day! Except Charles. You should have married him, Angèle."

"Perhaps, Nonc' Etienne," she always replied.

Angèle looked at Melodie now, in the full bud of sixteen years, and felt a warming of her heart. She had her mother's beauty. But my spirit, Angèle thought, seeing herself in this child of Clothilde's. Not rebellious but willful, set on going her own way, a sensible way for the most part, but often unconventional.

". . . and Genée Boudreaux, who sings beautifully, and Carmen Herrerra, who has hair I envy—like spun gold it is. . . ." Melodie was speaking of her friends from the convent school who would be attending the ball. Watching Jeffery, Angèle thought, *He is too sophisticated to reveal himself too soon, which is well.* After all, he would be going away to school in the fall. Melodie was a very wealthy woman in her own right, the only heir of both her father and her grandfather. She would have many chances to marry before Jeffery returned.

And she would marry. She had shown no inclination to manage her own property, such as had obsessed Angèle at her age, an obsession that still ruled her life. Unfortunately, neither did Jean-Philippe. His failure to share her almost mystical feeling

193

for La Sorcellerie also reminded her of his father, and roused a familiar anger.

"May we go alone in the carriage, then?" Melodie asked.

"Alone? I am also invited," Angèle said, her voice tart, "and not only as chaperone, I want you to know. But Jean-Philippe may act as your escort, if you wish."

They looked at each other, the three of them communicating with their eyes, as they had always done. "Jeffery too! They will both escort me," the minx said, laughing.

Angèle was amused to see that it was Jeffery whose fair skin revealed a faint flush, making her certain she was right about him. "It is something I have always wanted to see," she observed, dryly. "How three people manage their feet when they dance together."

She finished her coffee, and stood up. "Jean-Philippe, your education will begin immediately. There are things you can learn here that Paris cannot teach you. Starting tomorrow morning you will ride with me each morning when I inspect the fields." She rose and walked through the doors and into her study without waiting for his reply.

"Merde!" he said, too low for her to overhear.

Melodie and Jeffery both laughed, but Jeffery noted the anxiety in Melodie's eyes as she looked at her cousin.

Having the young people around for the summer, Mimi thought, made La Sorcellerie a livelier place. She sang at her work, and Ouma's handsome face wore a continual smile. After Duval's death Angèle had made Ouma her majordomo, and because he helped her with her accounts—Angèle herself had taught him his letters and figures—she assigned him two bright young Africans to train as footmen. Mimi still ran the house, but now she had many more house servants to supervise, with a cook, two cook's helpers, and several cleaning maids as well as madame's and m'selle's personal maids.

In the fields her own Jean-Baptiste was still overseer, with twenty-three field workers and fifteen sugarhouse workers. The only men he did not supervise were the stable boys and grooms, who answered to Jules, and the gardeners and maintenance men, who had their own overseer. It was a good life they had on La Sorcellerie, Mimi acknowledged, enjoying as they did Angèle's complete trust. Although she was ten years older than her mistress, she had not as many gray hairs—and those she had came from worrying about her poor lost Minette.

Not a day passed that she did not remember Kitten's mischievous ways and her sunny smile, and think of the pleasure old michie had taken in her. Often she glimpsed her from the corner of an eye, still a child skipping around corners in the house, just out of her sight. But at night Minette returned in Mimi's nightmares. She was grown now and in need, or in terror in a frightening place. Not a night passed that Mimi did not beg le bon dieu in her prayers to keep Minette safe.

Ever since she'd begun to hear talk of Jean-Philippe going to Paris to school, she had planned to ask whether he could look for Minette. She chose the morning hour, when she went over the food inventory and menus with Angèle.

"Paris is a large place, yes?"

"Yes." Angèle looked up from her desk, instantly on guard. Something in Mimi's unexpected timidity warned her what was coming. "Larger than you can imagine, Mimi."

"But there are ways to find someone, even in a large city, yes? As in New Orleans, one could go to the *cabildo*—"

"If you are thinking of Minette—"

"I am thinking of young michie Philippe going to Paris in the fall," Mimi said. "If he could just find out if she still lives?"

Apprehension tightened Angèle's throat. Not for the first time, she wondered how much Jean-Philippe remembered of his first two years. Surely it couldn't be much. She had hesitated long before deciding that she must allow him to go to Paris for his last two years of schooling. It was expected of a young Creole of his position.

There was little chance that he would meet any of the friends who might wonder why she had never mentioned a son who must have been two years old when Philippe was killed. Napoleon's court was no more. The Bourbons were back in power with Louis XVIII, the guillotined king's brother, on the throne. Napoleon was in prison at St. Helena, and word of Josephine's death of a chill had reached Angèle five years ago. The de Rémusats had fled the White Terror unleashed by the royalists and were in exile, probably in Switzerland.

"Don't you know that I would have found Minette if anyone

could?" she asked Mimi. "I even had the police looking for her!" She could not meet the other woman's imploring gaze. "It's hopeless, Mimi."

"If I could just know that she lives. . . ." The eloquent eyes, so like Minette's, filled with tears, and Angèle had to fight her impulse to confide everything to her, as she had done as a child.

"If Minette is alive, she could have sent a letter. Someone would have written it for her. Isn't it possible she doesn't want you to know what she is doing?" Angèle could say that much, confident that it was true. There had been no word at all from Minette. And there would be none. Minette would not risk the exposure of their deception.

When she glanced back at Mimi, she saw the anger in her eyes. Angèle said quickly, "I'm sorry, Mimi, but the police suggested that to me. There is little else a girl like her could do to keep alive. Please don't ask Jean-Philippe's help." She added lightly, "It would give him too good an excuse to neglect his studies. Do you understand?"

Mimi's pink lips tightened.

Mimi awaited her opportunity, and it came a few weeks before Jean-Philippe's sailing date. His friend Jeffery had already left for his school on the east coast, and his mother and M'selle Melodie were making a morning call. Jean-Philippe had slept late, and when he came downstairs ordered coffee and a roll on the galérie, saying it was too hot for anything more.

Mimi took the tray from the maid and carried it herself to the galérie. "Good morning, michie," she said, pouring his coffee.

He picked up the cup. "Thanks, Mimi."

"You will go away soon to France. France is very large, yes?"

"So they tell me." He drank and began buttering a roll.

"It will be difficult for you to find your way there?"

"I think I'm up to it," he said, and yawned. "Mon dieu, but it's hot. It will be good to get on that ship."

"But it will be difficult to find a person who lives there?"

He blinked at her. "Where?"

"In Paris, michie."

"What are you getting at, Mimi?"

"It's my daughter, Michie Jean-Philippe. I'm not supposed to say anything to you, but my heart is bleeding for her. If, when you get to Paris, you could inquire about a woman named

Minette who ran away from your maman's house and disappeared . . ."

He looked blankly at her. "In Paris? When maman was in Paris?"

"And your father was alive—"

"Mon dieu, Mimi, but that was years ago! I was an infant when he died!"

"Oui, michie."

He stared out toward the bayou, but he was not seeing the morning mists that softened its gleam and wove mystery into the silvery strands of moss hanging from the oaks shading its bank. He had very little memory of his first years in Paris, only a few vague impressions, and they were not visual. He could not remember his father's face, only a sense of his presence, large and loving, and a man's deep laughter. But the name Minette seemed to strike an echo. After a moment he said, "I think that was my nurse's name—Minette."

Mimi looked startled. But she immediately veiled her expression, as all good servants did when they heard something they were not supposed to hear. Jean-Philippe thought, What the devil?

"I'm sorry, michie. It's too long ago, isn't it? Please forget I bothered you with it." She left him.

Jean-Philippe sat sipping his coffee and worrying that name over and over in his mind. Minette. *Don't forget your Minette.* The admonition popped into his mind from nowhere he could identify. He must have had a nurse by that name. So she was old Mimi's daughter? And she had not returned home with them. He wondered idly what had become of her.

"I'm going to miss you like the devil, Melodie," Jean-Philippe told her. His sailing was twenty-four hours away. Last night they had attended a farewell moonlight picnic some of their young friends gave, much like the picnic two weeks ago which had ended in their waving good-bye to Jeffery as his ship lifted anchor and sailed down the river toward the gulf, on its way to Boston. Tomorrow another vessel would carry Jean-Philippe toward England, and eventually France.

Tonight Melodie and Jean-Philippe were alone. After dinner Angèle had gone into her study to work on her accounts. "My last night," Jean-Philippe said bitterly, "and she must do her accounts. She is glad to see me go."

"Jean-Philippe! She can't bear to think of your going! That is why she works."

"She hates me."

"No, Jean-Philippe! She loves you! How can you doubt it?"

"Easily," he said gloomily. "It isn't always that she hates me. But there are times when I feel it so strongly—"

"You imagine it," Melodie said. "She gets angry with me sometimes when I am being annoying. Come, let's walk out on the galérie and watch the fireflies like we used to do." It was the last time they would be alone together for two years.

"It will never be the same again, will it?" Melodie mourned. "You and I and Jeffery. Nothing changed when I went to the Ursuline nuns' school, but this will change everything. How I will miss you! You will both be having new adventures, meeting new people, while I will just be waiting. . . ."

She was thinking of Jeffery and his last night, when they had wandered off from the fire where the fish were frying and he had taken her in his arms. It had seemed so right to be held close against his heart, that she had lifted her face as though to kiss him would be the most natural thing in the world. The moon cast its light over her shoulder on Jeffery's face, revealing the tense look of his mouth and the anguished passion in his eyes, and for the first time she realized the depth of his feeling for her. Then he kissed her, and his kiss had opened a new world of sensations, a new awareness both of him and of her own self— just as Jeffery was leaving!

Beside her Jean-Philippe was aware of the soft mass of her body, close to him against the galérie rail, and of the sweet swell of her breasts beneath her bodice. Looking at her with eyes sharpened by his coming absence, he saw things he had taken for granted: the rich abundance of her hair, the light way her dark curving lashes lay against her magnolia cheek—like a butterfly poised to lift away—and the brilliance of her moon-bright gaze when her lashes fanned upward. He was aware, too, of her preoccupation.

"You will be having new experiences here, Melodie. You will be smothered by attention from beaux. I'll probably come home and find you married," he said disconsolately.

198

"I'll not marry *anyone* until you can come to my wedding! I promise you that, Jean-Philippe!"

"Did Jeffery ask you to wait for him?"

Melodie felt the flush that rose to her cheeks in the darkness. "He said he wouldn't ask that of me, but . . ." *He loves me!* She could not repeat his words. They were still too new and too private. She would wait for him. She was sure that Jean-Philippe knew that without being told.

"If we were not cousins," he said fiercely, "I would ask you to wait for me. But if you have to marry someone else, I'd rather it be Jeffery."

She cried, "Oh, Jean-Philippe, I love you both so much, so much."

Chapter 15

Paris. 1821.

THE café in the Palais Royal was crowded with after-the-atre diners, the talk on everyone's lips the death of Napoleon Bonaparte in his prison at St. Helena. France was at peace and the royalists in power, the portly Bourbon, Louis XVIII, on the throne. Paris was once again a city of pleasure.

The Salle de Trône at the Café des Mille Colonnes was filled with the murmur of discreet voices with an undertone of soft laughter. Light from hundreds of candles in the glittering crystal chandeliers struck sparks of emerald and ruby and gold from the women's jewelry. Satin hissed and velvet whispered as they moved, and wine gleamed red or golden in the delicate glasses they lifted to their lips.

Suddenly a young voice rose above the murmurous conversation, angry and slurred with drink. "The devil you will, m'sieu! I pay my own debts!"

In the second of appalled quiet this outburst produced in the room, a deeper voice said with quiet fury, "But you don't buy an aperitif for my woman, you drunken pup!"

With the others at her table, Minette looked in the direction of the disturbance. Her gaze froze on the young man who had spoken first. He was Philippe resurrected, Philippe at a younger age than she had known him. Could it be . . . ?

My son. Her heart almost stopped, and a warm weakness spread through her body while her eyes moved hungrily over Jean-Philippe's face and form.

Mon dieu, he was fumbling for his card! Was he such a young hothead that he was going to challenge a man like Monsieur Daudet?

Panic pushed her up from her chair and across the floor to the group standing before the "throne" of the woman known as the Lemonade Queen, who, behind her array of glasses and goblets, was already gesturing to her husband, the proprietor.

Minette stumbled gracefully, falling between the two men and against Jean-Philippe. His hands rose instinctively to keep her on her feet, but he staggered under her unexpected weight and she surrendered to an irresistible desire to embrace him.

"Ah, m'sieu," she murmured, "you have saved me from an undignified tumble. I am so grateful."

She released him, standing between him and the angry Monsieur Daudet, smiling up at Jean-Philippe with all the warmth flooding her heart. He responded with a dazed, pleased smile, and went docilely with her when she drew him away from the men standing around the limonadière's dispensary. He had forgotten his quarrel with Daudet, and when she suggested some air, went willingly outside into a summer night that troubled the senses with its scents of roses, mown grass, and fecund earth from the Parc Palais Royal.

Minette hailed a coach and Jean-Philippe climbed in after her without needing assistance. But as soon as the coach began swaying to the slow trot of the horses, he fell into a drunken sleep on her shoulder.

He is still a boy, she thought, giving in to her almost insupportable need to touch him. Gently she smoothed his hair. For this night only she could give him a mother's care. She gave the address of her apartment to the driver, and for the short space of the ride, with Jean-Philippe's head resting against her and his breath fanning her bosom, she basked in ineffable pleasure, thinking neither of the past nor of the future, but enjoying his presence, letting her love pour silently over him as the coach rattled over the cobbled streets, past the misty halos encircling the street lamps.

At her apartment she instructed her coachman to enlist the help of the concierge to carry him up the stairs. "Show them to the guest room," she told her sleepy maid.

"Oui, madame." The middle-aged woman eyed Jean-Philippe suspiciously.

"He is a silly lad who has overindulged," Minette said carelessly. "He was on the point of challenging Monsieur Daudet. I have saved him from disaster."

"Mon dieu, indeed!" The woman looked compassionately at the young man laid out on the bed in his soiled best, looking vulnerably young in his alcoholic sleep, and began gently tugging at a boot.

"I leave him to you," Minette said, repressing the urge to grasp the other boot.

In the morning Jean-Philippe wakened with a headache so painful he resisted opening his eyes. When he did, they rested on the canopy over a strange bed. Gingerly he moved his head an inch and saw a strikingly beautiful woman standing beside his bed, holding a cup of coffee toward him. He blinked, trying to remember events of the recent past leading up to this intriguing present.

He had gone home with a woman? But he could not remember taking her, and the bed he was in had obviously not been shared. Anyway, she looked like a higher-class woman than he could afford. Her pale café-au-lait skin suggested that she was a half-breed, but he could not guess from what races. Her features were pure French. She was wearing a deep rose velvet dressing gown, and the room's furnishings behind her were luxurious.

He raised himself, holding his head and cursing softly. "Did I make a fool of myself last evening?" he asked, with an echo of Philippe's charm.

"Mildly." Minette smiled. "I rescued you from serious folly."

"Then I thank you, Madame . . . ? I don't believe I've had the pleasure . . . or have I stupidly forgotten?"

"Take your coffee, m'sieu. It grows cold." Her voice was soft, he noted gratefully. "When you have completed your toilette we will talk."

He took the cup and sipped the hot dark liquid. Her velvet

skirts moved toward the door of his chamber and she disappeared.

When he had finished the coffee, he climbed carefully down from the bed and found the withdrawing room. A servant was waiting to help him into his clothes when he returned to the chamber. They had been brushed and pressed. He followed the direction indicated by the servant and found his hostess in a charming room overlooking a small garden, sitting at a table with a steaming coffee pot and plates of rolls and winter pears before her.

She was older than she had appeared when he first opened his bedazzled eyes, but she was a beauty. He was experienced enough by now to recognize the arts she practiced to appear always to her best advantage.

He bowed. "I am Jean-Philippe, the marquis de l'Eglise, madame. Since we are obviously not lovers, may I assume that the reason you brought me home with you is one I would just as soon not hear?"

She laughed, a contralto laugh with a hint of mischief in it. "You were about to challenge Monsieur Daudet, who would no doubt have put a bullet through your heart."

"Mon dieu! Did I have a cause?"

"None but too much Spanish wine."

"Then I am grateful to you. Madame . . . ?" he questioned a second time.

Her expression was enigmatic. "Do you remember Minette?"

As soon as he heard the name he realized that her laughter had been familiar to him. But he blinked again, in surprise and disbelief. *"You?* My nurse?"

She smiled a mysterious smile, nodding.

"You are Mimi's daughter, then?" It was incredible!

She nodded again, her eyes glistening with sudden tears. "She is well?"

"She is very well, but she wonders why she has not heard from you. She asked me to try to find you."

"Jean-Baptiste? And Ouma?"

"Both well."

She was stunning! Of course she had learned how to practice a woman's arts—how to dress, how to gild the fading lily. And she was speaking good French. A thought turned his amazement to eagerness. "You knew my father," he said. "Tell me about him. I can remember nothing."

"You are very like him."

He thought he had never seen a lovelier smile, and wondered if he had been wrong to think her an expensive courtesan. But no, for a daughter of his mother's slave it was the only road that could have taken her to her present position.

"And you, M'sieu Jean-Philippe, you are a student at the Collège de St. Louis?"

"At the Collège de France."

"Ah! That is an old institution, no? I understand it survived the revolution?"

"It was established in 1530 by Francis the First as a college of humanism."

"And do you enjoy studying there?"

"I enjoy my extracurricular pursuits more," he said, laughing. "We are given much freedom."

"Spoken like a true aristocrat," she said, her eyes crinkling with amusement. She knew there were no fees at the Collège de France, and anyone could attend without matriculating. "I would have expected your maman to enroll the future master of La Sorcellerie in the discipline of a Catholic school."

Smiling, Jean-Philippe said, "She did. She does not yet know I have changed schools."

"So you are a secret anarchist." The amused, half-mocking smile in her eyes made him feel very worldly. "And your maman, has she remarried?"

"Non! She spends all her days supervising the planting, the cutting, the grinding and boiling of sugarcane. Then the selling of the sugar. It is her life. She makes a great deal of money."

"And it will one day be your money and your life?"

"I suppose so. She expects me to like cultivating sugarcane as much as she does, but I find it mostly a bore. . . . You speak very good French, Minette."

"Why not?" She shrugged. "I have been in Paris sixteen years."

"Why haven't you sent word to your family in all this time?"

"A runaway slave? Here, I am a French citizen."

His glance around the apartment was eloquent. It took in the carved and brocaded chairs, the muted rich colors of tapestry and rugs.

"I have a protector," she explained, and added a bit sadly, "I think my mother would prefer not to know how I live."

He drank the last of his coffee and leaned back in his chair. This was very pleasant. "You know more about my years in Paris than I can remember, Minette. Tell me about them."

But she said, "What is there to tell? You were born, and I—"

"Where?"

"In the rue de Nevers."

"Were you my nurse from the beginning?"

"Yes, until you were two and a half."

"My wet nurse?"

Her face changed subtly, became a beautiful mask that put distance between them. "Yes."

"What happened?"

She hesitated. "Your father was killed—surely you've been told about that?"

He nodded.

"Your mother returned to Louisiana, taking you with her. I . . . stayed."

He studied her. He had the strongest feeling that she could tell him more, something important to him.

"Who is your protector, Minette?"

She shook her head, her eyes smiling but her lips mute.

"What shall I tell Mimi when she asks why you didn't come home with my mother and me?"

Minette hesitated. Then she said gently, "Tell her . . . I fell in love."

Jean-Philippe began to feel uncomfortable. There was a strain between them now. He sensed that it was time to take his leave. He rose and asked, "May I come again?"

A strange, sad look came into her luminous dark eyes. "It would not be wise, m'sieu."

So she was faithful to her protector. He wondered again who the man was, and resolved to make inquiries. Jean-Philippe felt extraordinarily drawn to her. When he went out into the narrow street, he looked about to see where he was and noted the number beside the gate in her wall.

He shared two rooms and a servant near the college with

Jacques Gautil, a tall, narrow-shouldered young dandy who had introduced him to the sport of gambling. He found Jacques there, waiting to see if he was going to attend a lecture that morning.

"I suppose you slept with a tart?"

"How discerning of you, Jacques. You shouldn't have waited for me."

"Was it good?"

Jean-Philippe kissed his fingers and rolled his eyes.

"Where can I find her?"

"Find your own tarts, Jacques."

"Selfish dog."

"What did you do last night?"

"I discovered a small casino where students are not questioned too closely. Very profitable too. I'll take you there tonight in exchange for the name of your friend."

"No dice."

Without confiding in Jacques, Jean-Philippe made a few inquiries, but found no one who knew Minette. He was forced finally to the conclusion that she was known by another name, and even having her street number did not help him to identify her or discover who was keeping her. In a few days the incident had begun to fade from his memory. After all, what was his former nurse to him? She had said herself that Mimi would probably rather not know what kind of a life she was leading.

Jacques could not resist taking him to the new casino, where they met girls all too willing to help them spend their winnings. Jean-Philippe found the sport so exhilarating that his last months in Paris passed like a dream.

It was not until he had booked passage to return to Louisiana that he thought again of Minette. On a whim he returned to her apartment to ask if she had messages for her family, and was told by a servant that madame was in the south of France.

Chapter 16

La Sorcellerie. 1822.

*A*LL the candles were lit in the dining room, their light reflecting on the exquisite china and crystal Cousin Angèle had shipped from France, penetrating the ruby wineglasses to throw rosy shadows on the damask cloth. Jeffery Archer was home from Boston, and Angèle had invited him and his father to La Sorcellerie for dinner. Melodie sat across from Jeffery, annoyed at herself for still feeling oddly shy with him.

Charles Archer, who had become very prosperous in his wholesale business in New Orleans, was talking about the rapid rise in the price of sugar and the rush of planters to engage in sugar culture as a result.

"It's extremely profitable," Angèle agreed, "but I can't increase my acreage without buying more slaves, and it's not easy today to find a planter willing to sell a good worker."

"There are still auctions in the swamps, where one can buy from smugglers like the Lafittes," M'sieu Archer said.

Angèle's eyes flashed. "Illegal auctions, you mean."

"If you would like me to buy for you—"

"Thank you, no."

His expression as he looked at her was quizzical. "You're a tough businesswoman, Angèle, tough as any man in your dealings. This sentiment of yours surprises me."

She considered him, mulling over his comment. Charles was a shrewd businessman, but without the abrasive American ways that offended the Creole business community. He had enormous appeal for her, but in the end the attraction had not been enough to overcome the remembered ecstasy and pain of her marriage. However, their intense but brief love affair had left behind a strong friendship.

"I grew up with slaves, but I've never purchased one." When his looked questioned her, she said, shrugging, "They breed. The children are trained as they grow. La Sorcellerie's work force has more than doubled in one generation. Actually, Charles, I'm now cultivating all the land that's drainable between the swamp and the bayou. With my new sugar mill I can crush cane for my neighbors and increase my income in that way."

Melodie was only half listening to their conversation, looking across the low silver bowl of floating magnolias at Jeffery and marveling at how handsome he had become. He looked manly and proper in his formal clothes, not at all like the ruddy-haired tease who had been one of the Triad.

But then, she had not expected to find him the same. At least his hair was still red, although it seemed a shade darker. She was relieved to notice that a stray lock was rising at one temple to ruin the smooth curve of his hairline.

His blue eyes had a warmth when he smiled at her, and her response to it made her wonder about the girls in Boston who had seen that smile and undoubtedly been rendered as vulnerable by it as she felt. "How many American hearts did you break, Jeffery?" she teased, and Jeffery's father, smiling, turned to listen to his reply.

"Do you think she's jealous?" Jeffery asked Angèle. "It's true that the girls in Boston are more ladylike than Melodie—"

"Oh, he lies!" Melodie exclaimed.

"They never interrupt," Jeffery said blandly. "I was going to say, but none can hold a candle to her for looks."

"Now he exaggerates," Melodie said, her eyes sparkling with a pleasure she could not conceal. He was still a tease. "M'sieu, is that why you sent Jeffery to Harvard, to acquire a silver tongue?"

"What better equipment for a lawyer, my dear?"

"Jeffery, is that what they taught you in that school?"

"It's going to take me a very long time to tell you what I learned there," Jeffery said with a grin. "I think we should start immediately."

Angèle listened, amused, while with a look or a gesture she orchestrated the serving of the several courses that Petra, the cook, had prepared, outdoing herself to welcome Michie Jeffery home with the Creole foods and sauces he could not find in Boston: shrimp and crab "gumbo," as Petra called the okra with which she flavored the hearty rice and seafood soup, followed by braised quail and breast of wild duck with mushrooms.

Later, while Angèle shared a brandy with M'sieu Archer in the salon, Melodie and Jeffery walked out on the galérie and stood at the rail, looking down at Angèle's gardens: smooth lawns stretching toward the bayou, and flower beds in gorgeous bloom.

"I missed the fireflies up north," he murmured.

"More than you missed me, I'm sure," she teased him. But she knew he was remembering how the three of them—he and she and Jean-Philippe—had caught the mysterious little creatures and imprisoned them in a bottle to make a "lantern."

"And more than I was missed, I'll wager!" he retorted. In the moonlight her beauty was making him ache. A delicate scent rose from her warm white skin. He wondered how many arms had held her in the popular waltz while he was sloshing through snow on the campus walks in Cambridge.

While they spoke lightly, there was a silent communication going on between them, a careful testing of their former relationship.

"I stood just here with Jean-Philippe the night before he left," Melodie confessed. "Watching the fireflies and thinking about you. Wondering if you would really come back to New Orleans."

"I told you I would come back, Melodie." His voice had deepened a note in the years he had been away. In the pale light his features were stronger; they had lost some softness of youth that had been there when he left.

"I wanted to believe you would, but you wrote so much about going into Boston, about what a fine city it was. . . ." Her voice trailed away.

"It is a fine city. You'll see . . . some day."

"I was born a Yankee, did you know that, Jeffery?"

He burst out laughing. "You may have been born in Philadelphia, but you'll never be a Yankee, Melodie!"

He tilted his head to listen as a mockingbird sang in a tree close to the galérie, a long joyous warble. Above the oaks the moon looked down at its reflection in the bayou.

"Jean-Philippe wrote me that the nightingale sings more prettily than our mockingbird. Do you think that can be true, or was he teasing me? Won't it be wonderful when he comes home next week," Melodie exclaimed, her tone lilting, "and the three of us are together again? I can hardly wait! Oh, Jeffery, do you think he will be much changed?"

"I'm anxious to see Jean-Philippe," Jeffery said. "But I think we've outgrown a threesome, haven't we, Melodie?"

He took her gently in his arms and she raised willing lips. His kiss was questioning, very sweet. He sighed deeply and pressed her head against his shoulder. "How I've longed to hold you like this!"

To be in his arms again was good, but also a little strange. There was a different smell to his clothing, something that said *Boston* to her. Would he want to go back? He'd as much as said she wouldn't fit in.

After a moment he took her face between his hands and tilted it, looking searchingly into her eyes. The warmth of his touch poured down her body. "You've waited, Melodie? There isn't anyone else?"

"I'm just the same," she said, her voice unsteady. "There's never been anyone I cared about but you and Jean-Philippe."

"I would hope that you care for me in a different way than you care for your cousin," he said dryly, releasing her.

"Of course it's different, Jeffery! Jean-Philippe and I grew up together. You know we've always been close. While you—" Once again she broke off without finishing her thought. She turned to gaze down the stretch of lawn. "You've changed, Jeffery."

"I? How have I changed?"

"I don't know." Her expression was troubled.

"I've always loved you, Melodie. I've always known I would marry you, or no one. When I left, I thought you felt the same way I did."

After a pause he found painful, she said, "Your letters were . . . different."

"My letters?" he said, in surprise.

"They were so serious, with such deep thoughts. They were about things you never talked about when we were together. About why we're here on earth, and what is federalism, and the politics of money, and . . . and some things I didn't understand in the least. It was as if they came from a stranger."

He was stunned. "Melodie, those letters were me, the real me. I was putting myself into them."

"You used to be more lighthearted," she reproached him.

"Because we were always a threesome, always playing games! In New England I was learnings things. I wanted to share my thoughts with you."

She turned a searching gaze on him. "And now you even look like a stranger."

"I've become a man?" he asked, smiling.

When she did not reply, he said, "Melodie, why do you think we're here on earth?"

"God put us here. Why question Him?"

"It's natural for man to question. Everything we've learned began with a question."

She regarded him thoughtfully. "Well, I will have to become better acquainted with the 'real you.' "

He asked, tenderly, "Did you understand when I wrote 'I love you'?"

"I *understood,* but . . ." She didn't want to say it again because she didn't want to hurt him, but the words had somehow lost their meaning, coming as from a stranger from so far away. She was looking for the companion who had first come between her and Jean-Philippe and then become part of their life at La Sorcellerie.

"Melodie?"

"Yes, Jeffery?"

"Kiss me."

She lifted her arms and embraced him. Her lips were soft and warm and they parted willingly enough. He kissed her deeply, with all the passionate longing that had been bottled up in his heart.

At last she drew away. His father and Madame Angèle came out on the galérie just in time to hear Melodie say, "Jeffery Archer, you've been practicing, haven't you?"

Jeffery went with them to meet Jean-Philippe's ship. They picked up Melodie's grandpère at his apartment in the Pontalba overlooking the former Place d'Armes—renamed Jackson Square in honor of the American general who'd saved New Orleans from the British—and went to the levee in Angèle's carriage with one of the footmen sitting beside her driver, to help him with the trunks. The river was spiky with the masts of schooners flying flags of many nations, the ships lying at anchor with their sails furled, their deckhands scouring the decks and working on the rigging. Tied up at the wharf was a square-rigged British merchant vessel whose cargo was being unloaded.

When she saw Jean-Philippe walk down the ribbed plank and step on the dock, Melodie gasped, "How grand he is!" He looked taller, or was it the high hat that sat so jauntily on his black hair? The smooth fit of his fawn-colored suit said *Paris,* and his cravat was elaborately folded.

"A Parisian dandy," Jeffery said, laughing. "He'll put the Creole girls in a spin."

Melodie ran down the levee to meet him, and they embraced. His dark eyes glowed with pleasure. "You've grown into a rare beauty, little cousin," Jean-Philippe said, the surprise in his voice making her flush with pleasure. Together they climbed back up to where the others waited. Jeffery stood back while Grandpère Roget took Jean-Philippe in a great bear hug, and grinned at Jean-Philippe's expression when he caught the wine-rich breath of the portly old gentleman. Etienne Roget's hair was still only steel gray, but his prominent nose was veined and enlarged, marks of the serious drinker.

When his uncle released Jean-Philippe, Jeffery stepped forward and clasped his hand while laying a familiar arm on his shoulder. "Welcome home, Shawn!" he exclaimed.

Melodie caught the amused twinkle in Jean-Philippe's eyes, and they shared a quiet laugh at Jeffery's pronunciation. Her cousin had not changed, she thought fondly.

Angèle's heart was pounding as she awaited her turn. In disbelief she thought, *He could be Philippe resurrected!* The resemblance had become so great it was painful. The love that flooded her was very like her response to his father, a witches' brew of emotions. While he was still on the ocean she had received a long letter from the Catholic school in which she had enrolled him, asking if she knew that her son had withdrawn from his classes after receipt of a letter requesting that he return home because of her ill health, and was now discovered to be still in Paris attending the free and liberal Collège de France. There was also a second request for payment of gambling debts he had incurred during the past year. She doubted that he had been able to clear them before sailing. His insouciant charm and his appearance, that of a gentleman dandy, both tickled her pride and fueled her ire.

Jean-Philippe felt her disapproval in the quality of her embrace, and his pleasure in his homecoming was threatened by memories of the adolescent despair that had attacked him in moments when he imagined his mother hated him. He thrust that youthful shadow behind him. He had become a man in Paris, after all. Why else had she sent him there? Mon dieu, his mother had no one else!

Except Melodie, of course. What a beauty she had become!

Leaving the servants to gather his baggage and take the horses to the livery stable to be fed and watered, they walked across the square to a restaurant for a meal. During the stroll they met acquaintances who stopped to greet both Jean-Philippe and Jeffery and welcome them home.

In the restaurant they were met by an old friend of Angèle's, Henri Devaux. He was an attractive silver-haired man of great distinction who, Grandmére Roget had once told Melodie, had been a suitor for Cousin Angèle's hand before she married Jean-Philippe's father.

"Ah, we have the Triad back," he greeted the three young people. "Now our balls will be lively again!" His appreciative eyes slanted a teasing glance at Melodie. "You'll have competition from our other Creole belles for the attention of these young scholars," he warned her.

"Melodie can hold her own against any I've seen," Jeffery said, smiling at her.

"My sweet cousin could hold her own in Paris," Jean-Philippe told M'sieu Devaux.

Melodie, with a hand tucked under an arm of each of them, laughed and said, "My chevaliers!" She was happier than she had been since they left.

Angèle invited M'sieu Devaux to dine with them. He and Grandpère Roget consulted together and ordered a wine to be served with the succulent shrimp rémoulade and the gently fried oysters from Barataria—so tender they melted in the mouth—which Jean-Philippe expressed a hunger for. The meal became a merry one.

When they returned to La Sorcellerie, Jeffery would have ordered his horse, but Jean-Philippe insisted that he remain to see the gifts he had brought. All the house servants had lined up on the front galérie to welcome him, and when they had finished bobbing their heads to him, the children came up, their scrubbed and shining black faces split by shy grins. That ritual over, he and Jeffery shared brandies in the salon and Melodie and Angèle sipped coffee. Jean-Philippe presented Jeffery with a handsome dueling sword, with a blade of the best Toledo steel so flexible it could be bent double. He basked in Jeffery's pleasure in the weapon, and Melodie's heart swelled with love for both of them.

For Melodie he had a small jewel casket which played a tinkly minuet when the lid was lifted, a gift that utterly delighted her. He had also brought a collection of beautiful fans for both her and his mother, and Melodie amused them all by fluttering a fan in each hand as she waltzed about the salon, wickedly imitating some of the grandes dames of New Orleans.

"And for Maman," Jean-Philippe said, drawing a delicately tinted porcelain shepherdess out of its voluminous wrappings and presenting it to her.

Angèle stared at the figurine in shock, making no move to take it. "Why did you choose that for me?"

The shepherdess was exquisite, Melodie thought. In one hand

she held a crook fluttering a fragile ribbon, while the other lifted her draped skirt. A wide hat tilted back from her porcelain features. In the small silence Melodie watched the expectancy fade from Jean-Philippe's face and felt his lurch of surprise.

"Don't you like it?"

Angèle, fighting panic, told herself it could not be a coincidence. How much did he remember? Had he deliberately chosen it to tell her that he remembered that day in Paris when she had given him a figurine very like the one she took from his hand, a toy he treasured all the month-long voyage to Louisiana? Could he possibly have been in touch with Minette over there?

"Why?" she demanded again.

Jean-Philippe shrugged. "I thought it was something you'd like. It reminded me of you."

"A *shepherdess* reminded you of me?" She made her tone self-mocking. "I think it must have reminded you of the time you broke a figurine very similar to this one."

There was a challenge in her tone that Jean-Philippe interpreted as anger. He flushed. "Then it's high time I replaced it, isn't it?"

His tone was so stiff that Melodie leaned forward to open the lid of her jewel casket, but the mincing tinkle of music only heightened the forced quality of her voice. "She's so pretty, Jean-Philippe! And you couldn't have found anything more delightful than this music box!"

"Or this beautiful sword!" Jeffery exclaimed.

Angèle looked at the wicked shining steel and said soberly, "I hope you never have to use it." She set the shepherdess down on the small table beside her, rose from her chair, and left the salon.

"Damn her!" Jean-Philippe muttered. "I'm never able to please her."

"Well, two out of three isn't bad," Jeffery said, laughing and flexing the Toledo blade. They made plans to meet again the next day. Jeffery took his leave and ordered his horse from the stables.

"Why do you and Cousin Angèle always get off on the wrong foot with each other?" Melodie demanded when she and Jean-Philippe were alone.

"Damned if I know." He sounded depressed.

She sensed his deep disappointment and ached for him. Why had Cousin Angèle spoiled his homecoming? "Do you remember breaking a figurine of hers?"

"Oh, I don't doubt that I did. That's probably why I was reminded of her when I saw this thing. But I don't remember it, no. Mon dieu, why should she bring it up now? What does it matter after all these years?"

Melodie put her hand on his. "It doesn't matter at all. Cousin Angèle was probably upset about something else. She works very hard, you know."

Jean-Philippe smiled and squeezed her hand.

Late that night Melodie was wakened from sleep by loud voices. She had retired after Cousin Angèle had requested that Jean-Philippe join her in her office to discuss his future. She recognized their voices now, carried up to her chamber from the room directly below it through the open shutters. Lying in her cocoon of mosquito netting in the moonlit room, she heard Jean-Philippe shout, "Why did you send me to Paris, then, if you expected me to live like a worker's son? My father gambled. You've told me so."

"Your father *won!*"

Oh, Cousin Angèle! Melodie thought. She was fair with the servants, with the cane workers, with her beautiful horses—why was she so hard on Jean-Philippe? Melodie rolled over in her bed and covered her ears. The loud argument went on for a while longer, ending with a slammed door. Neither of them came up the stairs before Melodie went back to sleep.

In the first and largest of the slave cabins built from bricks the slaves themselves had made, Mimi heard the shouting. Jean-Baptiste, who was up with the sun and in bed shortly after it set, was sleeping. Mimi rolled carefully out of the bed without waking him and padded on bare feet to the door. She opened it and sat on the stoop in the dark doorway. The moon was high, throwing a white light on the stones that marked the pathway to the big house.

Lights shone from Angèle's study, between the jalousies on the lower galérie. Mimi listened unashamed to the quarrel between her mistress and Michie Jean-Philippe. She had suspected before Jean-Philippe left for Paris that he was Minette's child. Angèle's attempt to conceal her panic when Mimi asked if he could look for her daughter had slipped that notion into her head. She had not dared give it voice, even to Jean-Baptiste. But sometimes she felt the secret swell inside her until she wanted to burst out laughing. Was it possible that the future master of La Sorcellerie and all its sweet wealth was her own grandson, son of her daughter by Michie Roget? She burned with curiosity, but guessed that only two living people, her daughter and her mistress, knew the truth.

And what about Minette? Mimi recalled Madame Astride receiving the sorrowful letter from Angèle telling how Minette had "run away." Had she really gone to secretly give birth? Mimi wondered. Jean-Philippe thought she had been his nurse. Had Minette posed as wet nurse for her own infant, then?

If Minette was his mother, obviously he did not know it. He had the unconscious arrogance of someone who had grown up with no lack of slaves to obey his every whim, no matter how crazy or what time of day or night. She felt the laughter rise again, silently shaking her belly.

Listening to the voices coming through the shutters of the big house office, she heard her own name. They were not shouting now, but they were still angry.

". . . one more thing! Did you go looking for Mimi's daughter? Don't lie to me, Jean-Philippe! I know she begged you!"

"Yes, dear Maman, she did. I didn't go looking, but Minette found me."

"What?"

"Minette is a notorious courtesan, Maman."

A low groan escaped Mimi. *Ah, my baby!*

Jean-Philippe's voice was deliberately taunting. "She found me in the Café des Mille Colonnes, very drunk, and she took me home with her."

Mimi started up. The silence in the lighted room at the end of the path was so loud that it buzzed in her head. She knew that Angèle must have swallowed her breath, because she certainly had. Her suspicion seemed confirmed, but she no longer felt like laughing. Instead she felt a dark foreboding, like dread.

"I must say she is doing very well for herself," she heard Jean-Philippe say.

Mimi wrapped her arms around herself and rocked in pain, remembering the love Michie Roget had lavished on the quadroon daughter he could not acknowledge but who had captured his heart.

She sat in the shadowy doorway long after the candles in the big house had been snuffed and the oil lamps extinguished, and her shock lessened as she mulled over the words she had overheard. She had heard the youthful bravado in Jean-Philippe's angry tone. He was showing off for Madame Angèle, she told herself.

When she silently returned to Jean-Baptiste's bed, she was convinced she knew the truth. She thought it very likely that Minette was Jean-Philippe's mother, and that it was as a mother and not as a courtesan that Minette had taken him home.

She vowed that nobody, no time, would ever hear the secret from her.

In the morning Melodie found no one in the dining room when she went down for breakfast. "Where is everybody?" she asked the maid who brought her coffee and rolls.

"Madame hasn't come down, and michie rang for his breakfast from the *garçonnière*."

So Jean-Philippe had already moved into the bachelor quarters that had been built for him. Remembering the pleasure Cousin Angèle had taken in planning the octagonal *garçonnière* and how she had furnished it, occasionally sending Jean-Philippe a commission to buy some piece of furniture she wanted for it, Melodie was even more bewildered by the anger that had flared between them yesterday over a trifle like Jean-Philippe's gift. She finished her roll and went out on the galérie, down the steps, and across the lawn to find him.

The *garçonnière* was a quaint two-story replica of the *pigeonnier*, with a dome for its roof. Its lower floor had been furnished for Jean-Philippe's personal use; the upstairs provided guest rooms when friends and relatives stayed overnight.

Brilliant cardinals and their lovely, more restrained mates flew up from the stoop where they had been feeding on crumbs before the open door to his sitting room. Melodie knocked lightly on the doorjamb and entered. Jean-Philippe was dressed and breakfasting from a large silver tray set on a table before his chair. He sprang up and came to meet her, giving her a hug and a quick kiss. "Good morning, sweet cousin! Have you come to lick my wounds?"

"I couldn't help hearing last night. You and Cousin Angèle were shouting."

He grimaced. "A loving welcome home. Come in. Have you had breakfast?"

"Just now, thanks."

He went to a small cupboard which held some cups and glassware, and took down a saucer and a cup. He filled it from the silver coffee pot on his tray, and when she was seated, handed it to her.

"Why is Cousin Angèle so angry?" She added quickly, "Don't tell me if it's something I shouldn't know!"

He laughed. "It's nothing, really. She is furious about having to pay some gambling debts I left in Paris. Mon dieu, she can afford them! From what I heard aboard ship, sugar planters are all rolling in wealth."

Melodie sat back and frankly enjoyed looking at him. He was wearing a loose white shirt with no cravat, and his strong tan neck rose out of its open collar with the kind of physical beauty she associated with Cousin Angèle's thoroughbred horses. His hair was soft and dark, curling a little over his ears and down behind them, and his eyes had a luminosity she found oddly moving—they were almost as moist as tears.

"Please don't quarrel with Cousin Angèle," she begged him. "If you only knew how she has been looking forward to your return, fussing over preparing your rooms and Petra's menus. She loves you very much."

"She has strange ways of showing it."

Melodie thought it prudent to change the subject. "Mimi is dying to ask you if you found her long-lost daughter. She has been able to think of nothing else since Cousin Angèle told her you were coming home."

"I found her. Or rather, she found me." He told her how he had goaded his mother the night before, confessing that the night he had spent in Minette's apartment had been wholly innocent.

Melodie laughed, but said, "Oh, Jean-Philippe, for shame!"

"Actually, Minette saved me from making a complete ass—perhaps even a corpse!—of myself in a duel," he confessed. "I'll tell Maman about that when I get over being angry with her."

"Is Minette really a courtesan?"

"Undoubtedly. And a very high-class one, I'd guess."

"I want to know what she wore and everything about her apartment. Everything!" Melodie demanded.

"What's so special about her? There are plenty of quadroon courtesans in New Orleans! I've been trying to remember Minette, and I think I do. Hazily, that is. I rather think she must have been my wet nurse."

"A courtesan wet nurse!" Melodie exclaimed with a scandalized giggle. "No wonder you torment your poor maman."

"Is she still angry?"

"She had breakfast in her room, and she hasn't left for her usual field inspection."

"That's another thing," Jean-Philippe said sourly. "She wants me to begin riding with her or with Jean-Baptiste every morning. Today we're inspecting the new sugar mill she's building. I'm afraid that's going to interfere with my social life. I rather fancy getting to bed about the time they start their ride."

"In that case I'll have to ride with Jeffery, because I like to ride at dawn too."

He groaned, and Melodie laughed.

"You needn't worry about your social life. There are dozens of balls on our schedule," she assured him. "Cousin Angèle is giving an enormous one to welcome you home. But I'll not tell you about any of them until Jeffery comes. I'm looking forward to showing you both off."

They smiled at each other. Nothing had changed, Melodie thought happily. The closeness they had always enjoyed was still there. The physical maturity she sensed in him added something to it, a little secret glow. She had been lonely without him, and it was wonderful to experience again the extraordinary way they read each other's thoughts.

But this time Jean-Philippe was not sharing her thought. His mind was lingering on something he had said earlier. Had Minette been his wet nurse? It was just a feeling he had; he couldn't expect to remember something like that. But the impression had brought a jarring new thought to his mind.

Why had his mother used a wet nurse? Could it mean he was adopted? But he had been told often how much he resembled his father. Mon dieu! Was he *illegitimate?* The child of a mistress his father had insisted his mother accept? Was that why he and Maman were so often "at odds," as Melodie put it?

He pushed the unsettling thought away. Many wealthy women used a wet nurse in order not to be inconvenienced, didn't they?

Chapter 17

*L*A Sorcellerie was a glowing jewel in the summer dusk, light spilling from all its wide open French doors onto its galéries, music wafting out into the warm evening, and the mingled scents of jasmine and honeysuckle drifting up between its slender columns from the gardens below.

The drive under the oaks from the bayou road to the mansion was strung with paper lanterns to light the way for the arriving carriages. At the steps young black boys dressed all in white ran up to stand at the horses' heads while the guests stepped down, and then lead their drivers to the stable yard. Guests were met at the wide door by a dignified Ouma, who directed them to their hostess. In the salon Angèle awaited them with Jean-Philippe by her side.

To Melodie, standing at Jean-Philippe's other side, with Jeffery beside her forming the familiar Triad, it was an evening she knew was being etched in her memory for all time because it was utterly perfect. Candles winking from the glittering crystal chandelier overhead gleamed on a rainbow of silken colors worn by the women, many with tiaras of flowers in their hair.

The scents of flowers and perfumes mingled exotically in the moist warm air. Cousin Angèle's two young footmen, Loti and Ti' Mouche—looking quite impressive in their buff livery—moved among the guests, carrying large silver trays holding glasses of punch.

Melodie felt very feminine standing between Jean-Philippe and Jeffery in a simple white dress with an empire bodice, its skirt encircled by rows of small ruffles. They were resplendent in their tight-fitting white breeches and creamy waistcoats, Jean-Philippe in a coat of dove gray and Jeffery wearing royal blue, which deepened the blue of his eyes. She laughed and teased the guests who came by, confident and lighthearted in the love that surrounded her now that the three of them were together again.

Later, when Angèle signaled the orchestra and said, "It's time to begin the dancing, Jean-Philippe," he turned to Melodie. But Jeffery said good-humoredly, "Surely you mean to lead with your mother?" and offered his arm to Melodie.

Jean-Philippe scowled briefly, but bowed and said, "Maman?" The guests applauded as he and Angèle moved out on the floor which was cleared for them. Jeffery waited until they had circled the room, then led Melodie out. She was still surprised at how much taller he was, and felt a quiver of excitement as he placed his arm around her. Throwing back her shoulders, she smiled up into his eyes as she pointed her toe to the right, ready for his signal to begin the waltz.

For Angèle, who was pleased to discover that Jean-Philippe had become an excellent dancer, the little exchange between him and his friend had opened a door to the past. She was reminded of the ball she had given to introduce his father to their friends when he was courting Melodie's mother, how he had turned to her when she asked him to lead the dancing and she had refused, insisting he dance first with Clothilde.

As she moved gracefully to the music, she wondered what Philippe would think of his son if he could see him now. He was so much like him, tall and slenderly built, but very masculine, with his father's beautiful face and aristocratic carriage and manners. Unfortunately he seemed to care as little as his father had about sugar culture. And he *must* care! Angèle thought. He must be made ready to take over La Sorcellerie when she was ready to pass it on.

After adroit questioning of Melodie, in whom Jean-Philippe confided things he would not speak of to her, Angèle's worries about his encounter with Minette had quieted somewhat. After all, Minette would not want to disturb their arrangement any more than she herself would. But it annoyed her to be reminded of Minette's claim on him. For years she had been persuading herself that Jean-Philippe was her own. She could almost believe that Minette was a surrogate mother, little more than a wet nurse for her son.

And what would Clothilde think, she wondered as Jeffery whirled Melodie past them, if she could see the lovely young woman her child had become? Would she approve of Jeffery? He was so obviously deeply in love. A charming couple.

Angèle swayed and whirled in Jean-Philippe's expert arms, finding it gratifying how intently the young women among her guests were watching them. Inevitably one of them would take him away from her. Which one? She would have something to do with his choice, she was resolved on that, and in her mind began going over the eligible girls she had invited tonight. She would have to be subtle. Jean-Philippe had inherited some of the Roget pride and willfulness her father had given her.

"Thank you, Maman." The music had stopped, and Jean-Philippe was smiling down at her. "It's a lovely ball."

She pulled his face down and kissed his cheek. "Welcome home, my dear."

Across the room Jeffery had not released Melodie from his loose embrace. "You're going to marry me, aren't you, Melodie?"

"I expect I shall," she said fondly.

His arms tightened around her and his eyes glowed.

"Jeffery!" she warned in a whisper.

"May I speak to Madame la marquise? May we set a date?"

She hesitated. "Won't that break up the Triad? I'm afraid Jean-Philippe won't feel comfortable with us anymore."

"I'm sorry to disappoint you, darling, but marriage was invented for two people, not three."

"I know, isn't it horrid?"

"Minx!"

"Jeffery, Jean-Philippe is just home. Can't we just . . . have fun for a little while?"

Jeffery looked down into her vivid face, saw the love shining in her eyes, and sighed with mingled joy and frustration. "I see I'll have to find a girl for Jean-Philippe."

Everyone said it was the gayest spring season anyone could remember, as balls and treasure hunts and breakfast rides were given by friends of both Jean-Philippe and Jeffery. The warm nights rang with music and laughter, with shouts and the thunder of galloping horses, but the days lengthened and grew warmer. Melodie slept all day with nothing but a sheet covering her and her hair braided to keep it away from her damp skin, only reviving after the sun sank low enough to cast long shadows across the lawn, when she arose to take a cooling bath and dress for dinner and the evening.

In the past few weeks summer heat had settled heavily over the river and bayous. The parade of balls and soirées slowed, to Jeffery's relief, for American businessmen had not adopted the Creole custom of a long sleepy luncheon with wine and a p'ti' siesta; he was often snatching sleep in the carriage as he rode to New Orleans with his father.

Life slowed for everyone except the planters, who had to watch over their slow-growing crop with unceasing vigil. "The cane can never be allowed to fully ripen here, as it does in the West Indies," Angèle told Jean-Philippe. Right now the cane workers were chopping out the weeds which grew with jungle ferocity. In July it would be "laid by" and the cane workers could augment the force working to complete the new brick sugarhouse before the harvest season.

"We must continue to check the cane daily," Angèle said, "because we must choose a time for cutting when the sugar content is as high as possible without risking storm damage. When the cane begins to tassel, there will be a lavender haze over the field. Then . . . ah, then, you begin to gamble with the weather!"

Jean-Philippe sometimes had a little difficulty staying awake on his mount. The heat shimmered on the cane like white gold, blinding his gritty eyes. His mother's voice was a buzzing in his head. "That field over there—see it? We'll be cutting it first."

"Beautiful," he murmured. But when he looked, wavy ripples of green and white danced before him and he saw images. He was being offered a long cold drink . . . he was naked, stepping into a cool bath . . . Melodie was in the tub, holding up creamy white arms, her breasts two perfect mounds. . . .

"Cane is a thirsty crop," his mother was saying, "needing constant rain. If we don't get it, we must flood it from the bayou." Yes, yes, he thought, but let's get it over so I can go back to my rooms and fall across my bed. Those two cold winters in Paris had made him vulnerable to this tropical sun, and after an hour under it he felt murderous.

The last ball of the season was the one Jeffery's father gave at Bellemont to repay the many social obligations his son's return had entailed. Melodie walked through the rooms of her old home with great interest, seeing herself as mistress here, listing in her mind the furniture of her mother's and her grandmother's, which she would return to the spot in which it remained in her memory, after she and Jeffery were married.

The night was very warm. Only the youngest guests danced; their elders sat on the galéries and were fanned by black children while they drank punch and talked lazily about cockfights and stallions, Paris vogue, Madame la marquise's new sugarhouse, and the price of sugar.

Inside the ballroom there was none of the usual gaiety and high spirits; instead the atmosphere was that of a drugged sensuality. The beat of the music had a slow tension. Played by black musicians whose faces dripped perspiration, its rhythm was torpid and smoldering. Melodie felt languorous and ripe as Jean-Philippe turned her in slow wide circles, and she became very conscious of the warmth of his hand at the small of her back.

"It's too hot to dance," she murmured, and yet she wanted to go on losing herself in the pleasant languor spreading from the small of her back down through her legs in slow, sweet waves.

Suddenly she was jerked rudely from Jean-Philippe's arms and looked up into Jeffery's angry face. "Damn you, Shawn!" Jeffery said in English, then in French. "Come outside, if you please. I want to talk to you." They left her standing there. A little dazed by the suddenness of it, she followed them through the open long windows in time to see them exchange a few words, then straddle the rail and drop to the grass below. She did not hear what Jeffery said, his voice was low, but she was across the wide galérie in time to see Jean-Philippe swing at him.

She cried out, "Somebody stop them!" Immediately there was a rush to the galérie rail.

A house servant came running across the grass. Charles Archer appeared around the corner from the front galérie, where he had been sitting. He called sternly, *"Gentlemen!"*

Melodie was elbowing her way through the guests crowding her at the railing, and running for the front galérie and the steps to the lawn. When she reached the two of them, Archer's servant was already there, and a small group of spectators had gathered around them. Jean-Philippe was saying, grimly, "It seems you'll have sooner need of that damascene blade than I thought!"

"Please!" Melodie cried, putting herself between them and catching each by an arm.

Jeffery looked pale. He looked down at Melodie's anguished face, then said, "No, Shawn, I'll not challenge you. We've been friends too long."

Jean-Philippe glanced down at Melodie, then back at Jeffery. After a tense moment he relaxed. "You're right. It's too hot to fight."

Jeffery laughed and put out his hand. When Jean-Philippe took it, Melodie joined in the relieved laughter of the small audience that had gathered around them.

When they returned to the galérie, they found that Cousin Angèle had ordered her carriage. There was no opportunity to talk privately with Jeffery, and Melodie could only answer the anxiety and the remorse in his look with a gentle pressure of her fingers as he took her hand.

As they drove away, Cousin Angèle asked Jean-Philippe, "What was that unseemly fuss about?"

"A simple misunderstanding, Maman."

Angèle said nothing more, but later, after Jean-Philippe had left them to go to his rooms in the *garçonnière,* she asked Melodie, "Why did those two quarrel?"

"I don't know, Cousin Angèle," she replied, but felt very uncomfortable, and could not meet Angèle's eyes.

"You must know something, my dear. The three of you are thick as thieves. What do you *think* they quarreled about?"

Melodie shook her head, feeling sad. She knew only that the beautiful closeness the three of them had shared was ruptured, and it seemed a beginning of the end of something very important to her.

"Mon dieu, you and Jean-Philippe are both adults now! You need no longer feel this big-sister responsibility for what he does. And another thing! It is childish of you to insist on keeping this threesome up, childish and selfish."

Melodie looked at her, appalled. Warm blood flooded her cheeks.

"Answer one question for me. You do love Jeffery Archer, Melodie? You've waited long enough for him!"

"Yes, Cousin Angèle."

"Have you told him so?"

"Yes."

In an exasperated voice Angèle said, "No wonder he feels frustrated. I think perhaps Jeffery is growing weary of having your cousin following the two of you around everywhere you go. I suggest that we decide on a wedding date and announce your betrothal. That will not only give Jeffery the time alone with you that he wants, but it will relieve the minds of several girls who have been seeking Jean-Philippe's undivided attention. Don't you agree?"

Melodie lowered her gaze. "Yes, Cousin Angèle."

"Ask Jeffery to call on me." Angèle turned away, her mind already moving to something else.

That night Melodie lay awake under her mosquito net and watched the moon shadows wheel across her wall. She had never imagined jealousy could threaten the Triad. She'd thought Jeffery understood how necessary Jean-Philippe was to her. "Blood calls to blood?" he'd teased her, when she'd been talking about how uncannily she and Jean-Philippe were able to communicate without speaking. Did blood make a difference? After all, their mothers *were* first cousins.

Jeffery was not the only one who was jealous. She had felt the strangest qualm when Cousin Angèle had mentioned the girls seeking Jean-Philippe's attention. The trouble was, she thought, turning restlessly on her damp sheets, that she loved both men.

Both! So deeply! Was it natural to love one's cousin as deeply as she loved Jean-Philippe?

Tonight some serious questions had been raised in her mind. She remembered Jeffery saying, when she'd claimed she loved them both, *I'd hope your love for your cousin is different,* and how she'd said of course it was. But tonight, dancing with Jean-Philippe, she'd felt stirred in the same exciting way that Jeffery's kisses stirred her.

Perhaps Cousin Angèle was right: it was time she married.

The next morning was hot and muggy, with the gray clouds rolling in from the gulf forecasting a summer storm. Angèle was edgy about the weather, fearing the lush stalks of ripening cane would be beaten down by a rain too heavy before it was time for cutting. She pointed out the danger and the possible losses to Jean-Philippe as he rode beside her.

Jean-Philippe had wakened with a headache, feeling a painful remorse for swinging at Jeffery the night before. His head still ached, and the air, heavy with moisture, pressed down on it. He regretted the quarrel, and he regretted upsetting Melodie. They were the two people in all the world he cared most for. He was also feeling guilty about an erotic dream he'd had about Melodie. It was not the first time it had happened, and remembering that last waltz with her the night before, which had probably triggered his dreams, he suspected that Melodie had known what holding her and inhaling her perfume and body scents was doing to him, as they moved to the sensual music in that hot room.

Had he imagined her response? No, he couldn't have, if Jeffery had sensed it. *Merde,* but it was a damnable thing to do to her! To both of them. He would have to get control of himself. He resolved to go into New Orleans alone that night. He'd heard there were decent casinos. Or maybe there would be an octaroon ball with all the lovely mixed-race virgins on display with their mamans. Could he afford an octaroon mistress on the allowance maman granted him? Then he remembered that he and Jeffery were obligated to escort his mother and Melodie to the Theatre d'Orléans that night to hear a touring singer, and he groaned inwardly.

He had heard little of Angèle's speech about the cane, but

when she referred obliquely to last night's quarrel, he jerked to attention.

"Perhaps it's a mistake to try to revive your three-cornered friendship anyway," she was saying. "I know Melodie is sentimental about it, but it seems a bit childish now. Jeffery doesn't need your help in wooing Melodie, I'm sure."

Through a sudden, blinding rage Jean-Philippe stared at the trembling tassels dusting the green and pale gold stalks. "Quite right, Maman," he said savagely.

She sensed his anger. All at once she felt a certain helplessness, and with it a great unease.

"I'm going back to the house," she said, turning abruptly. "Will you ride over to the mill and see how they're getting along with it? You'll find Père Baptiste there, with his crew."

He spurred his horse and rode away from her without speaking.

While he was in France, Jean-Baptiste had become Père Baptiste, the patriarch of the slave quarters, and his mother had picked up the title, probably from old Mimi and Ouma. Now that Ouma had been made secretary and bookkeeper to the plantation, he irritated Jean-Philippe with his quiet self-confidence. In a few minutes he was approaching the yard where, after the cutting, the great millstone would still be turned by mules pulling a beam around in an endless circle to crush the stalks of cane fed to it. From the grinders wooden troughs would carry the juice to a series of iron pots—each smaller than the last, set over wood fires—in which it would be boiled down into cane syrup and finally into half-crystallized brown sugar. Père Baptiste was watching a half-dozen slaves, stripped to their waists, who were completing the brick walls going up around the mill. More bricks were being made at a brick kiln, a little distance away but still close enough so that the fire heating the oven added to the heat of the already sweltering day.

"Good morning, michie," Père Baptiste said, touching the black felt hat he wore, rain or shine.

The half-Spanish overseer had gradually come to resemble a bull, with his grizzled head set forward on his massive shoulders by the slight hump of age that had developed in his back. Ouma was with him.

Jean-Philippe nodded, and his nostrils distended when Ouma

merely nodded also. He thinks he's white, Jean-Philippe told himself angrily. His head was pounding, and his stomach contracted from the odors of the swamp, concentrated by the heavy humidity. He had forgotten, too, how the sweetish odor of boiling cane juice clung to the mill from harvest to harvest, soaked into the woods of the apparatus during innumerable boilings.

Ouma was familiar with Jean-Philippe's childhood, and knew about his temper. He now looked up at the arrogant and hostile young man on his fine horse, and recognized his rage. Ouma thought of the conversation he had had with his mother in the kitchen over coffee early that morning. Already Mimi knew every detail of the quarrel between michie and his close friend the night before. She had them from the maid who had ridden over to Bellemont with madame and m'selle to freshen their coiffures when they arrived. Its beginning had been witnessed by the musicians and speculated on endlessly after the playing ended, when they were fed in the kitchen. His mother had been extraordinarily distressed by the story of the fight.

Jean-Philippe's restless horse had sensed his mood. He reared on his hind legs, moving sidewise, and his pawing hoof grazed Père Baptiste's black hat.

Père Baptiste stepped back, looking startled. Ouma sprang fo ward and grabbed the horse's bridle. "Watch it!" he said sharply, and the other slaves straightened to stare, stopping work.

"Back off," Ouma advised Jean-Philippe. "You're too close to the workers."

Jean-Philippe glared. "I don't take orders, I give them!"

"Oui, michie, but if you can't control your horse, you should not come so close to the work," Ouma reproved him gently.

His paternal tone snapped Jean-Philippe's control. He said, furiously, "Let go of my bridle, you black bastard!" and raising his whip, slashed it down across Ouma's face.

"No!" Père Baptiste bellowed and started toward them. Jean-Philippe, seeing through a red haze the old man charging forward like an angry bull, raised his whip again and brought it down across the rounded shoulders, knocking off the overseer's felt hat. There was a chorus of protesting cries from the angry, frightened workers. Ouma lunged forward with his arms up before his face, shoving Père Baptiste aside and putting himself between the older man and the horse. He staggered backward as Jean-Philippe, beside himself, rained blows on his head and shoulders, missing him as often as he struck him as his frightened horse danced about, but ripping his shirt from his shoulders and laying his flesh open in half a dozen deep cuts.

The overseer, as enraged now as Jean-Philippe, bellowed like the bull he resembled and ran at the horse's head. The animal screamed and reared back so suddenly that Jean-Philippe had to grab his reins with both hands, dropping his whip, and hang on as his mount galloped wild-eyed for the stables.

Ouma staggered and Père Baptiste caught him in his arms and eased his fall to the ground. Then he sent one of the workers for a piece of canvas they could use for a litter.

The need to calm his frightened horse brought Jean-Philippe out of his red rage. When he dismounted finally at the stables, he was lucid, but trembling. He ordered the grooms to walk his mount and wipe him down, and lurched to the *garçonnière*. In his rooms he poured himself a drink, downed it quickly, then threw himself across his bed. He was drenched with perspiration. *Melodie . . . Melodie . . .*

Chapter 18

*M*ELODIE dreamed she heard Mimi scream. With her heart beating in wild alarm, she opened her eyes to bright light. The sun was long up. But the screaming was real; it went on and on, a mindless repetition of shock and grief. Over it she heard other voices, and Cousin Angèle's quick steps on the polished floor of the downstairs hall, leaving her office. Melodie slid out of bed and snatched up a light cotton robe, pulling it on as she ran barefoot for the stairs.

The screams, reduced to shrill sobs now, were coming from the rear of the house. She could hear Cousin Angèle's shocked voice and Père Baptiste's deep rumble.

Melodie turned at the foot of the stairs and ran out on the rear galérie. Two cane workers came through the door of Ouma's room in the kitchen annex, across the rear galérie from the pantry. One of them was carrying a bloodstained tarp. They glanced sidewise at her from under lowered eyelids, their faces sullen and angry. The small room still seemed filled with people. Melodie glimpsed Ouma lying on his bed. His forehead was split open to the bone and Mimi was wiping the streaming blood from his eyes. His shirt was in ribbons, revealing bleeding cuts on his café-au-lait shoulders.

"Who did this?" Cousin Angèle demanded.

"Michie Jean-Philippe," Père Baptiste said reluctantly, and Melodie gasped. "I tried to stop it, madame, but michie raised his whip on me. Then—" His voice cracked. "Ouma stepped before me."

Melodie could not believe what she was hearing. *Jean-Philippe* had done this terrible thing? And to *Ouma?*

Her cousin's lips tightened, but she said calmly, to Père Baptiste, "Send for Aimée. Tell her to bring her needle. She will have to take stitches."

"Oui, madame." Père Baptiste left the room to get the cane worker's wife who helped the seamstress.

"Dr. Boudin?" Melodie spoke impulsively.

Cousin Angèle turned and saw her. "Dr. Boudin won't come for one of them. Melodie, get my box of medicines from my office. You know where it is. And tell Petra we'll need hot water and cloths."

Melodie turned and ran to the kitchen, where she found a perspiring Petra already heating water. Then she returned to the house, took the medicine box from the shelf in the office, and hurried back to the annex.

"Thank you," Cousin Angèle said. Aimée was just coming in. "Melodie, you find Jean-Philippe and tell him I will see him in my office in half an hour."

Melodie left, and still barefoot, ran over the prickly grass to the *garçonnière.* She knocked on the door, and when there was no response, opened it. His sitting room was empty. "Jean-Philippe?" she called.

Her heart, beating hard and fast, was the only sound she heard. She crossed the room, pushed open the door of his bedroom, and saw him lying prone on the bed. She cried, "How could you do that to Ouma? Oh, Jean-Philippe, how could you?"

When he sat up, she saw the misery in his face and her heart twisted with pity. Whatever he had done, he was not happy about it. She moved to the bed and sat down beside him, holding him and comforting him, as she had when they were children.

234

He moaned and put his arms around her waist, laying his head against her breast.

Until that moment she had forgotten that she had practically nothing on under her light robe. Now with the warmth of his hands on her back and his cheek heavy against her breast, she felt a stab of pure desire move down through her body. She stiffened.

Abruptly his hands fell away and he lifted his head. "Mon dieu, Melodie, go and put some clothes on! Did you just get out of bed?"

"Mimi's screams wakened me," she said, her voice as unnatural as his. "Cousin Angèle sent me. She wants to see you in her office in half an hour."

"Mon dieu," he said again, falling back on the bed.

Melodie stood up. "You'll go?" she asked anxiously.

"For my tongue-lashing? Oh, yes, I'll go."

She ran back across the lawn to the house, tears streaming down her cheeks.

Jean-Philippe lay without moving for fifteen minutes, then got up and poured himself another drink. He sluiced his face with water and combed his hair. He was waiting in her office when his mother came in, her face set. Energy radiated from her, but it was the energy of anger. She was forty-two years old and still a handsome woman, Jean-Philippe thought, with detachment. He was aware that the whole parish considered her an eccentric, but socially acceptable because she was a rich one. He saw her as a dragon.

She remained standing. After a moment he seated himself defiantly.

"Slaves have never been flogged on La Sorcellerie," she said. "My father wouldn't allow it, and I won't have it. I want you to understand that, Jean-Philippe."

"I'm sorry, Maman. I lost my temper."

She stared fixedly at him for a few seconds. "Why did you pick Ouma?"

"I didn't 'pick him.' He got in my way."

"He got in your way," she mocked him. "Ouma will bear the scars you gave him all of his life—if we can keep infections from killing him. Have you forgotten how, when you were a child, he followed you everywhere you went to keep you from harm? He adored you! Mon dieu, when are you going to become a man, control your temper, and think of others?"

"Do you?" he demanded, straightening up and leaning forward. "Do you know what it's like for me to live on a plantation that by law should be mine but is run by my mother? My *mother*, a woman who not only takes everything into her own hands, but keeps me on a tight rein! Mon dieu, how do you expect me to become a man?"

Her look was incredulous. "Are you saying that you think you should manage La Sorcellerie when you are reluctant even to ride with me each morning to inspect the crop?"

"No, Maman, that is not what I'm saying. I've always hated the cane. I hate the heat and the sweating slaves; I hate the flies that swarm to the crushing, and the smell of boiling syrup sickens me!"

His attack made him sound so eerily like Philippe that she was put off balance. "Then what do you want?"

"What I'm saying, dear Maman, is that I'm tired of being held like a bug under your thumb." He stood up and twisted his thumb on her desk in graphic illustration. "You don't squash me, you just hold me tightly enough so that I can feebly wave my legs but can't get away. Well, *no more!*"

Angèle sank into her chair, her face paling.

"You had better send a note over to Bellemont if you want M'sieu Archer to escort you to the theater tonight. Jeffery is coming over anyway, isn't he? Me, I'm going in to New Orleans." He added, with emphasis, "I don't know when I'll be back."

He walked out, leaving her shocked and staring. After a few moments her mind began working again. Word of Ouma's beating would move swiftly up and down the river, she knew. If she and Melodie did not appear at the theater tonight, the story would be exaggerated and distorted out of recognition. Ouma would be accused of trying to murder them in their beds, or of raping Melodie, or some such nonsense. She pulled a piece of parchment toward her, dipped her pen in ink, and scrawled across it, "Dear Charles, I need your help!"

Then she paused, thinking how natural it was to call on Charles Archer for help. Now she wondered if it would not have been better for Jean-Philippe if she had married Charles when he begged her to. At the time she felt that she could not betray Jean-Philippe's secret, and she could not marry Charles without telling him. If Jean-Philippe had had Charles for a step-father . . .

It was too late now for second thoughts.

A sound roused her from her disturbing memories. She watched through her window as Jean-Philippe rode her new bay gelding past the front of the house and down the drive to the bayou road. She had still been emotionally bound to his father, that was the chief reason she had not married Charles— bound by a crippling cauldron of emotions similar to what she was feeling right now for Philippe's son: something that was neither love nor hate, but a boiling mixture stronger than either.

She picked up her pen and wrote: "More specifically, I need an escort for the theater tonight. I shall be forever grateful if you will come with Jeffery when he calls for us this evening."

That should sufficiently intrigue Charles's curiosity so that if he didn't have a prior engagement, he would come. She rang for Ti' Mouche and gave him the message to send to Bellemont, then went back to see how Ouma was.

Mimi had given him laudanum and he was sleeping. "Is he feverish?" Angèle asked.

"It's too soon to tell." Mimi had quieted, but tears were still rolling down her dusty cheeks. Her thoughts were still roiling, almost incoherent.

Minette gone—and now this. And my own grandson—and yours, michie—has done this! Ah, michie, michie, did you think on those long ago nights there between the blue mountains and the purple sea, when you took me into your bed so quietly, and I so frightened, with the music of the rain dancing on the banana leaves outside your window—did you ever think that it would come to this? Our son, your only son, michie, my beautiful first-born, an upstanding man whipped like a stupid driver whips his horse?

She raised sad, accusing eyes to Angèle, who bent down and put her arms around the broad shoulders she had so often rested her head on for comfort. She inhaled the nostalgic smell of starched clean cotton and damp dark skin. "I'm sorry, Mimi," she murmured. "I'm so sorry."

When Angèle released her, Mimi bent forward, and with the

handkerchief in her hand, wiped the perspiration from Ouma's face.

There were four chairs in Angèle's stall in the dress circle, where one sat to see and be seen, at the Theatre d'Orléans. Melodie and Angèle sat on the two in the front of the stall, as ladies did, the better to display their gowns. Jeffery and his father sat to their left and slightly behind their chairs.

"We will say nothing of what happened here today," Angèle had instructed Melodie that evening when they heard the sound of the Archer carriage wheels and trotting horses on their drive. "We must keep up appearances in order to prevent gossip."

But Jeffery knew them too well. "Where's Jean-Philippe?" he'd asked while helping Angèle step up into the carriage.

When Melodie hesitated, Angèle answered him. "He went to New Orleans earlier today."

"Then he'll meet us at the theater?" It was more a statement than a question.

"Presumably," Angèle said, and Jean-Philippe's absence was not mentioned again.

Now Jeffery was looking over Melodie's shoulder at a stall across the horseshoe and saying in her ear, "There's Jean-Philippe now."

Melodie lifted her gaze from the patrons filling the orchestra seats and looked across the theatre. Jean-Philippe was with another man and they were paying their respects to a young Creole girl Melodie remembered from the convent—a mere child then!—seated beside her duena. Clear across the intervening space Melodie could see the girl's blush when Jean-Philippe kissed her hand.

When some acquaintances of M'sieu Archer stopped at their stall and were chatting with him and Angèle, Jeffery murmured, "What is it, Melodie? You've hardly taken your eyes from Jean-Philippe since he came into the threatre."

"Oh, Jeffery, he's so miserable!" she sighed.

"Why? Has he quarreled with his mother again?"

"Shhh!" she warned him.

The curtains parted then, revealing a plump American woman with very fair hair, her fingers intertwined below her ample breasts. Behind her a pale young man sat at a pianoforte. The concert began.

During the entr'acte Melodie saw Jean-Philippe again, but he did not come near their stall. It would not have been pointed but for the quarrel at the Archer ball that had been witnessed, and was doubtless being discussed again. When the concert ended she could not have told the title of any song that had been sung, and she knew that Jeffery was worried by her abstraction. They left the theater and stood waiting at its steps as the long line of carriages slowly moved up.

"Will Jean-Philippe be riding back to La Sorcellerie with us?" M'sieu Archer asked casually.

Angèle answered, "He has my gelded bay," and no more was said. The carriage came and M'sieu Archer handed Angèle and Melodie up, then he and Jeffery sat facing them. All the long ride home, Angèle and M'sieu Archer discussed the singer, her repertoire, her delivery and her voice, which they considered slight. Melodie was quiet and Jeffery's blue gaze, seldom leaving her face, was anxious.

It was Jeffery who stepped down to help them from the carriage and to walk with them up the steps to the front door, which Ti' Mouche opened immediately. Melodie saw the look her cousin exchanged with her footman, a question about Ouma asked and answered, apparently satisfactorily. Angèle went down the hall and Melodie lingered, facing Jeffery.

She looked so troubled. He would have taken her in his arms, but Ti' Mouche was still holding the door open for her, pretending not to watch them.

Melodie saw the love and concern in Jeffery's blue eyes when he took her hand, and when he brought it to his lips, she curled her fingers lovingly around his, trying to reassure him. *Yes, Jeffery, darling, I will set a date,* she told him silently. *I would tell you so now, but this is an unhappy night. When I tell you, it must be our night.*

"May I come tomorrow evening?" he asked her. Melodie nodded, murmuring, "I'll send you a note."

He smiled reassuringly and bowed, then ran down the steps to join his father in the carriage.

In her bed Melodie lay awake far into the new day, listening for the heavy thump of the bay's hooves on the drive up to the house, but no sound punctured the trilling of tree frogs and other night sounds from the swamp to tell her that Jean-Philippe had returned—not before she slept.

After her morning ride Angèle dismounted at the stables and turned her mare over to her groom. She walked to the rear of the house, entering the kitchen annex, and found Mimi still sitting beside Ouma's bed. When Mimi looked pointedly at the riding crop she was still holding in her hand, she flushed with anger, but put her hands behind her.

Ouma was sleeping, the café au lait of his skin emphasized by the white bandages on his forehead and shoulders. "Is he feverish?"

"No'm, he's healing." There were deep purple circles under Mimi's eyes, and her usually pink lips looked gray.

"You haven't slept, Mimi? You need rest. I'll send for Aimée. She can sit with him for a few hours while you sleep."

"Yes, send for Aimée," Mimi said, getting to her feet like an old woman. "But I won't sleep till we talk."

Angèle wondered what good could come of talking. "Mimi, I've told you how sorry—"

Mimi glanced out of the open door. "Privately."

"In my office," Angèle sighed.

She left the room and told Petra to send one of the children for Aimée, to sit with Ouma and give Mimi a rest, then entered the house and went along the hall to her office. A few minutes later Mimi came in and closed the door. Struck anew by her drawn look, Angèle motioned her to a chair.

Mimi leaned forward and laid her arms on the desk between them, stretching her hands toward Angèle in a gesture curiously like pleading. Her brown eyes looked directly into Angèle's, demanding truth. "Jean-Philippe is my grandson, yes? Born of my Minette?"

Angèle returned her look steadily, knowing it was useless to lie. "How long have you known, Mimi?"

"I think when you sent Jean-Philippe to Paris. You were so jumpy when I wanted him to find Minette." She nodded. "Yes, I think that is when I knew surely."

"I might have known you'd guess." Angèle waited fatalistically for what Mimi would say next, realizing that events were moving out of her control but certain that Mimi would be a willing conspirator, for Jean-Philippe's sake.

But Mimi surprised her. "So your man, your marquis, seduced my Minette too," she said heavily.

"Too?" Angèle echoed, frowning.

"I saw Michie le marquis carry you into your room that night the rain trapped him here—and M'selle Clothilde still thinking he was going to marry her. We all thought so, Michie Etienne and madame too. She was enceinte, poor child."

Angèle's eyes widened, and for a few seconds she felt as if she had been kicked in the stomach. When she could speak, she said violently, "No! You're lying!"

"Non, ma fille," Mimi said sadly. "I've never lied to you."

Pregnant with *Melodie?* When she met Hector? "Oh, my God, it isn't possible!" If it were . . . how Clothilde must have suffered that fateful spring! Painful memories crowded to her mind, scenes she had tried to obliterate: the look on Clothilde's face when she walked around the corner of the house and found Philippe kissing her there by the stables; Nonc' Etienne calling alone to tell her of Clothilde's wedding plans and asking her, brusquely, *Have you decided to marry like everyone else?* She remembered she had denied it.

"Are you saying this is something everyone knew but me? Did my aunt and uncle know?"

"I don't think so. But Michie Hector knew. Why else did they insist on a hurry-up wedding so she could go away with him? Why did she have her baby so far away?"

"You're just guessing, Mimi!"

"Of course her *femme de chambre* knew."

"I suppose she told you?" Angèle said with a tinge of sarcasm.

"I have eyes," Mimi said obliquely, and Angèle knew she would get no closer to the truth than that.

She steeled herself against the woman she had trusted for most of the years of her life. "You are asking me to believe that Ma'am'selle Melodie is my husband's child?"

"Just like my Jean-Philippe," Mimi said painfully. "Can you look at them and not see him in both of them? Look at their eyes! And when I saw what is happening, I knew I must speak."

"What is happening?" Angèle asked coldly. "What are you talking about?"

"It's happening under your nose and you don't see it? But then, he is not yours, is he? I see how miserable he is. You want to know why he struck out at Ouma? Because he's so miserable he'd strike at anyone in his way. I tell you something else. If m'selle's going to marry Michie Jeffery, she should do it now."

Angèle said angrily, "You're dipping your fingers into someone else's bowl!"

"I speak when I see the need."

"I think you're giddy from lack of sleep. Go now. Go to your bed and get some rest."

"I'm going," Mimi said with dignity.

Angèle stood up and paced the floor of her office, trying to stem the rush of tormenting emotions threatening to render her helpless, as one wild impulse blocked another. It was as if a dam had given way and all the stormy passions of the past that she had hidden away in the dark corners of her mind were bursting out. While she was being buffeted, struggling against them, she looked back at herself, seeing a strong-willed young woman fighting marriage because she could not bear the thought of being as dependent as her sickly mother had been, until she was caught in the toils of a passion she could not resist, not even for Clothilde whom she loved dearly, not for her sense of loyalty, not even for common sense. . . . Nothing else had had meaning for her after Philippe made her love him.

And why had he seduced her? In his own words, because he could not resist a woman who was unhappy because she was unloved! He was never loyal, not to Clothilde, who gave him her trust, not to her, not even to the emperor he was petitioning for his lost estates. Yet even now some part of her mind was insisting, "But he loved me. He truly loved me." She could still be seduced by his memory!

And Minette, her father's "little kitten." *We're his night and day.*

She paused in her pacing, stopped by an unexpected flash of rage. But on the heels of that thought was another, more rational, but depressing. If Mimi told the truth, Melodie and Jean-Philippe had the same relationship as she and Minette. Closer, because they were the children of Roget first cousins, from the same father! Not for a minute did she believe Mimi's insinuations—but they had a right to know.

There was only one person she could talk to about this: Nonc' Etienne. She would risk hurting him if he did not know, but for the sake of Clothilde's child and the small grave boy she had claimed was her son, she had to know the truth. She yanked the bellpull, then stepped out into the hall. When Loti appeared, she told him to order her carriage. "I'm going to the city. Tell Petra I will be back for dinner," she said, and went upstairs to change.

Melodie slept late. Her first thought when she wakened was to wonder if Jean-Philippe had come back to La Sorcellerie. She rang for her servant and dressed quickly in one of her cool pale muslins. Running downstairs, she went out to Ouma's room. His door was open and Mimi was with him. He was sitting up in his cot, looking quite normal except for the bandages swathing him. They both smiled to see her.

"I'm glad to see you looking better, Ouma."

"I'm not badly hurt, m'selle. I'll be working on madame's books again tomorrow."

"You'll no such thing!" Mimi snorted, but Ouma laughed, and Melodie thought he probably would. When she left the annex, she met Ti' Mouche on the galérie and asked, "Is m'sieu up, Ti' Mouche?"

"He hasn't rung, m'selle."

"Take his breakfast tray to him and I will follow you," she ordered. "I must speak to him."

Ti' Mouche hesitated. "He be angry, m'selle. Michie come home very late last night."

Infuriated, she demanded, "Do you think he will beat you?"

His expression went blank.

"Do as I say. Immediately!"

"Oui, m'selle."

She sipped her own coffee on the galérie while she waited. When she saw him returning with the tray, she went down the steps and across the lawn to the garçonnière. The door was closed. When she tapped on it, Jean-Philippe said, sulkily, "Now what?"

She went in. He was sitting on a chair behind a small table, on which he had apparently had his morning coffee, still wearing his white cotton robe. He had not shaved, and his expression was guarded as he looked up at her.

"You're up early, dear cousin. Did Maman send you again?"

"No."

He regarded her with half-closed eyes and an enigmatic expression. "Have you come to console or to scold me?"

Her heart seemed to crumple and began beating erratically. "Jean-Philippe, don't shut me out!" she begged.

"I don't want to talk about it, Melodie."

"I just don't understand! Have you forgotten that Ouma took you fishing, that he once saved me from stepping on a cottonmouth down by the bayou, that he made whistles for us out of reeds, taught us how to keep our balance in a pirogue? Oh, Jean-Philippe, how could you?"

He muttered, "I'm sorry, Melodie—"

"It's bad enough to strike a slave, who can't strike back. But to whip Ouma, of all people, the gentlest on the plantation, the one most valued by your mother. Why, he and his mother are almost like family! Mimi is *suffering*. She sat with him all day yesterday and probably all night; she is still sitting with him."

"Stop it, Melodie."

"I'm not through! Jean-Philippe, you must apologize to Ouma, and to Mimi too. You did apologize to your mother yesterday, didn't you?" she asked anxiously.

His head came up and the impact of his anger startled her. "I did more than that. I declared my independence."

"You what?"

"I crawled out from under her thumb, dear Melodie. I told her I was no longer her toy soldier." He stood up and tightened the belt of his robe. It was short, and his tan shapely calves revealed he had no trousers on beneath it.

She eyed them uneasily. "You haven't even been in to see Ouma—"

"Melodie, you talk too much," he said irritably.

She took a step backward, sensing a difference in him. "That cut on his forehead—he will be scarred—"

"Melodie, I'm warning you." He was coming toward her.

Instinctively she took another step back. "Or there could be an infection. Cousin Angèle says there is danger—"

"Will you stop talking—"

"He could die, Jean-Philippe," she warned him, backing away.

". . . long enough for me—"

She began talking very rapidly. "Why did you ride off so fast yesterday? Did you go to confession? Because if you did, you should tell your mother. It would make her ever so much—"

". . . to kiss you?" he hissed.

". . . happier?" She was backed up against the closed door, and he was standing very close, his luminous dark eyes glowing with passionate purpose, the warmth of his body and the odors of his skin and his soap enveloping her in a pleasant languor. She was hearing again the music of the waltz to which they had moved in slow sensuous circles that night at Bellemont. She could not tear her gaze from his lips, curved so tenderly.

With an effort she closed her eyes. "This is wrong, wrong . . . Jean-Philippe, you may *not* kiss me. . . ." But even while she was protesting, her face was tilting to receive him.

Chapter 19

IT was the hottest hour of the day when Angèle's carriage entered the narrow cobbled streets of the city on that day in the hottest month in the year. It would be the middle of October b fore the winds off the warm Gulf of Mexico, with their ever-present threat of hurricane, would change, bringing cold dark clouds rolling down the Mississippi valley from the north.

The overhanging balconies, where Creoles sat and gossiped after the sun went down, were deserted. Few people were abroad on the banquettes, and those were servants or *gens de couleur libre*—the freed people of color.

Angèle patted her forehead with a handkerchief and reflected on where she might find Nonc' Etienne. Certainly not in his stifling little house. At the intersection of a narrow cross street was a three-story building with two rows of lacy ornamental iron galéries curving around it. She rapped to get Jules's attention, and he pulled his pair up beside the banquette, dismounted, and opened the carriage door.

She pointed to a door emblazoned MERCHANTS EXCHANGE. "Go inside and tell M'sieu Etienne I wish to speak to him."

Opening her reticule, she gave him a coin for the small black boy who had run up to hold the horses.

In a few moments Nonc' Etienne emerged. He had grown portly since he left Bellemont, and his large nose was darkened by broken veins, but the fullness in his face and his longer whitening hair made it less prominent. He was still an impressive man.

He crossed the banquette and climbed into the carriage to sit beside her. "Ah, my dear Angèle," he said, his breath redolent of spirits. "How do you manage to look cool on such a day?"

"I do not take whiskey, *cher* Nonc'."

"It is the only way I can endure it. What brings you out in it?"

"I have come to invite you to lunch with me. Are you free?"

"My dear, I am always free for you."

"Bien." She spoke over his shoulder to Jules, still holding the door. "Drive us to Le Veau Qui Téte," she instructed him.

The Sucking Calf was a restaurant and lodgings for travelers on the corner of the rues St. Peter and Chartres, across from the old cabildo, in what had been the residence of the late Baron Pontalba. They climbed the flight of stairs to the dining room. The maître d'hôtel, who was well acquainted with them both, led them to a linen-covered table and snapped his fingers for a waiter.

After choosing a partridge for their meal that he was assured had been well-hung, and an imported wine to accompany it, Nonc' Etienne gave his attention to Angèle. He asked about Melodie and Jean-Philippe, then said, "Something important brought you to me on a day like this, no? Is it a thing that troubles you?"

Angèle broke off a piece of the crusty bread the waiter had set between them and began playing with it, rolling little crumb balls between her fingers. "It's an old wives' tale Mimi is repeating. But first I must tell you what happened at La Sorcellerie yesterday." Briefly she described what she knew of the beating Jean-Philippe had given Ouma, and watched the surprise and concern grow in his eyes.

"That Jean-Philippe, he has a temper, yes? Is Ouma badly hurt?"

"His face will be scarred, but no—not badly, I think. He is

strong, and Mimi is guarding against infection. It has hurt Mimi more than Ouma." She paused. "That may be why she has come to me with this . . . this tale about Melodie—"

"What tale?" Nonc' Etienne demanded.

Angèle hesitated, searching for the least hurtful words. But there were none. In the end she blurted it out. "Nonc', did you ever suspect that . . . well, that Melodie was born too soon?"

To her acute disappointment, his eyes slid away from hers. He summoned the waiter and said irritably, "Where is our wine? We'll have it now, if you please!"

"Right away, m'sieu!"

When the man had gone, he said, "Why should I think such a thing? Clothilde was in Philadelphia when Melodie was born." He still did not look at Angèle, and her heart sank. "She was a baby like any other when she came to us. A little larger, a little smaller, of what significance is that? Your Tant' Astride, she—" He stopped, realizing he was saying too much, and asked indignantly, "Why would you ask me such a question?"

The waiter returned with a bottle of wine and two glasses on a tray. They were silent while he poured it, then Angèle's hand clenched around her wine glass and she took a quick gulp. When the waiter left, she said, "Mimi believes that Philippe was Melodie's father."

Her uncle had raised his wineglass to his lips. He sputtered, "Mimi is the one should be whipped! I never wanted you to hear that rumor."

"Was it a rumor?"

"Never more than that. Clothilde told us nothing. But her mother . . . well, Astride was always adding two and two. And sometimes getting five!"

The waiter came with their partridge, beautifully browned and surrounded by garden vegetables. "I recommend this sauce, m'sieu," he said, setting down a steaming bowl of liquid. The fragrance of herbs rose between them.

Nonc' Etienne nodded, and they were silent as the waiter split the bird and served it. When he had gone, her uncle said, "You were happy with him, weren't you?"

"For a time I was in heaven." Angèle picked up her fork and made circles on the napery with it. "But then . . . there is something I haven't told you. Jean-Philippe is not my son. His

248

mother—" She swallowed, trying to stop the words she had sworn never to speak aloud, but her need to speak was too great. "His mother was Minette," she whispered. "You remember—"

"Min—" He stopped himself from shouting out the name by picking up his wineglass and gulping its contents, but his eyes remained wide and disbelieving. The waiter came quickly. While he refilled both glasses, Nonc' Etienne stared at Angèle with a stricken expression on a face that was slowly growing apoplectic. When they were alone again he said in a low, venomous tone, "If I could pluck the marquis from his grave in order to murder him, I would do it! The *canaille!*"

"It's true, then? What Mimi said?"

He glared at her and repeated, *"Canaille!"*

Angèle was beginning to wish she had insisted on their having this talk in Nonc' Etienne's little apartment in the Pontalba Building. She shook her head, fighting tears. "You would kill Philippe, and you say Mimi should be whipped for telling tales, but what about my father? He was your brother, Nonc' Etienne, but you didn't horsewhip him or call him names. What about my mother—" She broke off and picked up her fork, then laid it down again. "For years I pretended I didn't know that even before my mother died Mimi was more important to him. Or that I had a half-brother and a half-sister. . . . I'll always love Mimi. She was more my mother than my own, but . . . to have my father prefer her children to me—"

"What are you saying?" her uncle asked uncomfortably. "You imagine things! Did your father leave La Sorcellerie to them? Didn't he prepare you to manage the plantation? Of course he loved you! As he loved your mother—"

Her chest hurt with the effort to keep control. "Then why, *why?*"

Nonc' Etienne was looking very unhappy. He lifted his wineglass and stared into its ruby lights. Finally he said, "You were too young to understand, the terrors we experienced, *chère* Angèle. Your father and I—we escaped the torch and the guillotine in France only to face the torch and the machete in Saint Domingue. In France we'd had everything, but all we had left was our wives' jewelry, and we were threatened by unspeakable savagery. You probably don't remember much about that time, but you must have felt the tension, the fears in that house. . . . It was Mimi who saved us all from being murdered in our beds or burned alive."

A vision flashed before Angèle's mind—a vivid picture of leaning coconut palms against a smoky orange sky, a sunset where the sun never set, its terrible beauty receding as the boat slid silently over the reef in darkness. She was holding little Clothilde and clinging to Mimi, who cradled baby Ouma in her arms, all of them shivering in that thick aura of doom that was the boat's cargo.

"Your mother hadn't the strength to endure it. Your father—he was not the first man to find release in the body of a forbidden woman, a strong woman who loved him. Nor am I the first to find it in the bottle." He raised his glass to his lips and drained it. Then he said, "Shall we go?"

He called for the chit, and Angèle signed it.

The maître d'hôtel bowed effusively as they passed him, then went back to look at the food they had not touched. He shook his head and sighed. A waste of a fine partridge.

Jean-Philippe's kiss had changed everything. Melodie stared up into his familiar dark eyes, glowing with a reckless excitement that she recognized. Jean-Philippe was always the daring one, the initiator of their exploits, but she and Jeffery together had always kept him from going too far in his fantasies. Neither she nor Jeffery had been with him yesterday, when his temper had overreached the limits of what she felt was acceptable behavior. Nor was Jeffery here with her now when, backed up against the door with her lips tingling from Jean-Philippe's surprising kiss, she was scarcely able to breathe through the thick aura of his excitement.

His lips were so close to hers that she felt the small winds of his breath when he spoke. "You ask me for answers, Melodie. There's only one. I love you. I think I've loved you forever. I know I can't live another day without you. Melodie, darling, darling . . ."

She had not known how much she needed to hear his words of love, but that their love could be physical was an idea new and frightening. She knew it was not possible, but her longing to be close to him was intense. His lips touched hers again lightly, tasting, testing. When she did not immediately push him away, he thrust his tongue into her mouth and her response was so sharp she felt as if it were splitting her.

· Suddenly panicky, she tried to say *No!* but it was too late. The refusal came out like a moan while her lips clung to his, kissing him back. His long arms were around her slim body, holding her so tightly that his hands almost reached to her tingling breasts. They ached for his touch, and she pulled him closer, pressing herself against his chest, arching her hips against him. Their hungry kisses grew more frantic, their bodies trying to melt into each other, and they fumbled with the clothing in their way.

In moments they were on his bed, their light clothing discarded, and she was learning the shockingly delicious pleasure of sharing nakedness; everywhere her pale skin touched his, sun kissed and polished like gold, was a note of joy. She was learning new carnal delights from the touch of his hands everywhere, everywhere. . . . She moaned and twisted under his caresses as they explored each other's bodies, discovering what it could mean to be as physically close as they had always been in their minds.

When the unimaginable happened, it was not unimaginable at all, but something she longed for intensely, and the pain was small beside the unutterable pleasure of feeling him inside her and of surrendering herself to a union symbolic of their closeness. After that incredible convulsion of pleasure, he remained inside her for long moments while their hearts slowed gradually to normal, reluctant even now to end their connection. When at last they parted, he leaned over her tenderly to brush her hair back from her damp forehead.

"You're mine, Melodie. I'll never let you go," he told her, each word distinct. "We're going to be married. . . ."

Reality flooded back like the winter cold when dark clouds rolled down from the north, and with it came despair. *"Married, Jean-Philippe? Who will marry us? We're cousins."*

"Are we?" he said strangely. "Perhaps, but I don't think so."

She stared up at him, not able to read his expression. "What are you saying? Of course we are!"

"If we are, we'll run away, go to Barbados, become pirates—"

"Jean-Philippe, be sensible!"

He laughed. "No, it won't be like that, my love. I've suspected for some time that I was adopted. I'm going to confront my mother, make her tell me the truth."

"Adopted? Jean-Philippe, you're dreaming! Everyone says how much you resemble your father."

"I'm his son, certainly. But perhaps not hers. Don't you see? It's the only thing that can account for the way she has always treated me, blowing hot and cold." He gave a little bark of laughter. "I'm probably a bastard my father brought home to her and forced her to pretend was her own child. You know, Melodie, how often I've felt that underneath all that maternal love, she really hates me."

Melodie caressed his naked chest, her hand like ivory against his golden tan. "You're mistaken about that, Jean-Philippe. I know she loves you."

He put his hand over hers, but he said, "I want the truth from her. If I am not a Roget, nothing can separate us. But if what I suspect is true, I may not inherit La Sorcellerie either. I have to know the truth. I have to know whether I can support a bride."

She thought, We can always live at Bellemont, but did not say it because close on that thought came another: *And put Jeffery and his father out?* She was suddenly appalled by the implications of what had happened.

"But I thought you didn't want to be a planter?"

Hearing her troubled tone, he bent his head and kissed her, a long slow kiss that recalled a hundred new sensations he had taught her. "Darling, if I can marry you, I'll be the best damn sugarcane planter in the state of Louisiana."

She laughed shakily and put her hands up to his head to pull it down to her breasts. "When will you talk to her?"

"When she gets up after her little afternoon sleep. That will be the best time. Will you come back then?"

She nodded, but he made her say "I promise."

It was not until she closed the door of the *garçonnière* behind her and started for the big house, that she let her thoughts return to Jeffery. She remembered that today she had been going to tell him she would marry him, and her newfound happiness evaporated like bubbles of moisture in the sunshine.

Jeffery, Jeffery, darling, what have I done? She felt torn in two, and heavy with foreboding. The depressing thought came to her that she would never be completely happy again. How could she be happy without Jeffery? But how could she have imagined she could be completely happy *with* Jeffery, as divided as she felt?

It was done now. It could not be undone. And it had changed everything, everything. . . .

The creak of carriage wheels sounded on the bayou road, and before Melodie reached the house, Cousin Angèle's coach-and-four was turning in at the end of the long drive. Melodie fled to her room.

Angèle was enervated by her trip to the city in the heat of the day. Her nap and a cool bath revived her somewhat, but her spirits were still low. Why had Mimi told her? Better if she'd never known that Philippe made love to Clothilde before turning to her. It made her incredibly sad to know that she had collaborated in what must have been a tragedy to Clothilde. If she had known it was an affair, and not just an attraction between them . . . But would it really have prevented what happened? Could she have stopped loving Philippe, even then? Probably not, she thought, depressed.

She went first to see how Ouma was healing and found him sitting up on his cot, insisting to Mimi that he was able to resume his bookkeeping tasks in her office. Angèle forbade that, and went along to the office herself. But once there she could not concentrate on the plantation books. Her thoughts kept returning to Philippe. Philippe who had betrayed Clothilde as he had later betrayed her. How ironic! A man who liked women, who claimed he could not stand to see them unhappy! He had come into their lives, hers and Clothilde's, like an evil wind, and tossed them about like drying clothes on a line.

He had been dead for some sixteen years and was still able to hurt her.

There was a sharp rap on her closed door. It opened immediately and Jean-Philippe strode toward her desk. Angèle's eyes widened. With his uncanny likeness to his father, it was as if her dead husband were reincarnated and stood before her. Jean-

Philippe saw the look that leaped to her eyes, and his lips twisted sardonically.

She correctly interpreted his expression, and her own became more guarded. "What is it, Jean-Philippe?"

"I want the truth from you." He saw that she paled, and it confirmed his suspicion that he was not really her son. His leap of joy—*Melodie!*—was mixed with a sorrow he did not want to face. He said, "I know that I'm illegitimate."

Angèle drew in her breath sharply. "So Mimi's told you." A panic seized her, and her thoughts began whirling like a windmill in a strong wind. Who else had Mimi told? Jean-Baptiste? Mon dieu, she knew how gossip ran from plantation to plantation up and down the bayou! Was this Mimi's revenge for the beating Jean-Philippe gave Ouma?

Jean-Philippe grasped that Mimi must know the details of his adoption, but he ignored Angèle's remark. "Since I plan to marry, I must ask you about my prospects," he said formally. "Will I inherit La Sorcellerie?"

She heard him through a smothering fog of emotion. Was *that* what they wanted, Mimi and Ouma? La Sorcellerie? "No!" she said, eyes flashing.

Immediately she told herself it would have belonged to Jean-Philippe one day if Mimi had just kept silent. She was too upset to think straight, but her intuition told her everything had changed, and for the worse. She was no longer in control.

The immediacy and strength of her rejection stunned Jean-Philippe. He had been raised as a Creole gentlewoman's son, given every advantage, and at times had felt himself deeply loved. He realized that in spite of his suspicion that he was an adopted son, he had counted on being told that he was her heir. Naively he had wanted to believe that in spite of everything, she loved him.

"La Sorcellerie will go to Melodie."

His expression cleared. "Then it's all right, dear Maman," he said, his assurance returning with his relief, "because it's Melodie I'm going to marry."

Every vestige of color left Angèle's face. She looked as if she were going to faint. Alarmed, Jean-Philippe moved closer in case she slid from her chair.

But she held herself erect with an obvious effort and said,

"You wanted the truth, Jean-Philippe. All right, I'll tell you. Yesterday you took a whip to a man who has never been anything but kind to you, and you scarred him for life. That man is your mother's brother." He looked so blank that she began to doubt that he knew, but she had gone too far to stop now. "Your grandmother didn't tell you?"

"My . . . grandmother?"

"Mimi. She didn't tell you that Minette was not your wet nurse, but your mother?"

Jean-Philippe's mouth was open and he seemed incapable of closing it. He was in shock, his eyes wide and blank.

"Minette didn't tell you that when you saw her in Paris?" She had wondered about that, agonized over wondering.

He shook his head; it moved from side to side like a mechanical toy.

"She is also my half-sister," Angèle said, her voice cracking.

Jean-Philippe's expression did not change; if anything it looked more rigid. Angèle thought of the zombies in Mimi's stories. His lips moved stiffly. "Roget blood . . . I have Roget blood?"

She noticed how gray his face had become, and pity twisted her heart. "Yes. My father was your grandfather." She reached out her hands to him. "You can live here as long as you want, Jean-Philippe; you can manage La Sorcellerie for your lifetime if you prove yourself capable. But you can't inherit—not with Mimi knowing, and Ouma, and Jean-Baptiste, and I don't know how many other slaves. Do you see?"

"Melodie." It was a croak of pain.

"Oh, God, she is your half-sister," Angèle whispered. "Philippe fathered her too. She is not for you."

His eyes were terrible, no longer blank with shock, but blazing. "God damn you!" he said. "Why have you done this to me? Why did you raise me as your son and heir if—"

"Your mother brought you to me, Jean-Philippe. She did it because of what I could give you. What could she do for you?"

"Damn you, damn you! You bought me, didn't you?"

Her eyes filled with tears. "You were so much like your father. And I had lost our only child. I wanted you desperately."

"But not for myself." His terrible accusing eyes, so like Philippe's, were red-hot with hate. "Why did you raise me as the son of an aristocrat and then do this to me? You're punishing me for his sins, aren't you?"

"No! No, Jean-Philippe. It wasn't like that. I didn't know—"

"God damn you to hell, you and my mother both!" He whirled on the balls of his feet and slammed out of her office.

When the door of the *garçonnière* was opened so violently it banged against the wall, Melodie sprang up from the chair where she had been waiting for him. She saw in his face that something terrible had happened. He strode past without looking at her.

She ran into the bedroom after him and found him pulling out drawers and opening the armoire doors, throwing his clothing and possessions around wildly. "Jean-Philippe, what did she say? What has she done to you?"

He didn't answer her. He had found what he wanted. It was a case of dueling pistols that had belonged to his father. When Angèle had given them to him, he and Jeffery had taken them out into the swamp and for several days practiced shooting at knots on cypress knees the height of a man's heart.

He tucked it under his arm and picked up his riding crop. "Jean-Philippe!" she screamed. "What are you going to do?"

He rushed past her out of the *garçonnière* and she hurried after him. He was striding to the stables, his long legs taking him so fast she could not keep up with him. Her heart was pounding with terror, and she was almost breathless. Jules was there, putting tallow on the saddles.

"Put my saddle on Big Red, Jules!"

Jules took one look at his face and jumped to obey him. Melodie caught Jean-Philippe's arm, crying, "Speak to me, Jean-Philippe! Don't leave me like this. What are you going to do?"

He shook off her hand to help Jules cinch the saddle and test it. The red gelding sensed Jean-Philippe's black anger and would not stand still.

"M'selle," Jules warned her quietly when she clung to Jean-Philippe's leg as he mounted. The groom pulled her out of the way as Jean-Philippe dug his heels sharply into the gelding's flank. Snorting, the horse sprang forward, his eyes starting.

His hooves thudded down the drive, and Melodie's cry trailed after him.

She ran up the steps to the galérie and in the front door. Cousin Angèle's study door was closed. Melodie tried the knob and found it was locked. She knew her mother's cousin was inside. She pounded on the door, shouting, "Let me in! Cousin Angèle, open the door!"

She pounded, louder and louder, crying hysterically, "Jean-Philippe has gone! What did you do to him?" But there was no sound from inside the office.

Finally Mimi came, and putting her arms around her and crooning comforting words in her rich resonant voice, took Melodie away.

Chapter 20

MIMI led the hysterically crying girl up the stairway and to her bed, where she sat down and held Melodie tenderly against her shoulder until her wild sobs subsided. Then she eased her down on the pillow and lifted her legs up on the quilted counterpane.

Melodie rolled her head from side to side. "Why won't Cousin Angèle see me, Mimi? What did she do to Jean-Philippe to make him leave like that without speaking to me? It must have been something terrible! Oh, she is hateful, hateful!"

"Hush, *ma fille,* calm yourself." Mimi smoothed the hair back from Melodie's damp forehead. "Michie left La Sorcellerie because he loves you."

"No, no, he wouldn't leave me."

Mimi's rich voice was ragged with her own repressed tears. "It is terrible for him, m'selle, and not easy for madame either. Hush, and I will tell you what she has told him. Michie Jean-Philippe is your brother."

Melodie's body froze into absolute stillness, her eyes widening with terror. "No," she said in a whispery voice. "That is impossible."

Seeing Melodie's pallor, feeling her tremble under her hand, Mimi thought, Mon dieu! Jean-Philippe has already taken her.

"You had the same father—"

"No!" Melodie cried, more strongly. "My father was killed by the British!"

Mimi shook her head sadly. "Jean-Philippe's father seduced your mother before she married Michie Hector."

Life repeats itself, Mimi thought. She wondered if Melodie would conceive. If Jean-Philippe could not inherit La Sorcellerie, perhaps there would be a child of his as its master. *My African blood, that Michie Roget would not recognize.*

It was fitting.

But what about Jean-Philippe? With an ache in her heart she looked at the pale suffering girl he had loved.

Sitting beside his father in the carriage as they drove along the bayou road, returning home from their offices in the city, Jeffery was oppressed by a feeling of anxiety. He had not received the promised note from Melodie. Nor had he heard anything from Jean-Philippe.

He regretted the rift with his friend since their fight at Belle-mont. They'd both had too much of his father's punch! His jealous accusation must still rankle, he thought, since Jean-Philippe had avoided accompanying them to the concert. He resolved again to try to speak to Jean-Philippe about it. They had been friends too long for an estrangement between them to mar Melodie's happiness.

Madame Angèle's boat dock was ahead of them on the bayou. As they drew near the entrance to the drive between the oaks, Jeffery looked to his left and La Sorcellerie came into view, a jewel in its magnificent setting. It was almost erotically beautiful in this light. The rays of the sinking sun created a golden aura behind it, and pooled violet shade under the galéries, against which the white walls seemed to shimmer. From the slender pillars silhouetted against the golden light, streamers of shadow angled across the darkening lawn.

In Boston he had described the ambience of La Sorcellerie as one of serene beauty—at this hour its beauty was haunting and strangely disturbing, as if something distorted lay behind its elegance.

"It's witchery, isn't it?"

Jeffery looked at his father, surprised at how close their perceptions were. His father's face held the same sad bemusement he was feeling. "Bellemont is an early plantation house, too, and quite similar in its plan, but it doesn't have that special magic—"

"No," Jeffery agreed. But was it the house or who lived there that gave it its distinctive aura?

The house was fast disappearing behind the curtains of pale gray moss that hung from its trees, those strange light-absorbing streamers that reminded him of death and decay. He had seen no sign of life, no gardeners working in the flower beds, no black children playing, no movement during their brief glimpse of the stables, and that seemed to Jeffery unusual.

Nor was there any message from Melodie waiting when they arrived home. Jeffery sat at one end of the long table and his father at the other for their lonely meal, with a brace of silver candelabra and the etched crystal fly trap that had been a gift from Madame la marquise between them. When his father lit up his cigar, Jeffery excused himself, ordered his horse saddled up, and rode back to La Sorcellerie.

"Good evening, Ti' Mouche," he said when the footman opened the wide fan-lighted door. "Will you tell mademoiselle I am here?"

In times past, before he had gone to Boston, Jean-Philippe would have heard his voice and called happily from wherever in the house he was, and Melodie would have come running down the stairs. Tonight all was quiet.

"M'selle has retired, Michie Jeffery." An excessive amount of white was showing in the young footman's eyes, suggesting some inner tension.

The study door opened and Madame Angèle came out, greeting him with a warm smile. Before she closed the door behind her, Jeffery glimpsed two things: Ouma, sitting at the desk where he worked on the plantation books with her, had a white bandage wrapped around his head; and madame's pistol, the little silver weapon she always carried in a pocket of her riding skirt when she rode over her fields, was lying on her desk.

"Good evening, madame." Jeffery asked with the ease of an intimate of the family, "What happened to Ouma?"

"A little accident at the sugar mill. We're rushing to get it ready for the grinding. Was Melodie expecting you, Jeffery? I'm sorry, but she's not feeling well this evening."

Something had happened. He could sense it in the mysterious way an animal senses danger.

"I'm very sorry," he said, concentrating on singling out the clues that hinted at some disaster greater than "a little accident at the mill."

Madame Angèle put her hand on his arm. "Jean-Philippe left La Sorcellerie today."

So that was it. But why had he left? Jeffery wondered uncomfortably if he had contributed to Jean-Philippe's decision to leave.

"We had a terrible quarrel." To his surprise, her eyes filled. "We have no idea where he was going. Melodie is very upset." She paused, searching his face with an anxiety so intense it embarrassed him. "Jeffery, if he should get in touch with you . . ."

There was something more, he knew. Was it just coincidence that she had laid her pistol down between Ouma and herself?

He promised warily, "I'll certainly let you know if I hear from him."

"Merci. I'll go up and see if Melodie feels well enough to come downstairs," Angèle offered. "Is there a message you'd like me to take, in case she doesn't?"

"Tell her I love her . . . very much," he said, his voice suddenly unsteady.

Her smile was dazzling. Yet as he waited in the foyer, he felt like a stranger in the house he knew as well as his own. In a few moments she was back, saying, "Melodie begs you to excuse her tonight, Jeffery. She will send you a note when she feels better." She added, "Please take my regards to your father."

"But, surely, madame." He kissed her hand formally and left, feeling excluded, and rather pointedly reminded that as *un américain* he was not one of them. The pain of rejection was bitter. Even worse was his conviction that something was terribly wrong.

* * *

For a week after Jean-Philippe's departure, Melodie refused to leave her room or to see Jeffery when he called. Other friends were also turned away. On the seventh day Mimi came into her room bearing a tray covered by a linen serviette. "You are going to swallow every spoonful of this soup Petra has made especially for you, m'selle," she said firmly. "Then you are going to let your *femme* wash your hair and dress you to receive Michie Jeffery this evening."

"Don't think you can tell me what to do, Mimi," Melodie returned, with the first spirit she had shown.

"I shouldn't have to!" Mimi retorted. "You know as well as I do that you owe that young man an explanation. What has he ever done to deserve the kind of treatment you're giving him, tell me that? Now you sit up and make a lap for this tray."

That evening Jeffery rode his mount up the drive and turned him over to Jules, as he had every night since Jean-Philippe left. It had been a week. Surely tonight Melodie would agree to see him and let him comfort her, he thought. It was not in her nature to go into a decline, as some of the ladies in Boston were reputed to do. A dozen vivid pictures of her mischievous dark eyes laughing up into his came into his mind. Pray God she would again look at him like that!

Did she blame him for Jean-Philippe's disappearance? he wondered. She must know that Jean-Philippe's abrupt departure hurt him too. He must make her understand how he regretted that stupid quarrel which had boiled up out of nowhere when he saw Jean-Philippe holding her so close as he waltzed with her, and that he would do anything she asked to help find Jean-Philippe and bring him back.

He walked up the steps to the lower galérie and Ti' Mouche let him in. Madame la marquise came out of her office to greet him, as usual, and he asked, "How is she today?" It had become a nightly ritual. Always the same question and always the same answers.

But tonight Madame Angèle said, "She wishes to see you," and his heart leaped and began a hard beat.

"Please wait in the salon while I go up and see if she is ready to come down."

Jeffery walked into the room where he had spent so many

happy hours. The sliding doors to the dining room that had extended the space during La Sorcellerie's spectacular balls were closed. Jeffery looked at the white marble fireplace with its elegant carved mantel, and glanced up at the carved floral medallion on the ceiling from which hung the crystal chandelier. He ignored the graceful settee and chairs, and remained standing in the center of the pastel rug, listening for the sound of Melodie's step on the stairway and wondering if he could control himself if she walked into his arms.

Instead of footsteps he heard the thin tinkle of music. After a startled second he remembered the music box Jean-Philippe had brought Melodie from Paris. A slow red haze began misting his vision. Was that what she had been doing all week—sitting in her chamber playing that damned music box tune over and over? Because Jean-Philippe had given it to her?

It was the birth of knowledge, the beginning of death for his hopes. His heart drummed in his ears and his vision wavered.

Gradually, over the thunder of his heartbeat, he heard her coming down the stairs, not with the positive, running step he remembered, but tentatively, almost timidly. She stopped in the open door. A look at her pale, strained face told him his intuition was painfully correct. He knew why Jean-Philippe had left La Sorcellerie. He had left because of a love affair that was doomed.

For just a second Jeffery closed his eyes in pain. Then he braced himself to listen to what she wanted to tell him.

Melodie felt very weak. When she stood in the doorway and saw Jeffery standing tall and straight in the center of the Turkish rug, with his ruddy hair blown slightly about his ears and roughly smoothed down above his forehead, the last vestiges of strength drained out of her body. Her gaze fastened on his dear face—the steadiness of his eyes, so incredibly blue; his fair, open countenance, so typical of the Americans, who were straightforward and sometimes maddeningly self-confident, lacking in the Gallic guile and elaborate etiquette of her Creole kin. He was standing stiffly erect, as if braced for bad news.

That was when she realized that he knew. She steeled herself against a longing to throw herself into his arms, spill everything out, and beg his forgiveness.

"How . . ." His voice was hoarse. He cleared his throat and began again. "Are you feeling better, Melodie?"

"A little. Please sit down, won't you?"

He did not seem to hear what she was saying, he was concentrating so hard on his own speech. "Have you heard from. . . ?" She saw that he could not bring himself to speak Jean-Philippe's name, and wanted to weep because she knew then how deeply she had hurt him.

She shook her head, then moistened her lips. "I am not well, Jeffery, but I wanted to come downstairs to tell you that . . . well, that everything has changed." She said forlornly, "We were so happy once, weren't we, the three of us?" She saw him flinch and rushed on, "I have to tell you that I can never marry you. I'm sorry. I . . . I do love you, Jeffery."

She looked terrible, her eyes too big in her too white face. He knew she was suffering, but he was hurting too much himself to think long about her feelings. All he could think about at that moment was how she had locked him out of her life for a week while she played a tinkly little tune on her music box, and how close Jean-Philippe had held her when they waltzed. He wanted only to get away from her, from La Sorcellerie, before he broke down.

She put her hands behind her—if he touched her she would cling to him and beg for the comfort she so badly needed. "Good-bye," she whispered.

He gave her a jerky bow and rushed out of the house. He called for Jules and his mount, pacing up and down on the galérie until it arrived. Then he galloped off, but not toward home. He went tearing up and down the bayou road until his horse was exhausted, then allowed it to head back to the stables at Bellemont.

At La Sorcellerie Melodie climbed forlornly up the stairs, crawled into her bed, and lay back against her pillows. After a few minutes she picked up the music box and began winding it.

The days stretched into weeks and the harvest began. Angèle rode alone to the cane fields every morning, each time stabbed anew by Jean-Philippe's absence and her fear, almost a conviction, that she would never see him again. She ached for his return, regretting her bluntness. She should have made it easier for him. She could have if he had not come to her with his request when she was not only upset by his attack on Ouma, but stunned by Mimi's and Nonc' Etienne's revelations.

Ouma had insisted on checking the little pistol she had carried ever since her father had given it to her when she first began riding with him. She had never feared her slaves, but Ouma warned her that word of his beating had upset some of the cane workers.

It helped her to have to confront the urgencies of the harvest. The brick mill was almost complete and cutting had begun. It would continue for three to four months. This year she found no pleasure in seeking the slender stalks at the center of those ribbony leaves, to see if their pale green was streaked with lavender and gold. In the first field to be selected the knives were flashing up and down, slashing the leaves from the stalk, chopping it off at the ground, then decapitating it, for its head was unripened. Every morning she checked the bundles of stalks arriving by cart in the grinding yard.

She and Melodie had never discussed the night Jean-Philippe left. Angèle had entered her room the next morning, but Melodie had turned her head and refused to speak to her, keeping stonily silent when Angèle said, "Is there anything you want to ask me?" She was not sure just why or for what Melodie blamed her. Mimi said it was for her locked door the night Jean-Philippe left. She swore she had not told Melodie who Jean-Philippe's mother was.

"Plenty of time for that. She's had enough of a shock."

The smoke of the furnaces under the line of sugar pots rose through the new brick chimney and filled the air, and the smell of boiling cane juice blanketed the entire plantation. It penetrated the shutters of the long windows opening on the galérie from Melodie's room. The ever-present cloying odor made her queasy, and she sent back plates of food barely touched.

One day she asked, "Mimi, did my mother confess her sin?"

"How should I know? Most likely she did."

"I don't think she did."

"Why do you say that?"

"Would the priest have performed the marriage service if he'd known she was already enceinte by another man? Do you think my father knew before I was born? That I was another man's child?"

"Likely he did."

"If he didn't, my mother cheated him."

"Why speculate about something you know nothing about? Maybe the priest approved the marriage if she told your father the truth? Michie Hector loved her. And it made no difference in his love for you, no? Didn't he love you like his own daughter? If they did wrong, they were protecting you, M'selle Melodie, all of them, giving you a name to enter in the big book."

"All the same, she cheated my father."

Mimi studied the pale face framed by luxuriant dark hair. "They did it for you," she repeated, and ventured, "as you would want to give your child an even chance in life by giving him a legitimate name. Isn't it so?"

Melodie turned away. "I'm not enceinte, Mimi," she said coldly.

"Of course not, m'selle," Mimi murmured, hiding her disappointment.

When the social season began in New Orleans in the fall, Melodie Bellamy and Jeffery Archer were noticeably absent from the balls, as was Jean-Philippe, le marquis de l'Eglise. The story of his quarrel with his mother and his abrupt departure from the plantation was widely discussed. His quarrel with Jeffery Archer at the Archer ball was recalled and chewed over again. Since no explanation was forthcoming, many versions of what happened had been invented.

As the weeks went on, talk of various sightings of the young heir came to Etienne Roget's ears. He'd been seen with the Lafittes shortly after he disappeared from La Sorcellerie. Later someone swore he had seen him on a flatboat on the Bayou Teche near Poste des Attakapas. A traveler reported gossip about a charming fellow he'd bought an aperitif in a rough saloon in the prairies beyond Louisiana's border. He was reported to be one of a band that preyed on unlucky travelers on the frontier—but, mon dieu, he had the manners of an aristocrat! When he heard that story, Etienne hired a carriage and paid a Saturday morning call on his niece at La Sorcellerie.

He found Angèle on her mare near the grinding stone, a wide hat tied with a scarf to protect her head from the heat, her sun-crinkled dark eyes keenly observant of every detail of the work. *"Merde!"* he said. "You have a manager to oversee this operation, *n'est-ce pas?"*

His observant eyes had already spotted the small holster hanging from a belt around her waist. So she was wearing her pistol openly now.

"Yes, dear Nonc', but I like to remind my workers that a female sugar planter can be as vigilant as any male." She dismounted and came forward to receive his kiss on first one cheek and then the other. When her hat fell back, framing her face in its circle, she looked surprisingly younger.

"You should have a skin like leather, but you're as lovely as ever, my dear," he told her.

"Have you come to have a look at the new mill?"

"Of course. After you offer me a petite refreshment."

They walked toward the house, Angèle leading her mare. "Have you had any news from that young rascal?" Etienne asked.

"None. I lie awake at night wondering how he is eating, where he is sleeping. As far as I know, he took no money when he left."

"He came to me," her uncle confessed, "and I made him a small loan."

She gave him a grateful smile. "I'm glad. Did he tell you where he was going?"

"No. Only that he wanted to lose himself in a place where he was unknown."

"I miss him. And Melodie—Jean-Philippe left without speaking to her. She knows why he left, but she still blames me. I'm not sure why. . . ." She let her voice trail off.

"Does she know?"

"No," Angèle said quickly. "Mimi swears she told her only who her father was."

"She will have to know sometime, won't she?"

"I hope never."

"How old is she now? Twenty? She should be married. . . ."

Angèle shook her head. "Jeffery doesn't even come calling any more. And they were so close."

He made a clucking noise. "At her age you were already managing La Sorcellerie!"

"She is more like Clothilde, no?"

"But yes, that is so," he sighed.

Jules came to meet them and took the reins of her mount from his mistress.

Melodie was waiting on the galèrie. "Grandpère!" she exclaimed, and went into his arms for his hug and the kisses he planted on each cheek. "I heard your carriage and came down, but you had disappeared."

"I had to pry your Cousin Angèle from her latest project. Mon dieu, but I can feel every bone in your body!" he exploded. "Has La Sorcellerie lost her cook?"

Melodie smiled. She had missed her grandfather. "Petra is still here, and tempting me with every dish she knows how to make," she assured him.

"Then why don't you eat? Are you a bird that picks at nothing?"

"I will eat gluttonously if you will stay to dine with us."

"I'll make you a bargain. Ride with me over to Bellemont and I will return here for dinner. I must see my tenant, and we can have a nice private visit driving over and back."

All her joy at seeing him faded from her face. "I must beg you to excuse me, Grandpère."

"I will brook no excuses," he said firmly. "You and I, we have not talked in too long."

"Please, Grandpère, it is painful for me to visit Belle—my old home."

"I will stay only fifteen minutes. Agreed?"

How pale she was! Too weak to withstand his pressure. He felt like a bully.

"Agreed," she said in a small voice, "but I must change my dress."

Aha! Etienne thought. She still cares for young Archer.

Chapter 21

*T*HE days were shorter and the sun was already down, leaving its last waning glow on the mist the first chill of winter was bringing up from the still warm water of the bayou. Over the rhythmic beat of the horses' hooves they could hear the trilling chorus of tree frogs accompanied by hoarse bullfrog croaks. An owl hooted from deep in the cypress swamp. The smell of burning wood was stronger than that of molasses on the air.

Etienne took Melodie's hand. "It grieves me to see you so unhappy, *chère*. Put your grief behind you, as Jean-Philippe is doing. Don't worry about him. I gave him money enough to keep him for a time. Perhaps when that is gone, he will return. You must not let this disrupt your life. No real harm has been done, has it?"

"No real harm," Melodie repeated dully. Just a terrible sin committed and her whole life smashed. "Grandpère, must I confess what—" No, she could not even hint to this dear man what had happened! ". . . what I now know about my birth?"

"You mean should you confess your mother's sin?"

Melodie gave him a startled look. "I had not thought of it in that way."

Etienne hid his alarm. The confessional was sacred, its secrets not to be divulged. But that was the ideal, and ideals were notoriously unattainable. Besides, if the matter of the blood should come up—and it was always a possibility following any revelation of the trouble at La Sorcellerie; his brother Angel had caused enough gossip to ensure that!—wouldn't it be inscribed in the vital records of the parish and affect many generations to come? Etienne's private philosophy was that if a sin were discreetly hidden, it hurt fewer people.

"If you have sinned," he said, choosing his words carefully, "your conscience, which is the voice of God, must be your guide. You have been taught to confess your sins, so you know your confessor will tell you that you must repent in order to be forgiven. But to confess another person's sin? I would not take that upon myself."

Melodie bit her lower lip.

The gates to Bellemont stood open. As they entered, Etienne looked sourly at the garden, which had been much improved since Charles Archer had been his tenant. Astride had supervised the gardeners. After her death he had allowed the flowers and the lawns to be neglected until he could not bear to look at them any longer. That was one of the reasons he had moved to Nouvelle Orléans.

The driver pulled his horses up before the steps to the galérie. Melodie murmured, "If you will not be long, Grandpère, I will wait here—"

"Nonsense!" He said it so forbiddingly that she knew it was futile to argue.

Etienne's footman, whom he had leased with the house, was already opening the carriage door. "Good evening, michie and m'selle!" he said, offering his hand with such a sunny welcoming smile that she accepted it and let him help her step down.

"Is that you, Etienne?" Charles Archer stood in the open doorway. "You are welcome! Come in, come in. Ah, good evening, Melodie."

She had just stepped into the foyer when Jeffery came running lightly down the staircase and stopped dead when he saw her standing at its foot.

"It's a pleasure to see you both," his father was saying. "Can I send word to the kitchen that you will dine with us?"

"No, merci," Etienne replied. "My business is brief, Charles, and I have promised to dine with my niece. Can you spare me a few moments?"

"Of course. Come into my study. I am sure Jeffery can entertain Melodie."

Jeffery said, "Of course, Father," and came slowly down the rest of the stairs, breaking the spell that had held Melodie motionless, staring up at him.

He had changed in the weeks since she had seen him last. The bones of his face seemed sharper and his upper lip was firmer, taking away some of the softness of his mouth.

He did not take her hand to bring it to his lips for the conventional greeting—she was grateful to him for sparing her his touch—but waved her ahead of him into the salon and closed the door. To avoid looking at him, she remained standing, her gaze going around the room that was so familiar to her, the salon that she had expected would be her own as Jeffery's wife, with its mixture of Grandmère Astride's furniture and pieces that had belonged to Jeffery's mother.

He did not waste time in pleasantries. "Have you heard from Jean-Philippe?"

"No." After an uncertain pause, she said, "I do not expect to hear from him . . . for some time."

She risked a glance at him. His blue eyes held a baffled look, with something else in their expression that she could not read. When he moved, it was so unexpected that she was totally unprepared. His arms went around her, pulling her against his body with rough strength. He held her more intimately than he ever had before, and he kissed her lips with a hungry force and a passion he'd never shown her.

She felt as if he were ravaging her, but her lips were sweetly tingling under his assault and an intense hunger of her own blossomed in response, in spite of her angry but passive resistance.

When he lifted his head, she saw the fury in his eyes. "Is that the way he kissed you?" he demanded, still holding her indecently close. "Is that what you wanted, instead of the love I

271

offered you, the tenderness, the restraint? God, when I think of how I have let you dangle me!"

His arms tightened like a vise, and this time she struggled. He was stronger than she remembered from the days when the three of them had wrestled and fought each other like three boys. She twisted and turned in his viselike embrace, finally freeing one arm enough to draw it up between them. She was too close to him to slap him—her intention was to push his lips away.

He easily dodged her hand, but then brought his face back too quickly, in such a way that her elbow struck his nose and gave one side of his mouth a sharp blow. To her consternation, and his, his nose and lip both began to bleed.

"Oh, Jeffery," she began, stung with remorse.

He gave her one exasperated look, clapped his handkerchief to his face, and rushed out of the salon and up the stairs, leaving the salon door open.

When her grandpère and M'sieu Archer came out of the study and crossed the hall, Melodie was sitting primly on a chair with her hands folded in her lap, awaiting them.

"Where is Jeffery?" his father asked.

"Jeffery developed a nosebleed," she replied, standing and holding her reticule in front of the tiny spot of blood that had splattered on her dress. "He . . . he asked me to say good night for him, Grandpère."

Etienne looked at her with suspicion, but he could think of nothing to say except, "I'm sorry to have missed him."

Upstairs Jeffery bent over the basin of cold water his man had brought him. He heard Melodie's carriage depart with tears of angry chagrin in his eyes.

Christmas was approaching, and plans for the usual celebration were underway at La Sorcellerie. It was the tradition that gifts were prepared for every slave on the plantation, consisting mostly of money tied up in decorated parchment packets, except for Mimi and Ouma and some of the other house servants, who received more personal gifts. All the staff was busy preparing food for the feasts that would follow the distribution of gifts, one in the dining room for madame and her guests, the other for everyone else on the plantation on tables set up on the lawn.

This year the guest list was small. Nonc' Etienne always came out from town and stayed through Christmas and the New Year, and to Melodie's dismay, this year, as usual, Cousin Angèle had invited M'sieu Archer and Jeffery.

"They always spend Christmas with us," she'd said firmly when Melodie protested. "Your grandfather would think it very strange, and so would Charles, if we didn't invite them."

"Jeffery may not accept," Melodie said.

"He may not," Angèle agreed blandly, "if Edmée Giroux's parents invite him to spend the day with them. If he doesn't accept, then you have nothing to worry about, no?"

Melodie bit at her fingernails and didn't answer.

There was a good deal of money in the house, for it took time to wrap and tie enough packets for nearly a hundred slaves. Without Jean-Philippe and Jeffery to help, as in former years, it was necessary to depend on Mimi and Ouma devoting much of their time to the project. But they were busy, too, Ouma in taking several workers with him around to the north side of the lake, where the pines grew, to select and bring back the most beautiful tree, and Mimi to oversee the early preparations for the feasting.

The tree was placed on the front galérie and decorated there, where it could be seen from the bayou road by anyone passing by, and where it would dominate the festivities of the blacks who on this one night were allowed to use the front lawn. Standing beside the tree, Cousin Angèle, with Jean-Philippe and Melodie beside her, traditionally received each worker and his family on the galérie to wish them individually a Merry Christmas and give them the gifts of money to spend as they wished. While the blacks ate on their improvised tables below the galérie, the family retired to the dining room for their own meal and exchange of gifts. Afterward they returned to the galérie to watch the Africans dance and sing to the music they made on their primitive drums.

This year there would be only Cousin Angèle and herself, with Mimi and Ouma to help distribute the gifts. The wrapped and tied parchment packages were piled up in a basket in the office, and the extra ovens and grills were being assembled behind the separate kitchen.

Each day Melodie dreaded Christmas more. Jeffery's father had accepted for them both. It would be so different from the happy holidays when the Triad had been close and immersed in the special gaiety they had known. It was a time in the making of sugar when the boiled-down syrup was cooling in the vats, and it was part of the Christmas festivities to allow their guests to dip knotted strings of pecans in the vats to collect the forming crystals. Both she and Jeffery would be unhappily reminded of those happier times.

There was a difference in the way the blacks were responding this year as well. Mimi, as gloomy at times as Melodie felt, reported that there was still a groundswell of resentment about Jean-Philippe's treatment of Ouma. The incident had undermined their fragile sense of security on the plantation.

"They're speculating about whether michie will come home for Christmas," Mimi told Angèle.

"No one has heard from him," Angèle told her.

It was the last night before Christmas Eve. Melodie, feeling very tired and depressed, had gone to bed early. She thought Cousin Angèle was very well-organized, as always, but without her usual verve. But when she thought about Jeffery coming, after Cousin Angèle's remark about him and Edmée Giroux, she didn't know how she could get through Christmas Eve and the next day.

She had slept perhaps an hour that night of December twenty-third when she was awakened by the sound of galloping horses right under her windows. Her first thought was that Jean-Philippe had come, and she felt a surprising dismay, mixed with her leap of pleasure. Then she heard the coarse shouts, and from the snorting of animals and milling of hooves had a perception of how many mounted men were below. It confused her. There was a sound from her cousin's room. Melodie heard Angèle walk into the hall and saw the light from her candles coming through the crack under her door.

In the faint light she felt for her robe and put it on as she slid down from the bed. She heard a crash that sounded like the front door was flung rudely open, and saw the light under the door flare from torches. The shouts of men echoed inside the house. When she recognized Jean-Philippe's voice among them, she began to tremble violently.

"You'll find the money behind that door," Jean-Philippe said. "Get it while I get my woman."

Panic flooded her, dizzying her thoughts. Jean-Philippe had come for her! Where would he take her? Who were these rough-speaking men with him? She was frightened of the unknown, and could feel no happiness at his return. Her heart was pounding.

"Stop where you are!" Cousin Angèle's authoritative voice cut through the confusion of sounds.

Melodie's frozen limbs carried her through her door and into the hall. Her cousin stood tall and commanding in her silk robe at the top of the stairs, holding her candelabra above her head with one hand and with the other pointing her silver pistol down at Jean-Philippe, who had paused at the foot with his left hand on the balustrade, looking up at her.

He also had a gun, a large weapon that looked infinitely more dangerous and threatening than Cousin Angèle's dainty pistol. The light of a torch shone out from the open door of the study, and in the flickering light Jean-Philippe looked like a stranger. He was dressed in the rough shirt and trousers of the fron-tiersmen who came down the river on flatboats. His dark hair had grown longer and fell around his face like an Indian's, but his eyes, fixed on Cousin Angèle's little pistol, were the same beautiful luminous brown that Melodie had seen glowing with love for her.

"I've come for my inheritance, *chère* Maman," he said in French. "And for Melodie."

Melodie took a step forward and gasped his name.

He saw her then. *"Melodie!"* It was a cry from his heart, and it went through her like a blade.

He started up the stair, and Angèle pulled the trigger. Her gun made a curious little pop and absolute silence followed it. A dark spreading spot appeared on Jean-Philippe's breast. He swayed and slumped facedown on the stair, then slid back slowly, step by step.

A roughly bearded man ducked out of the office, his eyes starting as he saw Jean-Philippe. He raised startled eyes to Angèle and the pistol, now pointed directly at him. Dropping his own weapon, he slowly raised his hands above his head. One of them held the torch, wavering in his trembling hand but garishly lighting the macabre scene.

Other bandits appeared behind him, their hands full of the wrapped money gifts. One of them yelled, in English, "They got Frenchie!" and they poured out, jostling the first man into dropping his torch. At that moment from outside there was a single screaming cry, then the shouts of blacks and the wild neighing of horses.

"That was Obie!"

"The Africans're stampeding our horses!"

They all turned and ran, some of them dropping the money packets in their haste to get to their only means of escape. Ouma came running down the hall, picked up the dropped pistol and the torch, and began stamping on the scorched planks.

Melodie ran down the stairs and crouched beside Jean-Philippe's body, letting her hands wander over him, feeling for a pulse she couldn't find, murmuring his name and weeping so copiously she could hardly see.

Then Mimi and Ouma were there, pulling her up to her feet, putting their arms around her, saying—it seemed to her over and over—"He's gone, m'selle. Michie's gone." Saying, "There's nothing we can do. Come away now."

She lifted her head. Cousin Angèle was sitting on the top step, the pistol still dangling from her limp hand, her face gray. There was the smell of gunpowder and charred wood in the hall.

"Send for M'sieu Archer," Mimi told Ouma.

"I've already sent a message, Maman. He'll be here soon."

Melodie broke away from their loving hands and bent over Jean-Philippe's body, weeping wildly. It was Jeffery who lifted her again, and she turned into his arms, sobbing, "Oh, Jeffery, she's killed him. She shot Jean-Philippe."

Charles Archer went past them up the stairs to where Angèle sat. "You shot your *son?*"

Angèle looked up at him, her eyes suddenly filling. "Philippe's son," she said. "He was not mine. But I . . . loved him."

"M'selle Angèle!" From the hall below them Mimi's voice

rose much as it had when Angèle was a child about to do something that could bring her harm.

Charles Archer heard the warning in it. He looked down at the graying black woman, then pulled Angèle to her feet and said quietly, "Please, all of you, go into the salon. You, too, Mimi."

He steadied Angèle as she went down the stair and past the sheet Mimi had brought to cover Jean-Philippe where he lay sprawled at its foot. Ouma came out of the office with guns from old Michie Roget's gun case, and gave them to Ti' Mouche and Loti with some low-voiced orders.

Angèle looked back from the door of the salon and said, "Ouma must come too."

Charles saw the look Mimi and her son exchanged, one of unanswered questions. He was very curious, but at the same time was dreading the answers he meant to have. He waited until everyone had entered, then closed the door and motioned Mimi and Ouma to be seated too. Ouma took a straight chair near the door, but Mimi crossed the room to sit on the sofa beside Angèle.

Charles said to Angèle, "Do you want to tell us who Jean-Philippe was?" and he noted that Mimi took Angèle's hand.

"He was my husband's illegitimate child by Mimi's daughter, Minette."

Her leaden words fell like a crashing tree into the expectant silence of the room. Angèle looked at the stunned expressions on the faces of the three who had not known—Melodie and Jeffery and Charles—and went on in that curiously deadened voice, "Minette is Ouma's sister and . . . and my half-sister."

Melodie turned waxy pale, and when she felt the pressure of Jeffery's hand on hers, she clasped it as tightly as if she were drowning and he had offered her a pole.

"The Roget family had its . . . its secrets," Angèle said, in that scarcely human voice, "but it was a moderately happy family until Philippe de l'Eglise came into it. Clothilde and I both loved him. He discarded my cousin's love and her love child. . . ." Her dead eyes moved briefly across Melodie's face, and Melodie winced. "Our son was stillborn . . . and then he took Minette. But she . . . she brought me Jean-Philippe."

277

Her eyes closed briefly, and she murmured, "He looked exactly like his father."

A muscle twitched in Charles Archer's cheek.

"I didn't know he and Melodie were both my husband's children until Mimi told me . . . when I told Jean-Philippe, he left La Sorcellerie."

"M'selle Clothilde kept her secret well," Mimi put in. "For her child's sake."

Angèle looked directly at Charles. "I shot Jean-Philippe because I could not let her father's sins ruin Melodie's life too."

Jeffery was feeling ill, but he was not so absorbed in himself not to be apalled at what Melodie must have suffered and how she must be suffering now. He saw that his father was pale too. This was a tragedy that could destroy them all. A cool head was needed. He tried to throttle his raging emotions: a deep sorrow and pity for Jean-Philippe as well as for Madame Angèle; the pain of Melodie's doomed love for her brother; and his own feelings of irretrievable loss.

He spoke up harshly. "You shot him in self-defense, madame. F.e had a gun, didn't he?"

His father gave him a look of gratitude and hope. It buoyed him and helped him reach a more objective state of mind. After all, he had been trained as a lawyer, and Madame Angèle badly needed his help.

"I think, Father, that we must send to New Orleans for the authorities as soon as we are assured the bandits have left the region. Meantime, I would like to hear from each of you exactly what you saw and heard tonight."

He questioned Ouma first, and the big gentle man described how he had slipped out of his room in the kitchen annex to get help from the slave quarters when he heard the bandits ride up. "I figured they had come for the Christmas money."

"Did you know Jean-Philippe was with them?" Jeffery asked.

"I guessed, m'sieu. How else could they know about the money? They are not bayou men. They talked like men from the Mexican prairies beyond our border."

He had wakened Mimi and Père Baptiste and they had gone from door to door, alerting the slaves and sending a young worker through the fields to Bellemont to ask for help. Then they had planned how to overcome the man guarding the horses and stampede them.

Jeffery did not ask Angèle any more questions, but turned to Melodie. "What wakened you, Melodie?"

To her, his impersonal lawyer's voice was another flick of pain. She told him haltingly of hearing the bandits arrive, hearing Jean-Philippe's voice, and described how she had joined Angèle at the head of the stairs.

"He said he had come for me. He had a gun. When he saw me, he started up the stairs. That was when . . . when . . ."

"That was when madame shot?" Jeffery finished for her, keeping his voice matter-of-fact.

Shuddering, Melodie nodded.

Jeffery looked at his father. "The police can make nothing of that but self-defense, I'm sure. That's all they need to know." He looked at Ouma. "Are you going to reveal your relationship to Madame Angèle to the police?"

"Do you think *that* is a secret from Creole New Orleans?" Angèle said with weary cynicism. "It is one of those open secrets we never discuss. But Jean-Philippe—that is a different matter."

Ouma said slowly, "Madame is right. It is gunpowder, m'sieu. Not only in her world, but to us. It is dangerous for madame."

Mimi looked at her son, so fine-looking and so devoted to his half-sister, and the ache in her heart that he was so undervalued was more than she could bear on this night when she had lost her beautiful grandson. She stiffened her spine and snapped, "We want to protect madame and m'selle, yes! But we also wish to be freed, Ouma and I."

"Oh, Mimi!" To Charles, it seemed that Angèle came alive for the first time since he had entered the house. "How have I repaid you for all the times you've mothered and scolded and comforted me!" For the first time her tears began to fall. "Of course you can have your freedom! I've long planned it for you and Ouma one day, but I've selfishly kept you because I've needed you both so much.

"Whatever you want to do, I will leave La Sorcellerie in any event. I couldn't live here after— But you and Ouma cannot protect us from what I have done. Nor can you and Jeffery,

279

Charles. Don't you see that I must confess everything. How can I ever find peace if I don't confess it all?"

After a long silence Charles said, "You've taken the life of someone you loved, and I think I understand how you feel, but you must consider very carefully what you do and say in the next few hours because it will affect the rest of Melodie's life, and her children's lives for generations. In my opinion Melodie has been sinned against—and so, my dear, have you. I don't want to see you both pilloried after enduring this tragedy. Of course you must confess to your spiritual advisor, but please let Jeffery decide how much we will tell the authorities when they come."

"You must not lie," Jeffery said, "but if you tell them exactly how it happened, just as you have told me, *and no more,* it may be better for both madame and mademoiselle."

"And when they ask me why my son left La Sorcellerie?" Angèle challenged him.

"He wanted to marry Melodie," Jeffery said tiredly, "and as everyone knows, they were cousins."

The objective tone of his voice sounded to Melodie like cold rejection, and she could stand no more. She had lost them both, both Jeffery and Jean-Philippe, and she could see no future to her life. She stood up. "May I be excused now? I want to go back to bed."

"I'll take you upstairs, m'selle," Mimi offered, in her rich comforting voice.

"Take madame with you," Charles said. "Jeffery and I will stay here to make sure there is no more trouble."

After the women had left, Ouma said, "I will ask someone to prepare the spare bedrooms. You need not lose all your sleep. I've set a guard at the stables, and we have armed guards at the front and back entrances."

"Go to bed, Father," Jeffery said. "I might as well stay up. I will not sleep in any case."

A little later Charles found his way down the dim upper hall from the bedroom he had been given, to the one he knew Angèle occupied. As he expected, she was lying awake, her eyes wide open.

"Is that you, Charles?" she asked without surprise, although it had been five years since they had been lovers.

He sat on her bed and took her hand. "If you don't want to be alone tonight, I'm here."

She pressed his hand ever so faintly, and whispered, "Yes. Hold me."

He lifted the covers and got into bed with her, and she turned like a tired child into his arms. Neither of them slept, but he held her through the long hours until morning. It was not an easy night for him, but he had offered her comfort, and he knew a deep joy when she finally slept in his embrace.

Toward morning she wakened. He kissed her gently.

"Oh, Charles," she sighed, "if only I had met you first!"

"Don't think of the past. Think only of the future. I would like to waken like this with you in my arms every morning for the rest of my life."

She moved restlessly away from him. "You are pitying me, Charles."

"No. I think I know now why you refused to marry me. I think you still love me. Think about marrying me, Angèle."

"Maybe, when this is all over. . . ." Her voice trailed off into uncertainty. He had to be content with that.

The bandits did not return. Later in the morning the authorities came, and when they left, several things had been settled. Madame la marquise was charged with shooting her bandit son in defense of herself and her young cousin. She was taken to New Orleans to be placed under house arrest there until her hearing. Jean-Philippe's body was removed to New Orleans to be sealed in a lead coffin until a mausoleum of marble could be constructed for his place of rest, for in this swampland no graves could be dug that did not immediately fill up with water.

A morose Etienne Roget took Melodie back to New Orleans with him and settled her with the family of friends whose daughters had been at the convent school with her, both now married and raising families of their own. Melodie had scarcely spoken with Jeffery, who was busy all morning with the police interrogations, and she was in despair. It had seemed so natural to turn to him in her grief. Not to find him at her side had brought her a sharp awakening.

In this crisis, when her whole world seemed splintered, she was learning how much his deep, caring love meant to her, and how much she had depended on it. She had thrown it away in that wild hour of response when Jean-Philippe had taught her the delights of her own passion. Now she knew, too late, how strong and enduring her love for Jeffery was, and how much she valued him.

Too late.

The only comfort she had that long gray day on the eve of Christmas came from her grandfather. As she rode beside him in his carriage along the misty bayou road toward New Orleans, he said, "It explains the Triad, doesn't it? I always wondered about that curious threesome. Now I understand it."

"What do you understand, Grandpère. *I* don't understand anything!"

He put his veined hand over hers. "Remember that Jean-Philippe loved you, and think kindly of him. There was a natural affinity between you that you would have not have misunderstood if you had known of your relationship." He sighed. "We all share some blame."

The hearing was scheduled for after Christmas. On that day Etienne and Melodie were allowed a brief visit with Angèle in deference to the holiday. Her status was that of a guest in the mayor's house, which she was forbidden to leave until her case was decided. When the hearing was convened ten days later, the room in the cabildo was packed with spectators, avid with curiosity about the marquise who had shot her own son. But other than the ordeal of being publicly stared at and whispered about, the hearing was not difficult. It was more or less a repeat of the interrogation they had endured the morning after the tragedy at La Sorcellerie, and the outcome was the same. Madame la marquise de l'Eglise was acquitted of any crime, because she had acted in self-defense.

The spectators cheered and the judge rapped his gavel on his desk. Then the whispers began. Melodie could hear the whispering, see the eyes all turned her way, and imagine what was being said. *They were cousins—isn't it tragic? A love affair between cousins . . .*

Melodie stood, wondering if she could walk through that whispering crowd to the door. Then Jeffery stepped up beside her and offered his arm. She smiled up at him through tear-filled eyes and accepted it.

Charles Archer was waiting for Angèle to step down. They walked out of the government building together, receiving bows and words of congratulation along their way. A damp chill wind swept across the square to strike their faces, but when Charles raised his hand to summon a coach, Angèle said, "No. I am going to the chapel, Charles. Will you walk with me?"

He bowed silently. Their hands clung as they walked the short distance. He entered the chapel with her, but just inside she stopped and said, "Come back in an hour, dear Charles."

"Of course."

He lingered just inside the door while she made her way toward the confessional box at one side. The chapel was empty. He did not hear any sound when the priest entered the confessional, but he clearly heard Angèle murmur when she bent her head toward the screen, "Father, I have sinned," and he made a silent prayer of his own that the priest was not a gossip. This tale would cry out to be told and retold down the generations. He was not a man of prayer, but he prayed now. *For Melodie's sake, and for Jeffery's, let not the sins of her father be visited on her.*

He walked along the levee for an hour, oblivious to the activity on the flatboats tied up below and to the vessels riding at anchor in the river, trying to understand how it all had happened. When he returned to the square, Angèle was crossing it toward the convent of the Ursuline nuns.

"Where are you going now?" he demanded. "Let me hire a coach before you are chilled."

"I am on my way to call on the Mother Superior. I mean to ask permission to enter the convent."

Charles paled. "Not as a novice!"

"No, Charles. I will offer my services as a lay member, if I am acceptable."

"What in God's name will you do there? You won't be allowed to teach the girls!"

"There is a kitchen garden to tend, there are accounts to keep. There will be things I can do."

"You are choosing that in preference to marrying me?"

She paused and looked toward the river and the gulls circling the masts and furls of sail of the vessels anchored there, visible above the levee. The pleading cries of the birds rose above the grind of carriage wheels on the cobbles and the clatter of horses' hooves.

"Do you know what I am asking myself, Charles? Why did I take Jean-Philippe if I couldn't give him my whole heart? I taught him his way of life and gave him his expectations and then dashed them."

"How could you do anything else? You could not give him his sister!"

"I destroyed him long before I fired that shot. I thought I had made him one of *us,* but all along, somewhere in my mind, he was one of *them.* We Creole women have known all along that there is no *us* and *them,* only *we,* but it was a hurt so deep we couldn't talk about it, an open secret we couldn't acknowledge—"

"What would he have been if you had not brought him to La Sorcellerie? A Paris pickpocket? The son of a notorious courtesan?"

She said, "Please try to understand, Charles. For me the secret was not in a little house tucked around the corner on the rue Dauphin. At La Sorcellerie I lived with it. . . . You don't understand, do you?"

"I'm trying, but I'm feeling bitter. Angèle, I beg you to reconsider—"

"Charles, I cannot live with you until I can live with myself. Perhaps, when I have found peace . . ." She said softly, "I love you, Charles."

"I love you, Angèle. I'll always love you."

The gate was locked that had stood open during the Battle of New Orleans, when she had joined the Creole women volunteers who had driven their carriages out to the battlefield to help bring in the wounded to the temporary hospital the sisters had made of their convent, where other volunteers had joined with the nuns in nursing them.

She pulled a rope that rang a bell somewhere inside the building. Soon a nun came to let them in. Charles remained outside the gate and watched Angèle follow the nun up the walk. On the threshold she turned and looked back once. Then the doors of the convent closed behind her.

Epilogue 1830

*M*y eyes were blurred by tears, the tears I had not shed earlier in the day, when Cousin Angèle was laid to rest beside her parents behind the cathedral. She died of apoplexy in the convent, which was her last home. A proud and passionate woman . . . but she had renounced both pride and passion for service to others.

I had another stop to make before I could end this day of painful memories. Turning my back on La Sorcellerie, half hidden by the spidery curtains of gray moss which made it seem wrapped in cobwebs, I guided my mare along the overgrown path past the tumbledown *pigeonnier,* but had to dismount when she refused to enter the dark jungle that had grown up around the trees shading another mausoleum.

Cousin Angèle had had it made. No angel graced its roof. It was of a simple design cut in off-white marble which in the perennial dusk had a lavender cast. Above its sealed door was chiseled: JEAN-PHILIPPE, LE MARQUIS DE L'EGLISE, 1804–1824.

Nothing more.

Twenty years. So young to be doomed. But my half-brother

had been doomed from birth. What a waste of mind and spirit, of charm and of sheer masculine beauty!

The grass was scythed in front of his marble resting place, the creepers cut away, and a crockery jar holding water and a cut spray of creamy magnolias and leathery leaves stood on the ground. Likely Mimi had sent Ouma with them.

Standing there before the magnolias, I said my last good-byes. To the father I had never known, but whose diamond-and-sapphire necklace, last remnant of his family jewels, Cousin Angèle had bequeathed to me. It should have gone to Jean-Philippe, she said. I did not know the spot where our father lay, but perhaps someday I would seek it out. For who am I to judge him?

Good-bye to my cousin, the marquise, and to her adopted son, my half-brother, whom I had so dearly loved.

Then I turned and walked my mare toward Bellemont, feeling the beginning of peace steal over me as the dusk deepened. A tinkling cowbell told me the cows that furnished the children's milk were being brought into the barns for the milking. Candles were being lit in Bellemont. It was a much more imposing residence than La Sorcellerie had been, although it had never matched its sorcery.

We had added two single-story wings, one on each side of the original square planter's house to make room for Father Archer, and for Grandpère Roget, who was growing too old to live alone at the Pontalba. And last year we imported marble from Italy to cover the cypress floors.

Almost more money than we could spend came in from the sugar fields of the combined La Sorcellerie and Bellemont plantations, thanks to Cousin Angèle's long, dedicated management of them. A salaried Ouma, whom many planters had tried to hire away from us, managed them now. Cousin Angèle trained him well.

I rode around to the gleaming new stables and gave my mount to my groom, entering the house from the rear and going up the back stairs to the nursery, where Mimi was presiding over the children's supper. Mimi was also a "free woman of color" who chose to make her home with us. Her hair was completely white now, but her skin was still smooth, her lips had never lost their pinkness, and her eyes were as bright as a girl's.

"Maman!" Thérése exclaimed, but Antoinette, who was six and already becoming bilingual, called "Mumma!" Baby Alexander pounded his spoon on his tray and shouted, "Mum, mum, mum, mum, mum!"

I laughed, ruffling Thérése's dark curls, brushing Antoinette's fine red hair back from her forehead, and giving Alexander a hug which allowed him to smear my riding skirt with his porridge-covered spoon.

"Tsk, tsk!" Mimi said, grabbing a serviette.

"I have to change for dinner now anyway." I turned back from the door to say, "The magnolias are still fresh," and Mimi gave me a quick appreciative smile.

"What magnolias?" I heard Antoinette demanding. "Mimi, what magnolias?"

"Never mind. Eat your supper."

She was sharp-eyed, that older daughter. I thought of something my father-in-law had said: *It's a tale that will be told and retold.* The day would come when all three of them would ask questions. . . .

"Why the sigh?" Jeffery asked me as I opened the door of our bedroom. I looked with pleasure at him. He was still lean and erect, with the few lines at the corners of his blue eyes and marking the curve of his smile only indicating his maturity and the responsibilities he had assumed. To me he was handsomer than when he had returned from college. He came toward me with his arms outstretched, and I walked into them and laid my head against his shoulder. "Are you all right?"

"Yes, darling . . . I'll ride no more to La Sorcellerie."

"It could be restored, you know."

"I don't want it restored, Jeffery. Oh, maybe a hundred years from now, when I'm dead . . . if there's anything left of it then. I just want to let it die quietly." I was not yet ready to talk about my ride, and I changed the subject. "I stopped in at the nursery. Do you know what Antoinette called me? *Mumma!* Is it for that she must be taught English?"

"Melodie, we have not been a French colony for twenty-seven years. Besides, she can't yet pronounce *mother*. It comes out *mutter.*"

"I won't argue with you about the necessity for English lessons. I haven't time. I must change for dinner."

"Shall I help you?" He was nibbling at my ear and feeling for the buttons at my nape. I turned in his arms so he could see them, and he began nibbling my other ear.

"Ummmm," I said. "I'm glad Antoinette has your red hair."

My dress fell down around my feet and Jeffery began kissing and fondling my breasts. "Darling, *darling*," I murmured. "Hadn't you better lock the door?"

MALCOLM ROSS

**A rich West Country saga
in the bestselling tradition of POLDARK**

On a Far Wild Shore

Young, beautiful and newly widowed, Elizabeth Troy
travels to her late husband's Cornish home hoping to find
comfort in its fertile hills and valleys. But she is shocked to
discover the vast, decaying acreage of Pallas is now solely
her responsibility – a legacy as unexpected as it is
unwelcome.

Elizabeth's plans for her inheritance provoke the bitter
hostility of her sister-in-law, Morwenna, whose word has
been law at Pallas for thirty years. To bring the troubled
estate back to prosperity Elizabeth must look for help
elsewhere. And there are many very willing to be more than
a friend to the widow – David Troy, a poor relation whose
sober exterior hides some disturbing secrets; Courtenay
Rodda, the sensual newspaper proprietor; and James Troy,
the rich and worldly wise American cousin who begins a
thrilling but dangerous liaison with Elizabeth . . .

'The book is beautifully written, the characters depicted
with a passionate realism that held me entranced. I simply
loved it!' Patricia Wendorf, bestselling author of *Larksleve*.

FICTION   0-7472-3001-3   £2.95

More compulsive fiction from Headline:

The explosive novel of abuse and betrayal

Silk & Satin

MARCIA WOLFSON

They are known as 'The Sisters' – five charismatic women who seem to enjoy every luxury and privilege money can buy. But beneath the glossy surface, each one hides a dark secret – a secret that Mark Saunders' murder threatens to reveal . . .

Darleen – is she really the grieving widow?

Joy – she chooses to celebrate Mark's death in a provocatively sensual way.

Deborah – the councillor whose public respectability conceals dark appetites.

Aida – actress and drug addict.

Samantha – her Oriental fragility masks her ruthless ambition.

Combining the sensuality of LACE with the hedonism of HOLLYWOOD WIVES, SILK AND SATIN is the pulsing novel of power and revenge.

FICTION   0-7472-3007-2   £2.95

More compulsive fiction from Headline:

BAIT
OF LIES

HARDIMAN SCOTT
AND BECKY ALLAN

The tense political thriller of intrigue and treachery

Carolyn Hailston's student trip to Prague becomes a nightmare when she and her Czech lover are arrested by the security police. To ensure Josef's freedom, she must agree to collaborate with the Czech secret service on her return to England. No one would call Carolyn a promising recruit, except for one thing – her father is a government minister with access to secrets that can rock the delicate balance of power in Europe.

At home, her amateur attempts at espionage bring Carolyn swiftly to the notice of spymaster David Rackham. But her naive involvement in the politics of power and treachery only marks the entrance to a labyrinth of blackmail, murder and corruption that will endanger her own life, threaten her father's career, and bring the government to the brink of an international crisis of terrifying proportions . . .

FICTION   0-7472-3008-0   £2.50

THE

DIRTY DUCK

A Richard Jury Case

MARTHA GRIMES

Stratford-on-Avon is more renowned for its Shakespeare than its slaughter. And, despite its name, The Dirty Duck pub had enjoyed a blameless reputation until an innocent American tourist took her last drink there before being brutally murdered.

Superintendent Richard Jury, visiting friends in the neighbourhood, finds himself at the centre of the hunt for the killer. The only clue is a blood-stained theatre programme, left on the victim's body.

With the welcome assistance of the aristocratic Melrose Plant – and the very unwelcome attentions of Plant's formidable Aunt Agatha – Jury must track down a murderer who intends to kill, and kill again, until he has achieved his deadly ends . . .

'It is hard to overpraise this book . . . Miss Grimes may come to be regarded as the Dorothy Sayers of the 1980s'
New York Times

FICTION   0-7472-3004-8   £2.50

Headline books are available at your bookshop or newsagent, or can be ordered from the following address:

Headline Book Publishing PLC
Cash Sales Department
PO Box 11
Falmouth
Cornwall
TR10 9EN
England

UK customers please send cheque or postal order (no currency), allowing 60p for postage and packing for the first book, plus 25p for the second book and 15p for each additional book ordered up to a maximum charge of £1.90 in UK.

BFPO customers please allow 60p for postage and packing for the first book, plus 25p for the second book and 15p per copy for the next seven books, thereafter 9p per book.

Overseas and Eire customers please allow £1.25 for postage and packing for the first book, plus 75p for the second book and 28p for each subsequent book.